BURNT DEVOTION

THE IMDALIND SERIES, BOOK FIVE

REBECCA ETHINGTON

Copyediting by C&D Editing

Production Management by Imdalind Press

ISBN (print) 978-1-949725-04-9

ISBN (ebook) 978-0-9914313-8-0

Printed in USA

This Edition, December 2018

❀ Created with Vellum

THE IMDALIND SERIES

CONTENTS

To My Kids
Who are strong

IMPORTANT NOTE

This book is an all new edition as of December 2018. The book has been cleaned, expanded and much of it rewritten. While the story and characters remain the same, the new addition boasts 13,000 new words, and a bit more kissing. Okay, okay. A lot.

Please note that the first few chapters of Burnt Devotion occur in tandem with Soul of Flame.

I hope you enjoy this expanded version, rewritten and cleaned until Wyn's tattoos shine!

1

WYN

THE ABBEY WAS AHEAD, peeking through the trees of the Spanish forest like a looming fortress. The crumbling stone illuminated in streaks of white as bright lightning cracked above us, making the decrepit building look like the Taj Mahal, especially after what we had escaped from.

We had left the cold, torturous dungeons of Prague behind, but the knowledge of Edmund and the massacre that had occurred there was like a ticking time bomb. There were only steps until we reached Ilyan, until we could tell him what had happened in the cave.

About my memories, about the fire magic, about what Ovailia had done, and how she had betrayed us all.

I peered through the trees to a lone illuminated window, the bright block of yellow light glowing in the dark. The last camp of Edmund's men that separated us from the abbey sat ahead, laughing boisterously around a fire. Leaves shivered in the breeze, carrying the smell of smoke on its back as a dark shape moved in front of the light, the figure moving through the block of yellow light at a run. My anger boiled, she was already here with him, in the Abbey. Ovailia was there, ready to strike.

We needed to get to Ilyan before it was too late. Judging by the mass of Edmund's army we had already weaved through to reach the ancient building, however, we might already be.

Well, maybe. But, not quite.

I had my memories back, and the fire magic, and was just in time to wipe out an army, it seemed. Perfect.

Talon would have loved this...

My heart pulsed painfully at the memory of Talon.

My husband. My mate. Gone.

My last minutes with him slammed against my chest, blending with every other memory I had chosen to forget in a rage of flaming magic and memories that licked against my skin, ready to explode.

"We are almost out of time."

I would let all that pent-up anger out if Sain didn't knock it off.

His raspy voice dragged me out of the pain like water against my soul, the overwrought words pulling my focus toward the decrepit man who still looked like he was locked in a dungeon.

"We must move quickly."

I barely restrained my scowl.

He had said the same thing for days, ever since the lid of Ilyan's tomb had enclosed us into the tunnel system under Prague. The tunnels had gotten us this far, but being stuck with him as he repeated the same phrase every night as I tried to sleep and each day as we walked towards Ilyan was more than a little trying on my nerves. It really didn't help that each time the phrase rolled off his tongue, his eyes moved over the lines that covered the left side of my body.

He was doing it now, and I kind of wanted to throw him twenty feet in the air.

The deep, jagged edges were a harsh reminder of my past, of what my father had tried to do to me, of what Cail had tried to stop.

The Zánik curse.

It was the worst form of punishment for our kind. A promise of a slow, torturous, death.

My father had embedded the cursed magic within me after he had discovered my centuries of treachery against his master, Edmund.

My brother, Cail, had only barely been able to stop it by binding it into my skin.

Seeing as I had killed my father, I would have assumed the marks to leave—as Cail had promised—but still, they remained, staring at me as dark as the sins that lined my soul.

Staring at Sain as he said the same thing Every. Freaking. Night.

"Look away, old man," I said through the grit in my teeth, shooting him a look that was all danger.

"Something is wrong." Sain whispered through the chilled air, not even flinching at the warning glare I was throwing at him.

"Obviously," I mumbled, looking away from him to the light that whispered through the trees.

I didn't need his Drak blood to tell me something was wrong. Strangely enough, I could make that out for myself.

I could feel it in the way the magic pulsed inside the Abbey, the way that the weak magic flared and the strong pulsed. It wasn't the castle full of strength and power that I had been expecting. Something was off.

I hated that he was right.

3

I pushed the parallels from my mind, not willing to accept that Joclyn—that anyone—within those walls was injured, that they were little more than sitting ducks.

For once, I wasn't sure if the addition of my magic would tip the scales in their favor.

Edmund and his freaking minions were taking a major bite out of my pride.

Lightning ripped above us, the low bellow of thunder following right behind in a blast that caused all the Trpaslíks in the camp before us to jump.

"We are almost out of time," Sain gasped again.

"Yeah, I got that. Thanks," I growled as I pulled him from the security of the trees and to my side, my shield wrapping tightly around us and blocking us from sight.

Concealing an exasperated sigh, I dragged Sain toward the drunken camp. Our heavy footfalls were loud and abrasive in the still air. The obnoxious laughter of Edmund's men was barely enough to cover the sound of crunching leaves and snapping twigs as we skirted their camp.

I sneered at the six rough Trpaslíks, my magic flaring abruptly as I recognized two of them from when I worked for Edmund. What I wouldn't give to turn them into crispy black wedges of death right now. One poof, bam, dead.

The image made me smile.

The trees around us flashed white as the sky broke apart, lightning illuminating the refuge that was only steps away. I reached toward them, expecting the thrill of calm that our destination promised. The relief of security. The moment my fingers made contact with the jagged edges of the tree's bark, however, my body filled with fire and acid.

It ran through my veins in an electric shock that snapped through my muscles like the bite of rubber against asphalt. My back arched as bones seized, muscles pulled, and pressure swelled like a balloon against my bones. I couldn't move. I could barely breathe. The pressure expanded against my skull until the world began to fade, black and white popping against the trees as I tried to reach them. Desperate to reach safety. To stop myself from falling.

It was all I could do not to scream, not to writhe. Edmund's men were right behind me. I couldn't fight them, not now. I finally reached the tree, collapsing into it as I bit my tongue in an effort to stay silent.

Blood filled my mouth, warm and salty, as the heat of my magic ripped through me, trying

to stop whatever was happening to me, but it was no use. There was too much. The heat only added to the acidic burn, to the tremendous pressure, until it too was part of the pain.

Clinging to the rough bark, I stared at the dark, jagged lines that ran over my hand, over my arm, as I waited for the pain to pass.

I was so used to the black tongues of flame that had been burned into my skin, that it took me a moment to realize that they were moving. The twisted lines had begun sliding over my skin like poisonous snakes.

Forcing my scream to remain locked inside, I turned in fear to the man beside me.

Sain hadn't been speaking of the battle that was coming. He hadn't been warning me of the camps that surrounded us.

He had been speaking of me.

I was almost out of time. And, judging by the dark, hooded look he gave me, he had known all along.

"If I can only bind the curse, not send it into Edmund, and I die before my father, then the curse will be unbound, and it will

be unstoppable. Wynifred will die. To save her life, my father must die first."

The deep boom of thunder rumbled through my bones as the words my darling brother had said so many centuries before screamed in my mind. He had made the promise to keep me safe. Ilyan had made the promise to keep him safe.

Neither had happened.

Now the curse was unbound, and I was to die like the others.

But how?

I had killed my father, I should have been set free, which could only mean one thing.

Either Cail had been wrong. Or my father hadn't died quite as fast as I had hoped.

Even if Timothy was the first to die, the Zánik curse was unbinding, and I was cursed to face the traitor's death, the most painful demise that my kind offered. To literally be burned from the inside out.

Biting down a scream, I clung to the tree, hands wrapping around the rough bark as I tried to support myself.

Sain looked at me with dark eyes, his impenetrable sadness feeling like a slap in the face. I wanted to yell at him, to shake him and demand answers. Instead, he gave me the same nonsense he had been spewing for days.

"We are running out of time."

"Sain?" My voice was a gasp as I reached toward him in anguish.

My fingers were distorted and broken as the dark lines of my scars snaked over my skin. They twisted as though the wires were on a string, tightening, choking. The sharp barbs carved into me and infected me with their poison, with the heat that spread from them.

"Please." The word barely escaped as the once bound curse slowly seeped its toxin into me.

Still, he didn't move. Only stared, a darkness taking over his eyes.

"Sain." The word was a whimper, a plea. It was a sound ground in agony before the heat grew, before my legs gave out underneath me, and my vision faded to black.

I wasn't sure if I had fallen. I wasn't sure if he had caught me. For all I knew, I had fallen through the earth and was trapped between layers of rock and stone.

Within moments, the world around me had become nothing except pain and pressure. Heat wound its way through me like knives and rope. I couldn't tell where I was. I couldn't distinguish my body from the pain, my voice from the screams, my thoughts from the heat.

The curse had covered every part of me. It had taken me away until all that was left was the curse.

There was only heat.

There was only pain.

There was only death.

I was the curse. I was the pain. There wasn't a me anymore.

There was only Zánik.

"We need to get you inside." The words flitted to me through the darkness, the voice distorted by my own screams that drifted in and out of my mind like television static.

I was trapped in a place that was only pain, where mind and body didn't matter anymore. I had lost them somewhere along the way.

Strangely, I didn't care, either.

Somewhere, deep inside, something screamed that I was giving in, that I was letting the curse destroy me. But that too was trapped behind the static that devoured me. My screams cutting in and out like a bad signal the only sound I could hear.

Until something else joined them.

The sound of voices.

Other voices.

Familiar voices.

They cut through the static in languages I didn't comprehend, even though I knew I should.

"I thought you didn't like to wake the dead?" A sneer broke through the low hum of noise and pain, my body twisting as someone shook me. The sudden realization of a world outside the static-filled room felt strange and foreign.

Pressure wrapped over my arm as someone held me, long nails digging into my skin as someone threw me around like I was made of nothing more than fabric and a little bit of stuffing.

The broken-stone courtyard of the Rioseco Abbey flickered through the dark as I was thrown around, streaks of what I was sure was blonde hair adding to the visual cacophony.

My screams plowed through the static like a steamroller as my they drowned me, before pain swelled and sucked me into the void again.

"I didn't make that decision for you, Ovailia."

Warm water rushed over me at the words, the heat a balm against the pain. The smooth depth of the accent cut through the static and pulled me out of the disconnected world.

I knew that voice.

I knew it, but I couldn't focus through the pain enough to know from where.

Thunder rumbled as air moved through my hair, strong

arms wrapping around me as if I had done nothing more than fly into them.

"Goodbye, Ovailia," the voice came again, the sound soft as his voice tickled over my skin. The familiarity pulled again, this time revealing the name of a King who had saved me so many times I could barely count.

"Ilyan." I wasn't sure if I had spoken aloud, if I had been able to control my mind enough to work over the screams that rattled inside of me.

The static came back and stifled Ilyan's voice and whatever words had been meant as comfort were lost in the room that the pain had trapped me in.

I was sure we were moving, I was sure he was talking, but I couldn't register that. I couldn't be sure. I could only hope that Sain would be able to tell him of Prague, that he had told him of whatever he had seen. If I was lucky, they were taking me to Joclyn. I could say goodbye.

I wished he would hurry up.

"Wynifred." Thom?

His panicked shout broke through the fog and slammed against both heart and memory so hard that for a moment the pain vanished.

Was I already dead?

I hadn't seen him in centuries. I wasn't sure if he was really there, or if it was a cruel delusion of the torture I was trapped in.

"Wynifred," his rough voice came again, breaking through the static like a battering ram, the sound so clear and embedded in my memory that, even if my mind had still been bound, I was sure the sound of his voice would have broken the cage wide open.

For the first time since the heat and pressure of the Zánik curse had begun to devour me, I could focus beyond it. It brought back a hope that I desperately wanted to cling to. To fight against the curse, to force my magic to battle, to force myself not to give up yet.

His hand was against mine. I could feel his fingers as they ran against my face, my tears as he caught them. The surface I had been laid on depressed beneath me as he sat beside me.

I still could not see him, but I didn't care. If this was what I heard, what I felt, before I died... There was nothing I could have wanted more.

"Thom?" I was sure I had spoken this time, even though my voice was broken and airy.

"I'm here." His hand tightened around mine at the shattered emotion of his words. The memory of how he had looked when he cried over Rosaline still so clear inside of me. The way his eyes pinched together, his hand instinctively moving through his short, brown hair, much the way that his brothers did. For a single shaky breath, a joy I didn't think I could feel again took over. As quickly as it had come however, it was sucked from me, swallowed by pain as my back began to arch and writhe.

"Am I dead?" The question came without prompting, the seemingly childish query more honest than I had meant it.

There was only dead and not dead yet, now. I couldn't ask if I was going to be okay. I didn't have that luxury anymore.

"Not yet, sweetie, but I'll stay here until the end," he said with an exhale, his voice shaking even though I could tell he was trying to be strong. Strong in the way he held my hand, the way his hand pressed against my cheek; even through the shake of his nerves, of his heartbreak.

It made me ache. It made my muscles twist and writhe.

It made my heartbeat reawaken with a painful pulse of regret and longing.

In the last moments of life, I felt more alive than I think I ever had. I focused on that, focused on the heat, focused on the hand that held mine, and the blackness that surrounded me fell away.

A dimly lit room that I recognized at once began to come into focus, and a man who even though he had changed— even though his hair was in long dreads and his skin more worn, his eyes slightly dimmed— was still the man who had taught me so much about life and love.

It was still Thom.

I looked at him, the pressure of his hands tight against mine, as I saw him for the first time in centuries. As I saw him for the last time.

I didn't dare say anything. I didn't have anything to say. He had heard it all before, felt it all, lived it all. So, I held his hand, staring into him as the world began to shift, and the black of the curse threatened to take me.

Watching the grey seep into the world, I waited for it to come, but instead of death, the bright courtyard of the Nuremberg Castle materialized before me. The world blended together as my mind took me to a place that I hadn't seen in what felt like years—the beautiful, perfect world that Talon and I had created inside our Tŏuha.

I hadn't moved, Thom's hand was still wrapped around mine, but I could clearly see the sanctuary that my bond with Talon had created.

Every brick in both stone and wall reflected the reds and greys that they had for over fifty years, the bench we had spent so much time on sat glistening and waiting, nestled into an alcove of the garden outside the castle. It was all the same, peaceful, calm. Home.

Except for the shadowed body of a man leaning against the wall of old stone.

My soul jerked at the apparition, the discolored, shadowed form seeming out of place against the dewy world.

"Talon?" my voice was soft with longing as I stared at the shadowed shape, the features shifting, moving as he turned toward me.

My heart clenched in expectation, wanting to see him, to run to him before the entire scene vanished into smoke and ash. Swirls of grey encompassed me, pulling at my hair, at my heart, before it began to fade and I was left staring at Thom's tear-streaked face, his eyes deep with understanding.

Pain rattled me as I screamed, the agony ripping at my throat as my heart was torn in two. Everything was torn in two. Two worlds, two realities. I was saddened Talon was gone, my heart throbbing for the return of the Tŏuha. Yet, I clung to Thom, to the past, and to the last moments I would have with him.

"He will be there, waiting for you," Thom whispered as he leaned close to me, the brilliant blue of his eyes devouring me. "He's going to be right there... and... and you know who is going to be with him?"

"Rosaline?" The word pierced me, my back arching with fire and gut wrenching agony.

Never before had I regretted my decision to forget, not because I had turned my back on a life that had been so good, but because I had run away from Thom. A man who was still mourning the loss of our daughter as I was. He was still filled with pain and agony. We had both chosen to run away, although in different ways.

You can't escape something that is wound so deeply in

your soul, however. I knew that now. I knew that in the way Thom's voice pulled me from the pain of the curse and the way Rosaline's memory bound us together.

"Yeah, sweetie, she is going to be right there with Talon. She's been waiting for you, waiting... for her mommy."

Everything ached at his promise, the pain from the curse slamming against me as he turned away in his own pain. Body writhing, I struggled against the scream that tried to rip itself out, against the black that wanted to take me away again.

In a way, it would almost be more preferable, but I didn't want to lose this, lose these last moments. If only I had a choice.

Staring at Thom, my vision began to waver, the same courtyard from before materializing around me. The same shadowed figure was tucked off into a corner; except, this time, he wasn't quite as shadowed, he wasn't quite as far away.

He stood before the bench, everything around him crisp and clear. He, however, was discolored in patches of grey and black, the color swathed around him like wisps of smoke and fog.

Swathed in dead, I realized.

He was dead, and I was not. Not yet. He was standing there, ready to take me into his arms, ready to hold me in death as he had in life.

"She will be there," Thom's voice echoed through the bright courtyard as if he was sitting right there, but I didn't see him anymore. He was only an echo of a life that I was leaving behind.

"Do you remember that big smile she had after she lost her first tooth?" His voice was a boon in my ear, but I couldn't look away from the dark pain in his eyes. "How she would always push her tongue through the little gap?"

I knew Thom wanted me to answer, but I wasn't sure I wanted to. I was locked in place, staring at this man, waiting for him to take me, waiting for the smoke that smothered him to swallow me.

"She's not responding..." Thom's voice was broken, the pain clawing against my heart.

I almost turned to him.

"You have to choose." A heavy masculine voice echoed over the courtyard, it cut through the fog and resounded through my head in such a way that I knew it had come from inside me.

Come from the man who stood before me, shrouded by death.

Talon.

I could choose to be with him. I could choose to die. Or I could choose to live.

But how? You couldn't choose to live through this, through this curse. I was going to die. There wasn't a choice, only a reality.

"Just keep trying," Sain's voice cut through the distanced thoughts, tugging me back into reality. I wouldn't follow. I remained staring at the shadowed man, the distorted body shifting as it stepped forward. The swirls of grey and black picked up as a hand reached toward me, fingers pressed through the cloud becoming more than a shadowed distortion. They became real. They were skin and calluses and a scar I recognized at once.

They became Talon.

I looked up to him, expecting to see his smile, but he was still smothered in the smoke. His body was out of focus, as if my eyes weren't powerful enough to see.

"Do you remember when we took her to the beach?" I could barely hear Thom now, even though his voice was right there. He was fading away.

"You have to choose," the deep voice came again, rumbling through me.

I wanted to tell him I didn't have a choice, that someone had already made it for me. I couldn't seem to find the words, though.

It didn't matter, anyway.

Talon stood, his hand extended toward me, beckoning me home.

I began to reach toward him, a warmth spreading through me as I approached, swelling, filling me with each step. The pain of the curse was almost gone now. Fading into nothing as I left it behind. Left life behind.

Except that I knew that wasn't right.

I knew that warmth. I knew that magic.

It was a soothing balm to the pain, but it wasn't supposed to be here.

Something was wrong.

Something was pulling me back.

No, not something—someone.

"N-n-need m-more." I recognized the voice at once, even through the broken stutter and the fear that trembled underneath it.

It was Joclyn.

It was her magic that I felt move through me.

It was her power that was trying to heal me, to save me.

I looked up to Talon. The smoke that had swallowed him slipping away to reveal his grey eyes, his slight smile. He was there, so clear I could almost reach out and touch him. I wanted to.

My heart was screaming.

But I couldn't.

I couldn't move.

Sain had seen this. He had seen every bit of this. His need to get me to Joclyn had been so sure, right from the start. It wasn't merely to say goodbye, either. They still needed me.

What was more, I still needed them.

I still needed to live.

"I'm sorry." I couldn't get any more out than that.

Talon smiled, the emotion clear, as if he knew what he had done, as if he had been planning it for years and was proud of it. Seeing that look, seeing the playfulness in his eyes, a look that was so distinctly him I couldn't have a hope of recreating it within my subconscious, I knew it was him. I knew it was real.

All of it.

"Be happy, Wyn," he whispered as the smoke began to swallow him once more, his voice soft in my ear as Rosaline's laugh echoed around us.

The warmth grew with his words, it smothered me as the smoke was smothering him. The two of us frozen as death took him, and as life took me.

"No," I tried to scream the word, to reach for him, to stop him from leaving, but I was trapped under the warmth.

A residue of pain swelled alongside the warmth, everything beginning to fall away as the healing aroma of damp sandalwood and pine assaulted me.

"Talon." I tried to gasp his name as he faded to nothing, as the world of our Tŏuha faded to nothing and reality returned in the form of a hard bed.

I tried to move, and although there wasn't much pain, there also wasn't any response to my demand. I lay like a sack of rocks.

A deep groan escaped my lips in irritation, the sound instantly met by a relieved gasp that was not mine.

My eyes snapped open in alarm at the sound, my heart beating a million miles an hour as they worked to adjust to the dimly lit space. The heavy buzz of agitated voices filled the air as my eyes went to the man who hovered above me, his cheeks stained with tears and long ropes of his hair pulled away from his face.

"You're awake," he gasped as the loud buzzing of voices disappeared into nothing. His lips twitched into a smile so rare I was sure no one had seen it in centuries.

I stared at him—at his eyes, his dimples, and the face that I had memorized hundreds of years before. My heart pulsed once in an emotion so strong it almost felt out of place given the calm I had left, what had happened, and the way my soul and heart had been split into two pieces of memories and life.

Be happy, Wyn.

"Thomas."

2

WYN

I HAD FALLEN asleep clinging to his hand, our fingers intertwined in a hold that was more friendship than passion. It was a grasp that was exactly what we both needed—a hand to hold, a reminder that someone was there.

When I woke, his hand was still there, the calloused skin rough and slightly sweaty from holding on to mine for so long.

The room glowed with a few lanterns that were scattered over my desks and tables. The flashes of lightning blended with a slight orange glow, giving everything a haunted look and far too many shadows for my liking.

At any other time, seeing Dennis DeYoung and the rest of Styx with half illuminated faces might have been cool. But waking up from the brink of death made it a bit too much.

Besides, nothing should be allowed to mar his beautiful face, strictly speaking.

Thunder roared through the abbey, the pained soul of the earth screaming as I lay on the soft sheets staring from

80s hair gods, to the necklaces that hung from the ceiling, to the brightly colored walls. They flickered with the light of thunder as my mind slowly began to wake up, blinking to life as everything that had happened over the last twenty-four hours swirled together.

More like slammed into me like a dead weight.

Roughly turning over, I brought my hand to eye height, peering through the dim light to the shadows of black that covered my skin. The marks had always been so dark, like ink scraped into my flesh, but now they were barely there. Now they were shadows, making me wonder if I was seeing them properly, if I was remembering them the right way.

If I was remembering anything the right way.

The pain.

The dream...

The massacre in Imdalind.

The reason we had come here slammed into me, my breath heaving as I tried to sit up, although it became crystal clear it wasn't going to happen. Any muscles I had been hoping to awaken seized, and I called out in pain. Expletives and screeches ripped from me in a ribbon.

This wasn't going to work.

"Wyn?" Thom was understandably worried but it wasn't enough to dispel the level of confusion I was having.

"I need to get to Ilyan," I knew I was speaking irrationally, even in my half-awake fog. "Tell him what happened ... in Prague. Tell him what Edmund did."

"He already knows." Thom's voice was full of regret, a dark cast moving over his features as he shifted closer, his hand tightening around mine. "Sain told him last night."

The tension in my chest increased like I was in a vice, the soft bed suddenly feeling like a slab. I should have been happy that I had been spared that conversation, but I couldn't be. Not with the way Thom stared into the darkness, his shoulders hunched and broken, lost in thought as he always was when he was brooding.

Part of me wished he would say something. That he would talk. That I could ask him a million questions, dig into his soul and discover everything that happened over the past hundred and fifty years. However, there was another part that wanted to curl up in a ball, cry, mourn, and ask this seemingly unfamiliar stranger to leave.

And that was part of the problem.

I had thought I had figured all of this duo-personality mess out before, but as I lay there both wanting to cry and punch something, it became clear that there were too many parts of me now to have anything be that easy.

There was the part that killed for sex and money, hunted, and spied on my own people for centuries; there was also the mother, the mourner, the lover; the part that loved Talon and the part that loved Thom.

Sitting here with Thom, in the room I had decorated with Talon, was mashing them all together in that irritating "pretending REO Speedwagon is a decent band" kind of way.

REO Speedwagon was not a good band, and I clearly didn't know who I was.

I was laying amongst band posters and brightly colored comforters, trapped beside a life that felt unfamiliar while staring at the man who owned my heart long before Talon had been around.

It made me want to roll my eyes, which made me want to slap myself.

This was not going to work.

I tried to sit up, as if the motion would shake off the stale air, but my muscles were still refusing to respond.

"I'm sorry, Wynifred," Thom whispered into the dark chill of the room as a brilliant crack of lightning smacked against the walls. I jumped like a panicked dog.

All those muscles and bones that weren't moving before pulled painfully at the movement and I groaned, the sound escaping like a slow leak.

A slow, whiney, leak.

While I was grateful for whatever Jos had done to save my life, it also seemed to be the equivalent of getting hit by a Mack truck covered in protruding knives. And probably with a herd of deer following behind. I was sure, if I looked close enough, I would find a few hoof shaped bruises.

"Why are you sorry? It's not like you could have stopped anything with that magic of yours," I regretted the question the second I asked it. I regretted the way my voice snapped as it always had and the anger that flowed freely behind.

One part of me was kind of a jerk.

I opened my mouth to apologize, to take it back, but Thom only smiled, his bright white teeth flashing in a straight line behind slightly chapped lips. I started at the response, my heart beating fast in confusion before it sunk in—the reason for his smile, and why my knee-jerk reaction seemed so comfortable to him.

It was me.

The me he knew, anyway.

The jerky me that spoke without thinking and had limited value for human life.

My stomach flipped at the knowledge, my body shaking in exhaustion as I forced myself to look away, to look anywhere other than at him.

Of course, doing that pulled me face-to-face with Talon. Well, memories of him anyway.

Stupid room was full of too many stupid memories.

"They said you had changed." Calm washed through me at the slight laugh in his voice, so freaking familiar, and handsome. I still refused to look. "I'm glad to see it's not too much."

"I have changed." I snapped at him as if that settled it.

It didn't. He chuckled but I still didn't turn, choosing instead to stare at a goofy picture of Talon and I that had been framed in the 70s. It was taken back when every picture came out sepia toned and far too yellow. We looked like we had taken a bath in yellow mud, and it didn't quite wash off.

I stared at that picture, the calm rhythm of Thom's breathing the only sound in the room.

Calm, and somehow so right that it hurt. How did he do that?

"I had a different life... a hundred years..." My voice faded away as I looked from the picture to Thom who was still staring at me, awed that I was back from the dead.

Which I was.

I snapped my eyes shut, the memory of Talon standing in the white shadows of my dream flitting itself into place.

Screw this.

Once again, I tried to force myself up, desperate to escape now. Once again, muscles and bones only greeted me with a terrible agony. I wasn't even able to sit up all the way, I just flopped over like a fish.

"Ilyan told me," Thom said as he moved beside me, carefully reverting my pathetic attempt at escape and helping me back to bed, the old bed frame creaking under the movement. "Right after it happened, he told me about how you forgot everything, how you fell in love with Talon..."

"He fell in love with me, too." The words burst out, desperate to be heard.

More importantly, for Thom to hear it from me and not from Sain or any of the other gossips in this place.

Which I did, I realized with all the frustration of a teenage drama queen.

With our past, we couldn't pick up where we had left off. There was no way that would happen.

"I'm not surprised. You're easy to fall in love with." His voice was calm, sweet. Perfectly understanding. It was Thom.

Recognition flared inside of me in the most awkward of ways. A chuckle erupted from my throat that was equal parts flirty and smug, the two emotions, the two halves blending together until I sounded like a strangled duck.

A psychotic strangled duck.

"That's rich," I spat, needing to expel both the duck laugh and the look of dread Thom was giving me. "Seeing as making people fall in love with me used to be the last thing they would remember."

I let it flow—the haughtiness, the warning, the irritation that had been trying to fight its way out for the past few minutes. Memories of blood flowing down my hands came with it, more questions and confusion rising right alongside.

I needed to destroy something, the heat of the fire magic rising to the challenge at once as I sat up, fire and magic numbing any pain before I collapsed against the wall my bed was pushed up against.

I still had a strong desire to wring necks. I was fairly certain it wasn't a good thing.

"At least they had one good memory before they left."

"Lust or love? Neither is a good memory," I shook my

head, looking down to my hands twisting in my lap as I tried to expel the lump that was building in my throat.

"I'm still in love with you," he spoke as the sky rolled with sound. The power of the earth magnified his declaration. My eyes widened as the words slammed into my chest, sucking my breath away into the chilly air, taking the images of blood and death with it.

I searched his face, my eyes running over old scars and the dreads that were quickly growing on me. I was frantic to find the lie in his eyes, to have him break out into a laugh and declare his words only in jest. Instead, he held my focus, the warmth in his eyes wrapping around me so tightly that his gaze might as well have been holding me.

I couldn't move if I had tried, the wall held me against it as if I had been strapped there.

I needed to, though. I couldn't let those words float between us with hope, commitment, and devotion on their backs like everything was the same.

It wasn't.

Not anymore.

"That's part of the problem, Thomas. Like you said, I've changed. Everything has changed." I tried to keep my voice strong, to keep the same depth of the person he knew intertwined with each word, but the person I was faded into nothing as I wilted under the warmth he projected toward me.

I might as well have been singing a 1920s love ballad for all the good my attempt did me. The 20s were a terrible time for music.

"Change is not always a bad thing, Wynifred. Sometimes, it has to happen to show us who we really are and set us on the right path." He spoke as if my foolish attempt to push him away had been just as pointless as batting at a fly.

A heavy weight pressed against my chest as his words began to sink in, my already pained heart beating faster, rebelling against him. Rebelling against each word as though it was spoken with acid.

I didn't want this change.

I didn't want Talon to die. I didn't want to be set on the right path. I didn't care if it was meant to happen. It upset me. And me thinking like a child was upsetting me more.

"Well, this change hurts," I gasped, my voice cracking as I clung to the blankets that lay over me, the soft cotton that I was sure would still smell like Talon if I got close enough.

"I know." Thom reached forward, his hand smothering mine in a heart stuttering motion that sent both uncomfortable tension and eager palpitations through me. "I know. To lose someone you love—"

"It's more than that." My voice was stronger as I pulled my hands away from him. "He was my mate. He was my other half. And I loved him as much I did Rosaline, as much as I did you."

"Is that a problem?"

"It's confusing trying to decipher if the love was real, if any of it was."

My heart had forgotten how to beat. The heavy, lead cage clamped so tightly around it I was sure it would fall right to my toes, a solid mass of bleeding, useless flesh.

That was it.

That was what it was about.

More than who I was and what I had become, it was knowing the most treasured parts of my life were real— Thom holding me at night and reciting poems in French. Talon bringing me flowers and dancing with me in the lamp light. Rosy cuddling into my collarbone, her breath hot on my skin as we tried to sleep.

They all felt like a dream and not like a life I had really lived.

I had to find the reality.

"The love was real," Thom said, his hand pressing through the blankets against my knee, the warmth of him seeping through the heavy layers of cotton. "You know it was. Change does not detract from the promises and the realities you know. It's all true. Some of the facts may have been hidden from you for a time, but that doesn't change what you know."

I wanted to believe him. I wanted to let his words seep deep and become real. They only floated somewhere in the air between us, however.

Thom seemed to see that. He sighed heavily as he crawled over the bed to sit against the wall next to me, the frame and mattress creaking and shifting dangerously underneath us. He sat there, his hand still wrapped around mine, the pressure soft and careful as he leaned into me. The bright blue of his eyes deepened as they soaked in what little light we were surrounded by and saw the man I had spent so many years with, whom I had cried against.

Who I wanted to cry against now, but there was still Talon, the man I had bonded myself to. The man I had said goodbye to and watched disappear into a fog with a smile still on his face.

Be happy.

Pain, frustration. It all vanished as the memory of Talon faded back into the yellow sepia photograph. Then the part of Thom's words that I had so diligently ignored banged against my skull like a bass player on a sugar high.

Sometimes, change has to happen to show us who we really are.

So we can find ourselves.

"Thom?" I asked, the word choking on its way out.

He only shook his head, his eyes shining as he wrapped his hand around mine. Then he pressed his forehead against mine, leaning into me the way we had done so many times before.

"The love," he whispered, his voice soft in my ear. "The life you had, the life you built; the memories you hold, the memories you will make; and every whispered word, every shared laugh, they were all true, Wynifred. I still find you very easy to love."

My heart restarted as the words seeped into me, as the pain in my chest eased enough that I could feel my heartbeat.

I sucked in breath then pulled away from him as he did me, his hand pulling away so softly I almost missed the movement.

"You always were wise beyond your years, Thom."

"Everyone keeps saying that lately. I'm about to go back to not talking. As irritating as pretending to be mute is, at least I wouldn't have to put up with being known as the Dalai Lama."

"To you perhaps." I sighed, my muscles already tightening at the admission I was about to make. "I've missed talking to you. I would miss it still."

"Do you remember, Analine?" Thom asked, the sheer abruptness of his question catching me off guard. Not because it had come out of nowhere—something that was standard practice for him—but because of what he was asking about.

Of *who* he was talking about.

"Your mother?" I almost couldn't get the words out. They felt foreign.

"Yes."

"Of course." I don't think I could ever forget the woman who, at the time, was regarded as one of the most beautiful in Europe, a French princess Edmund had quite literally stolen off the throne. There were still portraits of her hanging throughout the world, except no one knew who she was anymore, just a nameless beauty whose memory Edmund had squashed into oblivion.

I had known her quite well before Edmund had ordered me to remove her heart. The memory of her tear-stained face came to me without prompting. She hadn't even fought me. She had only rambled in French about her son. The man who now sat before me.

"Before she was taken away, she told me something about my father that I didn't believe until after I had left. Something about how he loved me, but he didn't know how to show it, because he had never felt love before."

"I find that hard to believe." I couldn't keep the scoff out of my voice, not like I really tried. The idea of Edmund loving was painfully laughable.

"So did I. Because I had never felt love before, either. I had never known love strong enough that losing it destroyed me. Losing Rosaline destroyed me. Losing you..." He paused, his voice catching in his throat as he looked down to our hands, to our fingers sitting so close to each other I could feel the heat of his skin radiate against mine.

I reached forward without thinking, my hand pressing against his in a desperate show of support, a plea to remind him I was there. Despite not wanting to, I was feeling the same things he was.

Even after three hundred years, her death still hurt. It always would.

"You can't show love unless you know what it is to feel it. You can't recognize it until you've lost it." His voice muffled toward the thick bedspread, the silence following his words drowning us until the room illuminated with a forked streak right outside the window, his body continuing to shudder under my touch.

"You know it's real, because you feel the pain of the loss. You know it was real because you are showing me love even now."

"I've changed, Thom." I spoke softly, hating the way my words punctured into his soul, the way they deflated me.

My hand dropped from his back as he rose to face me, the room roaring with noise as he looked into me. Stared into me.

"Everyone changes. But you have not changed as much as I was expecting. There is softness in your eyes that wasn't there before. Even after Rosy was ... born," he ended lamely, his eyes leaving their intense focus to look at his large calloused hands as they writhed over each other.

"Is that why you are sorry?" I asked, my voice so soft and meek I wasn't even sure it was mine.

I waited for him to answer, knowing I needed to give him time but anxiously hoping that whatever he was going to say would help me solve the swirling identity puzzle I was trapped in. It was like an intro to a Yes song, long, meandering, and hopefully ending in something great.

"No. I'm sorry for leaving you behind."

I froze, every muscle tightening in tense ropes as I stared at him, my heart a thundering pulse at the apology he had shared with me.

He had left me behind.

However, he had also held me as we cried, as we mourned the murder of a child we had both adored. That loss—that moment when we had watched her soul slip from her body and into the red-tinted knife that Edmund would later use against me—had destroyed us more than I think either of us had realized.

He had withdrawn into himself, mourned and cried in inconsolable sobs that scared me, something only Sain understood. I, instead, had chosen to lock the emotion away, killing hundreds of Draks and thousands of mortals.

It had been the only outlet I could find.

I had needed him, but he couldn't be there for me. He couldn't, because he was as broken as I was, and inside that shattered soul, his only recourse was to flee, leaving me behind.

Another pain had been added to the mound already there. That pain threatened to cripple me as he reached for my hand, his hot fingers wrapping around my cold ones. His eyes searched mine, waiting for a response, for an acknowledgement, for the forgiveness I wasn't sure I could give him.

Not now.

Not when the emotions, the sadness, the memories of abandonment were so fresh.

With only a few words, he had brought all of them back. The gauntlet swelled inside of me so fast I could barely breathe. It built in a wave of magic and anger that I felt sure was going to explode.

I wanted it to explode.

I wanted Thom to hear, to feel the depth of what he had done to me.

I wanted to make him hurt as I had so many others.

Yet, that part of me wasn't the only bit anymore. It wasn't

the only emotion I had, the only memory I clung to. Yes, it was me, but there was more—more understanding, more compassion, more forgiveness that Thom had never been able to instill inside me.

I was more.

I was more because of what had happened, because Thom had left. I was more because of Talon. And, although it hurt, I don't think either of us could have come to terms with our monsters if we had stayed by each other's side, if we had let the demons that plagued us grow together into a roaring beast.

Now, as we sat across from each other, his hand wrapped around mine, the soft bed I had shared with Talon sagging under our weight, I thought I understood.

Not in its entirety, and I don't think I ever would. There was too much in this world to understand, too much to make sense of, too many lives to meld together. However, as I squeezed his hand and let myself fall into the emotion in his eyes, I at least grasped the first step of the thousand-step journey I was about to take.

I had said it before in the belly of Imdalind with my legs shackled to a wall.

I am Wyn.

Sometimes, you didn't need to overthink things, and I had definitely been doing that.

Be Happy.

"But you came back," I whispered, my voice cracking as tears silently fell down my cheeks. "And that's all that matters."

Thom smiled at me as his hand tightened around mine, sighed and opened his mouth to speak. Any words that he would have said were swallowed when the bed shifted so abruptly I was sure I was about to fall out of it.

Thunder roared, and the abbey groaned, but I knew at once it was more than the fit the earth was throwing. It was something magical, something that had erupted from inside the walls.

"Are we under—"

The abbey shook again before I got my question out, the hallways echoing with the sound of an explosion. Dust shook from the rafters as a shout echoed over stone, a fine layer of dust falling over us in some type of ridicule.

"I don't know. Can you find them?" The bed groaned loudly as Thom jumped up, standing over me as he looked out the window, searching the fields and forests that surrounded us for signs of movement, war, and who knew what else.

"Of course I can," I answered with a snap, immediately pushing myself forward in what would have ended in a head-first dive off the bed.

My body screamed in protest at the motion, the soft mattress feeling like a branding iron as I landed on it and dropped my hand down to the old hewn wood of the floor. The surface was smooth after a couple hundred years of feet and furniture, the wood feeling like warm satin as it too began to heat, its hidden magic welcoming my own, right as I plunged my power into it.

Even through the weakness that Joclyn's healing ability had left me in, I knew I had enough energy to at least try to find the enemy. Battling was probably out of the question, unfortunately.

Well, at least that's what I would tell myself.

My magic moved through it as I searched for the pinpoints, searched for the little pressure of power that I could always feel.

I hadn't even reached the exterior walls of the abbey

before the panicked screams echoed through the hallways and into my room, rendering my search unneeded.

"I don't need you!" The words came loud and clear as my depleted magic snapped back into place, my exhausted body sagging against the bed as I slunk over the floor.

The anger and frustration behind the shout was terrifying, but there was something else that was even more frightening: the magic that followed on its heels. The voice that was unmistakably Joclyn's, followed by a man's, and while the words were undistinguishable, I recognized the panicked tone at once.

Edmund had turned Ryland into a weapon specifically to hunt and kill Joclyn, and somehow, they had found each other. If Sain had told Ilyan what had happened, Ilyan should know better than to let the two of them find each other.

Something was wrong. I needed to get there.

Gripping the side of the bed, I immediately worked to push myself up, bound and determined to go help my friends, to stop the massacre before it began.

"Stay here, Wynifred. You will only hurt yourself." Thom said as he jumped off the bed, attempting to hold me back.

"Yeah, right..." My grumble was barely audible as I pressed against his palm, defying his silly need to protect me.

It probably would have worked too if I hadn't looked up and been frozen in place by his eyes.

Deep blue and full of so much... affection.

"Please." I had never heard that level of desperation in his voice. It was like sticky syrup against my soul—warm, yet I wanted to wash it off before it dried there.

I nodded in numb disbelief.

Thom returned the gesture before he ran, the echo of

the door snapping shut behind him settling over the still room as I sat, staring after him.

Listening to the screams of my friends.

To the thunder of magic echo through the hall.

Screw this.

What in the world was I doing?

Thom should have known better.

I couldn't ignore this. I needed to be there for my friends.

My legs shook as I pushed myself to stand, the skinny limbs already quaking in fear of having to hold my weight. My arms were an unset gelatin as I gripped the mattress, the treacherous thing giving far too much way, and I almost went down before I was able to catch myself.

Perhaps this was a mistake. Yes, I needed to help them. But I could barely stand, my stubbornness was going to get me in trouble.

I probably would have stayed still if another shake of magic hadn't surged through floor and bed, awakening my magic with a pulse that empowered me.

Yeah, I needed to get there and pull Ryland out of the hell his father had created for him. I needed to see Joclyn, to know she was okay.

I burst from the bed, barely reaching the wall before everything began to shake and give out, the cold stone turning into a slick support. I wasn't even sure how I was staying upright with the pain that raged through every inch of me. My fingers didn't seem like enough as I dug my nails into the groove of bricks, my toes curling against the floor.

Each step brought a new agony, each one ignored as I practically dragged myself along the wall, following the sounds of screams and magic as though they were a beacon.

Another explosion of magic nearly sent me to the

ground, my fingers barely enough to keep me upright as I pressed my forehead to the stone, as if it could help me not tumble down. I waited for the pain to stop, for the strength to continue, only to have the silence broken by a scream that pierced my heart, a plea that never should have seeped past that girl's lips.

"I want to kill him!"

"No, Joclyn, you don't," Ilyan's voice came right after hers, the pain behind it only adding to the shock of Joclyn's plea, to the knowledge of who she was speaking of.

"I do!"

"No, my love, no," Ilyan consoled, his voice strained with a patience and love that, given the situation, seemed very out of place.

His footsteps grew louder as they approached, the heavy taps of Ilyan's shoes frantic against the stone as they walked through the hallway right in front of me. Ilyan held her tightly against him as she fought and wailed, beating on his back with fists clenched so tightly they were pure white.

I took the last few steps as quick as I could, my body dragging along the stone as I leaned against the corner, pressing my face to the smooth, rounded stone. I watched Ilyan's retreat, watched Joclyn as she screamed, as her blood red eyes looked past me to the battle she had faced and the boy she wanted so desperately to rip limb from limb.

The streaks of color in her eyes screamed with agony and madness, and my heart dropped. The same lunacy I had seen in Ryland so many times before now stared at me. A broken spirit trapped somewhere deep inside a mangled soul.

"What have they done to you?" I whispered more to myself than to her.

I should have killed Edmund when I had the chance, I

should have seen his actions for what they were when I was only a child.

Joclyn's screams faded to nothing more than echoes as Ilyan carried her away, leaving the abbey in the sobs and rumbles that came from somewhere behind me, from the men who carried Ryland's immovable figure.

His lips were tinged blue, blood dripped over his skin, his mouth lolling in the same way it had when Cail had beaten him, when Edmund had used him. His heart and soul were as battered as they had been his entire life, a loveless existence that he had been forced to endure.

It was him that I followed.

3

RYLAND

"I WANT TO KILL HIM!"

Joclyn's screams rumbled through my head, bouncing off the stone hallways of the abbey, or what was left of them. We had destroyed most of the walls in that room in our attempt to kill each other.

"I want to destroy him!" Her scream mixed with my father's laughter, rattling against my skull as I lay on the remains of the wall I had been thrown through. The screams, the laugh. Together it was so loud it was hard to ignore.

Or rather, it was hard to find myself amongst it.

She tried to kill you. The filthy Drak almost killed you.

I know...

I know.

The second I acknowledged his rambling my rage picked up. My magic flared in sparks and screams, each one desperate to kill Joclyn, to chase after her. I needed to get her. To kill her.

She almost killed you.

The attack Joclyn had hit me with when she sent me

through the wall, however, made that nearly impossible. My magic may be sparking, but my body was seizing in a painful near-death.

She doesn't love you anymore.

No... no...

I groaned at the voice, trying to silence it as I lay in agony. Cold hands pressed against my chest as someone tried to save me, chasing away whatever miniscule grip on reality my death would have brought. Precious sanity slipped away, retreating back into wherever Edmund had taken it.

You heard her. She doesn't need you. She tried to kill you.

She tried to kill me. I told her to kill me, and she tried.

She doesn't love you anymore.

I know.

You know what you need to do.

I need to make her pay.

Stop wasting time.

And then I screamed.

I writhed against the burn of my throat as my lungs ached from the air that was finally finding its way back into them after the last few minutes of denial.

Joclyn should have worked faster. She should have sucked the life out before they'd had a chance to stop her, before they had restarted my heart and plunged me back into this prison of madness.

At least then I wouldn't hurt anymore.

Perhaps then I would know who I truly was, and not be trapped behind torture, forced to watch the last memory I knew was mine slip away.

That Joclyn loved me. That I loved her.

You don't know love.

Now, I had lost the only thing I had. I couldn't be sure of anything anymore.

Kill you. Joclyn tried to kill you.

Except for that. I could be sure of that.

Words filled my mind like acid against my soul. I would normally fight my madness, fight to keep hold of who I was, but laying there, feeling the pull and tug of hands and magic and who knows what else as I was carried away from her, away from her screams. I couldn't find the strength.

My father's voice was right, she had tried to kill me.

The familiar surge of ownership and desire that I always felt at the mention of her name was suddenly nothing more than a bothersome fly in the back of my mind.

A fly that echoed my emotions back to me in a cruel nightmare. There was only anger, hatred, and a reckless need to find her, to hurt her, *to kill her.*

To kill her.

The words blended with my moans, with the echoes of her screams, and with the unfamiliar voices that chattered around me until I could barely tell my madness from reality.

Everything mashed together, as whoever had grabbed me carried me away, their magic pressing against me in healing. In comfort. In control? I couldn't be sure anymore.

The idea of comfort was too foreign.

Don't let them touch you. You need to get back to her.

I know. He took her.

You need to find her.

I tried to fight, although whether it was with the hands or the voice, I wasn't sure. No matter how hard I screamed and writhed, however, my body didn't respond. I was trapped inside my own mind.

It was the worst possible place to be.

Deep down, I knew what was going on. I knew what he had done to me, and how he was controlling me. That control was slipping thanks to the distance of my father from me, but I still couldn't pull past the screams. I still couldn't drown out the ridicule my father had implanted inside of me.

Find her now!

I was still a prisoner.

"Her, too?" The mumbling voices that had surrounded me broke through the madness, but the voice was unfamiliar and my panic turned into a bass drum in my head.

"I suppose keeping them away from each other is going to be harder than we thought." Sain's familiar cadence punctured a hole right in that bass drum. Heart, mind, everything slowing as something familiar, something comforting, smashed against me.

If only it was enough to stop his voice from filling my mind.

You had the perfect opportunity to kill her!

"I don't like this." The unfamiliar voice was strained as I was jostled again, they were clearly carrying me somewhere.

"You think I do?" I tried to focus on Sain's response, to let it drown out the madness and allow the fragile pieces of sanity I had left to take hold. "We're surrounded by an army! We have two children inside who are trying to kill each other and two adults debilitated..."

"Edmund has thought through his plan far too well." The second voice returned, the tone so dark that it acted like a trigger, sending my heart and muscle into a terrifying tango. It felt as though I was being run through a meat grinder, combining that with the muscle pain from my near death was not something I was interested in continuing. "You sure you didn't have anything to do with this, Sain?"

Go back and find her!

"Even if I did, do you think I would have been able to stop it?" Sain snapped, the voice slamming against me and I groaned, the sound the first one I had been able to muster. "You rescued me from that place all those years ago, you even helped in controlling me. You know I have no say in the matter."

Kill her.

"I know. It's just…"

Kill!

"Don't you trust me?"

"Kill!" The word burst out before I had even reached a fully conscious state. Every command I had sent to my body over the last few minutes broke through the barrier at once, and I flailed, arms and legs tangling one over another as my magic reacted.

The men called out in alarm as I slipped from their hold, falling onto the hard stone floor like a hundred-ton weight. A ripple of pain shook through me, pulling at bones and muscles that were already ripped and broken. I screamed, the sound more in frustration than pain, as tiny droplets of blood sprayed over my hands, making the taste of blood in my mouth grow.

She tried to kill you.

Find her!

I'll find her.

Kill her.

"Kill her!" The words ripped out of my chest as I attempted to crawl away from Sain and the stranger, to find her in any way I could. I needed to. I needed to finish the job. The thought was unstoppable.

I hadn't moved more than a few feet before their hands were on me again, pulling me back. Dragging me through the stone lined hallways of this wretched place. Everything was tinted an alarming shade of red from the blood that still flowed through the gash in my head. Crimson rivers drenched my hair and landed in droplets on my eyelashes before drying against my skin in sticky pools. Everything was the color of death, it wasn't helping me regain a grip on my sanity.

"Let me kill her!" I tried to fight the men again, but their grip increased. Although, they had given up on carrying me, and were now dragging me across the rough wood floor. The sound of grinding wood cut through my shouts as a table skidded away from us on its own, the ancient wood slamming against stone and splintering with a loud crack.

I wonder which of the two had done that. Probably the dreadlocked stranger, I was pretty sure Sain didn't have it in him.

Cold stone slammed against my back as I was thrown into it, the red in my vision flickering to black before strobes of green and grey detonated, casting the room full of dark, haunted shadows.

Just like the dungeon.

Sain may not have thrown the table. But he did do that.

Welcome Home.

I slammed my head against the wall, as if the motion would expel his voice from my mind. Instead, it only enraged him more, his laugh pounding against my skull.

"Breathe, Ry," Sain whispered from somewhere beside me, his shadow stretching over the tables and chairs that filled the wide room.

"Shut up," I hissed through clenched teeth, that small desperate hope rising up to defeat my father.

"Excuse me?" That rough voice snapped, but I didn't

turn, I stared into the black and green abyss, letting it be my stable ground.

"He's not talking to you," Sain hissed, his shadow moving closer as he came up beside me, obviously intent to pull me out of the hell I was trapped in. Doesn't he realize how impossible that was?

You can't escape me.

"No... Nonononono... No... no..." Words seeped from me the same way they always had, my whole body tightening together as I clawed at my hair, pulling at the blood-soaked curls in an attempt to escape the madness. Pain ran over my scalp with each tug, the pressure giving me something else to focus on.

"Don't let him in," Sain said as he sat down to face me.

His eyes were filled with the same kindness, understanding, and sympathy that I had always known from him. Except, there were no bars between us, only the dull, green glow of his magic.

I stared at him from between my scarred and filthy forearms, from behind the blood that dripped from my hair, wishing it was enough to drown out the demons my father had infected me with.

Kill him, too.

Kill Sain?

Kill them all.

No.

"Ryland, it's okay. You're okay." Sain's voice was calm, his hand soft against my arm, his eyes patient and... *just like hers.*

No.

You saw her eyes.

Black, dead eyes.

The eyes of a dirty Drak.

43

My heart rate sped up, panic and desperation infecting me as my father's rumbling scorn returned. Twitching, I tried to cover my ears, but it was pointless. Instead, I focused on the aged face of Sain and the pale man whose voice I hadn't recognized before.

Now I did.

Thom.

"I need... Kill..." I couldn't keep the words locked away.

"No, Ryland," Sain and Thom said together, but it did no good.

Kill.

"Kill." I slammed my back into the wall.

Kill.

"Kill." I slammed my head into the stone.

Kill.

"No, Ryland," Sain soothed again, placing his hands around my head to stop me from the deranged motion.

"I need to find her," I groaned, as he held me in place, his face inches from mine as the dull roar of his magic seeped into me. "I need to find her."

"You don't want that." Sain hissed, the cracks in his perfect calm beginning to show. Little cracks of gasoline that added to the roaring flame.

Yes, you do.

"If I can't have her," I growled as I tried to pull away from him, "then no one can."

"You don't mean that, Ryland."

"Need... Now." I hissed as I yanked myself away, moving right back into a rocking, mumbling mess.

"This is pointless," Thom said in a growl from somewhere in the dark, his words laced with a pity that only enraged me more, and I screamed. The loud feral sound ripped from my throat and made everything taste like iron.

"Ryland," Sain whispered, but this time he didn't try to stop me. He sat there, his body calm as I glared at him from behind the damp strands of my hair.

"They are nowhere near here. The blade is nowhere near here. You are safe."

You are never safe.

But he said...

Not from me.

"You are safe," Sain repeated as if he could hear the battle raging within me. I tried to keep my focus on him, but it was nearly impossible. My eyes kept drifting, my body kept swaying. It was hard to control my body, hard to control my mind. "You're safe, Ry."

Safe.

My heart clung to the foreign word like a lifeline. Although I could still feel the tension that rippled through every muscle, the rocking slowed, my breathing slowed. He pressed his hand against my bicep in a reminder of the reality we were in.

Reality. Sanity. It was a fine line that I fell from easily. All it took was Cail's taunts. Ovailia's smile. My father's laugh. I pressed my head against the stone wall, trying to focus on the icy chill of the rock and keep myself from falling off the high wire I was attempting to balance on.

"You are safe, Ryland."

My hand shook as I placed it against his arm, my fingers leaving streaks of blood on his elbow as I pulled him toward me.

Calm. Controlled.

"I want to kill her." We both jerked at the calm mellow of my words.

I hadn't meant to say that.

Other words had been forming in my mind, words and thanks, yet those were the ones that had escaped.

Sain's face blanched as the pressure of his hand increased. I could feel his pulse through my skin, feel it accelerate as mine did, as my body tensed at what was coming.

"I want to kill her." The words felt sane. My voice wasn't of my madness, yet I knew they had been wrought in the same subconscious place. I knew they were real.

It scared me.

That's my boy.

I flinched at the feigned love that oozed through it. My heart sped up at the acceptance I had always wanted, despite knowing what that meant.

And perhaps how doomed I was.

Kill her.

"Kill," I hissed.

Sain's lips pressed into a tight white line. He knew what was coming as much as I did.

"I want to kill her."

"Ryland." His plea was useless.

"I want to kill her." My roar echoed round us, the light of his magic fading to black as my power smothered it, as thunder rumbled alongside.

"No, you don't." I jumped at the new voice as much as the snake that lived inside me did, the slimy creature reacting with a violent spark, as if it was reacting to an enemy.

An enemy to attack, or escape.

I needed to pick one, the thought had nearly formed when a bright orange light joined Sain's green one. Its arrival was a frightening unknown, and I jerked, pressing myself into the wall in a need to escape.

The colors blended awkwardly, leaving us sitting in a puke-filled room as Wyn slowly meandered toward us, clinging to the wall as if it was part of her. Thom groaned loudly, swore in a snap and rushed to her, practically peeling her off the wall as he hissed at her in a language I couldn't quite make out. She waved him off, keeping her dark eyes trained on me as she shuffled over.

"I need to," I hissed through gritted teeth, wishing there was a way I could restrain it, wishing I wanted to.

Then go.

"I need to go."

"No, Ryland, you don't," Wyn's face was wrinkled in a pained grimace as Thom helped her to sit before me, her arms shaking as she supported herself. As she leaned into me.

The shaking increased under the intensity of her stare, and my back hit against the wall. The same stone, the same chill, the Wyn.

Then why was I so scared of her?

"I do." The words were a moan.

"No," Wyn said, a smile turning up the corners of her mouth, pain still haunting her eyes.

Her pain hit against my heart, her agony peeling away the crazy and letting my worry peek through in torturous empathy. I had seen what my father had done to her. I had heard her screams too.

I wanted to reach for her. To hold her and apologize for everything. To make her madness go away. But I couldn't even expel my own.

I couldn't guarantee that I wouldn't wring her neck instead. Hurt her to get to Joclyn.

I slammed my back into the wall with a little more force, wishing I could break through and escape.

"I need to get to her," I whimpered, "I need to ki…"

"You don't, just as she doesn't want to kill you," Wyn continued as if nothing had happened, her tone still kind. Her eyes didn't even hold a scrap of worry, or fear.

She's lying. She wants to kill you, too.

No, she's good.

Don't fool yourself.

She wants me dead.

I want you dead, too.

The truth of the phrase was a lightning bolt, the power behind the tiny piece of will I still held snapping through me.

"I want you dead, too." The flash of lightning painted the room yellow as I spoke, the roll of thunder right behind bathing the room in a dread that caused Wyn's smile to flicker.

My words were clear, honest, and although I knew I spoke them to my father a tiny part of me spoke them to her, too.

"No." Wyn's voice was more forceful than it should have been, given how weak she appeared. The strength behind it moved through me with a jump that pulled my wavering focus back to her. "You don't. Edmund does. The demon that Edmund has placed inside of you does. You need to stop listening to him, Ryland. Don't listen to your father's voice." Her words were calm, full of more knowledge and experience than I would have given her credit for.

Kill them all.

His voice was a laugh.

Did she know? How could she know? Did she hear him, too? Did she hear him yell and scream? Did she have the same memories of pain as I did?

Looking in her eyes it was clear that, even though she

knew, it wasn't the same. There was still something else there, though, some other pain I couldn't quite place.

You saw her... Don't listen...

"How?" I asked, the word broken as I forced it past the madness, past the voice that only grew louder.

"How do I know?"

I nodded once, my sagging curls falling over my face and dropping in my eyes, I didn't dare look away from her though.

I needed this answer.

"Because he's done it before, Ryland," she whispered. The gravelly edge of her voice was so different from what I had heard before that for a second I wasn't sure it was really her.

"To you?"

"No." Her voice caught in her throat as heartbreak pulled past her words, the sound so raw and honest it yanked at my soul, bringing some long-forgotten memory to life.

I only barely registered that I wasn't rocking anymore.

"He did it to Cail before he became what he was. He did it to Mym, your sister. He did it to Rosaline, my..." Her voice caught again.

I wasn't sure if I was breathing. I leaned away from the wall, desperate to hear.

Thom's hand wrapped tighter around her, bringing her closer as he enfolded her in comfort and support. So kind, so gentle. When was the last time I had felt the same? Their connection tugged at the tiny thread of sanity I felt, before it all unraveled with one feral shout in my ears.

Lies!

Don't listen to her. You know you need to find her.

But Wyn knows something...

Don't trust her.

But I do...

Make her pay.

Make them all pay for what they have taken from you.

I cringed as the voice came again, strong and powerful, and my muscles twitched in fear and anger. My hands moved up to my ears in another desperate attempt to lock him out, but I knew it would only keep him in.

"Don't listen to him, Ryland," Wyn whispered.

Find her.

"How?" I moaned, the word grinding behind clenched teeth. "Too loud."

Before I knew what happened, I was rocking again, slamming the back of my head into stone as my hair bounced before my eyes. Words repeated on my lips as they did in my mind, the hatred flowing in time with the rhythmic pounding of my back against stone.

Kill. Pay. Death.

They consumed me.

Until, with the touch of the soft hand that wrapped around my wrists, it began to slow. A burning heat of unfamiliar magic flooded me in a painful wave that sparked against my nerve endings as though they were being electrocuted.

The fire-filled pricks ran over my body with the force of a thousand tiny knives, the pain growing as the heat did. I tried to move away, I tried to escape her touch, escape the fury in her eyes as she leaned toward me, gripping me. She only clung tighter, Sain and Thom holding me in place as I began to scream.

"No!" The word ripped from me as the scream did, as I writhed and tried to fight, but it was no use. The pain continued, the screams continued, the words 'kill,' 'destroy,' and 'no' mixed with my screams until it was nothing but noise. Nothing, but the gasps of those who sat before me, who held me.

And then there was only... nothing.

Nothing except heaving breaths and tense waiting.

My screams stopped as abruptly as they had begun, the voice in my mind silencing into nothing but a memory.

Silence I hadn't heard for months. Silence that I wasn't sure I had heard in my entire life. He had always been there, whispering, criticizing, ripping me apart. Now there was nothing.

Nothing but me.

My mind was clear.

The pain was still there, wrapped around my arm in a white-hot wire that cut right to my bones. Compared to the freedom my mind now felt, however, the pain was bearable. The pain was unimportant.

I looked up to her in wonder, moving from the shadowed markings on the hand that held mine to the girl who leaned against Thom in such a weakened state she could barely keep her eyes open.

"Wyn?" I asked, the steadiness of my voice sounding unfamiliar to me.

"That's how," she breathed, the words taking far more effort than should be necessary.

Her eyes fluttered open from where she leaned against Thom, a playful smile dancing on her face at what she had accomplished.

"Are you okay?" I asked, fighting the desire to pull my hand away and protect her.

This wasn't good for her. This couldn't be good for her.

"I used to do this to Cail. Although I wasn't recovering from a near death cursing then," she gasped, forcing a laugh as she squeezed my hand. "I would bind his heart with a shield. It kept Edmund out of the Štít and his mind. It gave him freedom. You feel it, don't you? Free?"

I could only nod. "A Štít? Is that what he did to me?"

"No," Sain answered, his voice sounding louder without the competition inside of me. "What he has done to you is much more dire. You are his son. You are his blood, so he can control you without such complex methods. You will never escape the seed of his mind that he has implanted in you. Instead, you must become stronger than it."

My stomach dropped. I didn't need to hear more. I knew he was right, I had a million memories of what I'd had to endure as Edmund's son to verify that, to magnify whatever he had infected me with. Every beating, every snub, every moment I was ridiculed.

It was true. Right then, however, with my mind free from my madness, I didn't feel like it had to be.

Right then, I felt a whisper of who I wanted to be, as if I still had a chance to be good.

Who I used to be had been killed many months ago by the man who gave me life. To give life, only to then take it away seemed to be the sole thing he was good at.

"Right now… Everything is clear… like when we were in the waiting place."

"Yes," Sain said, kneeling down beside me. His hand was still on my shoulder, as if he expected me to fight him. "Even in the waiting place you were plagued by the monsters Edmund placed inside your soul. Wyn has only shielded your heart from the monsters, but the memories and the emotions are still there. She has just made it easier to decipher them."

He was right. Even though the voice was gone and I felt more of what I used to be, I wasn't whole. I still had the memories of Joclyn hunting and hurting me, memories of a distorted version of me that he had used against me from the moment he had broken my mind, when he had begun to take 'me' away.

I had more to defeat than the voice. I had to rise above what Edmund had done to me from the beginning.

What he had created.

What I had become.

None of this was me.

I was still dangerous.

"Don't give into it, Ry," Wyn said, her voice shaking as I felt the shield begin to slip, her exhausted magic retreating back into her.

I wanted to plead with her not to leave, but I knew there was nothing I could do to stop her. She was collapsing before me, just as I was slowly shattering inside. What little calm I had been given had been a lifesaver. Like a reset button, it had given me another chance to gain control of my mind.

I lay back against the wall as I prepared for the onslaught and steeled my mind against the voice that was coming. I promised myself I could defeat it, even if I felt as weak as Wyn looked.

The stone was strangely comforting as I huddled into it, wishing that somehow I could fall asleep and escape the voice for a little while longer.

This much anger, this much hatred wasn't me. Well, it didn't used to be. Not before my father took control. Not before he changed me.

He had taken away all the hope and love that Joclyn had given me.

I pressed my body into the stone again, right as it began to shake. Feral sounds of a never-ending pain echoed through the abbey, rippling through my bones until it was as if I felt it for myself.

"What was that?" Wyn voice rattled with fear as the building shook underneath us again.

"Ilyan," was all I said, grateful when my brother's name on my tongue didn't insight another onslaught of anger and fear.

"Ilyan?" Wyn asked, more in surprise than in question. "What happened? They couldn't have been fighting, could they?"

"They better be," Thom grumbled from beside her. "If their porcelain chamber pot didn't break soon, I was going to smash it against the wall. It's about time they went at each other's throats."

Wyn smacked Thom's arm as the yells continued, the abbey continued to shake and tremble with his pain. We sat there in silence, waiting for it to slow, to calm. It never did, though. It only grew until my heart began to ache with him.

"Shit storm or no, I am beginning to wish Talon was still here," Sain said, Wyn flinching into Thom's arm as my surly brother gave the Drak a glare.

I waited for some kind of explanation, but none came. Knowing Sain, however, he deserved more than a glare.

"I guess I better stop it before it gets to out of control." Thom spoke as though it was the most unsavory thing in the world, a severe lack of disinterest making me question his intentions. Then again, as the room rumbled and yet another scream of pain and heartbreak surrounded us, I could see why he wouldn't want to go to his brother.

Our brother.

Dust fell around us like rain, the abbey rumbling right alongside it. Without another word, Thom sighed, stood, and moved toward the door, his dreads swinging wildly with the movement.

"You coming, Ry?" Thom asked before he had moved more than a few steps.

I froze at the question.

"I'm sorry?" He couldn't be talking about me, could he? He shouldn't be. Putting me before Ilyan right now would be madness.

Thom only laughed. I guessed madness was his forte.

"He's your brother, too. You know, family sticks together and all that. One of the many lessons our loving father taught us."

"But, it might... I mean... I know why he's..."

"So do I." Thom spoke sadly as he looked toward the sound of breaking glass and crumbling stone. The first real sighting of emotion in him seemed very out of place against the tough biker guy that stood before me.

"I would only try to kill him."

"Your choice." He shrugged. "Soon, you will have to get to know who your family really is." He walked toward the door before he had finished, leaving me cowering against the wall with Sain's hand firmly on my knee, the pressure keeping me in place more than anything.

"Oh, and Sain," Thom turned as he stood in the doorframe, his forehead wrinkled in an emotion that didn't quite meet his eyes. "Will you take Wyn back to her room... or at least pretend to? We all know she has no intention of staying there, after all."

His voice was so flat I couldn't be sure if he had spoken in jest or in truth, but Sain only laughed and nodded in agreement.

I didn't know what to make of Thom. He was far too

quiet and sarcastic for me. The idea that we shared a father, that we were related, seemed impossible.

Thom stuffed his hands in the pockets of his leather jacket then walked out of the room in a shuffle, his shoulders hunched as if he had been born with a hump.

I watched him go, the voice growing steadily louder as I fought it, fought the pull to follow Thom, though I knew it was an impossibility. I couldn't fight the voice for much longer.

No matter how hard I tried.

You should kill him, too.

Thom and Ilyan.

You should kill them.

I should?

4

RYLAND

As if Thom had somehow known exactly what Wyn had in mind, she left shortly after he did. However, unlike Sain had promised, he made no move to stop her.

Wyn and Sain had stared daggers at each other in some silent conversation I didn't even try to follow before she had pushed herself to standing, and Sain remained sitting by my side.

It wasn't as though she was running away either, she was still so weak she had to lean against any available piece of furniture as she made her way out, and to, I assumed, Joclyn.

Months ago, I would have been the first to stand, the first to offer her my arm and lead her away. I would have rushed to Joclyn so we could all eat hamburgers and talk about whatever problem had come up between her, her mom, or her twelfth grade science teacher. But not now.

Not anymore.

She was gone, taking her orange light with her.

Now, it was all I could do to focus on the chill of the stone against my face as I leaned into it. To savor the last few moments of fleeting sanity. To stop myself from rocking, stop clawing at my hair.

Even if everything was loud and confusing, I could remember what sanity felt like now. Wyn had given me that.

She had given me a hope of escape.

Stop messing around! Get up. Find her.

I don't have to listen to you anymore.

Don't listen to that fool girl. She doesn't know you. She doesn't know how you killed your own mother. She doesn't know how wicked you are. I own you. You are nothing without me.

I didn't...

Don't lie, Ryland. You are just as wicked as I am. Just as worthless as all of my children.

I'm not.

You are nothing.

No.

Nothing but a murderer. Worthless.

I groaned, a long throaty exhale rattling my chest and filling the air with more pain, the sound of my father's laugh accentuating it. The pressure of Sain's hand against my leg increased at the noise, the touch sending a jolt through me and I jumped, moving away from him and into the wall.

"What is it, Ryland?" Sain's voice was lined with that same paternal calm that had soothed me from the very first time I had heard it.

My focus turned to him before darting away again, my heart rate picking up to a speed that felt both painful and impossible.

"He's coming back." Getting the words out was like wrestling a rabbit from its hole. It kicked and pulled, and in the end it only screamed louder.

Tell him what you did.

The words sliced through the sanity, pulling at the

strands of it as I pulled at my hair. Tugging, pulling. Perhaps if I pulled hard enough I could pull him out of my mind.

With each yank, however, the echo of his laugh increased, the sound rattling through my soul in such a way that it only brought more fear.

I was sure he was standing right beside me. I could almost feel his hand on my back, prompting me to kill them all.

"Ryland?" Sain's voice filled with that calm depth I had come to expect from him. "No one is here. It is only you and me."

He's lying.

Ilyan is here.

Not far away.

Close enough to kill.

Kill.

You can still hear him.

You can reach him.

He's not far…

No! I can't. I won't. I won't.

It's just me and Sain.

That's a lie.

I'm here, too.

"No!"

"Don't listen to him, Ryland," Sain continued, ignoring my outburst.

You're never alone, my son.

"He's not here."

I jerked toward Sain again, the constant pull of my fingers through my hair lessening as what he said seeped in.

"How did you know?" I asked in a whisper, surprised at the clarity of my voice.

"I know because I've lived through what you have."

Sain's voice was dark, the gravely base filling the room with a haunted echo as he leaned closer.

The dim green light of his magic cut across the heavy lines of his face, casting him in monstrous shadows that made me twitch. I knew it was Sain, I knew him. But for a moment the green of his eyes looked more menacing, his smile darker, and I saw a monster inside of him that I wasn't quite sure didn't exist.

I pressed myself into the stone as he moved closer still, "The voice you hear? I heard it, too. I *hear* it, too."

I had been surprised at what Wyn had told me before, about Cail. But somehow, that seemed like peanuts compared to this. He heard him. He knew. But that didn't make any sense.

See? He lies to you, too.

They all lie to you.

His voice was such a growl of accomplishment that I couldn't even find it within me to rebut.

After all this time, my father was right.

Sain and I had been imprisoned together. He had helped me pull away from the beast I had been infected with. Why had he said nothing then?

I knew it shouldn't matter. With everything we had been dealing with, this small piece of information was as inconsequential as bread, and yet... it felt like a betrayal.

"Why... why... didn't you tell me... you knew?" Each word grew in decibel as my anger did, my father laughing right alongside.

Sain didn't flinch at my outburst. He didn't seem to acknowledge me as both magic and breath picked up into short, ragged, bursts.

He lied. He lied!

"He did. He lied," I answered the voice aloud, mumbling as I began to rock and pull at my hair.

He lied.

"He should pay."

"Ryland." I heard Sain's snap, but I didn't look up at him. I was too consumed by the voice. Too lost in its madness.

"Ryland." Sain's voice was a boom of thunder in the dark, his voice echoing back as the green of his light buzzed and grew. The sound, the pressure of his hand against mine, it all pulled my focus, leaving me glaring at him, ready to attack. He didn't seem to care. "It wasn't my choice not to tell you. My sight did not show me of what was to come until now."

"Do you always follow what your sight says?" My question was more in irritation than honesty. I already knew the answer. I had asked him the same thing more than once, and the answer had irritated me more every time. Something Sain very well knew, which is why he only chuckled derisively at me, the sound deep and abrasive.

More lies.

Don't waste your time with him. He's nothing but a filthy Drak.

He's not lying.

Kill him, too.

I flinched at the voice, barely able to maintain control of my mind.

"My father... he controls..." The broken words were all I could hope to get out through the schizophrenic conversation that was rattling inside of me. "Filthy Drak."

It was the same as always—broken words, broken mind.

Luckily, Sain caught my meaning as perfectly as he always had.

"Edmund attempted to control my mind and my sight

for centuries before you came along," Sain said, his voice a touch darker than I had expected it to be. "He was much less successful than he believes himself to be."

The laugh faltered inside of me as my confusion smothered it. From the broken fragments of sanity I found in the dungeon, I had watched my father manipulate and control Sain, use his sight for his own good.

While I couldn't be completely sure of what I had seen, it sure looked a heck of a lot like my father had control of him, and his sight.

"What... do you mean?" It took a lot to force those few words out.

"I control my sight more than you know." His voice was lined with a menacing undertone I hadn't heard from him before.

I recoiled, sure I had seen a demon in his eyes before he smiled, and waved his hand to the side as though it was nothing.

"I am the first of my kind, the first to control my power. All the power of the Drak flows through me. I see what all others see and control the flow of that magic. It is the same with your father. He is the first of the chosen children, his first mate was the immediate descendant of the first of the Skříteks. All the magic of the Chosen flows through him. It is why he is so powerful."

I opened my mouth, desperate to ask more, but no words came, only a haunting laugh that alone seemed to confirm what he had said. I could only stare at him, the depth of what he told me sounding more like a prayer than a secret. Perhaps it was both.

"All the magic is connected, like some sort of waterfall?" It was the only analogy I could think of through the broken pieces of my mind. A waterfall, a steady flow from the top to the bottom, a ribbon that flows through everyone.

Sain only nodded in assertation, his face twisting into an odd little grin.

"Why didn't I know this?" It took all my strength to keep my volatile anger at bay, and even then, it nearly exploded with one snap from my father.

You aren't worthy to know.

I jerked at that. Thankfully, Sain ignored it.

"I'm not sure even Ilyan knows. And, if he does, he is using it to his advantage. Ilyan is powerful for a reason, you know."

To protect Jos. The thought was simple enough, a fact I had been told time and time again, but it was one that had always hurt.

Protect? More like steal.

So much for keeping my anger at bay, the anger and madness that came with the thought of her was taking over.

He took her.

I know... I couldn't deny it.

Stop playing around.

Kill them all.

I slammed my back into the wall as I tried to fight it. Tried to throw the voice and emotions and pain out of me. Hitting my head against the cold stone, the voice grew louder. It seeped out.

"Kill... kill... kill.."

It bled from me as though I was possessed.

Perhaps I always had been.

"Focus, Ryland." Sain's voice tried to break through my insanity, but I barely heard it, barely felt his hand against my shoulder. "You can do this."

"No... nononono... Kill..." The words kept coming, the

image of Joclyn attacking me floating through my mind with more blood and hatred than I was sure had been there when it had actually happened.

"Ryland"—the pressure grew—"you are stronger than it."

"Nooooooo…" If agony could be put into words, that would be it. It would be the phrase that would encompass my soul and the sound that seeped from me, the echo of a breaking heart. "No."

"Yes. You can do this, Ryland."

You can never defeat me.

Do what I ask. Maybe then I will set you free.

Maybe?

Kill them.

"Don't listen to him." Sain scooted closer, his fatherly voice a deeper calm than I had come to expect from him.

Sain was the strong support I had spent my entire life without, his presence a painful reminder of what I had been missing in my upbringing.

"It took Cail centuries to master; me, decades. It can take you weeks. You are stronger than us all."

"How?" The word sounded as broken as I felt.

"You were calm before Cail would pull us into the nightmares," Sain said, his eyes sparking a brighter green. "How did you accomplish that?"

I knew the answer already. He had told me the very first time when I was pulled into the blade, when we had met and I could think clearly for the first time in weeks. I had felt like myself. It was the blade. It held what my father had taken from me.

I would always be broken until I got it back.

"I want my heart back. I want my soul back." The words were more of a sob as I stared at the dim dawn light that had begun to stretch over the ceiling. My heart clenched at the normality, my battered soul wishing the comforting green would never leave.

"You can get it back," he whispered, pulling my focus from the grey stone.

"How?" I asked, attempting to drown out the laugh that had begun to filter through me, the joyful strain an overture to the answer I already knew was coming.

"We will have to get the knife from your father. To do that, you will have to face him." He tried to make his voice lower, as though it would lessen the blow.

It didn't.

"You will have to fight him."

"I... don't... I can't..."

You're right. You can't.

You never could.

And now is no different.

"If you can get me that knife, I can fix everything," Sain said, the laugh in my mind making his voice sound darker. Sound like my father's.

The sound of it pulled me further into my madness.

"I need..." I gasped, my hand pulling at my hair, wishing I could pull out enough that the voice would fall away.

What do you need?

"I need..."

Say it.

"I need to kill..."

Sain shook his head in disappointment, a move so parental I was surprised I reacted the way I had seen teenagers on television do so many times before, considering it was something my father had never done. My father's way of parental scolding was something more along the lines of torture or forced destruction.

"You don't need to kill Joclyn."

"I do... I need..."

What are you waiting for?

Kill her.

"Kill... Kill... kill."

"Look at me, Ryland. Look at me."

I repeated the word over and over, the call for blood flowing from me, until Sain grabbed my chin and forced me to look at him. His hard eyes dug into me enough that I could focus on not pulling away, even if the word kept coming.

"Focus. Think of the space before the dreams, the space where your heart and soul are one. Think of how you felt when Wyn placed a shield over your heart... that calm. You said it yourself. You want your heart back. You want your soul back. That's what you want," he repeated, his hand dropping from my face, his now bloodstained fingers looking broken in the dim light.

Sain was right, it was what I wanted. But in order to find that, in order to reach that, I would have to face my father.

Face me.

It was that thought that destroyed me.

Edmund's laugh echoed inside of me as if he knew the impossibility of what was before me and found joy in watching me fail.

He always had.

Try. You will fail.

The thought was a painful stab, and I jerked, causing my head to slam into the stone in a move that was both a comfort and pain.

"The soul's blade," I whispered, the acknowledgement of where my sanity was kept filled me with more fear than hope. Fear because I knew what it was, knew what it had been used for. Fear because I knew where it was. More than guarded by my father, it was within me, as well.

"Yes." Sain's voice was little more than a whisper, the depth filled with a gravelly yearning that was similar to the growl my father would make when he saw a woman he desired or someone who possessed magic he wanted to take.

Desire and greed all wrapped together with enough malice to melt a brick.

But from Sain?

My stomach wrenched, my jaw clenching in expectation of seeing my father before me. But it was a disheveled old man with skin like battered leather.

"Yes," he repeated so normally I was sure I had only heard the words in my head. The clarity had me questioning my sanity even further.

If that was possible.

"It is with my father." I sighed. "It is inside of me." The word was a gasp as I tried to get him to understand, and my hand pressed against my heart as the painful throb I had felt since I had first stabbed the thing into my own heart pulsed painfully.

You will never get your soul back. The voice was a laugh.

"Ryland?"

Just look at you.

You need to kill them.

"Ryland?"

Now.

Now?

Before it's too late.

"Ryland!" His heavily accented voice should have been enough to pull me out of the psychotic prison I was trapped in, but it only ignited it more. The owner of the voice was the last person I needed to see right then.

Ilyan.

It's him.

It's time.

Kill him!

I rushed the blur of long blonde hair before he even came into focus. I didn't need to see his ridiculous blue eyes and haughty expression to know who it was, I could tell by the accent in his voice.

The monster inside of me collided with the monster I had become, exploding out as I erupted off the wall, my body flying toward him while my magic flared, ribbons of red and black streaming from me in a mad attempt to wrap around him, to devour him.

Kill it!

"Kill!" I screamed, a tiny voice inside of me pleading for me to stop. It wasn't enough. It would never be enough.

Destroy him.

"Kill!"

I had barely moved more than a few feet before everything froze. The magic that had been streaming away from me slammed into a wooden table, shattering it and recoiling painfully back into me, throwing me back against the wall where I had started. Suspended above the ground, Ilyan's magic held me in place, a thick shield moving around me, yet whether to protect me from myself or him from me, I wasn't sure.

Not that it mattered, with the rage in Ilyan's face it could have been both.

Everyone had heard of Ilyan's temper. He was known for it. What was more, although I had seen it before when I had helped him to escape my father, to have it directed at me was another story. Terrifying was not a strong enough word.

What are you waiting for?

You weakling, attack him.

Kill him.

I can't.

He's right there.

Do it now.

Kill!

Ilyan glared into me, filling me with the knowledge that he would destroy me with nothing more than a snap.

Seeing the warning in his eyes wasn't enough to quiet the monster inside of me, however.

"You!" I roared as his magic pressed into me, restricting me against the wall as I snarled like the wild animal Cail had turned me into.

"Yes." Ilyan stalked to me slowly, his eyes sparking as though they were on fire, and not the blue we had all inherited.

He's right there.

Now is your chance.

I can't reach him!

You can break this barrier.

You weakling! Kill him!

Kill him!

Kill!

"Let me kill you!" The words ruptured as my magic did, the powerful spark slamming into Ilyan's barrier with a crack that echoed over the empty stone. I slid down the uneven wall, collapsing into a broken pile of flesh; bones and muscles that were flaring in agony. I wasn't even able to lift my head before his magic snapped back against me like a rubber band, slamming me into the wall once again.

I knew it was foolish to fight my brother. I knew I couldn't win. Yet, the laugh continued, the madness swarming me and giving me no other option than to fight him.

"Like you tried to kill Joclyn? Like she tried to kill you?" Treating me like the wild animal I was, he stepped toward me slowly, every motion calculated as his eyes bored into me.

"I should have killed her first," I yelled alongside the voice, the outburst earning me another glare.

"No, Ryland." He was trying to disguise his rage. It didn't work.

It only added fuel to my fire.

Kill him!

All he does is lie to you!

Everything he says is a lie.

Don't let him lie to you!

"You lied to me!" The roar matched the creature that dwelled inside of me.

"I lied?"

He's still lying!

"You said I could have her, that you were keeping her safe. But she's not safe. She's broken. She's an ugly Drak, and she doesn't love me anymore!"

Sain flinched, Ilyan snarled. I didn't care about any of it. It irritated me how precisely Sain followed his sight as much as the knowledge that Jos was just like him did. I had been raised knowing that Draks were nothing more than dirty servants. Slaves. It was why Sain served us. It was that imbedded knowledge that was leaking out now.

No matter how much my heart screamed that it was wrong.

"You did that!"

"I did that?" He laughed, his blue eyes flashing

dangerously as he took another step toward me. "I made her want to kill you?"

He was so close now that I could feel the heat of his magic against my skin, the burning power of it scalding. My gut constricted in fear, everything tightening in warning. The tiny voice in my subconscious screamed at me to back down, yet I couldn't stop myself.

The voice wouldn't let me.

"You lied to me!" I yelled again, fighting against his restraints, ready to throw myself against him and claw his eyes out if I had to.

I would.

I wanted to.

No.

YES!

"LIAR!"

"I kept her safe," Ilyan said calmly, his anger rumbling against the surface, pressing against his magic until it was white-hot against my skin. "I could not stop him from destroying her. I could not stop her from being tortured and breaking your bond. I did everything I could, but sometimes, things do not turn out the way we plan."

"You liar!" The words erupted from deep inside my broken mind as I fought against the heat. Fought against the pressure.

"No, Ryland." I could tell he was trying to calm me, to soothe me, it wasn't going to work. I wouldn't let it. "Whatever our father has done to you—to both of you—it is deeply rooted in your souls. It is dangerous."

Ilyan's voice rumbled with regret, his god-complex so thick it made me uncomfortable. It made me mad.

He had taken everything. Like hell if I was going to let him lord it over me.

That's my boy!

"You are saying that because you want her for yourself. Because you think you love her!"

I wanted the words to stab. I wanted them to hurt. They struck home.

"I do love her!" The words roared with ice and flame, the strength and power slamming against my heart with enough force, enough anger, that I knew they would ignite the monster that Cail had implanted inside of me.

They should have, they should have given me the strength to defeat him.

They didn't.

It was a cold water bath to hear the truth, even more so to hear the emotion behind it that Cail had almost missed. To hear the love.

Silence punctuated the icy chill in my heart as Ilyan sighed, stepped back, and ran his hand through his hair.

"I have loved her for eight hundred years." Ilyan continued, his eyes digging into me in confidence and commitment, "I have loved her since the sight was first given that showed her to me, since the first time our magic bridged the gap of time and let me hold her in my arms. Her. Her laugh, her smile, her wit. I love the way her eyes sparkle when she plans a trick and the way she laughs to herself when she thinks of something funny. I love the way she sleeps curled into herself. I love her. And, because I love her, I would give her the choice. I would let her return to you if that's what she wished. I protect her so she can make that choice."

"Why are you telling me this?" The words choked in my throat, barely able to escape. I wasn't even sure he heard. He continued on as though he was the only one in the room.

"All you two wish to do is kill each other. She is so

terrified of you she cannot form complete sentences, and you cannot hear of her without the voice in your head exploding to life. Do not play me, Ryland Krul. I know what that look in your eyes means. I have seen it in her as well."

More lies.

No. These are different.

His rant sucked all the anger from the room. The powerful pressure of his magic ebbing from me as he paced, the fire in his eyes extinguishing to a low rumble of passion.

His absent-minded motions made it clear it was my chance to act, to attack, and yet... I could not move.

Kill him. Stop waiting.

I barely heard him.

"You love her?"

"Yes," he whispered as he turned back to face me. "More than anything. Don't you?"

The question was honest and rooted in a deep caring that kept me sane somehow. The way my brother sat before me, waiting for my answer, kept the incessant voice calm.

Kept *me* calm.

"I thought I did," I finally said, grateful when his magic began to loosen, my tense muscles relaxing. "But now I am not too sure. Everything seems broken. I know she doesn't love me. Everything has been shattered."

I slid down the wall to sit before him, fully aware that despite the fact that his magic was no longer pressed against me, it was still there. A protective barrier between us, keeping me restrained. Keeping both of us safe. Even though I had escaped that dungeon, even though I was fighting the voice, I was still a prisoner.

I sat still, watching the shimmer in the air before I turned back to him, grateful to see much of his fire had left, though I could tell it was still there, right under the surface.

"Edmund did that."

I could only nod.

"Our father does more than he should. But his meddling was foreseen by sight long before he ever dreamed of playing his little game of hearts and souls."

He's lying.

I twitched at the voice, pushing it out of my mind as I stared at my brother and let his words play on repeat in my mind.

It was an interesting way to put it—a game of heart and souls—but I guess, in a way, that was exactly what it was. My heart, my soul, had been shattered then bound in a knife. Just like so many others. I wondered if Joclyn's soul was locked inside the blade, as well.

That was my father's game.

He who holds the blade, holds the key, much like Sain and his so-called fountain of magic.

"I'm sorry this happened to you, Ryland. I am sorry for your pain," Ilyan said as he stepped closer to me, his shield flexing and moving. While I was still completely shrouded, he stepped closer his hand extended out in a show of support and kindness.

As my brother.

"So am I." I took his hand slowly, fully aware his powerful shield was between us, preventing any and all skin contact.

"If I have learned anything in my long life, it is that we are all only a piece of a bigger puzzle, and each piece is placed where it is for a reason. I believe soon that reason will be made clear to us."

"Because of Jo... Joclyn?" I could barely get her name out without slamming my head against the wall in agony. He wanted me to, anyway.

Kill them all!
They hurt you!
They lied to you.
No.

"Yes, my daughter has a bigger part to play than even she realizes at this point, than any of you do," Sain said as he looked at Ilyan.

Ilyan tightened his hand around mine as he met the old man's gaze. He looked at him, his brow furrowed as he contemplated what to say, before turning back to me. The silent warning making the old man back away a step.

"You are my brother, Ryland. And my promise to help you still stands. What can I do to make you well?" He spoke in Czech, the familiarity of the language almost enough to incite fear, but where my father had always used it in retribution, in hatred, Ilyan used it honesty, the familiar words sounding like any other to me. "What do you wish for, Ryland?"

I stared at him, trying to decide what I could say, and most of all, if I could really trust him despite the screaming that was moving through me.

I knew I could.

More than that, I already knew what I needed.

"I want to be myself again. I don't want to hear our father's voice in my head."

"Then I believe I have something that may help you in your journey." The corner of Ilyan's mouth twitched in a way that instantly put me on guard and I pulled away from his hand that was still wrapped around mine and pressed it right against my heart.

Ilyan watched the motion, that uncomfortable twitch on his face returning.

A smile.

A greedy smile.

"What?" I snapped, letting my fear pour out of my voice at his action, second guessing him.

Did he want the blade too? Did he know about it? About what it held?

I couldn't be sure if he understood my need to find the soul's blade, to return my fractured soul to one piece.

Could I trust him with that? I wasn't sure. I wanted to. Something inside of me was stopping that however, and it was more than the voice in my head.

"I would like to help you," Ilyan finally said.

I bit my tongue and nodded, unwilling to put voice to the fact that, all things considered, Ilyan probably already knew.

"If you will let me bind your heart, Joclyn has requested to speak to you. She would like to give you something, in the hopes of bringing your heart together, of giving you peace."

I stared at him.

He didn't know. Heart not soul.

It was only one piece of the puzzle.

"Will you consent to this, Ryland?" His voice was calm, that same deep rumble as he tried to lord over me.

You are better than him.

You don't need him.

Looking up to Ilyan, the voice repeated through me the drum of the words growing louder with each beat of my heart. Hearing it so loud, being swallowed by the thunder, made it hard to remember what I really wanted—if I wanted to be myself or if I wanted to kill Ilyan.

Either way, having him help me would put him in the path of both outcomes.

Kill him.

"I will."

5

RYLAND

"It's your necklace... on the floor."

Joclyn's voice was muffled as she spoke through the heavy wooden door that separated us. Sain's breathing filled the hall behind me, blending with the subtle whispers of scrapes and bumps from where Ilyan and Joclyn were cloistered away. Just behind the door. The sounds bled into an echo that bounced over the stone, duplicating the laugh that festered in my mind.

I waited for the monster to come alive and growl in violent vibrations of animalistic destruction.

Nothing happened, though.

Ilyan had bound my heart and mind so tightly, that I could think clearly. Well, clearer than normal. It wasn't like when Wyn had placed a shield around my heart, but it was close. It was still freeing.

I pressed my forehead against the door, trying to talk down the part of me that was desperate to be close to her, and stared at the swirl of a silver chain and the deep red of the diamond that lay on the floor. Glimmering.

As if it had just been dropped there by accident and not cast away.

Picking the necklace up carefully, I wrapped the fine chain around my clumsy fingers, careful not to let the stone touch my skin.

It looked so much different than it had the day I had purchased it from the snot-nosed salesmen at the jewelry store in New York. It was still the same diamond, still the same necklace; it just held something inside of it, is all.

It held me.

I had traveled to the city with Cail the summer before I had given it to her. We were following a lead to what we had hoped would be Ilyan's capture while taking a few select souls from their homes and into the dungeons where my father conducted his experiments.

It was something I had done a hundred times before— tried to capture my brother, taken innocents and given them to my father.

I had never enjoyed it, though.

How could I?

But, I didn't have a choice. I was trapped.

As much as it made my stomach turn, I had gone through the motions. I had done everything as I was asked so as not to uncover my father's wrath, despite my mind being full of thoughts of my best friend and the summer following when she would be pulled from me forever.

I had a foot in two different worlds—the one I wanted and the one I was forced to live in.

Perhaps that was why the store had called to me.

I could see the blue frontage from the hotel room. I saw it as we walked from place to place. I saw it in my mind as I took life after life. The more I thought of the world-renowned name, the more the idea began to cement itself in my mind.

A simple gift, holding the most precious thing I had to give her. Something that, even though she would not realize it at the time, was more than a simple token of my affection. It was my affection.

And it would keep her safe.

A piece of my heart.

It was all that I had wanted, and it had done anything but.

"When I made this, I had no idea who you really were," I whispered, unsure if I was talking to her or to myself. Perhaps it was both. "I wanted you to have it forever because I knew I would never see you again. I was going to run away and try to disappear. Anything to keep myself from what Edmund had planned for me. My father had been training me for years to hunt Ilyan. I wasn't even going to school." *You were working for me.* "He was going to send me and Cail on a kamikaze trip to kill my brother." *I already have, you know; he's right there. And you are going to kill him for me.* "I guess, in some ways, that still happened. And then, when I found your kiss, and I knew I could use you against my dad to make him hurt the way he had made me hurt. Hurt. Hurt."

I retold the story to her, desperate for her to know. To hear. Even if she didn't care anymore, I needed her to know that I had loved her.

However, the more I talked, the more my mind shattered, the barrier breaking away until it was little more than rice paper. The voice sparked in and out of my mind mixing with the rumble of Sain's voice as he tried to stop my descent.

Please don't let it be too late.

"I need you to focus right now," he whispered in my ear.

"I don't know if I can." I could barely get the words out.

I know you can't.

"Fight it, Ryland. I am right here with you." I stared at him as the voice battled back and forth inside of me, the intensity growing.

"Hurt." I hadn't meant to say that.

"Focus, son. If you can get through this, I know you will find a piece of your sanity that you thought you lost. You will regain a piece of yourself that your father hasn't been able to touch." His voice was deep with the sound of the Drak as he leaned over where I had collapsed on the floor, the heavy reverberation seeping through my bones. "Once you have this piece, you will have the strength you need to get the next. You will be able to get the knife for me. You will take your soul back, son."

His voice lulled to nothing. The waver of the sconces that flickered around us shimmered against the grey stone until he was cast in lengths of shadow that stretched over his face like a sheet of hair.

I stared at him, my rocking slowing as I realize just how right he was.

Inside of this diamond was not only a piece of my heart, but a piece that had not been infected with the torture of my father.

It hadn't been destroyed.

It was pure.

The last untarnished piece of me.

"Will you keep the necklace, Jos?" I asked, my voice shaking as I tried to get this final request out before it was too late.

She doesn't want the necklace. Didn't you hear?

"I can't..." she began, but I couldn't let her finish. I didn't think I could stand to hear her rejection or have that pain return.

"No, not my heart. Just the necklace. A promise that maybe we can try to be friends again." My voice caught as I tried to make her understand, to make her see why I needed this. Why it was important.

"Of course."

I barely heard her voice through the door, the whisper of agreement not quite enough to grant me the acceptance I was looking for, but enough that I knew she would at least uphold her side of the bargain.

It was enough.

The large stone spun through the air as I held it by the chain, the firelight bouncing off the faceted surfaces into millions of refractions that covered the hallway in tiny specs of the deepest red. To anyone else, they would be nothing more than the glint of the diamond.

"You can do it, son." Sain's voice was a deep root of confidence that embedded into my soul.

You are a fool. Stop playing games. Kill her now.

Shut up, Father.

"I know," I whispered in desperation. "I don't know what's going to happen when I do this, Sain. If I..." I couldn't even bring myself to finish the sentence.

I ripped my focus from the necklace to the old man. His eyes were wide and welcoming as he nodded his head once.

Even without the explanation, he knew the dangers. For all we both knew, the transition might destroy me.

Maybe that wouldn't be a bad thing.

Lowering the necklace into my palm, a surge of magic and pain ignited through me the second the stone pressed against my flesh.

It rippled over me in both heat and agony, as if it was

threatening something I didn't quite understand. Death maybe?

I don't know. It didn't matter. I pressed my palm against my chest. The hard nob of the gem indented into my skin, the painful pressure now both heat and an intense stabbing that caused me to call out.

My shout echoed louder as the pain exploded, the force so strong that I was sure I was being ripped in two. No, I *was* being ripped in two, my chest opening as the tiny shard of my heart was returned to its rightful place.

My agony echoed in my scream, the sound moving over the hall, alongside the mournful laugh of my father, and the sharpened gasp from Sain.

It had hurt so much more when I had removed the piece of my heart and placed it inside the necklace. When I had done that, I had gone to the ring of trees in the forest where I had always taken Joclyn, gotten drunk enough that I couldn't feel anything, and then cried for hours until I had finally passed out.

This was pain, but it was the pain of recovered love, my heart moving right back to where it belonged.

As quickly as the pain had come, it left, my breath heaving as it faded to nothing more than the dull throb of a deep tissue bruise. My hand fell away, the diamond nestled in the center of my blood-covered palm, the crimson fluid sliding from its surface.

"It looks just like your eyes," I said the words aloud, feeling the bind Ilyan had put on my mind slipping away, taking the clarity with it. I needed to get the words out now before it was too late. Before I wanted to kill her again.

"Wear it always." It was a gasp in my throat.

Sain's hand curled around my arm, his grip tight as he lifted me to standing, guiding me down the hall.

I leaned against him as we moved, feeling Ilyan's bind slip off my mind, the last thin shield he had provided me with fading into nothing.

I cringed as the voice returned, and the sharp claws of my father dug back into my soul.

I expected it. I expected the madness. I expected the anger and the hatred.

But, for whatever reason, it didn't come back, not as it was. It would never be like that again.

I wasn't free, not yet, not even close.

However, Sain was right; it was a stepping stone, a brief reprieve and bolster for what was coming. I had recovered enough of myself that, while the road before me was nowhere near the simple path I would hope, it was a bit clearer.

The footing a bit more sure.

With this one piece of my heart, I would take back not only the blade, but my soul, as well.

Just as Sain had said.

6

WYN

ROSALINE'S LAUGH echoed in the same childlike joy that had driven me mad to the point that I had willingly sacrificed my memories. I had given up who I was to find an escape from that laugh, to run from the lighthearted joy that I never thought I would find again.

Hearing her laugh now was a painful, gut wrenching, run-over-by-a-unicorn reminder that I had experienced joy at some point. It made my face heat with ugly, spiteful tears that I could feel run over my cheeks. I batted the treacherous things away, cursing their existence, cursing the return of her laugh.

Although, I was quite aware that it had never really left, it had always lived in my dreams. Right now, however, I was trapped with it.

As an added rub-salt-in-the-wound bonus, I was also trapped in the freaking stone hallways of the castle Talon and I had built our Tŏuha in.

I would say I was dreaming, except this was officially a nightmare, and had been since Joclyn had healed me nearly a week ago. Every night since that last moment I had seen

Talon standing in the courtyard, trapped in the glittering fog of death, my dreams had dragged me to this prison. To this empty shell of what once was.

It made me want to rip out my own heart just for the chance that I could escape this emotional prison.

Even then I wasn't sure it would work.

This must be what purgatory felt like.

The haunted laugh bounced around the endless hallway I stumbled down. The sound made everything echo; heart, laugh, and stifled sob melting into my agony.

Into my panic.

I couldn't take it anymore!

Heart pounding, I bolted down the hall.

Desperate to escape the sound.

Desperate to escape the memories.

Desperate to reach her.

But I was trapped in the stone maze of the castle.

I sprinted down a twisted staircase that I knew would lead to the large courtyard. Instead, it was only more stone, more twisted hallways that threatened to swallow me whole. Panic rattled against my chest, but I ignored it. The ridiculous emotion was not welcome here.

Centuries of practice promised me I could handle this. Although, I might feel the need to kill someone before too long.

I ran until the only sound was the slap of my sneakers against the stone, the rhythmic thuds dull and lifeless against the heavy chug of my heart. Matching my steps to each ragged breath, I began to slow, forcing myself to relax in the quiet.

My muscles however, remained wrapped in tight lines of sinew, just waiting for the next painful explosion of her laugh. Waiting to see her standing around the next corner.

Not knowing if she would be smiling, or if she would be screaming.

"Knock it off," I scolded myself, running my fingertips along the ridges of the cold stone, letting them bounce along the ripples of the crevices. Each impact sent little drops of ice down my spine. Over my skin. I could have sworn that someone had turned on an air conditioner with how I had begun to shake.

I could officially see my breath.

It really was a freaking horror movie. I didn't need her laugh to remind me of that, but it came anyway.

My breath snatched in my chest and I pressed my back into the stone, staring out of the high windows that lined the hall. Normally, streamed ribbons of sunlight would cut through the casements, cast over the halls in a glimmering glory. A beautiful Tŏuha.

But this wasn't my Tŏuha and the disturbed windows hung dull and dank, a sheath of grey clouds covering the sky and dripping their dreariness into everything.

"Damn it," I said to no one in particular. Cursing whatever foolish gods had trapped me here. They better hope they never meet me.

Focusing on the sound of my Converse against the stone floor, I ignored the distanced chimes of her laugh, the sound rippling like wind moving through the trees. It was so broken I wasn't sure if it was her laugh to begin with.

Muscles tensed, breath shook, and I ground my jaw together in a combination of pain and spite, my fists wrapped into tiny boulders that beat against my thighs.

"Wynifred?"

I froze.

Talon. The deep grind of his voice was so familiar, yet

there was still an undertone of joy, like he was always ready to laugh at the world.

"Wynifred?" It took everything in me to resist the urge to call out to him.

I had been sure I was the only one in this haunted space the last few nights.

Well, except for her laugh, but I wasn't going to count that.

It couldn't be him... and yet my foolhardy soul was already running circles around me in an attempt to get there.

The sound of rubber soles against stone was loud in my ears as I cautiously moved closer, waiting for it to come again, rejoicing when it did.

"Wynny?" It was louder, more joyous.

I ran.

I didn't question it. I didn't wonder if I was only following the voice into a nightmare, if Rosy would be there.

I didn't freakin' care anymore. I just wanted him. Chilled air flew past me as the laugh echoed, as he called, and as those same traitorous tears dripped from my eyes like the acid they were.

"Wynifred?"

I turned another corner and froze, the maze of hallways that had been my prison dissolving into our courtyard. Large stone pavers, perfectly groomed topiaries, massive rose bushes that giggling maidens would hide behind.

It was all as it had been, right down to our bench.

Well, except for the sun, that was still smothered by the low clouds that made everything feel a bit too much like a veil of death for my liking. Especially with the dank everything-is-dying feel it was giving the beautiful courtyard.

The trees sagged, leaves curled, and even the stone had lost its luster.

But it didn't even matter. Because he was there. Right there, staring at me with the widest grin I had ever seen him have.

"Wyn." His voice was the same as always, his large arms reaching out to me.

I didn't need more of an invitation. I ran across the courtyard, slamming against him as he enveloped me into him, pressed me against the barrel of his chest like I was little more than a paper doll.

I willingly let myself be crushed, let myself get wrapped up in the woodsy smell of his skin, and his far too hot breath that brushed over the top of my head.

It was him.

It was him as he chuckled. It was him as he pressed his lips against my neck, and yet...

"Talon?" My voice was panicked as I yanked myself away from him. He reluctantly released me, albeit not that far. My tiny frame was still pressed against him as I looked up to him, his large, warm hands still wrapped all the way around my waist, pressing against my back. "What's going on?"

I tried to keep the accusation out of my voice, but it didn't quite work. Talon's face sagged at the question, the light behind his dark eyes dimming enough that every muscle in my back was flaring in warning. I was half expecting him to peel his skin from his face or some crap, but there was nothing in this dream-nightmare.

"What do you mean, Wyn?" He answered my question with a question.

Ummm, no.

Like an off-key note in a Styx cover, something was

bothering me. I couldn't quite put my finger on it, but the more I looked at him, the more my panic grew.

I changed direction, responding to his question, with yet another question. At any other time, I was sure it would be comical. Right then, I was just trying to figure out how I could wake myself up if all of this went horribly, disastrously, face-meltingly, wrong.

"What are you doing here?"

His smile spread further, my unease infecting me just as quickly.

"This is our Tŏuha, Wynny."

This wasn't a Tŏuha. It couldn't be. Not after his death, not after the choice I had made. I had given this up. This life, this beautiful place that linked me so closely to my mate, to him—it was gone now.

"No." It was all I could do to keep the explosion locked inside, the frustration and confusion were sure bubbling up —and fast. "I chose to live."

"You did," he said succinctly, as if commenting on his distaste in my choice of music.

The response only added to my confusion. I was positive it showed on my face, Talon chuckled the same as he always had, the sound deep and low and feeling like warm soap sliding over my back, just like his hands.

I shivered at the touch, his chuckle drifting through me.

"We should talk," he whispered, his low tone matching the calm of his fingers against my spine.

I couldn't even bring myself to respond, I was sure only a mumble came out.

So much for the badass assassin that owe going to destroy the face melting monster, I was already letting him lead me over to our bench.

"Then how...?" The butterflies of emotion were so

tangled now that the words were swallowed. I was sure I was going to give myself permanent wrinkles from the amount of concentration I was doing.

I sunk down on the bench, Talon kneeling before me on the old cobblestones, his large hands wrapping around mine.

Just like when he proposed.

Oh, hell no.

I moved to bolt, but he held on tighter. He seemed so much larger than he really was when he sat like that, the sheer bulk of his muscles and width of his chest turning him into a bolder. I couldn't hope to escape that. Not without some serious firepower, which I didn't have.

Because I was trapped in this nightmare.

"You chose to live," Talon parroted, his voice near a whisper as the pressure of his hands against mine increased. "You let Joclyn heal you so you could help them... so you could be with them."

"When you say it like that, it makes it sound like I chose them over you."

My stomach twisted. I had made the choice, and while I don't regret being able to help them—to be with Joclyn after her fight with Ilyan, to help Ryland fight his monsters—I did regret not being with Talon.

I regretted his death and that I couldn't follow him.

Yet...

"I know you didn't," Talon cut over my thoughts, pulling my focus as he finally came to sit beside me.

"So why are you in my dream?" I only barely caught myself from saying nightmare.

Or worse, from saying Tŏuha, I really didn't want to put that label on it right now. I didn't think my heart could take it.

I mean, this *was* our Tõuha. Now that my memories were back, I recognized it as the yard of Nuremberg castle. It was the reconnaissance spot Talon and I would meet at when I had spied for Ilyan so long ago. It was the only place we would meet one-on-one. It was the first place our hands had touched.

I smiled at the memories, at the knowledge that he had loved me even before my memories were gone. He had loved every bit of me, even the parts that had worked for Edmund for so long.

The thought was comforting. It made everything seem more real.

It also made everything hurt like salt against an open wound.

"It doesn't feel like a dream," Talon responded in a whisper, his arm wrapping around me as he pulled me closer. "I feel very real. You feel very real…"

His voice faded away as his hands trailed over my body, the rough pads of his fingers somehow soft against my skin. I gasped at the touch, at the sensations that shivered through every nerve.

It was so similar to how our magic had always connected inside of this space. Although much the power and the emotion behind it was missing, I could still feel it. I could still feel him.

He was right, it was all very real.

My breath shook in exhale as his fingers moved over my neck, only to have both of us freeze at the childlike laugh that moved through the courtyard. The sound was high and joyous, despite my body refusing to register it as such. Everything tensed, rage and pain preparing to see the bloodied child standing before us. It was only the sound, however, only the echo of a life that was trapped.

I knew that now, but it didn't stop the panic and tension from taking over. All I could feel was the heavy, painful pulse of my heart as I looked over the courtyard. Talon's touch was all but gone.

"She is very real," Talon whispered beside me, his voice sounding far too distanced as another echo of a laugh encompassed me.

"Rosaline."

Did I speak in longing or fear? I wasn't sure. My heart felt both, and it scared me.

"Yes."

I turned toward Talon at his one word response, my eyes wide as I looked at him and begged him for an answer I knew I needed, even if I dreaded what it would be.

"Have you seen her?"

The air pulled with dread as I waited for his answer, searching his eyes for some clue as to what he knew. There was only understanding and love as his hand came to rest against my cheek, as if the touch would somehow soften the blow.

I don't think anything could.

It only made me, or rather the assassin in me, want to punch something.

"No. I have searched for her—I have followed the laugh —but she is not there. Her soul is still trapped."

Her soul is still trapped.

The words dug into my heart as the memories of that night assaulted me. Of Edmund's torture and the way he cut my daughter apart, locking her soul into that blood red blade.

Days before now when I escaped Prague, I had vowed to Edmund that I would release her soul from that blade. I had promised I would set her and my brother free from the extended torture I knew he had wrought on them.

Hearing it again, hearing the reminder of what had happened to her, only renewed my desire to live. I would hunt down the man who had destroyed so much and hurt so many.

My jaw clenched together, the powerful magic that had stayed dormant until now raging to life. My fingers burned with the energy.

"Rosy." It sounded more like an anthem than a name. Perhaps it was now.

It wasn't just Joclyn that needed me. I wasn't alive just to help them escape.

I was alive for her.

I would make Edmund pay, I would gladly rip his head from his shoulders to make that happen.

My fists wrapped back into their boulders as I stood, certain that if Edmund was before me at that moment I wouldn't hesitate to destroy him.

The laugh came again, loud and joyous in my ears, and I flinched, the flare of determination waning as the pain attempted to swallow it.

Instead, one single piercing scream ripped from my throat as I forced all the anger, and pain, and anguish out.

I stood long after the echo of my scream had left, staring at the dying roses, feeling the heave of my chest.

"Don't worry, Wynny." Talon whispered as he stepped behind me. "One day, you will be brave enough to follow that laugh."

Hair whipped around my face as I turned to him, exhilaration and panic flooding through me in equal parts of ice and fire. I wanted so much to agree with him, to say how right he was. But I couldn't, not right then. There was too much guilt right then.

"You and Thom, both. You will find peace. Happiness." Talon's voice suddenly seemed to be a million miles away.

Thom.

Rosy's father. The man who had tamed the assassin, a man I still desperately loved.

Blood drained from my face, guilt taking over as I turned back to Talon, to his wide smile. I opened my mouth to say something, but nothing escaped. I wasn't sure anything could with the weight that had taken up residence in my throat.

"I want you to always be happy, Wyn." The words were a stab to the gut, the phrasing exactly what he had told me only moments before he had died, before I had chosen to live and left him for what I had thought would be forever.

"Be happy." He leaned down and whispered the last words in my ear, his voice so soft and gentle as it ran down my spine in a ripple that took all my confusion and guilt away.

I shivered at the touch, the chill fading away as the grey sky broke open, the smothered, golden light breaking through in ribbons as it escaped its confines. It bathed the courtyard in a yellow glow that made everything glitter and come alive. I breathed in the warm air, turning my face to the warmth the same way I had every time we had met in this place, in our place.

"Our Tŏuha," I said it, but I didn't know if I believed it.

"I am not sure how this works," Talon said, as calmly as if he was answering my thoughts. "I don't know if this is our Tŏuha. I don't know if it is real or if it will be here again. If I will be."

Any remains of the assassin in me melted away at the

touch of his fingers against my neck, at the gentle breeze of his hot breath against my skin.

I sighed and leaned closer, needing him, wanting him, all the while cursing the effect he had on me. Cursing the eternal youthful girl who loved him so much she was literally melting into goo inside of me.

Warm, delicious goo.

"I hope you will be. I know you will be." I was determined to make both of those things happen. Force them if I had to.

"So do I." He sighed into my ear, "But, if I'm not here the next time you find this place, know that I love you, that I adore you, and that I will see you again soon."

I recognized that tone in his voice, the sad longing bringing back the volatile snap of my emotions.

"Talon…" I tried to stop him from continuing, stop the goodbye or whatever nonsense he was trying to spew. But he stopped me cold, singing one of my favorite songs, from one of my favorite bands.

"You gave all the love that I needed… You're my lady."

Foolishly, I had worshiped Styx since I had first found them in the 70s, from that moment Talon had playfully declared his distaste for them. As he sang the song now, however, it was an adrenaline shot right into my heart. Powerful enough that I could feel tears threatening to break free.

"Go save that beautiful girl of yours. I can't wait to meet her."

His words faded as the brilliance of the sun washed everything into a bright white glow. Warmth spread over me in a flame as the Tòuha faded into reality, leaving me gasping on my bed as I was shoved into the dark chill of my bedroom.

Awake. Alive. And with an ache in my heart that felt a bit more like a hole than it should.

I blinked, the room I had spent most of the day ripping apart, and removing all traces of Talon and who I had been, slowly coming into focus. The dim light of what I could only assume to be dawn, spread over the ripped remains of posters and the pile of bedding I had thrown into the corner. It was all unfamiliar, all but the ancient, wooden rafters above me.

I stared at them, watching the wood glitter in the morning night, remembering far too many mornings when I woke up here, dreaming of Thom.

Nope.

That memory hurt too.

I groaned, hit my pillow and rolled over, every single muscle catching on fire with the movement. Even though it had been a few days since Joclyn had removed the curse from my body, I still ached, like a body flu mixed with a muscle transplant surgery. It was only then I realized I wasn't alone.

"Good morning, Wynifred." Sain's voice was soft as he leaned down to face me, his deep green eyes only inches from my own. I flinched in shock, my need to fight or kill flared bright and strong.

"Back away old man, unless you want me to remove your nose from your face."

The threat was based more in reaction than in reality, but it didn't matter, he only laughed at me anyway.

"Those self-preservation skills don't go away easily, I see."

Sain sat in an old chair near my bed, a wide grin plastered to his face as he slowly sipped on the disgusting filth both he and Joclyn now called food. My stomach twisted a bit at the memory of Joclyn, sitting surrounded by all those feathers after her fight with Ilyan, shaking and broken as she drank that stuff.

Black Water.

It was truly bizarre how everything had changed, for the both of us. Too much change, too fast. Jayne would want to blow something up. I would, too. Good thing I wasn't in a space western.

"Good morning." All signs of my previous threat was gone, but my voice was still stuck in its 'I just woke up and need water' gasp, something which Sain took note of as his smile widened. He walked away from me, toward the table where a couple of plain, ordinary, everyday water bottles sat.

"Sorry, it's just me today." He said as he retrieved one of the water bottles. "Thom is on watch, so I volunteered to take his place. It seems you were talking in your sleep, and he preferred some time away."

Sain handed me the water bottle as I slowly pushed myself to sitting, the aches rippling over me with a deeper intensity. I, of course, stubbornly ignored them.

"I was talking in my sleep?" My voice sounded flat.

"Yes, seemed to upset Thom some."

Ugh. I knew why, and it made me want to break something, or at the very least keep from tearing apart my room. My blood pumped in disappointed irritation. I suddenly felt like I had been hit in the chest with an elephant gun.

"I wonder why that would be." Sain spoke succinctly, his eyes digging into me with the same intensity I had always hated from Draks. Even as a child, the way they looked into me creeped me out. I was *so* glad my best friend was going to start doing that, too.

Sarcasm is a beautiful thing.

"You tell me." I didn't even try to restrain the snap.

Yes, I was surly, but I had every right to be. Thom should know better after so many years and bondings and everything that went with it.

He should know.

Nothing would be the same.

"I have no need to tell you what you already know."

Of course, he had to answer my grumpy rhetorical question in that irritating Drak way; open-ended, all-seeing vultures. He might as well be wearing purple robes and carrying around a crystal ball.

I slammed the water bottle down on the side of the bed with a thunk, droplets flying from the lip from the force. Sain moved away from them as if they were poison, his lip curling into a sneer of disgust.

"He was my husband, Sain." I snapped, fixing him with a glare as the water in the bottle beneath my hand began to boil. "Talon was my mate for over a hundred years. I can't walk away from that and back into a life I willingly left behind. It doesn't work that way."

"You know as well as I that your heart is fighting the same as his. He does not expect things to be as they were. He knows of the life you led. Do not place all the blame on him."

He did not roar, he did not even raise his voice, but the result was the same. My anger froze in place, realizing exactly what he was saying.

Thom was fighting the same thing. The same joy of finding each other. The same pain of loss. And the same realization that we had both lived entire lives without each other.

Thom wanted to move forward, and part of me did too, but we both knew that that wasn't possible.

Especially given the dream I had.

Be happy.

That same Mack Truck heartache returned, and I cringed.

"Sain?" I asked, my voice faltering a bit with nerves at what I was about to ask. "Can you still have Tôuha's after your mate has passed on?"

Sain froze, his mug having only made it partially to his lips. He looked at me from over the ridge, his gaze hard, before it dropped down to his waist, staring at it as though it had wronged him.

"I wouldn't know..." he said after a moment, the hard, clipped edge to his voice startling. "My mate is still alive."

The regret at the question was strong, my breath shaking with an exhale before I aggressively drank from the water Sain had given me, my forehead furrowed in agitation.

Sain may insist that he no longer loved Ovailia, I knew better as much as he did. Love didn't simply go away. It was always there. It was just that sometimes it was hidden, sometimes it was a little more pain than passion.

But all of that, it didn't matter. That love, that connection, had been stolen from him by the same man who had murdered my daughter.

That pain I understood.

"But Dramin would."

I hadn't expected any response, and that one was worse. Sain had said it so simply, so casually, that it almost seemed like a gross overreaction when I nearly choked on my water.

"Dramin? Your son?" The words were little more than a squeak.

"Yes."

"He's... he's here?"

Sain would only nod, his eyes lowered as he drank from his mug.

The last time I had seen Dramin was in a cave in Africa, a cave I had filled with the blood of his children, his grandchildren.

I had slaughtered them all.

I had walked through the pools of their blood in my attempt to reach him, the hem of my dress soaked with the deep, red magic that had once held the power of sight. I would have gotten him, too, if his mate hadn't flung herself before me. Before I could finish her off, he had already gone.

"You are aware of my tie with Dramin?" I could barely get the words out.

"I am. After all, it's the same tie you have with me. You killed all of my progeny, as well."

Let's just add to the dread, why don't we?

He had brought it up before, but it still seemed like pouring salt on an open wound.

"I still talk to you."

That doesn't help Sain.

I stared at him, eyes narrowing as I tried to figure out what to say, tried to understand what he meant and what the peculiar look he was giving me was. It wasn't the anger I would have assumed. Not the heartache, either. Something was there that I didn't understand. Something that was fueled with an emotion I knew all too well, the same one that had fueled so many of the murders I had committed.

Greed.

Although why I saw it in him right at that moment, I wasn't sure.

"I can't..."

"My son is currently unconscious, but he will be waking

soon." Sain interrupted me, rolling over my quiet rebuttal like it didn't exist. "You should ask him then."

I swallowed.

Sain's mate may not have died. But Dramin's had.

I was the one responsible. And now he was the only one who had the answer I was looking for.

Nothing about this situation could get any more traumatizing.

Even if the son of the man before me didn't have the answers, at least he would have a clue.

I only needed to ask him.

I only needed to face another of my past sins.

Choosing to live had been the easy part, it seemed.

7

WYN

THUNDER WAS NOT MY FAVORITE.

And it really wasn't my favorite now that I had been trapped with it for the past week. Yes, it had only been a week since my miraculous recovery, and already I was cursing the earth for its never-ending, freaking ridiculous, thunderstorm.

Yeah, I got it, the earth was pissed.

Didn't need to throw a hissy fit about it. And Ilyan certainly didn't need to talk about it like he was ready to jump ship and join the "Mother Earth Cult."

As if on cue the rumble of thunder broke directly overhead, one single bolt of lightning breaking through the sky directly above me.

"Yeah, yeah, I hear ya," I scoffed, giving a massive sigh and leaning against the ancient stone work of the bell tower. The tiny cylindrical room was all too familiar, and far too homey. This wasn't the first time the abbey's high point had been used as some sort of watch tower, nor was it the first time I had been locked away in here helping to 'ensure everyone's safety.'

This was, however, the first time I was up here when I shouldn't be.

Or rather, when Thom wouldn't want me to be. I doubt anyone else would care but Thom. And Thom would be pissed. He certainly had turned into the hovering mother bear. But, alas, Thom was sleeping, Sain needed a break and I was bored out of my mind staring at rafters all day.

It felt good to stretch my legs, and my magic.

I sighed again, but this time it was with that deep contentment of my escape. Of mind, body and magic. The last of which was probably the most important, and the most exhilarating.

Pressing my fingertip into the ridge of stone, I let a tiny line of fire free as if to prove the point. The miniscule flames rippled over the rock like a snake, the line of destruction following the ancient grout as though they were rivers. They glowed like a pathway to heaven.

Or hell.

It all depended on the way you looked at it.

The beauty of the fire reflected against the stone in ripples of light. Fire, death, and destruction all glowing inside of the flames. It was a beautiful piece of my magic, no matter how small it was. It still did exactly as I wanted.

A smile stretched over my face as the heat began to swell, that wicked little part of me threatening to take over. It was a weird feeling, wanting to destroy while also wanting to keep everything safe.

Just another little piece of the schizophrenic tango my mind was stuck in.

I could tell this was going to get old fast.

I knew why I was still alive and I knew what I needed to do to accomplish that task.

Get to Edmund, rip his freaking head off, and free my daughter from that damn blade.

I could do it, especially if the anger that was now coursing through me was any indication.

I was more powerful than the bastard king and it was his turn to burn.

My magic sparked as my frustration and anger did, the flames growing to a roar that surrounded the bell tower like a beacon.

"Crap!" I practically screamed the word as I doused the flames, returning my magic to me and smothering the tower with an additional shield. As if that could help to cover the "Look at me, I'm over here" lighthouse I had just turned the tower into. Not like it mattered, they knew right where we were. But the less I helped launch us into battle the better.

Yeah, this was going to go over well.

Forcing myself to take deep breaths, I turned from the now blackened rafters to the forest that surrounded the abbey.

The tall trees stretched far into the distance, their bows shifting in the wind as the sky once again broke open with thunder and lightning. The deep boom cracked right overhead, and I jumped, my fingers sparking right alongside.

"Whoops," I mumbled, keeping my focus on the tiny, glimmering fires that marked each camp. Of course, I couldn't tell if those camps were empty, full, or leading a magical charge right toward me.

Thunder cracked again, louder this time. Lightning sparking through the sky above me to hit hard against the roof not a hundred yards away from where I was perched.

I did more than jump this time. I let out a yelp and ducked behind the half wall that made up the tower.

Awesome. Band-geek me was scared of lightning.

Grinding my jaw, I attempted to ignore the sharp spine of shame that was digging into my heart, when thunder and lightning cracked again.

The thunder louder, the lightning closer. So close it sent an electric charge through my veins, the impact point only feet away from me as tile and bits of wood from the roof it hit danced into the air.

This time, I didn't react. I watched the rubble slide down the side of the roof, slipping toward the forest where a storm that was just as intense raged.

Right near the edge of the forest.

My magic picked up dangerously as electric buzzing rumbled over my skin.

Magic. I realized with a start. *Magic I knew.*

My own power shot through the hole in my sneakers, spreading through wooden rafters and stone until it reached the soft dirt of the ground. Fire ripped through the soil as my magic sped past camp after empty camp, only barely tasting their dying fires as my panic grew.

This couldn't be leading to anything good.

The thunder above me cracked again, the rock beneath my fingers slipping as I leaned over the ridge of stone, watching the forest along the edge, where the lightning was.

Where I was sure he was. I felt the ugly barbs of his magic before my magic even reached whatever lied at the edge of the forest.

"Well, damn it," I growled, the words still echoing in the air as I tore out of the watchtower.

Joclyn stood in the middle of Ilyan's room, overly baggy pajama pants that I was sure were Ilyan's hanging on her hips. She looked at me with a scowl so severe I was sure it would give her permanent wrinkles. It didn't help that the ripples of light that shimmered from Ilyan's lantern made her features seem darker, angrier.

More than that, they made me sure that she didn't recognize me.

Well, more like she recognized that something was drastically different.

Painful, but it made sense. Nothing about me was the girl she knew. I wasn't wearing a single bangle and had traded the band shirt in for a beaded chemise from the 1700s. The thing used to be considered underwear, but it looked great with Thom's leather jacket.

It wasn't just my clothes that were different, either. I stood and snapped at Ilyan in a voice that Jos hadn't heard before, and that he had heard far too many times to count.

Her eyes grew darker as we stared at each other, Ilyan shuffling around that massive map of his as he processed the new information I had come to give him and Joclyn had confirmed.

The magic in the forest had changed. Edmund might well be there.

It was huge and frightening, and I would be lying if I said it didn't feel it. Right then, that was the last thing on either of our minds.

The question of who I was seemed like a much bigger demon.

I hadn't seen anyone look at me like that for a while. I hadn't seen that look of fear mixed with disgust in centuries.

It was more than fear, more than confusion. It was the look you gave someone you did not like, someone who had hurt you. Before, it was a look that I treasured, because it meant I was striking fear in those I was about to kill, into my subordinates.

It meant I was doing my job.

With Joclyn, however, she was seeing who I truly was. She saw the real me. She saw the woman who struck fear and disgust into thousands. She saw the blood on my hands and the murder behind my eyes. She saw what people had seen for centuries, and she didn't like it.

Because she didn't understand.

I, like a fool, hadn't had the guts to tell her why she saw that.

Maybe it wasn't guts I lacked. Maybe, I didn't want her to know. I didn't want to hurt her with the truth.

Seems I had done that anyway.

Awesome. Best friend status revoked.

I cringed as her look deepened, as if in confirmation of the demotion I had just granted myself. The best friend wanted to cry, the assassin, however, wanted to snap and tell her, or maybe myself, to grow up. Neither were going to help, not right now.

"I need you to wake everyone, Wynifred," Ilyan suddenly announced pulling me from my internal battle and right back to the emergency at hand. "Tell them to strengthen their portion of the shield, and inform them that we will be meeting in the dining hall at ten."

"Ten?" I practically yelled in exasperation. I tell him Edmund is here and he acts like I invited him to tea. "Why so late? If he is coming, we don't have time—"

Ilyan stopped me with one look, I may have just pushed his patience too far. Although I wasn't totally convinced that that was a bad thing.

Yeah, he had let me break quite a few of his rules over

the last hundred years, fueled by his guilt for what had happened, I was sure. Now that I was back and all my memories returned, though, I wasn't going to get away with that anymore.

Fine by me. I liked this dynamic a bit more, anyway. He was quite fun to prod at.

"I need *everyone* there, Wynifred," he scolded in that same tone, "and I will need to prepare Joclyn to meet Ryland face-to-face. Please tell Sain to prepare Ryland to do the same."

His command ripped behind his words. Edmund's perfectly placed game was tightening around us. More than just sending Ryland to kill Joclyn; it was putting a weapon right in the middle of us.

No, I corrected myself, my eyes darting to the broken girl in front of me. *Two weapons.*

Joclyn was one, too, even if she didn't realize it. They had broken her the same way. I was a fool not to have seen that from the way they used him in Imdalind. I was a fool not to understand.

We all were.

Well, all accept Ilyan, it seemed.

Two men stand, one will fall. Blood will drip. The game is played, and those with the most pawns will take the stage. Take your man and play the game, but be careful where your trust is laid.

Sain had said those words to Edmund when the sight had been forced from him and now, on the other side of the rotting jail cells, it meant so much more. The game was so much more than anyone other than Edmund understood.

Now we knew, and Ryland was here, perfectly placed to play the game Edmund had commanded him.

Freakin great. I didn't want to have to kill him, but I knew I would if it came to it.

Both of them.

Like serendipity, Jos caught my eye and my stomach flipped.

I swallowed once and curtseyed, the movement feeling awkward without the massive dresses I was used to. "Yes, my lord."

Joclyn's confused eyes sucked me in, and I couldn't help it, I smiled. I smiled the way I was used to. I smiled the way she had always seen. And while the tension in her shoulders lessened, the confusion inside of her only grew.

Great.

I would have to tell her.

But now was not the time.

I left the room without another look.

The snap of the closing door echoed through the long, stone hallway in a ripple that made me jump, as though the door closing was a snap of a gun and a call to arms.

The analogy seemed way too close to the truth right then.

I pulled Thom's jacket tighter around me then took off down the hall, letting the buzz of Joclyn and Ilyan's voices fade into nothing as I practically sprinted toward Ryland's room. Sain would more than likely be with him, nights were hard for him, and the incessant thunderstorm sure wasn't helping.

I cringed, Sain was really not going to like this. Getting Ryland settled down from thunder was one thing, but ready to face Joclyn in a "not a death match" table meeting? I didn't know if that was possible in such a short amount of time.

Sure, I could shield his heart, but that needed skin

contact, and I wasn't sure if that was going to be possible, or if I was strong enough yet to keep the shield strong for the entire meeting.

I exhaled roughly in spite of myself. We might as well set up the boxing pit, or ring, or whatever you box in. We had our work cut out for us.

Between Ryland and Joclyn's hitman personas and Dramin's endless comatose, I had no clue how we were going to get out of here alive.

Unless we had access to an invisible hot air balloon, we were pretty much doomed.

At least I would get to kill people as we all went out with a bang.

I was sure that alone would make it worth it. I didn't even try to stop the greedy smile from spreading over my face, although the chill of the abbey wiped it away so fast I might as well have been slapped.

Slapped by the breeze as it tangled my hair, and tugged at the jacket as though someone stood right beside me, trying to get my attention. I should have been concerned about where the draft had come from, about the way it wrapped around me, but with the slight breeze all thought of what I had been ordered to do was wiped from my memory, déjà vu taking its place.

It was like the dream. I tensed, expecting the sound of her laugh to ripple beside the breeze and pull me right into the hallways of my Tòuha.

But nothing was there.

Nothing but her memory as it burst through the wall I had built and danced among the shadows. There was only her shimmering grin lighting up my mind, making everything seem light for the slightest of moments. I couldn't help it. I smiled.

I smiled, and then I ran.

I ran right to her.

Right to the door that I had tried so hard to forget, to the room that I hoped time would have eaten alive.

But it was still there, looking the precise, traumatizing, way I had remembered it.

After a massacre in the 1700s Ilyan and his people had begun traveling together, safety in numbers, I guess. That also meant, however, that in each safe house everyone had their own room.

In Imdalind.

In the Motel.

And here.

This room was mine. Not the one I had been staying in, that one was one shared with Talon. This one was from before. Back when I worked for Ilyan, and stabbed Edmund in the back as many times as I could. I couldn't even count the amount of times I would come to this room, in fear of having been caught.

Ready to die among the relics of the life I had chosen to forget.

The door creaked as I pushed it open, the dust motes springing to life as the light gust of air moved over them, swirling them through the darkness in inky spirals that made everything feel heavier.

Haunted.

Maybe it was. No, actually, I was sure it was. There were too many memories in here for it not to be.

I stood there in the doorway of the room, the dull orange glow of my magic flaring on its own, casting burned shadows through the pitch, over the sheet-covered furniture, over the old Indian rug, and the ancient furnishings.

I stared at it, my heart pulling me to go in and yank the sheets off the life I had left behind like some kind of unveiling on a gameshow. You know, if the game show was all about skeletons, or ghosts, or whatever people keep in their closets.

Everything was still in the last place I had left it, like those creepy ghost towns you find in the midwest states. I just got up, left, and promptly forgot everything about myself.

The silver hair brush that Cail had given me was still lying on the table, a petticoat thrown over the headboard, a book open on the nightstand.

It was as if I had walked out a few days ago, on my way to Texas. Except, it wasn't. Everything was covered by dust and sheets. Everything was as forgotten as I had wanted to be.

My heart was thundering so fast I could feel it in my throat, the pulse powerful enough to make it hard to swallow, let alone breathe. Something that was proving to be impossible, anyway, as I pulled the sheet off the tall wardrobe, a pillow of dust flowing into the silent air and falling around me like snow. I felt them fall on my hands, on my arms, on the tip of my nose, but I didn't look away from that wardrobe, even though my heart was trying to burst out of my chest like an alien baby, devour my intestines and lay more alien eggs in my brain. I couldn't hope to escape, even if I tried.

My fingertips traced over the designs that had been carved into it when the French Revolution was all anyone would talk about. Flowers, hummingbirds, a dancing bear.

So beautiful. So painfully, terrorizingly beautiful.

Screw the bear, and screw the alien that was trying to lay its eggs in my brain. I threw the wardrobe open, revealing the carefully hung dresses, each and every one preserved as though they had been made only days ago.

Red velvets, blue gingham, lace cuffs, and corsets—dresses I had used to entice males for centuries, to visit kings, to murder kingdoms. Dresses that were tailored to fit to my body, accentuating everything.

It was a freakin' walk through history but it wasn't a revisit of the Elizabethan Era that I wanted.

An electric buzz vibrated through my skull as I moved the dresses to the side, revealing a large, wooden chest covered in a carved seaside scene.

The waves, the sand, a sun setting off in the distance. It was exactly as Thom had carved it all those centuries ago. Precise. Perfect. It had taken him months to create the replica of the day he had met me at the beach a few months before Rosaline was born. It had been the first time we had felt her magic within me.

He had felt her move.

It was the moment that we had connected, not only to her, but to each other. We might not have been granted marriage, but that had been our ceremony. It was the moment we had created a family.

Thom had made this chest for her so she would always know that, even though our family was a little broken, we still were one.

I stared at it, my hand frozen against the soft cotton of the dresses, the light flickering over the surface I had opened so many times since that day.

I wouldn't open it now.

I didn't need to.

I could see it all.

The deep blue dress that brought out the darkness of her eyes; the fabric doll Thom had made her for her second birthday, the stitched eyes pulling slightly from where she would rub her nose against them; the white night cap; the petticoats; the flower crown that I had watched her make in my dreams for years.

I knew how they were laid.

I knew how they were folded.

I knew how they felt.

I knew it all.

Because I had cried over that box every freaking day for hundreds of years.

Because I had touched those things as I had longed for her.

Because I knew her.

My hand slid down the fabric of the dress as I sunk to the floor, my legs folding awkwardly beneath me as they forgot how to support me. The weight of my body against the floor sent a plume of dust around me, but I barely noticed.

There were only memories.

Only pain.

Pain that grew and grew until it ripped out of me in a scream that echoed every pain, every heartache.

The sound of my agony shook the room, layers of dust falling through the air in sheets of grey that slid like snow drifts, piling in mounds around me.

I didn't stop the emotion.

I didn't think I could if I tried.

I let it come.

I let myself feel it.

Never before had I let it out. I felt the pain of Rosaline's murder. I felt the agony of Talon's death, the betrayal of Thom leaving me behind, the heart stuttering loss of my brother who had been the only support I had known for hundreds of years. I felt the stabbing loss that Joclyn had given me, that one look saying more than she could ever know. Not because it showed me what I was, what I had become, but because it showed me what I had given up.

I felt the pain for the first time as something snapped inside of me and the weight I had carried around for centuries slipped into the piles of dust.

What Edmund had done was unforgivable. What I had lost was insurmountable. However, by holding it inside and letting it fester, I had forgotten the person Thom had taught me to be. I had forgotten my child.

I had become something else.

I was more than pain. I was more than bloodshed. I was more than joy. I was more than the confusing bits that made up who I was. Those were part of me, yes, and someday, I would explain all those parts to Jos.

My agonizing wail faded to nothing as I stood, tears slipping over my face as I searched through the orange bathed room for the one thing I would take from this place. It was the only thing I wanted.

I moved through the ghostly forms of furniture as I ripped off sheets, unsheathing the room as I opened boxes and drawers and wooden chests in a mad rush to find it. The need only grew with each step, the dust filling the air so heavily I could barely breathe.

I didn't care.

I needed to find it.

"Wynifred?" Thom's voice drifted from behind me in a wall of worry that froze me in place, my hands hovering over the lid of a heavy, oak chest I didn't remember.

I tried not to let his tone dig into me, tried not to let the deep concern that lined his face bring about the confusion I had been fighting.

It did, anyway.

How could it not? He was looking at me with the same calm face, the same calm eyes I had fallen in love with all those years ago.

As if I needed a reminder how much I was still so desperately in love with him.

Curse him.

The heart twisted, a sharp stabbing pain ripping through me, like a vice grip with nails.

Except instead of ripping apart, it was as though the shards were trying to piece themselves back together. With a nail gun.

It hurt so much more than it really should.

Pressing my lips together in an attempt to keep the emotion inside, I went back to digging through the belongings I had hidden in the back of the room.

"What are you looking for?" Thom tried again, the soft sound of his footsteps echoing around me as he moved closer.

"Her blanket," I said, knowing I didn't have to elaborate.

Thom said nothing. I only heard the sharp intake of his breath before he walked right up to an old trunk that had been hidden in the back, the top lifting before he had even reached it.

"I had the other one on my bed in the cave in Italy," Thom said as he lifted the old blanket from the trunk, the heavy woven fibers as bright as the day the travelers had given them to her. The nomads had doted over her long hair and the way her eternal flame glowed, they could feel her magic even though they didn't understand it. And they loved her for it. "To always keep her close. Keep you close."

Thom's voice was soft as it rolled into me. I collapsed into him, and his arms enfolded around me as he covered us with the old blanket, wrapping the edges around us and trapping us together.

"I know it's hard," Thom whispered, "but I will help you through this."

His hand moved up my back as he held me against him. The promise was a deep rumble of sincerity that I had always known from him. The question, the motion, was almost like stepping back in time.

The thought, while true, was slightly ridiculous.

So was the sudden desire I had to kiss him. And that really wasn't helping.

"I'm not sure that's possible, Thom. You are part of the problem..." His chest hardened before I had even finished, the muscles tensing underneath me at my admission. I tried to move away, but he held me against him, his magic flaring. Mine answered his warmth like it was some kind of homing beacon and instantly flared to meet him, wanting to meet him.

Breathing was suddenly becoming very difficult, but not just for me.

"I'm still in love with you, Thom." I said it very quickly, bolstering my courage in a need to tell him the truth. A sharp intake of breath made me almost lose track of what I needed to say to him. Almost. "But I am also still in love with Talon. My heart hasn't quite gotten the memo about having lived two different lives."

"Your heart is smarter than your head, then." It was a whisper in my ear, the warm air of his breath rushing over my neck. "They weren't two different lives. It was just one life. Love as many people as you want."

The words were honest. But they were also a stab in the gut.

An echo of a memory of two teenage girls laughing on

the floor of a punk rock bedroom stabbed alongside. Styx had been playing in the background, and my own voice had broken over the music with advice that at the time seemed insignificant. Not so much anymore.

"It's okay to love. I think it makes you a better person. At least then you know what it feels like to love instead of living without ever knowing. I love a lot of people I know will never love me back, but I am happier because of it."

I had been speaking of my brother, of my father; however, hearing those words roar through my head now, I knew it was so much more than that.

"I know. I wish that would take away the anxiety, the way everything feels like it's crawling around inside of me."

"Are you saying I need to find you something to kill?" His arms loosened enough to let me look into the face that was more a part of my memory than any other. Even when I had forgotten him, even when Ilyan had taken that life from me, he still had been with me in my dreams. I guessed, in a way, he had always been there.

"Something like that."

Thom chuckled, his voice low and deep as it rolled over my skin. I clung to him at the sound, which only made him laugh more.

"I think I can arrange that. Give me a few days."

I knew I should laugh, but I couldn't make the sound come. He was right. I really did need to kill something. It was what I had always done, after all. Why should now be any different?

"Wynifred, you have always had a habit of overthinking things and taking the smallest bit of information and dwelling on it until it sits on your chest, and you can't breathe."

Sometimes, it scared me how well Thom knew me.

"Stop it." The kindness in his voice was gone now and I flinched. "Stop overthinking. Your heart and your mind know what to do. They know who you are. They know what your answer is." His voice was a whisper, while I wasn't even sure I was breathing. "Trust it."

I stared at him, at the dimple, at the dreads, at the shallow scars on his chin and...

"Thom," I began, but he only smiled, his hands pressing me against him again as he stopped what I was about to say with that gruff irritation of his.

"Don't say I'm wise," he growled. "I don't think I could take it."

I couldn't help but laugh. He just didn't realize he always had been.

8

WYN

"For Sdens."

My voice was a grumble, the drunken slur the last rumble of the night-before-battle ritual that I was trapped in.

While no one had died at the Joclyn-Ryland meet and greet of a few hours before, it didn't guarantee that we were all going to be alive by this time tomorrow.

Edmund was here. The forest was infested with little bat demons and Dramin had woken up, leaving me another invalid to take through the forest to safety.

We would be lucky if we made it.

So I drank.

I drank to each person who had died in this centuries long war, in a tradition that had carried on just as long. Probably longer. Who knows, maybe Sain was the one to start it. He seemed the drunken memorial type.

"For Villin." I slurred, taking another drink. "For her life. For her death."

Thom had fallen asleep, Jos and Ilyan were long gone. But I continued on like a woman possessed.

I couldn't stop. Which, knowing what I was heading into was a terrible, terrible mistake.

Crickets chirped through the partially opened window, the sound vaguely familiar as it slurred with my tears in a buzz that made my head spin as though it was begging me to knock it off and go to sleep.

I knew I should—my body very clearly wanted sleep—but I couldn't, not yet.

I still had too many names to go through before I began our deadly attempt to get everyone out of Rioseco and to Prague.

Prague, you know, the city that Joclyn had just *seen* in deranged Vilỳ bloodbath alongside her father during that table meeting a few hours before.

So, you know, even if we made it through the armies that surrounded us here, we were still totally doomed.

Which seemed a whole lot scarier when Jos said it in that creepy as heck Drak deadpan. It was the first time I had heard her true power in her voice, and I really didn't want to hear a repeat.

Creepy.

I took another shot, letting the liquor burn my throat as I tried to wipe the freaky sound of her voice from my mind before I returned to my toasts.

I poured one shot after another, moving like one of those weighted birds that old men kept on their desks.

Pour. Name. Pour. Name.

Up and down.

Over and over.

I needed a top hat.

As my drunken state descended, so did my list, shifting from those we had lost in the war, to those whose life I had ended.

To every person I had wronged.

With each drink I sealed my fate with the admission of my sins and grievances.

If only the heavily fermented drink was enough to wash them away.

I was sure the people who had first built this abbey would think it was. Either that, or they would hang me, my sins too great for any form of redemption.

"For Carin." Drink.

"For Prek." Drink.

"For Vahan." Drink.

"For Dramin." My tongue slurred around the words, and Thom exhaled in such a way that if it wasn't for the snoring I would have thought he had heard me.

But it was only me and the crickets.

I sighed, and this time, I downed the drink straight from the bottle, liquid pouring down my chin, the taste more like acid than liquor. I didn't care. It didn't really matter, anyway. I was already far too inebriated for my own good.

I had seen the youth of society do it enough as I dragged Talon from concert to concert. I guessed it was my turn.

Pouring again, the glass and bottle slammed against each other thanks to the shake in my hand. Nothing came out.

There was no more. I had, foolishly, consumed every last drop.

I stared blindly at the now empty glass, my mind feeling blank and hollow as I tried to think of the next name, the next person that I had sold bits of my soul to betray.

Nothing was there anymore. The massive list had disappeared with the mention of Dramin.

He was here, in this abbey, and he was awake.

The one person who would know the answer to my question.

I had to know if my Tŏuha's were real or if they were dreams. I had to know if Talon was *real*.

As far as I saw it, there was no better time to confront the man whose mate I murdered right in front of him and ask if he still dreamed about her.

Jeeze, I wish I had more booze.

I didn't give my confidence, or my insanity, a chance to waiver before I bolted through the door, my shoes slapping loudly against the stone as I ran, or maybe stumbled, through the pitch-dark hallways.

Thanks to hours of drinking, my normally heightened senses had dulled, leaving me stumbling through dark that I would normally be able to see through. Like a cat.

This was what mortals must feel like in an old building. Creaks were louder, shadows longer, and everything was dark. I couldn't be sure, but I swore there was a hunched man following me.

No wonder horror movies were so popular.

I had never seen the pull, but now that I was in one, I didn't know if I wanted to keep going or press pause and find a way to escape.

So, like a foolish mortal, I ran. I ran around the last corner and right into the old, weathered door of the room I had vacated only hours before.

Yes, into it.

My head smacked into it with a bang and I stumbled back staring at the door as if it had wronged me.

Even the door didn't want me there.

Suddenly, I felt a strong pull to turn around and avoid this conversation altogether.

"Grow a freakin' back bone, why don't you," I chastised

myself, placing my heavy-as-a-bag-of-rocks hand against the door. The wood was rough against my palm, my fingers dragging against it as I pulled it into a fist.

My knock was an explosion of sound that caused me to jerk back. I don't know why I did, heck, I don't know why I knocked. I ran into the freakin' door. I was sure he already knew I was here.

Didn't stop the nauseating anxiety from duplicating as his voice called back.

"Enter."

Here we go. Don't lose your cool.

I could do this. Even when drunk.

Back straight, I walked into his room, my forehead wrinkling in agitation as I let my eyes adjust to the dim blue light that streamed in through the windows.

Towering bookshelves lined the walls, stretching high above me in elongated mouths, looking as if the room itself would swallow me whole.

My intoxication was causing me problems.

"Ah," Dramin sighed from inside the monster's jaws, the sound more like a deflating balloon than a person, "I had a feeling it would be you."

Of course he did. Darn Draks and their infallibility. If I had been accompanied by Captain Mal, he would have had the same reaction. If he knew who that was, of course. Well, and if he was real, but I wasn't going to get hung up on logistics.

Captain Mal was real enough. Didn't matter if it was a TV show. It was the greatest of all time.

Yum.

"You saw me coming, I take it?" He laughed at my question, and my shoulders stiffened, my feet stopping their slow advance as I froze in the middle of the room. Scanning the dark, I finally found the withered, old shape that I was sure was him, his chest rising and falling calmly as he lay on his bed.

"No, my father told me of your conversation yesterday. He warned me that you would be visiting."

"Warned." I guessed I deserved that, all things considered. "Is it okay that I am here?"

"Of course, but if you wouldn't mind turning on a light? As much as I enjoy chatting in the dark, I like to see the people I am to be friends with."

His comment caught me off guard, the light, calm nature of his voice was so out of place that my alarms were screaming 'trap' before I could calm them. No matter what I had heard about this man, no one could easily turn things around after what I had done to them.

No one.

Except Talon.

After all, I supposed Talon had done the same. I had killed his sister, yet somehow...

My breath shook, my pulse quickening at the not so gentle reminder for what I had come here to do in the first place.

My magic jumped at the emotions and the few lamps that were littered throughout the room sparked violently as the fire magic washed over them, giving life to the dry and dead wicks for the first time in what I could assume had been decades. Judging by the state of the room, it might have been longer.

Those earthen mugs were everywhere, tucked amongst the misshapen piles of books that covered the shelves, the tables and any other available surface. I had been so preoccupied with restraining Ryland and memorizing battle plans earlier that I hadn't really noticed we were having a battle meeting in the middle of a minefield.

Those poison filled mugs were everywhere. It made his room look like the disheveled library of a mad scientist, something you would see on an old TV show. I didn't know why, but even with all the death mugs that were ready to tip over and burn the crap out of my skin, it made me comfortable, almost like I was walking onto the set of a show I used to love.

"That wasn't exactly what I had meant, but it will do," he said, his lighthearted chuckle pulling my focus.

From here, I could sense his magic tucked between the layers of his blankets, healing flowers and water folded into the fibers of cloth. It was one of the most basic and powerful forms of healing magic. We had done the same thing to Joclyn after she had broken her back, but this was different. It was as if the magic within the blankets was all that was keeping him alive.

Looking at the way he melted into the bed like putty, I was sure I wasn't that far off. He looked tired and his incredibly unkempt hair made him look the part of the mad scientist.

"Tatinek seemed to think I would sleep, and so he left me in the dark, something that wouldn't have been a problem if I had the ability to light my own lanterns."

"Can Draks not ignite lights?" I asked, fully aware that I had lived under Sain's green lights for nearly a month.

"Normally, yes, but there seems to be something wrong with my magic. It doesn't look as if it is interested in working properly." His voice dragged mournfully, a sadness erupting in the undertones that smacked me hard.

I understood that pain all too well. To lose something so instrumental to your being was a lot like losing an arm.

"It seems that whatever the Silnỳ hit me with did more damage than anyone thought. Of course, I could also be dead, so I must look on the bright side."

He tried to smile, but the emotion didn't reach his eyes, it didn't breathe into the room like it had before. It slid to the ground, pooling on the floor like sticky syrup that made me sure living wasn't quite a 'bright side' to him anymore.

"But she healed you." I was fully aware of how childish the statement was, but I didn't care. At this point, I was more interested in keeping the conversation away from the real reason I had stumbled over here and bringing it to something light and airy, instead.

Like not dying... Yeah... This was not going to work.

I had obviously lost my nerve, which was pretty damn infuriating.

"I guess you could say that," he said with a chuckle. "Of course, she saved you, too, didn't she?"

I could only nod.

The skin around Dramin's eyes wrinkled in a smile, the emerald green dancing in the light. I stared at the color that was so similar to Sain's and wondered if that was what Joclyn's eye color used to be. She had told me once that her eye color had changed when she had received her mark, and judging by her family...

Family.

The word seemed dead after I had watched them all throw verbal mud at each other. My brow wrinkled and I stepped away without thinking, the parallels from her family and mine making me uncomfortable.

Of course, my family didn't just yell. They also tried to kill each other.

"Am I to take that as a yes?" he said with a low chuckle, the sound out of place against my reverie.

I didn't know what the man found so joyful, but he certainly did smile and chuckle a lot. It was as if he kept all the joy of the world inside of him, and he alone was responsible for distributing it. Being around him was making me feel light, the dread that had escorted me into the room flitting away into nothing.

"Yes," I finally answered him. "She took the Zánik curse from my body."

"Ahhh," he sighed with the contentment of an overjoyed parent, his body sagging down into the bed. "My little girl is growing up."

I couldn't help it, the tiniest of smiles crept over my face. He sounded like one of those TV families. I could practically see him smiling, side-by-side with his wife...

Damn it. His wife.

I couldn't ignore it any more. I had come here for a reason. It wasn't like me to lose my gumption.

Of course, it also wasn't like me to start any kind of conversation with, "Hey, I'm sorry I killed your wife and your kids... and well, everyone else in your family, but can we powwow about these awesome dreams I have been having?"

Well, it wasn't like either of me.

The murderer wouldn't care. The rocker wouldn't have killed anyone for fun.

"Can I ask you something?" I took a tentative step forward as he turned to look at me, his face so kind and understanding that some of the tension left my over-taut muscles, my chest deciding it was okay to breathe normally.

"Of course. You came here for a reason, after all. But, I cannot promise you will get the response you are looking for. I cannot promise you peace."

Like the snap of a rubber band, the tension ripped

through my shoulders, the murderess roaring to life in my mind as intoxication gave way to defensive anger.

Or rather, the anger rose in an attempt to smother the heart-wrenching guilt and vehemence.

Guilt.

The darn emotion was so strong that even if my personal filter was working at full strength, which it wasn't, I was sure I couldn't keep it restrained. As a result, everything flew out in a rush.

"I'm sorry for what Edmund made me do. For what I chose to do. It wasn't right, and I didn't feel like I could make a choice. I was trapped. If I could go back, I would let him take my life over every single one I murdered."

The words weren't enough. They weren't powerful enough. They weren't deep enough. But I didn't know how to make them stronger, so they lingered, the silence coming back as though it lived there.

An unwelcome guest, like a vampire, sitting on my chest and sucking my life away. It made it hard to breathe, hard to see past the burning heat in my face as angry tears began to break free, sliding over my cheeks in burning ribbons.

The room evaporated into nothing except smoke, silence, and air that was too thick to breathe.

"We all make choices." Dramin said, his voice breaking through the strangled gasps that were emanating from my chest as I tried to avoid crying. "Every day, we make new ones. And all of those choices are based on what we know to be right and true at the time. It truly is a miracle that our knowledge within this life gets to grow and change. Otherwise, we would keep making the same choices, the same mistakes, thinking they were the right ones."

"What are you saying?"

"You killed my family, Wynifred." His words were harsh,

filled with the anger that was clearly printed on his face. They cut through me like the blunted knife they were. Slow, painful, caustic. I let them. After all, I deserved it.

"You massacred my wife right in front of me. I felt her soul disconnect from mine as her blood sprayed over my face, and it has haunted me for centuries."

There were no words I could say in response to that. If sorry was not enough, then there was nothing within our language that would cover the sins I had committed, that could seek forgiveness and hope to receive it.

I didn't deserve it, anyway.

"I know." It was only two words, and while it was not enough, they said so much more. They were understanding. A shared heartbreak.

"He did the same to you."

I could only nod, trying to keep the memory of Rosaline's last moments out of my mind even though it was already there, playing on repeat.

"Is that when you knew? When your faith in him began to change?"

"It was before. When I felt her move inside of me for the first time."

"When life became something real."

Something real.

Those words froze the world around me. I didn't think I could move if I tried. I didn't see Dramin anymore, even though he was only a few feet from me. I knew he was there, but I was seeing the beach. I was seeing Thom in his ugly hat. I was seeing life and love and remembering that moment so clearly—the feeling of another person inside of me, of tiny hands and legs pressing against me.

I had disposed of life for centuries before that moment, and every time I had thought nothing of it. People that, in some cruel way, had become nothing more than a pig on a slaughtering block. However, feeling my daughter, that child, a person. Feeling her grow, move, and become alive inside of me, had made it real.

Life had become real.

It had become more than sprays of blood and hearts in boxes.

It had become something I wanted to protect.

Something worth protecting.

"Do you regret it?" His calm whisper pulled my attention, my eyes drifting back into focus.

"Regret what?"

"What you have done," he clarified, his eyes kind through the pain I could see behind them. "What you chose to do?"

"More than anything." Once again, words were not enough to convey what I felt.

"Then you may ask your question."

It wasn't an act of forgiveness, for I wasn't sure I would ever gain that from him, but it was an open door, some kind of acceptance I wasn't sure I would ever understand.

"I have been having dreams—"

"Of your mate?" he interrupted me, his voice shrouded with a hard edge that for the first time of all of my existence made me doubt myself.

I could only nod.

"Are they a Tŏuha?" he asked, the unrelenting hope sprouting up in my chest, my heart swelling with need.

Need.

Love.

Guilt.

Worry.

Confusion.

I suddenly found myself trapped in a cyclone of emotions, everything blending and erupting against each other until my magic reacted with a white-hot flame that rolled over my skin. I let it burn, burn away the foolish, feminine, emotions that were smothering me.

"What do you feel they are, Wynifred?"

I squished my face together in concentration as I rephrased my question.

"They feel like a Tòuha. We are in the same place, and he's there. It doesn't feel like he's gone... it's like he's still somewhere in the world connecting with me. But I know he's gone. I can't feel his magic inside of me. I..." My words stumbled to a stop as the memory became too much, as the haunted cry rang through my mind.

I should have never come here.

"I see my mate every night when I sleep." The unexpected calm of his admission was ice water against my soul, his pain mirroring my own so perfectly that I was sure they cancelled each other out. "I see her in the forest that we spent every one of our Tòuha's walking through. We talk, she holds my hand. And, for years after her death, I was sure they were real. I was sure that it was really her."

"It wasn't?" I could barely get the words past the jagged stabs that were running over my chest.

"No. I was too blind to see that it was only my memories replaying. It was only my mind pulling at what I knew to be there and creating a shadow."

He looked at me from where he lay, the dim light from the lanterns flickering around us, and this little piece of what we were, this common ground, cemented itself between us in a thread of understanding whether we wanted it to or not.

"But, why...?"

"Because part of your soul is missing, and each night when you sleep, you search for it. You search so hard that you create something that is not there, if only to keep you going."

My soul. For years, I had been searching for my soul. Even before Talon's death, even before I regained my memories. My soul was still searching for what had been ripped from it. For years, haunted by dreams and nightmares, I watched Thom and Rosaline move through my subconscious. But in reality, I was searching for them.

And now, without Talon, my dreams were left to dwell in the parts still missing and the parts now gone.

I was right; losing parts of who you were and then being forced to relive them was like a special place in the underworld reserved just for me.

"Purgatory."

"I'm sorry?"

I hadn't even realized I had said the word aloud.

"I had that thought, being there. Being trapped with... him." And her... but I wasn't going to say that. Not aloud and certainly not to him. "That it was purgatory. Being with someone that you want so dearly, but not being able to."

Dramin gave me the same look Sain always had, the intense stare that Draks always had, I corrected myself. Except this time, something was missing. A light or intensity that I had paired with the stare was missing. I didn't shy away from him, instead I looked at him as a deep groan seeped past his lips, and he rolled over, patting the bed beside him.

Ummm... I know we had a moment, but I really wasn't sure if we were there yet.

The kind smile he gave me though was making it really hard to say no.

I hesitated for only a minute before I closed the gap between us, my body tense with nerves as I sat beside the one person I had harmed more than any other in this building.

"In a way it is," he whispered, his weak hand patting my knee comfortingly. "Being forced to relive what you can no longer have is a form of torture I wouldn't wish on anyone. Not even on you."

"Thank you... I guess." The words were swallowed by my poor attempt at humor.

"You are welcome, I guess," Dramin said, his inflection matching mine as he patted my knee once more. "Besides, I am putting my life in your hands tomorrow. I must learn to trust you."

I stiffened at the reminder. The two halves of myself beginning their usual internal battle. I was filled with dread, while the other half was ready to run into the forest and begin the massacre.

Sometimes I wondered if I was turning into a true head-case.

"Does that mean you forgive me, then?"

"I didn't say that." He rolled back onto his back with a groan, his face as calm and unresponsive as an old man reading the newspaper. "It means I must learn to trust you."

Well, when you put it like that...

I wasn't sure if Dramin was kidding, being serious, or somewhere in the middle. By the amount of laughter he had infected the room with and the way his eyes shone, somewhere in the middle, suited me just fine.

Even if I would never gain his forgiveness, I would gain his trust, and in oh so many ways, that was enough for me.

I stood without a word, grateful when he didn't say anything to stop me, and softly padded toward the door, my magic flaring as I turned the lights off, hoping it was the right thing to do.

"Go dream of your mate, little girl," he whispered from somewhere behind me. "And I will dream of mine."

I froze, staring into the dark room, wishing there was something to say. Something that could make everything better.

I think that was part of the problem.

There wasn't.

And there never would be.

9

WYN

"LET ME GO, WYN!" Ryland's shout was the bang of a gun in my ear, the close proximity of the shout making the sound even louder as it echoed through the kitchen.

We had been waiting in this kitchen for nearly two hours for Ilyan and Joclyn to make their appearance. I was still hungover, my head was pounding thanks to Ryland's screaming, and my patience had reached its end. Ryland's had too, either that or he liked to hear himself scream.

"No, Ryland!" I growled as loud as I dared and tried to grab his arms again, to push my magic into him enough that I could forcibly calm him down.

Keeping contact with him was like wrestling a greased octopus in a mud pit. He kept fighting me, his body thrashing as whatever demons his father had impregnated him with grew stronger.

The closer Edmund came, the worse he got. This battle that we were minutes away from entering was feeling like an impossibility.

We were so dead. Especially if I couldn't get Ryland to "calm... the... freak... down..."

I said the last words aloud, trying to wrestle the muddy octopus as his hand latched onto my plate and sent the last of my cantaloupe salad flying.

"Great," I groaned as Thom finally, slowly, lethargically, moved to help me.

I gave him a look that held more daggers than thanks, but the grumps ignored me. I couldn't be mad for long, the added hands gave me enough leverage that I was able to find skin. My magic flooded Ryland in a rush of heat and ice that calmed him immediately.

"No!" he called out again, but his interjection was halfhearted. His voice sunk as he did, right into the battered bench between me and Thom. Then his hands fell into the plate of food before him, sending tomatoes rolling.

"That was fun," I sighed, collapsing against Ryland, careful to keep skin contact with the boy in question.

"For who?" Ryland's voice was more like a whimper, the dejected growls barely audible.

Talk about a stab to the heart. It sucked, but I knew there was nothing I could say to that. No words of comfort, no inspirational speeches. I couldn't fix it, this shield was the best I could give him.

When it came down to it, it just sucked, plain and simple.

"I know, Ry." I leaned my head against his shoulder, my hand tightening around his in what I would hope was a show of comfort. "I know."

Ryland stiffened underneath my touch, his muscle pulsing beneath my shoulder. Crap, I had forgot that he hated contact. Being there like this seemed so natural. I almost pulled my head away, but he relaxed a moment later, pressing his head over mine as Sain burst back through the old double doors.

Dramin perked up from where he sat at the round table across from us at the return of his father. It was the most movement I had seen from the guy in the last few minutes, his food was still untouched before him. Of course, he could have been doing the tango and I wouldn't have noticed with all the octopus wrestling I had been doing.

"He's coming." Sain grumbled without looking at anyone. "At least, I hope he is. I don't want to have to go back down there a third time."

It appeared that Sain's irritation and hostility when concerning his daughter and Ilyan lived on. The man was so red-faced I was questioning if I needed to run over and check that he was breathing.

"He will come, Father. Have faith in our king." Dramin spoke calmly from across the kitchen, his focus on one of the two mugs that sat before him.

"I will have faith in him when he starts making choices that are more conducive for all of Imdalind." Dramin may ignore Sain's scorn, but the hatred in the old man bristled my anger. Before I could say, or do, anything about it however Thom scoffed loudly from the other side of Ryland, his dreads swinging as he threw his head back and laughed.

Not a good laugh mind you, but a weird hostile sound that was clearly meant to egg his friend on.

I had a feeling I didn't want to be here for this.

"Yes, because your choices are so effective for everyone," Thom exclaimed loudly, his voice echoing around us like a bass drum.

"I speak only for the Drak."

"Well, I speak for the half-breeds, and they don't seem to be complaining," Thom growled, the bench we sat on shifting as he leaned forward, his eyes sparking viciously.

"Well, they should be. Those half-breeds aren't in charge

of everyone." Sain's return was a snap, and obviously cut too deep for even Thom to ignore.

He practically jumped off the bench, sending Ryland and I rocking.

"He's your King, Sain! Just because you are a first doesn't make you a God!"

Ryland jumped at the rough bark in Thom's voice, the outburst igniting every reaction that I had spent the last forty minutes trying to repair.

"Crap!" I yelled as Ryland was reduced to a howl of fear that wrenched through my muscles and sent both men rushing to his side, whatever face-off that had been about to take place forgotten.

We needed to get out of here, start moving, start fighting. Anything to ease the tension that was starting to infiltrate the abbey like two teen boys on steroids.

Ilyan had said we were to leave before sun-up when we had set a plan last night. Well, the sun was up and we were still sitting and waiting for them to make their appearance.

It really didn't help that everyone could feel the violent waves of magic from the armies that surrounded us. It was like an anger virus and I had just about enough of it.

"I was afraid of this," Sain's voice was low as he stood over Ryland, his hands on his shoulders as he, too, attempted to comfort him.

"You were afraid that he would turn into an uncontrollable weapon right as we are about to leave?" I couldn't keep the snootiness out of my voice, a fact Thom seemed to enjoy as he laughed darkly beside me.

Wasn't helping, but it was true. Edmund and his perfect little sabotage. The man was a villain of the worst kind, he had effectively made our escape that much more impossible.

No matter how much I loved a challenge, this was not one I was looking forward to. I cared for these people too much. I needed to protect them.

Even Dramin.

If only to prove to him that I was sorry.

"I'm sitting right here," Ryland sighed, his voice broken as he dropped his head into his free hand, the long fingers pulling at his curls roughly. I clung to the other one tightly, refusing to let go.

"Sorry, Ry." The words were starting to feel pointless, never mind that they were true.

My voice was a whisper against Ryland's labored breathing, Dramin's pained exhales, and the exasperated sighs of both Sain and Thom. All the sounds combined in a wall of unsaid fears and worries that were starting to feel more like a plague.

A plague that I had to destroy.

I knew how to do it, the words were already there, ready. Perhaps it was because I had sung the song to Joclyn only hours before, or because I had woken up from yet another dream with Talon, but they were there. The words were a calm comfort to me, a pleasant reminder of so many positive memories.

"*I know you feel these are the worst of times, I do believe it's true...*"

"What?" I smiled at Thom's question, at his lack of knowledge of something that, to me, was so common.

"It's a song from this band—"

"Styx, I know. I lived through the 70s. The 80s, too. Although I preferred Queen." He smiled as I did, my mind trying to wrap around the millions of possibilities that one statement could hold for me.

He knew Styx, and he liked Queen, that while clearly

not as good as Styx, was still a good band. Oh my, this was very nearly the best news ever.

I opened my mouth to ask as Ilyan and Jos walked in, and anything I had been planning to say was instantly gone. Gone as if it had never happened, as if the air had been sucked from the room.

Yes, he was the king. Yes, she was my best friend. It should have been a boring normal entrance, except it wasn't. Not by the way they stood next to each other, not by the way his hand rested protectively on her back.

My eyes were wide as I stared at them, fighting the smile at what was as clear as day, even without the long, golden ribbon that trailed from Ilyan's hair.

It should have been normal.

Everyone who came from Imdalind knew of the length of the royal line and what it meant. However, for Ilyan to wear the long golden ribbon somewhere it could be seen, and for Joclyn to be wearing a hoodie that covered what was normally an absolute mop of long, black hair... It wasn't normal.

I knew at once what it meant. Just as everyone else did, it seemed, guessing by the number of wide eyes I was surrounded by.

I guess my meddling hadn't been in complete vain.

So glamorously, wonderfully, perfect.

After everything she had to face and what Edmund had done to her, I was happy for her.

I was happy for them both.

"Surprise, surprise," Thom chuckled from beside me, his voice low enough only I could hear.

I only rolled my eyes at him. Saying something about this new development so close to Ryland was only asking for trouble.

Shaking my head at him in warning, I went back to helping Ryland who was now whimpering beside me like an injured dog, thankfully oblivious to the new development. I didn't want to know what he would do if he found out they had bonded.

Bonded. I was so giddy that the upcoming bloodbath we were about to swim through didn't seem quite so ominous anymore.

"My lord," Sain greeted Ilyan formally as he approached them, and I had to forcibly restrain an eye roll. Of course, he was all proper and courteous now, whereas earlier, he had seemed about ready to start a coup.

Joclyn watched us, a deep pain bowing through her features before she moved to sit next to Dramin.

She looked entirely calm, entirely controlled compared to how I had seen her only yesterday—the scared, volatile girl who cowered in corners and clung to Ilyan like a lifeline. She stood straight and tall, her face happy. There was no wonder at why she was happy.

Joclyn laughed at something Dramin had said before turning back to us, the worry that was taking over her features sliding away as she caught my eye. Normally, she would have smiled, made a face, done anything, but she merely stared at me so guilty that if there had been any doubt, she took it all away.

I wanted to laugh; instead, I smiled with a grin that was all plot and no pleasure.

Great. The assassin had made an appearance at entirely the wrong time.

"Ryland." The low rumble of Ilyan's voice pulled me away from Joclyn's stare and back to the whimpering boy who rocked back and forth beside me, his brother surrounding him in what was part comfort, part security.

The loss of my touch, and my shield, had put us right back where we had started.

Wrestling baby tigers was never fun, no matter how cute you thought the stripes were.

"Ryland," Ilyan tried again. This time his brother's focus snapped right to him. "I need you to look at me. I would like to help you."

Ryland moaned at Ilyan, the sound so low and mournful that it felt like the sound of a dying animal. It echoed around us before he began to rock with much more force. He was clearly trying to find something to press his body against.

I fought the need to reach out to him, to wrap my hands around him as Sain and I had done for so many weeks and even months as Cail destroyed him. I wasn't the only one, either. Sain stood behind him, writhing his hands in the same agony. Needing to comfort him, but not being able to. Yeah, it sucked, but I couldn't hold his hand and shield him while we fought our way through the armies in our attempt to reach the cave.

I was good. Not that good.

Ryland needed to be able to at least partially control himself, and I was starting to question if Ilyan was going to be able to deliver that.

It was not that he wasn't trying to calm his brother, not that Ryland wasn't trying to be calm. We had simply run out of time, we were out of time before Ilyan had even showed up. Edmund and his freaking games. He may as well have won, just like the sight had said.

Ugh. The sight. With the way Ilyan's focus was now boring into Sain I obviously wasn't the only one to think of it.

Sain's eyes narrowed into a scowl at the look Ilyan was giving him, as though he knew what was coming.

Creepy Drak probably already did.

One of these days, I was going to say something that Sain didn't foresee. I didn't see that happening, but at least I was going to try.

"Sain," Ilyan began, his voice harsh. "I need to know the exact moment my father will arrive—"

"You know Drak magic doesn't work that way, Ilyan," Sain interrupted him, the breach in conduct visibly bristling Ilyan.

I stepped back. I had been on the receiving end of that wrath one too many times as it was, and I wasn't interested in testing my survival skills.

"I understand this, Sain." Yep, one foul step away from explosion. "But I need you to get me as close to the exact time as possible."

The two men locked eyes in a silent match for power. Whatever had upset Sain before came back full force as their magic bristled. I may fear Ilyan's temper, but this matchup was only comical to me. I knew the power Draks held, and it wasn't much. What was Sain playing at?

A Chihuahua could not defeat a Great Dane, and it would be foolish of them to try.

Although, I kind of wanted them to, if only for the show.

Unfortunately for me, the staring match ended with a nod from Sain, and then his eyes instantly dipped to the haunting black the Draks always had. I looked away, preferring not to watch. The memories of the horror movie hallways from the night before were quickly increasing my freak out factor.

I must be losing my nerve. Either that, or I had too many

nerves, the anticipation from the *exciting challenge* of what I was about to face too much. It could go both ways.

"Under the flashes of magic the sky breaks apart. The man will come bathed in flames. The time is soon when the sun will break the clouds. Then it will be too late." Sain's voice was that low rumble again, and I shivered, the magic in his words moving into me the same way they had before.

He had barely said anything before Thom took off toward Dramin and Joclyn, his shoulders hunched as they always were, but this time, it had more to do with the fact of what Sain had said and what that meant for all of us.

"Can't you bind his memory, his heart, something to make it so I can get him from point A to point B without a massacre falling on my head?" Ilyan's eyes widened at my question, his distaste in memory binds shining through.

I knew he hated them as much as the next person. It had taken sheer bribery to get him to perform one on me, but I really didn't see how we had an option here.

As far as I was concerned, we could either bind him so tightly that he barely knew who he was and what was around him or risk him turning on me before we reached the cave that was our only chance of escape.

I wasn't very good at fighting people when the sole intent was supposed to be on keeping them alive.

Killing, yes.

Restraint, no.

I would make a terrible police officer.

Ilyan locked eyes with me as Ryland's whimpers continued below us. His hands were wrapped around Ilyan's as he began to plea for help, for assistance, for his brother to take it all away.

The sound was so similar to how Cail used to plea with me on especially bad nights that it broke me.

"If you won't, Ilyan, I will." My voice was hard again, a fact Ilyan obviously noticed. His lip twitched a bit before he stared me hard in the eye.

"And hold onto him all the way to Vitoria?"

I already knew I couldn't, leave it to him to call my bluff.

"There isn't another choice, Ilyan. If we don't do this, he *will* attack us. He will turn on us. I don't want any more innocent blood on my hands." Both Ilyan and Sain flinched at my comment, but I plowed on, unwilling to give in quite yet. "You heard Sain, if we don't leave soon, we will all die. This isn't a question of morality anymore. It's a question of survival."

Ilyan didn't look away from me, but luckily for him, I was stubborn enough for the two of us. The hard stares beat neither of us down. That was, until Ryland began to cry, one word seeping from his lips on repeat as his soul flaked away and left him open and raw and dangerous between us.

"Please."

Ilyan's eyes pinched shut as he ran his hand through his hair, his resolve failing as he looked away from me in defeat.

"You're right."

He said nothing more, but it was enough. I would probably never hear something like that from him again, so I locked it away and turned to Sain as Ilyan began whispering to his brother about what was going to happen.

I didn't need to hear this. I had lived it, and the old man seemed as uninterested as I did.

"We'll need to move as quickly as possible," I began, my voice a whisper so as not to interrupt Ilyan and Ryland's powwow. "I know we talked about you escorting Dramin before, but I want you with Ryland."

"Ryland?" Sain's chest puffed up at the suggestion, the action making him look like an explosive puffer fish. I was torn between laughter and fear at the image, my body settling for tense muscles and an odd choking noise as I tried not to laugh. "I need to travel with my son. I need to protect him."

The tension in my shoulders grew at his comment. Any chance of a laugh was gone as he once again played favorites. I knew I shouldn't care. After all, Jos and Sain really didn't know each other. Hell, I didn't even know Sain. But Jos was my best friend, and how he treated her was so similar to how my own father preferred Cail over me. It was like watching reruns of The Partridge Family, except with magic and sights and people dying.

I exhaled, not really wanting to get in a death match this close to the actual death match, and stood as tall as I could before him. I was fully aware that I wasn't even close to tall enough to make this as ominous as I needed it to be. I also wasn't going to unleash my prowess on my best friend's dad.

Ew.

Of all the teenage things to have stuck with me.

"I understand that, Sain"—I was trying to be diplomatic, but I was sure it wasn't working—"but you can calm Ryland down quicker than anyone. That will be more important to all of us if the bind breaks. Thom can keep Dramin safe because, if this doesn't work, and Ryland still erupts, I doubt you would be able to save your son then."

Sain's face whitened to a shade so pale I was sure he was going to be sick. Then his teeth clenched in what I wasn't certain was irritation or stomach issues. I waited, every part of me tied in knots as the reality of what we were about to face sunk into me, my magic prickling in both eager anticipation and cold-hearted fear.

The cave may be a sanctuary, but the chances of us making it there were dwindling by the minute.

Sain nodded in agreement as Ilyan stood, and we didn't wait. We swept Ryland from the kitchen without another word.

While what we were about to venture into seemed a little bit more of a possibility now, it was anything but a sure thing.

I only hoped the bind was enough to keep Ryland safe.

And to keep me from killing him.

10

WYN

FACING JOCLYN IN THE COURTYARD, moments away from battle, the sky ripping apart with lightning and doom, was not the right time to tell her about my past.

To spill about babies and marriages and everything else that I was hiding. And everyone I had killed.

Yet, I wanted to.

I wanted to spill everything, let it cut through the air like the jagged lightning that broke across the sky. Hot, quick, and precise. I wanted to plead with her not to run into that forest, not to die, while knowing neither she nor I had a choice. The battle was here. She would go in one direction with Ilyan, and I would go in the other with the invalids. We couldn't stop it.

I was over four hundred years old, and I stood with a teenager wishing we could go back to girl talk. I had, miraculously, come full circle.

Jos smiled sadly as the sky broke open in a roar of thunder, the storm was getting worse as the final moments ticked down.

A countdown to doom.

Joclyn looked to the sky at the sound, and I didn't wait. I bolted, running away from her and Ilyan into the forest after my disabled party like the coward I was.

A perfect chicken.

I had been avoiding her for days because I couldn't find the strength to talk to her, to spill my guts.

And now it was too late.

The wrong time. The wrong moment.

She needed to focus on what her and Ilyan were heading into.

Perhaps there would be a miracle and she would survive. Perhaps I would get another chance.

Thom and they others were a few hundred yards into the tree line, the tall conifers hiding him and the others as they stood away from the abbey. It was a little resting spot before we ran for our lives, and they were already taking advantage of it.

Dramin had found a sturdy fallen tree to sit on, his body looked as aged as it had last night. Being out of bed wasn't doing him any favors, and neither was Sain. He hovered around him like a nervous mother, fingers fluttering as he mumbled something. And Ryland? Ryland was hitting his head against a tree.

We were already off to a great start.

Thom looked to me as I approached, my head held high as my fingers buzzed, ready for the release that I hadn't been able to give them these last few days.

"Ready to kill some of my cousins?" I said with a smile, glad when Thom laughed at a joke I had made far too many times before.

I chose to ignore the grimace that lined the Draks' faces. I couldn't walk on eggshells all the time, and right now, I needed to have my head on straight if they expected me to get them through this. As a result, they would have to deal.

Ilyan and Joclyn were already waging their own battle in a mad attempt to distract Edmund's armies enough to let us get out of there. Wasting those precious minutes to help them feel comfy would only put everyone else in danger.

"You mean other than Edmund's little puppets?" Thom said as he came right up beside me, his laugh fading much quicker than it normally would have. "I think we have a problem."

"Besides the fact that we have to travel through piles of armies to get to a cave with three basically useless invalids." I didn't even try to keep the mockery out of my voice.

"That and neither of the Draks can shield themselves."

I looked at him like he had cancelled a Styx concert all on his own. Murder, pure vengeful murder, flashed in my eyes. Thom took a step back, his hands plunging into the pockets of his leather jacket and shrugged. The Thom-ism for 'it is what it is.'

Great.

"Having them shield themselves was the only thing we had going." I tried not to yell, but I was not positive it worked.

"Well, we do always have the option to turn ourselves in. I am sure Edmund would love that." His voice lingered near eruption, the emotion only increasing as thunder rumbled above us once more.

Double great.

An angry Thom, a quickly unraveling Ryland, and some useless Draks.

I was feeling like this exciting *challenge* was heading more in the direction of *massacre*. I didn't think we would be on the massacring side, either.

Triple great.

"I guess we will have to run as fast as we can." It should have been comical, but instead we were lingering somewhere more near insanity.

Ryland might already be there.

We couldn't change the plans in formation. Sain needed to stay with Ryland and try to keep his mind somewhat stable. Well, at least stable enough that he wasn't resorting to self-mutilation. That poor tree was looking a little too battered as it was. And Thom was the only one physically capable enough to drag Dramin through the forest, weather by magic or pure brute strength. Knowing Thom it will be a combination of them both.

"Run like the wind and hope that Ilyan's plan will work..."

"It will work." I interrupted him with a sigh.

I was confident, while Thom was not, and the loud, obnoxious laugh that rang through the forest proved it. I couldn't keep myself from glowering at him.

"Have Ilyan's plans ever not worked?" I was obstinate, but I didn't care. His lack of confidence was grating on me. Not that I had much to spare, but I was stubbornly clinging to every last drop. "Don't be so cynical."

I didn't know if I spoke more to him or to myself.

Maybe both.

Probably both.

All of Ilyan's plans had been rocky, yes, but successful. I was holding tight to that even though this charade already had more than the normal hiccups. This was a drunken man's belch as far as problems go. I wasn't ready to admit that.

Besides, even if we wanted to deviate I was sure Ilyan

had bound us to his plan. If we stepped a toe out of line, he would know.

I shot him a look and popped my hip out, ready to dig into my stubborn positivity. Another bolt of lightning dragged across the sky and stopped any rebut in its tracks. This time the light cut through the sky in streaks of angry red and white as it shot from wherever Ilyan and Joclyn waged their war.

I stared at the light, the angry beauty of it tensing through me as my magic roared, rejoicing in what was coming.

We couldn't wait any longer.

I couldn't be more excited.

"Time to break out the bubbly and get this crazy train moving." I gave Thom one last look in warning or irritation —I wasn't sure—and he moved away, everyone taking their place as if this was some grand orchestrated event.

If only.

I didn't even dare look at them. I began to run, hoping beyond hope that they were following behind, that they could keep up with me and that Edmund's Trpaslík army couldn't keep up at all.

The ground was rough underneath my bare feet, each little stone, each pine needle and stick pressing into the soft tissue in painful little points. It was more than pain, more than pressure of the foreign objects. It was power.

I had rarely worn shoes before Ilyan had wiped my memories, before he had bound my magic. After that, I could feel the power, but it was a shadow of what it had been. Even if I had recognized it, I wouldn't have known what to do with it beside create a handy warm floor for the winter. Now that I had regained control, however, I had regained the power that came along with it.

With each slap of my bare feet against the earth, my magic spread away from me, fanning through the soil and undergrowth like a virus, searching for others magic and burning away whatever traces of my own I left behind, making us nothing more than a little invisible army running through the forest.

Well, we would have been if it wasn't for the stupid Draks.

Ilyan's plan from the night before was laid out in my mind, the binding of it creating a red line of his instruction. The visible path meandered through the forest towards our destination. There shouldn't be any question of what we were supposed to do, but now that Thom had planted an obnoxious amount of doubt inside of me, I was suddenly wondering if there was a better way.

You know, other than dragging invalids through the forest.

Darn you, Thom.

Jaw locked together in frustration, I tried to focus on keeping my magic moving through the soil in search of enemies or dangers. With how fast I was running, however, I was constantly losing contact with the ground, making it impossible for me to scan very far. Sometimes, I wished I could feel people next to me like Ilyan did or whatever Jos did with her tiny smoke people that grew out of maps.

It would make this whole mess that much easier.

"Let me at her!" Ryland's shout ricocheted from behind me, echoing from the trees with such a snap that if any Trpaslík were around us it was ninety-nine percent guaranteed that they were officially headed our way.

Dead leaves and dirt sprayed around me as I dug my heels into the ground in a mad attempt to stop. Thunder and lightning ripped above us as I rushed back and help

Sain from whatever monster had erupted from the boy, making it seem as though the eruption was everywhere.

I flinched at the explosion of dirt, sky, and man as a tree no more than ten yards away from me went up in flames, casting the scene before me with an ominous flicker of reds and yellows. Sain was trying desperately to keep a hold on Ryland who was now twitching, his hands clawing at his hair, his body slamming into the trees as sparks of color flew from his fingertips.

Forget exploding tree, he was a bomb.

"Kill her!" he roared in explosion, his voice breaking through the forest so abruptly that I slammed my heel into the dirt, sure someone was already heading this way. "I need to kill her."

Throwing up a sound barrier in a mad attempt to keep us hidden, I ran at him, my shoulder ramming into his chest and taking him to the ground like I was some sort of bulky football player and not the wiry five foot, three inch Trpaslík I was.

He went down with a thud, the abrupt attack pulling him out of his insanity enough that he looked at me with wide eyes, the fear I knew all too well staring back at me.

"I'm not going to kill you, Ryland," I promised through gritted teeth as I placed my hands against his face, letting my magic smother his heart.

I had done this so many times before. This time, however, it didn't seem to be enough. Just as Ilyan's bind hadn't been.

Edmund was too close, the madness they had wound in him too deep to restrain it.

I really hoped I got to Edmund first, make him pay for all he had done. Who cares about the sight promising Jos to get there. Watching Ryland writhe and fight below me only strengthened my resolve.

"Wyn." His voice was a moan as he tried to fight the madness, but it was only one word before he fell into a babbling nonsense, his hand digging into the dirt as his eyes darted around me.

My muscles clenched as he writhed, my heart aching right along with his.

"Ryland." His name was a snap and his eyes darted back to mine, the bright blue filled with the same ice Edmund always had. "I know you can hear him, but you can hear me too. Can you focus on my voice? On Sain's?"

My heart beat wildly as I stared at him, my foot pressing against the ground as I scanned the forest for signs of an attack, for any sign that we had been seen or heard. Luckily, we seemed to be in the clear so far, something that was both comforting and disturbing.

Surely someone must have heard his wailing.

"We are right here with you, we are going to get you away from it," I said calmly, grateful when his breathing began to regulate and his powerful body began to relax underneath me.

"Good." I said, the knots of my tightly wound muscles easing back, just a bit. The release of fear was almost like a breath of fresh air.

Of course, it couldn't disappear completely, but not with the way the sky was constantly ripping itself apart, the inky black night flashing in colors of war that I was trying very hard not to dissect. I had been in too many battles not to know what was going on.

"Breathe, Ry," I prompted, even as panic began to knit its way through my heart, my scans finally returning what I feared.

Our luck had run out, there was someone there.

A jolt of negative energy burst through my magic, its source just on the outskirts of trees.

No, it was in them.

Sitting.

Waiting.

As if they knew where we were, knew how my magic worked, and knew right where to stand in order to go undetected.

"Breathe," I repeated the word even though I was no longer looking at Ryland. My focus was far away, as if I would somehow be able to see miles away, see who stood there, waiting for us.

Sain spoke softly to Ryland as I stepped away, staring through the branches as my magic stretched toward them. Long tendrils of my power wrapped around the angry flame of their magic, my power pulling at not only him, but several dozen others that popped into being with each step. Like little gophers.

Gophers with magical bazookas.

"What is it?" I barely even acknowledged Thom's approach.

"It's an ambush." The words were lead on my tongue.

There was no other reason for them to be standing there. No reason for them not to rush toward the fight that I knew Joclyn and Ilyan were currently raging on the other side of the abbey.

A battle for distraction, a battle to give us time to escape.

Useless.

Edmund had been one step ahead of us.

Again. So much for having three Draks on our team.

"Freaking bastard!" I snapped, a small tree a few feet away collapsing to ash with a single impulse of my magic.

I didn't even flinch, Thom however jumped so high he could have placed in the Olympic trials.

"I hate it when you do that!"

I guess it had been awhile since the full strength of my magic had been released. For both of us.

A sinister smile curled over my lips as the familiar maniacal joy took over, heating my blood and loosening my stress. We might not make it to Prague, even if there was anything left. Hell, we might not even make it to the caves.

But I was sure going to go out with a bang.

"Let's go." The depth of my voice had come back in one crashing blow.

Thom chuckled as he walked back to Dramin, leaving me staring at the trees before I turned, striding right to Sain who was still struggling with Ryland.

"Go help your son." I didn't give him a chance to rebut, I just grabbed Ryland, plunging my magic into him as I pulled him to stand.

"He's close," he moaned as I draped his arm over my shoulder, as if I was going to be able to somehow carry him on my own the rest of the way, he was easily twice my side. "He wants me to kill her."

"I know, Ry. I know."

His twitching stabilized as my magic began to take old. Instead of just shielding him, however, I basically knocked him out. His head lulled to the side as he collapsed, my magic catching him moments before he collapsed to the ground, arms and legs tangled like a jiggly pretzel.

He looked broken. No, he looked dead. But if it was going to help us get there without dying, I would drag him behind me like some kind of tractor if I had to.

With so much of my magic concentrated on keeping

Ryland stable, I wasn't going to be able to scan the forest anymore.

We might know that a herd of Trpaslík were shadowing us, waiting to attack, but now we had no idea when.

An ambush of a birthday party that no one wanted.

It only added to the fun, though.

Thunder ripped through the air as we began to run, the Ryland trailer soaring behind me as the two of us cleared the way. We may be running much faster than we had before, but it was the only thing that was on our side.

Carrying Ryland like this was putting more of a damper on my Trpaslík sonar than I had expected. I could sense nothing, which left me staring at the forest, waiting for a twig to snap, a bush to sway, or even an explosion to signal their arrival. At this point I would even take a clown popping out if it meant a warning for when they would attack us.

I didn't get a clown. I got the sound of our own feet stomping through the undergrowth, the wheezy gasps of Dramin, and the long, meandering line of Ilyan's plans.

I sprinted through the trees, following the path as the first of Ilyan's instructions came into view. A bright red line intercepted the path we were following, the map Ilyan had placed in my mind playing out like a blueprint.

Burn the trail here.

His voice echoed through my mind in a haunted echo. If he hadn't cast that trick on me before I might have been scared I had lost it, instead I slowed, the bind he had placed over all of us keeping me in perfect time with whatever they were doing on the other side of the forest.

Thom and the Draks sped past me as I came to a stop, my hand firm against Ryland as I pulled him into me, the full weight of his body coming to rest on my shoulders. Oh heavens, he was heavy! It was a miracle I was able to stay upright underneath his bulk.

My fingers dug into him as I tried to keep him upright, my magic pushing through the earth as I took the chance to scan our surroundings. I wouldn't have another opportunity until the next intersection Ilyan had made in the map, so best to make the most of it.

With the speed of the lightning that cut through the blackened sky, my magic spread through the soil in search of the same magic I had felt before. I found nothing, nothing but that same angry energy we had felt before. The toxic weight of it wound over my magic, weighing it down, holding it in place as if it could devour it.

Burn the trail.

His voice came again, louder this time, and I knew I couldn't ignore it. My magic recoiled back like a snake, the slithering tendrils moving through me like warm bubbles before I sent them out again, into the soil in a fan of heat and power that burned through the trail of magic we had created. Any remainders of our trail evaporated as I forged a new one away from us, through the forest and right back to the abbey.

It was an old trick, but one that almost always worked. Few people could actually feel and track the magic of those that were around them. The majority of the time, we all relied on good old-fashioned tracking.

Change the path, confuse your pursuers.

It was easy enough, yet something about it was digging into my gut.

I looked toward the trees, toward where I had felt the magic before, and fought the urge to scan again.

Just to check.

Any chance of that left with a bang, or more like a

scream from the boy behind me. The sound was so loud, and so quick, that I couldn't mask it if I tried.

"Let me kill her!" he roared. "I need to kill her."

I smashed my magic into him, knocking him out again as I twisted away, taking one last look into the trees before I bolted after the others.

So much for burning the trail, the alarm system I carried would still drag them right toward us.

The trees pressed against me, making the already dark night feel like an abyss, an abyss that was only broken by the snaps of lightning that came so fast the forest was nothing other than light and dark, I was trapped in a strobe of light that was making it hard to see where I was going. Even with my heightened sight, even with Ilyan's lines stretching before us, everything felt heavy. I had walked into a fun house maze only to get lost for hours.

My stomach twisted the more I ran, the longer it took for me to reach them. The tense ball calmed when Thom came into view, his squat frame lumbering besides Sain as they carried Dramin, who now appeared to be unconscious.

Because we needed that.

"Is he okay?"

"Keep moving," Thom grunted as I overtook them, only to stumble to a stop as the ground rippled and swayed beneath me, magic swirling beneath my toes.

The flood of power was different than when an attack was coming. It was almost as though an attack was being drained away.

Life being sucked out of the earth.

No, magic.

I had no time to question before the sky lit up like a firecracker and the entire forest was bathed in the color of blood.

A brilliant red pillar of magic cut through the sky, right from where Ilyan and Joclyn were fighting. The geyser of red towered over us, leaving us staring into the red lit world of danger and fear.

"What in the--"

Thom's expletive was drowned out by Ryland's scream as the roar of the explosion snapped the bind I had on him. I tried to grab him, my magic ready to slam back into him, but he broke out of my grip and darted into the forest screaming about death, blood and murder.

"Well, crap," I hissed, turning to Thom as the earth continued to rumble, the sky continuing to break apart.

This was it.

We didn't need to say it, the silent understanding was all that was needed before I bolted into the forest after Ryland, Sain following close behind as the red light faded back to the strobe of lightning.

Flash after flash ruptured the trees, my magic pressing through the soil as I searched for the mad prince. We needed to find him and get us back on our path before whoever was hiding the trees decided now was the time to make their move.

Screw the clown. I would be happy if Ryland would pop out and scare the bejeezus out of me.

But there was nothing, not even a whisper of his magic.

The forest cracked in black and white, the thunder shaking the trees as the sky broke apart.

"Ryland?" It was foolish to call out, but I didn't see another option. I couldn't feel him, despite knowing he had to be close.

"Ryland." I tried again, quieter this time, only to jump when the snap of a branch answered back, the sound harrowing in the roar of thunder right above us, loud and oppressive.

Whipping toward the sound, I stared into the dark as the sky flashed with electricity.

The boy stood only feet from me.

Staring at me.

"Ryland." The name should have been calm. I should have been overjoyed to see him, but the look on his face and the way his back eyes stared at me struck fear in me in a way I hadn't felt since the dungeons of Imdalind. A monster stood before me. No matter how hard I looked, I couldn't feel that monster's magic.

I couldn't sense him.

"Ryland?" My voice shook as the sky cracked again, the dark consuming the trees before the light snapped back, but he had gone.

There was nothing but the tall bending spires and the roar of thunder.

I jumped as Sain caught up to me, his dark green orb of light bobbing beside him, giving the forest a fluorescent glow.

The forest looked much safer with Sain's light illuminating it, but it wasn't enough to drown my questioning panic.

I had seen him.

Hadn't I?

I scanned the forest as we began to move, each crunch of undergrowth sounding loud beside my strained breathing. He had to be here somewhere.

"Ryland?" Even Sain's voice was shaking in fear, and the question that neither of us wanted to ask clear in that one word.

What happened if we didn't find him?

I looked at Sain, fully intending to ask, but he only stared straight ahead, his face dead and pale as he watched something I could not see, his lips moving in words that were drowned in the rumble of thunder from overhead.

"When the girl... Stays... take her blood..." I stared at him as the broken pieces of what I was sure was a sight broke his lips, his lips curling wickedly before the blank stare in his face broke, and he looked to me, eyes wide in a fear I had never seen in him before.

"Everything is broken," he gasped, a gravelly undertone taking over his voice. "They are coming."

Before I could respond, Ryland's scream broke the forest, the boy running through the trees in animalistic terror, yelling about our deaths as a jet of black magic poured from his hand, the ribbon of what was sure to be our end moving right for my chest.

11

WYN

I REACTED before I even fully understood what was happening. My instincts kicked in and I raised my hand sending a wall of fire ripping through the air and toward the dark magic that was heading my way.

Flying at me straight from Ryland's hand.

My red fire slammed against his black smoke in a destructive force that smacked through the air and slammed against my chest, sending everyone back and tumbling to the ground. Ryland's attack twisted harmlessly into the air in ribbons of smoke, the trees and undergrowth glowing with red embers from my fire.

I groaned, swore, and slowly began to push myself to my feet. I seemed to be okay. Well, I wasn't bleeding profusely anyway, I could only hope that Sain and Ryland had fared the same.

We were already behind and I didn't need to be reattaching an arm or something.

The dirt was warm beneath my bare feet as I pushed myself up, and I knew at once that Ryland was the least of my worries. Like a hornet to a candy jar the dozens of

Trpaslík I had sensed before had chosen that moment to attack.

The crazed prince had led them right to us.

Screams roared over the thunder as Trpaslíks streamed through the trees like ants, magic sparking, red eyes glinting in the lightning, ready for death. For them, for us, they didn't much care.

Unlucky for them, I wasn't going down. Even though I was the one standing by a useless Drak.

I was ready. It had been more than a century since I had a good fight.

Bring. It. On.

Throat ripping with my battle cry, my scream joined theirs as magic ripped through the air, a dozen attacks heading right toward me and Sain.

Unsurprisingly, Sain shrieked and dropped to the ground. I exploded.

Fire lunged from my fingers in a ring, wide circles enveloping the dark forest before they joined together, spreading into a wall of violently licking flames.

The mass of flame burned through the front line of assassins, while I sent a second wave of magic through the ground, speeding through dirt, undergrowth, and into the souls of the would-be-assassins right behind. None of them could even yelp in pain before they were burned from the inside out, turning to horrifying statues of ash, before even those began to chip and break apart in the large drops of rain that had begun to fall. They didn't even have a chance to fight back.

With a crash like an explosion, the sky opened up, drenching us as well as the remains of what had once been people.

"Watch yourself," Sain said from beside me. His voice

was full of parental guidance that ground against my spine and clamped my teeth together.

I know what he was about to say, and I agreed with him.

There was no way that could have been that simple.

Sure enough, one pulse of my magic revealed more of Edmund's men were already heading right for us, charging through the undergrowth.

"Now is not the time for lectures, old man," I growled. "Go fix that one before you criticize my attempts to keep both of us alive." I nodded to Ryland who was now attacking the next wave of Edmund's men, his face filled with maniacal laughter before he moved to slamming his head against a tree. "Now."

I really shouldn't have to ask him twice. I was not his mother, as he was not my father. His big head about being the first of his kind was really wearing on my nerves.

Sain left without another word, leaving me to attack the still arriving Trpaslíks and their wretched screaming barrage. One after another they sped through the trees and one after another I blocked their ugly magic and sent ripples of smoke and sparks through the air. I got every single one, laughing the entire way, until a bright blue streak of magic sped past my ear, singeing my hair before colliding with a tree behind me and showering me with splinters.

It had almost got me. My instincts were strong, but not fast enough it seemed.

It really didn't help that we were about to be overrun.

I could feel the hate filled magic of Edmund's men past the trees, they just kept coming. Wave after wave moved as swiftly as if they were nothing more than the flow of a tide.

I had wanted this fight, but this was going to try my ability to the absolute limit.

Challenge accepted, Edmund.

I fought without thinking, magic moving from my hands, streaking through the air before exploding in fireworks of color and energy. Attack, block. Attack, block. More than once, I felt the heat of them against my skin, the now stagnant attack burning potently into my flesh.

I had only destroyed the last man before five more broke through the trees. Ryland screamed to the left of me right as Sain called out, the sound loud and pained as I was sure whatever Ryland had done was injuring him.

I couldn't even turn to check.

I couldn't even help.

Not with the armies Edmund had sent after us... I might be powerful, but I wasn't Ilyan.

"Thom!" I screamed his name, my voice cracking with iron and salt as I transformed the five before me into ash, their bodies erupting in stone as the rain splashed against their once alive facades, streaking them with tears they could no longer shed.

"Thom!" I ran to Ryland before the next wave hit us, my magic rushing into him the moment I reached him in a desperate plea to calm him, to knock him out, anything. I might as well have been trying to turn carrots into glass. My hand was nothing more than ice against the heat of his skin.

He spun towards me at the contact, his black eyes a startling stab that only got worse when he smiled in a wide, wicked gleam that spread malice over his face.

"Ryland?" I asked, even though I knew, I knew as surely as my stomach had turned into one solid terrified stone that I wasn't looking at the boy anymore.

I was looking at his father.

"Edmund." The single word growled out from behind my clenched teeth.

"Think you can survive this, do you?" His voice was a

snarl of ice, it twisted through the air and attempted to slice against my confidence.

Tried, but I wouldn't let it.

I wouldn't back down from this black eyed monster. I would stand by Ryland.

I held on tighter to his hand, letting my magic flood the boy, unknown by the monster that inhabited him.

"You are a fool to think *you* can, Edmund." The words ground between my teeth like rocks, my body strained as I flooded Ryland with my magic. As I tried to fight off the army that was surrounding us; to get us all out of there.

Screaming in anger, I fought, I pulled, my magic spread in every direction until with one wave of fire through the ground I sent the army flying away, and with it, Ryland right into a tree.

He slammed into the bark with an almighty thud, his own shout echoing mine as his eyes opened to a thankfully bursting blue.

One task down.

I couldn't even welcome him back, I spun around as the next line of attack broke through the trees with a blood-curdling battle cry.

Sain rushed to Ryland, I rushed to the army, and with one massive pop of magic we were surrounded by enough fireworks for a whole country's independence.

I sped through the air with a leap, landing on one of the Trpaslíks with a violent force that sent both of us to the ground, my hand pressing against his windpipe as I burned it closed, his lungs seizing as the flame continued into them.

Moving as quickly as I could, I jumped from the body of the first, lunging into the second and sending him plowing into a tree trunk as a spider web of flame moved over his face, spreading down his body as the slow burn devoured him.

Ready to take on the third, I turned, only to see Thom burst through the trees, Dramin tumbling to the ground as Thom plowed his way toward Edmund's blood-thirsty minions.

Freaking took him long enough.

We were quickly becoming overrun, and I was just getting settled into the idea of us dying here in the middle of this depressing forest when Ilyan and Joclyn appeared beside us with the tiny pop of a stutter.

So, we weren't dead yet.

The idea was short lived, however. They were there, they were alive, albeit covered in sweat, dirt, and blood. But as glad as I was to see her, her being alive only spelled failure for the rest of us.

I didn't dare ask, because I already knew. Sain had spoken the words only minutes before that, in some way, had sealed her fate as much as ours.

Everything was broken.

"Welcome to the party," I couldn't keep the excitement out of my voice, although the emotion was more based in the battle I fought and not in the outcome.

I raised my hand again as she reached me, taking down another of Edmund's men, this time someone I recognized.

I had done that before, it was part of my job. But my hundred years of living as a perpetual teenager had done me wrong, and a twinge of guilt wrinkled in my brow, my heart falling at having killed someone I knew. Someone I had grown up with.

Stupid human emotions.

In my pain and frustration, I ignited a tree not far from where we stood, glad when Thom took advantage of the powerful fire and threw the trunk into a few of the mad Trpaslíks.

"Did you kill Edmund?" I asked her, as together we eliminated two squat Trpaslíks who had gotten too close.

"We have to get out of here!" Joclyn perfectly avoiding response was as much a guarantee to what was heading our way.

I nodded once in understanding, I could feel them too. While I knew Joclyn's magic was stronger, I was sure all of us could sense the danger that was very quickly pushing out way.

Knowing anything else would have to wait until we reached the cave. Then she would have to tell me everything —about the golden ribbon that was peeking out from behind her hoodie and everything.

I would have to tell her, too.

Right now, I needed to get us out of here, and sadly, I already knew how.

"Thom," I yelled to where he valiantly fought, the hunch of his shoulders showing his weakness more than he knew. "You take the Draks with Jos. I can stop them all long enough to give us a good start, but you all have to be ahead of me."

He nodded, knowing exactly what I meant, and took off, nearly dragging poor Dramin behind him.

I rushed the tree line as the sky opened in a noise that tensed through my nerves, moving directly toward where Ilyan was battling Ryland in an attempt to get him under control.

We couldn't wait any longer.

"Ilyan!" I screamed his name in an attempt to get his attention. If this was going to work, everyone needed to be in front of me. Luckily, he was already subduing our biggest liability.

"Ilyan!"

He threw a now unconscious Ryland over his shoulder, his magic flaring as two other Trpaslíks were foolish enough to attack him, but still, he did not hear me.

The Trpaslíks were almost here, so many that, if we weren't gone before they broke the tree line, I wasn't sure what I could do, even with Ilyan and Joclyn here to fight with me.

I opened my mouth to scream again, right as Jos came up beside me, her voice so calm and controlled that it felt out of place for the firestorm we were surrounded by, for the blood she was covered with.

"He's coming."

I didn't dare ask for clarification. There was so much more in her statement than calm, something that I was missing.

Yet another thing to ask her about later.

I didn't pry, not that we had the time, I let the fear fuel my magic as I turned from my retreating friends and faced the trees that in a moment would become nothing more than flame.

They used to say that there was a reason the fire magic was taken from the earth, that those too foolhardy to use it brought so much destruction that the earth was nothing more than flame and glass, which only made me wonder why I had been given such a unique gift.

Why me with my temper and my terrible sense of right and wrong? Why had I been cursed with so much power?

Back then, when I had Flared for the first time, it had scared me. That was when I had known.

Even with all the destruction I had done, even with all

the death I left behind me, it was something I never fully unleashed.

Even now, I wouldn't let loose. But they wouldn't know that. And they would still be burned in hell.

Throwing my clothes off and into my backpack, I let the magic built to a raging inferno inside of me, my power burning through my veins as it pressed against my skin, growing and pounding the inside of my skull. It swelled inside my bones and rattled them until I was sure they were going to fall apart, which was exactly what was happening.

It was a magic so strong that it devoured every fiber of my being. It controlled every part of who I was to work.

I was nothing but fire, nothing but magic. Nothing but destruction.

Flames licked against my skin in fingers of every color that moved over my body and slithered across the ground like snakes that only I could control.

Snakes of flame that would destroy everything in their path.

I fought the need to scream out in pain at the power that consumed me, my body shrieking as it became the flame that dwelled inside of me.

My eyes snapped open as the army burst through the trees. What Edmund had meant to be his last line of defense froze in place as they came face-to-face with the witch that was bound in an inferno.

A rippling serpent of flame moved over my skin, twisting and turning before it fell to the ground and devoured trees as if they were little more than pieces of tissue.

Fear pulsed from their eyes, the reflection of the demon I had become clear.

Beautiful. Demonic. Dangerous.

I smiled, the magic growing as my excitement did, ready

to take that last step and destroy Edmund's final attempt to do away with what he viewed as his enemies.

"Hello, lovelies." My voice echoed with a dead hollow, the magic rippling through me as though I had become possessed. My fire grew with each word, rattling through the trees as they sparked with flame, the clothing of those that stood closest to me beginning to spark and smoke.

A hollow laugh escaped my lips as the flames swelled down my arms, my hands pushing forward and sending the blaze right to their horror filled faces. A fan of flame soaked the air, shaking the ground before it seeped into the soil in a cylinder of heat that turned everything it touched to ash.

Turned the world to hell.

The army screamed as my fire consumed them, men turned to nothing more than smoke, trees evaporating from the sheer enormity of the pressurized explosion. With the force of an atomic bomb, it spread away from me, eating the world into nothing but flame, the once proud forest turning black and white with char.

No one would have guessed that an army had stood before us.

No one would have guessed what I had really held inside.

I wasn't even sure Ilyan had known.

Now he would.

Now they all would.

There was a reason I had wanted this power bound. It had never been a danger to me. I had learned to control it beyond all else. However, it was a danger to the world, and if Edmund got his hands on it... the whole world would burn.

And now he would want it more than before. Now he would stop at nothing to get it.

If he had ever been successful in all the times he had

tried, this was what the world would have become—this barren wasteland that I was now surrounded by. A ring of fire that would continue to burn until someone mistook it for a forest fire and came to put it out.

The fire in my soul began to extinguish, leaving me naked in what used to be a forest. A regret I had never felt before seeped through me like an unwanted poison, eating at me until I pushed it away. Refusing to let the bastard emotions take control.

There was no turning back now.

Pulling my singed clothes over my head, I turned to run, plumes of blackened soil erupting into the air with each step, the remaining embers still smoldered, devouring the tree skeletons that remained. I didn't even look, only ran, my magic moving into the earth as I tracked the quick progression of my friends, the frightful reality of their close intersection with the flames twisting through my gut.

If they didn't move faster, the fire would reach them. Then, not only would they see, but they would be in danger of having the same fire burn into them.

Time and fate were not on our side today.

"Run!" I screamed before I had even reached them, my feet moving faster as the disease I had plagued on the earth continued to move, chasing after my friends and threatening to destroy them, as well.

I only hoped they ran fast enough that they wouldn't see what I had done.

That they wouldn't find out that, this time... This time, I had enjoyed it.

12

OVAILIA

THE TALL, stiletto spike of my bright red heels were unstable against the charred earth. I fought for stable footing with each step, but I wasn't going to let the struggle show. Instead, I kept my head high, my jaw set as my long hair swung behind me, and chose instead to glower at the golden highlights in the hair of the man I followed, as if they had somehow offended me. Of course, they had in a way.

I knew he was a distant cousin—only the direct bloodline of my grandmother had blonde hair—but I didn't care anymore. Not with what he was leading me toward, anyway.

Ilyan's attack had begun moments before Edmund had arrived. I hadn't had a chance to speak to my father before the battle had begun. Before Ilyan and his whore had bust through our defenses in a perfectly planned attack that had destroyed the work we had spent almost a year putting together. Worse yet, we had failed.

Daddy wouldn't be too pleased about it.

It was that failure that I was on my way to answer for.

I wasn't the first one to be punished for our failure, either.

The blonde cousin let me past the writhing bodies of those who had already faced his wrath, the waste of perfectly good soldiers disgusting me. They screamed as Edmund's torturous magic raged inside of them, the weaker ones already succumbing to death as their bodies burned as the magic that had scorched the earth moved to destroy them too.

My nose wrinkled at the smell of char and death, the pitiful sounds making it more pitiful. They didn't even deserve a glance, I flipped my hair behind me, my hard glare focused straight ahead as I blocked the sound. If they were going to be weak under my father's discipline, they could at least do it quietly.

Edmund stood only a few yards away now, perched on the top of a high outcropping, his wide frame shadowed by both sun and ash in a smoky image that made him appear even more glorious. More than a dozen of his bodyguards cowered near him, the pathetic Trpaslíks attempting to do his bidding, even as they feared his wrath. It was a bad place to be, especially now that Timothy and Cail were gone. There was no one left to challenge him. No one to hold him back, not like either of them had.

Now it was only him and me, something I both relished and feared. To be trusted to be so close to him, to his greatness, yet to be close enough to receive the brunt of his frustrations.

My teeth ground together as I climbed the hill, my heels digging up burning embers as I trudged past the skeletal remains of the forest. Thunder groaned as if announcing my arrival, the incessant thunderheads still rolling overhead.

I wish it would just shut up.

The earth, the pathetic failures behind me. They should all be stronger than these hissy fits.

"Sir," the man I followed began, his voice shaking as he went down on one knee, ready to announce his arrival and a job well done.

I didn't even give him the chance. I breezed by him, knocking his unstable figure to the ground with the heel of my shoe, moving right up to where my father stood, his focus scanning over the still smoldering earth.

"Isn't it beautiful, Ovailia?" He groaned, the depth of his voice filled with more awe than I had heard in a while. I expected some new woman, a new prize to be standing before him with how he spoke.

It was only devastation, the bright red flames of magic still devouring the tree line in the distance.

Of course, he would be referring to destruction.

"If you enjoy death."

My heels sunk deeper into the charcoal the longer I stood behind him, watching the sky ignite with forks of lightning until the whole place looked like a barren wasteland pulled straight from hell.

"I am not speaking of the fire," he soured, his voice trailing over my spine like ice.

I flinched at the sound, almost expecting what was coming, and glared into the space before me.

"I am speaking of the fire magic. I am speaking of the destruction our dear Wyn has caused."

He might as well have been looking at a woman. It wasn't the destruction he admired as I had assumed. It was the power. Or, more specifically, the power that laid inside of a woman. A woman I had already known him to lust after for far longer than would have been deemed appropriate.

I narrowed my eyes as my chest tensed, my irritation

growing as I turned toward my father. Dark curls had loosed from his usual slicked-back style, falling over the piercing blue eyes that dug into me the moment I turned.

Hatred bored into me like the ice they were and I flinched. The jolt of my fear was subtle, but still apparent enough he had noticed, a reaction that only caused him to smile more.

"I must have it." The greed dripped off him as he took a step closer, his bulky frame coming level with mine.

I could not stop my eyebrow from rising or the twitch of my lip as I smiled at him. That was it? After everything, after failing to kill or capture any of them, after losing track of them and losing more than two hundred of the vile bats he had spent centuries creating, he wanted me to capture Wyn, to bring him her heart.

No punishment. No retribution.

There had to be more. There always was.

Back tensed, I waited, watching him for some sign of what was coming. He only stood in the darkness of his greed. The vile emotion colored his face until, looking into him, I felt like I was looking into my own death.

"I suppose you want me to get it for you." My tone was harsh, expectant even. I was treading carefully, waiting for the ice of his lies to crack.

They did, in a wicked glimmer of his greed that stretched his face into a maniacal grin. Unbidden fear trickled down my spine, though I kept the malice on my face, unwilling to let him see my reaction.

Shards of ice dug into my bones as his hand wound around my waist, pulling me toward him, the tips of his fingers pressing into the base of my spine.

My shirt lifted at his prompting, the icy chill of his fingers pressing into my lower back, rubbing against the painful scars that ran the length of my spine. I would have tried to move away, to stop what was coming, but there wasn't any point. He controlled me.

After so many years, I had come to love what he had done to me—the pockets of poison that he had placed against my spine and the power they gave me when he released it into my bloodstream.

As if on cue, his magic surged through the long lines of my scars, slicing through the tough tissue with miniscule dexterity and releasing the toxins into my body.

Into my blood.

A hiss of pain and fear seeped through my clenched teeth as the power ignited, the infectious fire spreading quickly through bones and veins and anything else it could find to infect. His nefarious grin grew as he watched me writhe against the venom, as he held me against him as one would a lover. To him, though, it was only control. It was only for a better view to watch me become what he had created.

My head fell back as the pain grew, the Vilỳ venom and black water seeping into me in an acidic burn.

The poisonous concoction took control and I sagged in his arms, my eyes staring unfocused at the orchestra of light and sound above us, it was though everything was dancing. It was the drug of the best, and worst, kind. My mind became a numb mass as any scream I might have thought of releasing lodged itself in my throat.

"Of course, I want you to get it for me," he growled, his animalistic voice rumbling in my ear as he pressed his lips against my jaw, the heavy breathing of his anger increasing the tension in my muscles. "But, if you for one second think that is all I am going to do to you after what you have done today, you are sorely mistaken."

His words cut like daggers against my skin. Slicing deep before he shook my limp body violently in his arms and dropped me to the smoldering ground, leaving me to crumple as the caustic poison ran its course.

If I thought I would be allowed to cower here, waiting for it to leave, however, I was only expecting more pain.

He towered above me, his raspy breathing picking up with a hunger that twisted my nerves further, his already tried patience was ready to snap. "Stand."

I could have screamed at the order, the pain too much to even fathom. Instead, I cringed and pushed the need to collapse away, pushed away the tears and the screams and stood. Each joint howled in agony as I straightened, my body swaying as I tried to stand before him, the height of my heels only making my attempt more precarious.

"What do you want of me, Father? Name it, and it is yours." My voice shook through the pain, the irritation I normally had wavering underneath the agony that was making it hard to see straight.

His smile spread before he moved away from me, leaving me swaying in the ash as the sky continue to rip itself apart. I didn't dare move. He hadn't beckoned me to follow, and approaching him when I wasn't wanted would only bring more pain.

He strolled back to me with an even wider grin, a tortured Vilỳ clutched in his fist.

Between the pain and the fear I wasn't able to stop myself, I staggered back in both exhaustion and pain. The action spread his grin into a cat like curl.

"Tell me what you have learned, Ovailia." His voice was soft as he brought the Vilỳ up to eye height, the creature snarling and lashing about. Edmund looked at it like it was a beloved pet, the twisted thing bringing more affection to the man than any of his children.

My lip curled at the image, my disgust at what I was seeing tensing in my gut.

"You spent several days among them, yes? What did you see?"

His fingers moved over the forehead of the thing, its teeth snarling as poison dripped from its mouth. I looked from the creature to Edmund, his icy eyes making me doubt if I had made the right decision, if I should have ever left Ilyan's side in the first place.

Then the image of Sain in the abbey came back to me, the lie of his supposed death that my atrocious brother had fed for centuries hurting more than the poison that still moved through me.

I couldn't stop the anger that twisted through me. I didn't want to. The strength of the emotion was a cooling balm to the fire that still ate away at my bones.

"Ilyan has a burn on his palm from Black Water." I spoke the words confidently, my chin rising in accomplishment as the hatred in my father's eyes was replaced by surprise. "He did not have it when I arrived, but it was there when I was dismissed. I think that is how he brought Joclyn back through the Tŏuha."

His hand was frozen on the head of the creature he held. The monstrous thing still lashed, even though Edmund's focus was far away from where we stood in the ash-filled debris of Rioseco.

"So, he has filled his body with that poison, has he?"

I said nothing. I only waited, swaying as we stood on the burning earth, the smell of soot and flame making me even dizzier.

"Does he have sight?" he asked after a moment. "Can he tap into the sights of Draks as you can?"

"Not that I can see, Father." I tried to ignore the irritation at his suggestion. It had taken me over a hundred years of work to master that ability after my father had placed the mud within my body. I doubted Ilyan could do it after only a few days and a little bit of water. He might be powerful, but I refused to believe he had an ability even close to that.

"But I believe Joclyn can..." Any thought of what I had been about to say was wiped from me with the look my father fixed on me.

My heart accelerated in both fear and expectation, the burn increasing as the tempo did.

"Joclyn can what?" he snapped, the anger in his voice the same every time the girl was spoken of.

"I believe..." I began, careful to choose my words as I steadied myself, "that Joclyn can 'see'. I believe she has inherited her father's ability, as you assumed."

My disgust at the admission grew as his did, my lips twisting into a snarl along with his, my heritage shining through as I stood beside my father, drowning in our malice.

"There is more." Disgust reigned in my voice, the tone a snarl that yanked at the pain in my spine. When Edmund made no move to look at me, I continued, my heart rate accelerating in anticipation. "My brother has bonded himself to the brat. She wears the délka vedení královsk."

He froze, his eyes unwavering, before he laughed. The sound was deep and rich as it echoed through the barren wasteland. The servants who cowered around him backed away slowly as the depth of his anger rippled in a sound that should have been joyful.

The marriage of his eldest son.

However, his joy was full of wicked manipulation.

"So, he has chosen his queen. I would like to see how long he plans on keeping her around."

He spun to face me, more of his hair coming loose and falling over his eyes in such a way that he only looked more mad, as if the insanity he kept within himself was about to explode.

"I will forgive this... travesty... that you have inflicted on us, Ovailia. But we must play our pawns in a much wider net if we wish to win, yes?"

"Yes, Father."

He smiled at my assent, the charcoal beneath his shoes crunching as he approached me, the twisted creature he held in his hands growling with a feral sound that flared through me. It was the sound of pain and eagerness, as if he knew what was coming.

A flinch shook my torso at the realization, the need to plea for commiseration strong.

I wouldn't let my weakness show, though—not to him, not to anyone.

"We will continue with the attack on Prague as planned." His voice was hard as it carried around us, the cowering peasants slowly righting themselves as they prepared for his instruction. "Send out word to begin closing off the city. I don't want any mortal coming in or out. Cut off their power, their water, and shield them."

One by one, the cowering Trpaslíks nodded in understanding, their bodies bowed as they ran away from their master and across the charred earth to do his bidding.

"Are you sure it is wise?" I asked cautiously, expecting the scold that would come from my impertinence. "Ilyan still lives. Joclyn is healthy and well from what I could tell. Everything could be for naught."

"Or I can destroy them as I do all others. Over a million

of my little pets descending on the city, and in the middle are Ilyan and his broken subjects." He laughed at the image, his joy feeling as dark as the thunder, the sound deep and low as if the earth was screaming at what had been decided, at what was going to happen.

There was no way Ilyan could stop it. There was no way he could survive it. He would be bitten like all the others, and if he was... He would become little more than Edmund's puppet at that point, just like everyone else the nasty little creatures would infect. Edmund's army, all of the magic under his control. It was only days away.

Finally, the golden boy was right where he was meant to be.

I couldn't stop the smile.

"Are you sure it will work? We don't even know if that is where they are going."

"I know," he said with a smile. "I have infected Sain's sight and Ilyan will do anything to protect that pathetic city he loves so much. He doesn't want me to control Imdalind, child. I know that is where he is going."

"Right into your hands."

My father moved so close I could see the blood vessels in his eyes, the red lines much darker than they should be, making his twisted face that much more nefarious as he leaned into me. His thick fingers lifted my chin up, holding me in place, holding my gaze as he sneered.

"Right into the end," he whispered, his breath moving over my face, and I tensed. "It's time to show the mortals who really owns the world. To show them how *safe* they really are. All the magic in the world belongs to me. I was the first to bare the mark of the Chosen Child. I saved the world from fire. The wells of Imdalind chose me to create the magic of the world into something more, and I am going to make sure it stays that way." He smiled as he stepped away, continuing to stroke the monster he held in his hands, his eyes scanning over the barren wasteland as if he was looking for something in particular.

"We may have failed today, but everything continued to work in our favor." His voice was like honey, and I tensed for what was coming. "But that means we have to work harder. We cannot fail a second time. If we do, only death will await those who fail me."

"Yes, Father."

He nodded once at my obedience, his focus still lost in something I couldn't see. The look made me uncomfortable as I stood straight and waited, careful to keep my body steady through the pain, my face fixed with the same powerful snarl I always held.

"I want you to start by taking Wynifred's heart. I have had enough of that girl. And, if this is the true extent of her power, then it is mine. It should have been mine from the beginning."

"Consider it done."

It seemed a simple enough request, but the look on his face promised of more to come. I tensed again, keeping my eyes on him as he walked, lightning cutting through the sky behind him in a warning I neither heard nor cared about.

"I want Sain back," he whispered, his voice making his desire sound deeper than I knew it to be. "I want you to lure him back to us, to you. I want you to connect with him and use his sight."

"I don't think that is possible."

"Oh, it is possible." The eagerness in his voice was communicable. "His mind is infected, and as much as he tries to deny it, he is too proud to admit he is damaged. He will not be able to escape the insanity for long. You need to create an opportunity to *help* him and bring him back to us. Arousal is a beautiful device." His hand was hot as it rested against my cheek, his thumb hard as it pushed against my skin.

I knew the touch was in warning. The way he looked at me promised that. I may have wanted to shy away from his touch, but I didn't have a choice. I had to do this whether I wanted to or not.

I supposed it was best to make the most of it

"Yes, Father," I said with a smile, the feigned eagerness cementing itself in place.

He smiled as I did, his eyes flashing as he pushed the tiny winged creature toward me, the instruction clear even without words.

I grit my teeth in understanding, careful not to let my displeasure shine through my eyes as I stripped my shirt from my body, turning away from him and presenting him with my bare back, the scarred flesh clear in my mind's eye.

The raised ridge of the scar ran the length of my spine, and riddled over all of it was the kiss of the monster my father held in his hands. Each one was an infection of magic as he worked to strengthen me and make me into the weapon he envisioned me to be.

That I wanted to be.

I held the black water in my body. My parents' powerful magic had been strengthened by his experiments, by the centuries of exercises and administrations.

I tensed as I heard him come closer, the ash crunching beneath his feet as the creature snarled, its claws digging into my flesh as it held on and bit down. It was then that I collapsed to the ground, the heat from the earth seeping into my body, the distant sight of the Draks flashing before my eyes.

13

JOCLYN

MULTICOLORED BOBBLES of our magic trailed behind us, drifting through the caves like enchanted Christmas lights, which I guess in a way they were.

Little bobbles of magic that followed their owners on our trek through the dank cavern. While the lights were bright, the cave was too massive and full of too many sharp edges, meaning the light only gave everything jagged shadows and dark corners that shivered with life.

It definitely didn't put me in the mood to sing Christmas carols.

Especially as I walked side-by-side with the girl who had become my best friend faster than I could have thought possible. Spunky, crazy, and stubborn enough to get past all my insecurities and oddities.

I loved Wyn, I knew Wyn. Well, I thought I did. The Wyn who was walking by my side was different somehow.

She wasn't quite as spunky and her scowl made her look a little bit like she was ready to rip someone's face off.

Which I guess was true with everything she had just told me.

No wonder she looked ready to de-face someone, she probably knew how to do it. Hell, she may have actually done it before, being a trained assassin and all.

Which was weird.

And cool.

I didn't know which anymore.

Two days ago I had sealed the cave behind us, trapping us in the endless cavern that was leading to who knows where. It had been two days of awkward small talk and growing agitation as we dragged each other deeper into the black. It wasn't until a few hours ago, when she had finally started talking, that everything had begun to make sense, no matter how confusing it still was.

Her personality had changed when I removed the curse from her—the way she moved, the way everyone interacted with her, and the way she seemed so buddy-buddy with Thom.

Okay, more than buddy-buddy, but I wasn't going to tell her that, especially with what she had just revealed to me. Thom's outburst into her well-being in Italy all those months ago wasn't so out of character anymore.

A relationship. An assassin. A French Prince. A child.

Admitting that must have been terrifying. Not knowing exactly what to say or how I would react. She hadn't just been concealing a dislike for shrimp, after all. This was a whole other life.

I needed her to know that she was my friend, no matter how hard it was to understand everything, or what had happened.

"Okay…" Or, I could just say that.

Well, I sounded like an idiot. At least Wyn knew me well enough to interpret it the right way.

She only laughed with a rich sound that filled the

confined space like honey, her arm draping over my shoulder the way she had done so many times before. And just like every time before she was so much shorter that she pulled me down until my back arched uncomfortably.

"So, you're a mother...?" That wasn't any better than the dreaded 'okay.'

"Yeah." Her voice was dead and hollow, not surprising.

Leave it to me to pick out the most painful fact of her past to talk about.

At least I hadn't chosen 'you're a whore' or 'how many people have you killed?'

Come to think of it, those might have been better, actually.

Anything was better than asking about someone's deceased child. My stomach is in a full-on rampage now.

Ilyan's magic filled me in a comfortable spiral, warming me from the inside, the contact a steady reminder of his support, even if I didn't feel I needed it right now.

There was something else I did need from him, however.

I looked up to where he walked several yards before us, his brothers at his sides as we all meandered through the tomb-like darkness, the imminent end having grown louder every day. However, they walked and talked and laughed as though we weren't traveling into certain death.

Wish I could be so positive. I knew too much, I saw too much.

'Why didn't you tell me about Wyn?' I couldn't keep the painful accusation out of my internal query if I tried.

'It was not my story to tell, my love.' I knew he was right, still irritated me though. *'Wynifred needs to come to terms with everything that has happened and who she is. The fact that she told you is a sign that she is doing just that. It's a good thing.'*

I tried not to roll my eyes at him, but it didn't quite work, and I ended up staring at the colored bobbles in frustration. Something that Wyn did not miss. She chuckled, or more like moan-sighed.

"Yes, I am a mother." Her voice was soft, the pain that had smothered her laugh giving way to the playfulness I had always known from her. "And Thom is a father. And, together, we had a baby. And that's as far as it goes. I am not going to be the one to give you the birds and the bees talk. But, dude, if you haven't had that already, then we have bigger fish to fry."

My stomach sagged right to my toes like someone had filled it with rocks. I may still be walking, but I had left my heart, stomach and most of my brain cells a few steps back. We couldn't be talking about this... we were so not talking about this!

I was lead, Ilyan was acting like he had choked on his own spit, and Wyn was laughing so hard I was sure this forsaken cave had turned into an insane asylum.

"Something you two wish to share with the group?" Thom asked with a bark of irritation from somewhere ahead.

Maybe it *was* an insane asylum, and I just hadn't gotten the memo.

Being trapped in a cave for days as we made a mad dash to a city that may or may not be under attack, while talking about past lives, sex lives, and everything else, had definitely addled our brains.

I don't think the cave had felt so restrictive until that moment.

Even if Prague was already under attack, I would like my escape pass from this tube of peculiarity, thank you very much.

"No, thank you, not needed. From either of you." The

squeak of words caught in my throat, my hands waving frantically in front of me to deter the eyes of all five of the very nosey men.

How in the world could we be this outnumbered?

Wyn continued to laugh even as Ilyan recovered. Thom was still looking between us as though he had missed out on some epic tale.

No Thom, just your everyday awkward sex talk. Nothing to see here.

"Glad to hear it, all things considered." Wyn tugged lightly on the golden ribbon.

Tripping over the uneven ground, I took a step away, although I wasn't certain I could escape my own embarrassment.

Wyn's expression flashed from the playful girl I knew to the saucy woman I had seen before so fast I was half expecting some undead spirit to emerge out her mouth like in a horror movie. I waited for her playful smile to smack back into place, but it never did. Instead, she eyed me with a weird trepidation that made my stomach pull into a large twisty knot. This version of Wyn was going to take some getting used to.

"Why didn't you tell me before?" I asked, trying to shake off the shiver that the wicked glint in her eye was giving me.

"About my past?" Thankfully some of her 'I could kill you at any moment' look had vanished.

I nodded.

"There was never a good time. I wanted to. I tried when I came to your room after your fight. But, I mean, you had just had a fight with Ilyan. There couldn't have been worse timing. After that..." She stuck her hands in the pockets of her jeans in much the same way Thom did. I smiled at the similarities, at the way she had already picked up on him or the way she always had. I wasn't sure, but either way, it suited her.

"Is that what you meant when you said you have trouble remembering who you are sometimes?"

Our pace slowed and her shoulders sagged, her lips pulling up as she gave me one twisted side-glance. I didn't miss that our slowed pace was creating an even bigger gap between us and everyone else, the darkness of the cave swallowing them as we were left behind, standing in the dark, stale air.

Staring at each other.

Which, would be creepy no matter which way you sliced it. I was definitely fighting the need to catch up, but I didn't want to leave her. I didn't want to leave this lingering unknown that had opened up between us.

She needed me to be here as much as I needed to. That much I could tell was needed by the way she looked at me. Her large, dark eyes were filled with enough sorrow to consume the world in grief.

"Yeah," she whispered, her voice just as broken. "It gets confusing, like two different people are jammed inside of me. Two different lives shoved into a box and locked up, forced to live together but so dissimilar there is no way they can co-inhabit in peace."

It was like the medical definition of schizophrenia, but so much more real. And she was trapped in the middle of it all.

"It's not, though..." She cut me off with a sad smile, her hand soft against my bicep.

"Oh, I know. I think I have finally got it figured out. Sometimes, life takes us on bizarre journeys, and sometimes, we just need to go along for the ride."

"You are as wise as he is."

"As who is?" Her voice rose an octave in sudden alarm.

"Thom." I smiled at her, the softness in her eyes increasing the grin.

I was sure she already knew that.

"But there's gotta be like a hundred years of..." So much for teasing. Anything I had been about to say was swallowed by a snap of Ryland's mania, the words indistinguishable through the echo of the cave, even though the meaning was as clear as day. Forget writing on the wall, we had a freaking cave screamer.

They were far ahead of us now, the faded lights of their magic rippling back to us just as Ilyan's emotions hit me, a wall of concern and fear that sucked the joy from the air.

Everything felt dead, inside and out. The cave. The air.

Even my soul was a rock inside of me.

"We're here." The words felt just as dead as the rest of me as I walked toward the pull of my mate's magic, toward the light and the voices that became clearer with each step, even if everything was begging me to run in the opposite direction.

"We can't be there already, can we?" Wyn was obviously as unwilling to accept this harsh reality as I was.

I didn't blame her.

She had just come through these tunnels from the other direction, and it had taken her a week.

We had been trapped in the dark, endless lengths of the claustrophobic space for only five days. Trapped with the spiders and the rats and the water that was always dripping directly above our heads, as though the leak had a personal vendetta against us.

I was glad to be free from it, but we still didn't know what waited for us outside of the dark depths of the space. We didn't know how much truth Sain was telling.

If the Vilỳs had attacked yet or not.

We could be walking into war, into ruin, or into some completely mixed up reality of both.

Or, even worse we could be walking into a trap.

No one knew, and thanks to Sain and his stubborn bullheadedness it could be anything. It was the battle of the sights in the worst possible way.

I just wanted to be prepared. At this point I could care less about who was right, and who was wrong.

"What is it, Ilyan?" Wyn asked the second we reached the tense knot of people in front of us, all of them facing what appeared to be a black wall, heads turned up as if they were worshiping it.

Weird. Maybe we hadn't made it to Prague, and something else was wrong.

A million possibilities hit me, everything from a wall of poisoned Vilỳs to Edmund himself coming through the dark, were running through my mind like an old broken-down slide show.

Then I felt the warm breeze that had caused them to stop, the heat of the swirling air so uncharacteristic of the cave that it clearly came from somewhere else.

Somewhere that smelled of cinnamon.

Somewhere familiar.

Not to me, however, to Ilyan.

Memories of his childhood flitted into my mind like paper airplanes sent off course. The fleeting images cemented with the smell of warm cinnamon bread, ancient wood, and a sunrise over the Vltava traveled on the back of the breeze.

We were here.

It was just ahead of us, hidden in the dark.

Prague.

Somewhere before us, was the city that Ilyan had been raised in, that Ilyan had even ruled over for a time. The city that Ilyan loved.

His home.

'Our home.' He corrected me, the warmth of his magic rushing behind before it was swallowed by my own panic.

I had seen this city destroyed in my sight, I had seen the sky darken as the Vilÿs devoured it in clouds of black. I watched their teeth gnash. I witnessed blood spill as they bit the mortals.

As they created an army.

I knew we were walking into a war. I knew it was dangerous, and everything in me was begging me to go the other way.

But Sain swore it had already happened, that the city would be safe.

In mere steps, we would know who was right, if Sain was telling the truth. Or, if the sight was right at all. The battle of the sights was on, and it was enough to turn my blood to ice.

"Ilyan?" I asked aloud, breaking the silence and pulling him from his memories.

His eyes darted to mine, the brilliant blue filled with the tense fear that had become more prevalent lately. The icy determination I was used to, the pain at losing a place that meant so much to him was new. It was that shared emotion that was ripping him apart.

'It will be okay,' I spoke the words into his mind, the fearful torrent of his magic calming as his lip twitched, his fingers reaching for me.

His warm touch tickled the side of my face, weaving strands of hair that had come loose from my braid back into place.

He said nothing. He didn't need to. I could hear it all as

his thoughts ran through me, his emotions swelling. I could feel his love, his pride, and more than that, I could feel his eager anticipation to introduce me to the city that in so many ways was mine, as well.

It was what could be on the other side of the doors that scared him.

"You aren't alone in that," I mumbled low enough that only he could hear, his smile twitching before he silently stepped away, gesturing us to follow.

Conversations about past lives, relationships, and who knows what else faded away with the snap of Ilyan's leather shoes against the stone, the heavy pad of tennis shoes, and in Ryland's case sneakers adding to the bizarre symphony.

The sound was punctuated by the heavy thunder of my heart, the pulse of Ilyan's just as loud in my ears. The silence of drums had never been so deafening.

Buzzing echoed around the cave, the magical sound roaring louder as another warm breeze swirled around us. A tall line of light spread across the stone, the warm color stretching between us like a divide. Ilyan and I on either end, the Drak's on one side, Wyn, Thom and Ryland on the other.

I really didn't want to read too much into that, but it was pretty much screaming at me.

The light grew brighter with each step, spreading over stone as though someone had captured the sun and drawn a line with it down the side of the cave, one straight staff that moved from the towering ceiling to the grimy floor.

Brightness flooded around us with one silent command from Ilyan, his golden orb turning into a spotlight revealing massive carved stone panels that grew from the stone. Light seeped through them in a beam of brilliance that shone over our battle worn party, showing all of the scars and bruises more clearly than I would have ever like to see them in.

We looked as though there was hope in the dark.

We looked nearly dead in the light.

The massive panels stretched farther than I could reach, they towered over head, and pulled over the expanse of the cave like a gate for horses, or houses. Or both. If it wasn't for the light that moved through the gap between the colossal slabs, I probably wouldn't have even recognized them as doors.

The stone walls of the cave moved from ragged, uneven terrain to that of smoothly carved designs so effortlessly that I couldn't even make out a hinge. For all I knew, they wouldn't even open at all.

Designs of medieval peasants danced against the heavy lines and gothic archways that had been carved into the stone. The intricate carvings swaying to imagined music as the bobble of light that floated above our heads reflected onto them. Churchgoers, children, a royal family that looked hauntingly familiar.

It was a million years of history carved into the stone, a million years of Ilyan's history, of magic's history, and now of mine.

The pace of my heart increased with each slap of Ilyan's shoes against the stone, his body hesitant as he moved toward the stream of light that leaked between the doors. A whispered babble of what I could only assume to be people flowed through the heavy panels and filled the once silent cave with noise.

No one dared breathe as Ilyan pressed himself against the doors, his body tense as he peered between the narrow gap. He stood, framed by the sliver of light, the pure brightness blinding as his body diffused it through the dark, illuminating the cave in its brilliance.

The breeze swirled around us one last time, the long slender ribbon that ran through Ilyan's braid reaching back to me as if it couldn't stand to be away.

I knew the feeling.

'Ilyan,' I whispered to him.

His shoulders relaxed ever so slightly before he turned from the door. His jaw set in a powerful line as he looked between each of us before settling his gaze on me, his magic surging as his eyes flashed with menace.

"Everything is calm." His voice rumbled through the cave as the breeze shifted through the door, tugging at the ribbon. I grabbed it as it danced in the air, holding it against me. "That doesn't mean it will be safe. I need to know if Edmund is close. I cannot assume he has stayed in Spain." His eyes held mine as his thoughts overran the words he spoke—the anger at Sain's lies, the fear over what it could mean, broken sights and mislaid trust.

Knowing the city was safe should have brought calm, but it didn't. It couldn't. Not with the new unknown that we faced. If the attack hadn't happened yet, when would it? What trap were we walking into? Was there was one at all?

"If he's stayed in Spain, then I'm about as desirable as a popcorn fart," Wyn scoffed with a laugh.

My eyebrows rose as I tried to decipher what she was trying to say. She didn't seem to care. She only rolled her eyes at me before looking back to Ilyan, her jaw tightening as an old magic came over her.

"I'll find him."

I didn't dare move as Wyn's magic swelled through the floor, the heat burning the soles of my feet again as we stood in silence, listening to the muted conversations of those just beyond the door.

"I can't find him, Ilyan," Wyn said after a minute, her body tensing as if she was preparing for the doors to open and a battle to begin. "There is something different there, but I can't tell what it is. It's a long way off."

"Silný?"

Squaring my jaw, I gave him one nod and let my magic surge in heat and excitement, as if the power itself had heard him and was ready to answer.

At least something was. I had no desire to feel Edmund's magic again.

Ilyan's magic surged, his lips twitching as he let his power move through our bond, the heat a heady reminder of support and love. I didn't even try to stop the smile that spread over my face as the heat grew, as my fingers flexed, and as Ilyan's voice filled my mind.

'Find him, my love. If anyone can find him, it will be you.'

You better believe, I can.

My heart picked up as my magic bubbled to life, the excitement growing as if Ilyan's words had been all that was needed to open the floodgates.

Ilyan's magic melded with mine, the power blending seamlessly as I closed my eyes and let the magic spread away from me, let it explore and search through the city that already felt like home.

I could still hear the excited babble of the people beyond the gates, feel the calm of the crisp fall day, the enjoyment of the mortals as they shopped in the markets. They went about their life as if nothing was happening other than the threat of rain the weather forecaster had given them on the news that morning.

Moving through the city streets, my eyes took in every

detail. The whitewashed stone walls, the ancient statues, the ruddy brown of the river.

My heart beat faster as I recognized many of the buildings from my sight, saw the red shingled roofs of the old town. Except, it was different.

There was no fire. There was no screaming. It was a city before the sight had come, a city as I had never seen it before.

It was beautiful.

It also couldn't be more frightening.

Sain was wrong, and whatever was coming was just waiting for us.

An odd pull that was laced behind the laughter, a fear was burrowing underneath the sunny cobbled streets. Something lived underneath the joyful exterior, something that only increased my fear.

It was different than the rancid magic of the Vilÿs, different than the pained swells of the earth I had felt when flying through the trees in Spain. It was a thing so raw and vile that it twisted through me. It was the pockets of fear that hid in abandoned buildings and the rippling agony that slithered through the sewers.

Tension moved into me, my muscles twisting in anxiety that should have been a warning to stop. I didn't. I couldn't. I needed to know where Edmund was, and more than that, I needed to know what was coming. How true my sight had been.

If it had been.

I pushed my magic farther, away from the center of town, away from the towering doors we were all clustered behind. The more I pushed, the worse the fearful plague grew. The more my magic buckled underneath it.

It crept into my soul with the same agitated fury I had

felt in Spain, the pressure and fear seeming to grow until I reached the forest that surrounded the sprawling city. Surges of magic swelled amongst the trees and farms that were clustered there, pressing against me.

Sucking my life away.

I knew I was close. I could feel the faint throb of Edmund's power now. I could feel his hatred. I could feel the black tar of his magic where it had leached into the soil and poisoned it.

I continued to push, my magic trailing after the ripples of power. The farther I stretched, however, the weaker the fingers of my power became, until it was only wispy shadows that retreated back into me like a tape measure.

Heaving for breath, I fell to my knees with a snap as my focus drifted back to the cave. Each inhale shook as I desperately tried to fill my lungs with air that seemed foreign and forgotten.

Wyn's hands were on my back before I even had a chance to focus on the uneven floor my fingers were spread against. Ilyan's magic flooded every inch of me as his shoes tapped loudly against the stone in a desperate need to reach me.

He sunk to the ground, hands shaking as he reached toward me. Even though his face was stoic and calm, I could feel his worry leech through our connection, my injury from Spain still weighing heavily on his mind.

"Was it a sight?" Dramin said from beside me, his voice weak as it echoed around the cave.

"No," I gasped, my eyes still not leaving the concern in Ilyan's face. "I found him."

"Where?" The concern on Ilyan's face vanished almost instantly, albeit I could still feel it tense through his body.

"There is a forest that begins near the farms that

surround the towns..." I began, hoping it was enough to explain. I wasn't familiar enough with the city to know how to begin, and I had a feeling saying, 'In the mud by a farm with tomatoes and funny looking cows,' wasn't going to cut it.

Thankfully, Ilyan understood. He released a tense breath with a sigh, his hand wrapping around my elbow as he helped me back to standing.

'I'm fine, Ilyan,' I added silently, grateful when the tension in his shoulders lessened a bit.

'I know,' he said, any chance of relief drowned with the next question. *'What else did you see? What did you feel?'*

I wasn't foolish enough to hide anything from him, despite being uncertain what the dread that filled the city was. Besides, his magic had been there right alongside mine. I was sure he had felt it, too.

'Fear,' I said, hoping it would be enough yet knowing it wouldn't. *'Not in the mortals, but in something else that was inside the city, something that was hiding.'*

He shot me a look that had as much confusion as I felt. Yes, fear hiding in the city did sound a bit crazy... but with everything we had gone through?

I only shrugged my shoulders, something he found quite humorous. His loud laugh echoed around the tension in the cave like a broken cymbal, the sound loud as it broke the fear like shards of glass.

"Ugh," Thom growled from behind me, the first word he had spoken in a while ringing with his typical irritation. "I'm going to start laughing randomly and answering questions from nowhere if you guys don't knock it off. Why, yes, peanut butter is delicious, thank you for asking." Thom rolled his eyes in frustration, but everyone else stared at him in utter disbelief.

Well, everyone but Wyn, whose high-pitched squeal broke against the stone.

"Yep, I'm hilarious," Thom growled, oblivious to his own absurdity. "Is it at least safe to leave the cave? I would really like a shower…"

Ilyan looked at me in question, his hand winding around my waist as he pulled me into him. I could hear the question on his mind without him having to even put voice to it.

"Nothing has happened. The city is safe. I didn't feel Edmund or any of his men inside the city. So, unless we want tomatoes we should be fine," I said, my voice sounding far too loud against the silence of the cave.

"Right." Ilyan moved away from me and back to the door, looking through the gap once again before turning back to us. "You will need to be under a shield if we wish to make it through the court without attracting too much attention."

I nodded with all the others, no one daring to second guess his proclamation. If we went out as we were, I was sure some kind of riot would break out. My shirt was still covered in dried blood; Ilyan was prickled in small cuts that, although healed, had left trail of dirt and blood behind; Dramin could barely walk on his own; and Ryland…

One look at Ryland sent my nerves into an electrified storm. The darkness that had taken over his eyes were back, a panicked fear rumbling through him and setting my desperate need to attack back into motion.

I looked away before it took hold, but not before Ilyan caught the whisper of my thoughts in his own mind.

Ryland had told me he was fine, because his father was too far away, because some blade was too far away. He *should* be fine.

But he was nowhere near fine. He looked like he was falling apart.

No, he looked as though he was being pulled apart.

"The closest safe house is above the clock about ten kilometers to the north. Stay close, but if you get separated..." Ilyan paused, the tension in the cave swallowing the temporary joy as if it had been waiting in the shadows the whole time. "Just make it to the clock."

Everyone nodded once as they began to break into groups. Wyn moved to Ryland, Thom to Dramin and Sain. It was the same grouping they had adopted for most of our trek through the dark, the bonds forged in hundreds of years, or months of forced survival that had driven them together.

Ilyan pressed me against him, the warm palm of his hand running down my bare arm before he stepped back to the crack in the door, toward the light that was now noticeably darker. The crowd's noises lessened.

"Be quick," Ilyan said, wrapping his hand around the massive iron loop that was nestled into the carving near where a doorknob would go. The ancient groan of handle and hinge echoed through the cage as if it was a monster that had been roused from its sleep. I almost expected the thing to erupt into a nightmarish creature. Ilyan's magic coaxed it along as the door swung open, flooding us all with blinding light as the stone itself bent to Ilyan's will and allowed us enough space to pass, unseen by the mortals.

We stood in the bright bath of warmth and light, the tattered group of survivors' mere steps from our next destination, from the next leg of the war for our lives.

Wyn sucked in breath as the door opened, her eyes flashing with panic before she glanced to me. A mischievous grin tried to meet her eyes, but it didn't quite make it. It stayed on her lips, the two Wyn's colliding in the middle.

She fixed me with yet another silent goodbye before she grabbed Ryland's hand, and her magic surged through the cave. I was sure she was shielding herself from view, even though the simple magic didn't work on me. It never had, there wasn't any reason for it to start now.

Wyn looked stoically forward, her jaw set in that powerful determination she had been trying to hide from me before she ran from the courtyard and into the cave. She and Ryland were followed by the already concealed Thom, Dramin, and Sain.

I stared after them all, passed the door and into the courtyard that was so bright it could have been the afterlife. The haloed shapes that moved and laughed through the courtyard could be nothing more than angels.

It was strangely beautiful the way the sun moved through the clouds and sent beams over the blissfully ignorant people in the ancient square. I was sure it would have been beautiful no matter what time of day or situation, but seeing it for the first time, combined with the flood of memories that flowed off Ilyan like a river, it actually felt like home.

Like I had known this place all along.

Ilyan said nothing as he grabbed my hand, leading me into the antiquated place.

The groan of the iron doors as they closed behind us was so loud I was surprised no one turned to look. It was like they hadn't even heard. Which I was sure they hadn't. Hadn't heard the noise, hadn't seen the doors.

Feet slipping on cobblestones, I tried to take everything in while keeping up with Ilyan's pace, my focus jumping from place to place like little ping-pong balls as Ilyan led me through the ancient square—the old stone houses, the antiquated carvings above each door, the old fountain that stood on the other end of the courtyard. I wished we could get closer to it. I wanted to inspect the medieval animals that spouted streams of water from their mouths, but Ilyan plowed ahead, taking us into a dim alley, following right behind Wyn and Ryland who looked to be running. Not that I blamed them.

Even though I had been so absorbed by the city, by the happiness of Ilyan's memories, I could still feel the heavy beat of my heart. Feel the worry that raged through Ilyan. I could still see the vivid images of my sight.

I picked up my pace as Ilyan did. His hand tightened around mine as we moved farther into the dark and around the corner that Wyn had disappeared behind moments before.

Nearly identical rows of apartments grew from the dirty stone street as if they were planted flora. They stretched to the sky, the normally bright blue tinged with red from the setting sun. It was claustrophobic, the sensation that the buildings were falling round us, enclosing us away from the golden light of dusk.

It was then, as the light from the setting sun broke in golden flecks over the red shingled eaves of the houses, and the perfect replica of my sight fell into place, that the world started screaming.

I stopped running before Ilyan did, my blood flaring in memory and magic as the Drak in me awakened, as the sight replayed itself as though someone was fast forwarding through an old home movie.

A movie full of screaming. Screaming that was everywhere. The sound came in ripples as the earth shook beneath us in what I was sure the mortals were assuming to be an earthquake. I knew better.

My heart raced in a pulse of panic as my muscles tensed in agony at the sounds, the panic, and the exhilarated fear moving over me.

Ilyan moved into a protective position, his magic flaring angrily as he tried to figure out what had happened and, more importantly, what he could do.

Nothing.

He could do nothing.

"It's starting," I said, but I wasn't sure if the words were mine or that of my sight. The depth of my voice was entirely dead.

I had barely spoken before the golden light of the sunset, the light that had been seen so clearly in my sight, was sucked from the sky and replaced with a sheet of red. The color was thick and all-encompassing, as though someone had thrown a thin blanket over the world.

I looked toward the sun, the red tinged orb that was trying to sink behind the skyline. As the earth rattled beneath me, the strength of a distant explosion rumbled through the ground as the red blanket of sky was streaked with pillars of black.

Thousands of winged creatures cut through the sky, through the red veil, descending on the city.

Devouring the city.

Devouring us.

14

JOCLYN

It was a trap, and we had walked right into it.

Sain had deceived us all.

Screams reigned through the city, they rippled through alleys and bled through the streets as columns of black erupted into the sky. Tower after tower joined the first, the screams increasing as the earth shook underneath our feet, the sky turning to a blood red overhead.

It was a mirror of the sight, everything was the same.

Every horrifying image was the same.

Creatures poured into the sunset on all sides of us, streaking over the blood red sky like bats. Flocks of the winged monsters were encapsulating the city from all sides.

Enclosing us in.

Trapping us.

Even if we wanted to escape the city, there was no chance of that happening now.

Edmund had drawn us here.

Herds of screaming people choked the streets around me and Ilyan; Wyn, Thom, and the others had vanished, the fray devouring not only them, but the calm from moments before.

The European city was only chaos now.

The chaos became mayhem as the Vilỳs hit the ground like wet rags, their screeches mixing with the people's screams of terror as the things then came to life with terrifying speed.

Wings unfurled, bodies glistened, teeth gnashed, and their sharp claws attached themselves to the humans like locusts, biting, ripping, and tearing at their flesh as they infected them with their poison. The once revered "kiss" was placed upon them like a disease, infecting them and their newly born magic with the same infection the Vilỳs held.

Edmund was creating his army.

I wanted to rejoice that my sight had been correct, that my magic was correct. But this? This should have stayed hidden in the shadows of my Drak blood. This should have never come to pass.

A car zoomed past us, at least twenty of the little things clawing at the metal, ripping it apart to get inside. Ilyan's magic flared in a violent surge that shifted through my blood, igniting my own magic and blending together in a wave of sparking fire similar to the fairy lights I had seen every time our lips touched. Except now, they were not wrought in love and passion. Now, they were bred from the flame of Ilyan's anger, the strength one I had only seen once before.

Now, the lights were dangerous.

Now, he was dangerous.

We were dangerous together.

Dropping our shields, we met the new battle head on, running into the tangled mess of blood and carnage.

Streams of magic surged from my hands, burning through Vilỳs and pulling them away from the battered people that were writhing on the ground. The magic was only a banner of our existence and they flew to attack us, to the danger we represented.

The mortals were easy pickings, even the ones who tried to fight back were felled in seconds.

But me and Ilyan?

It was as if they sensed that we could stop it.

A swarm of heavy leather wings charged at us in a wall of teeth and blood, magic erupted from me in an orb of white light that sent the cluster to the ground. It seemed like a good tactic, until the light alerted the hundreds of other creatures that hadn't taken notice of us.

The monsters froze, their ugly, deformed sphinx faces turning toward us in matching grins of malice that ran through my body like ice.

There wasn't even a chance to run. The tiny wicked little things moved too fast, swallowing the red light that bled from the sky. Hot wind beat against my face, the smell of excrement and blood filling my nostrils.

My head swam at the smell of their rancid magic, the nasty weight of it infecting me the same way it had in the forest outside of Rioseco. My Drak blood boiled against it as it fought to take over, fought to drown me. The power of my sight was a claustrophobic pressure that made me fight to stay upright, to not fall to my knees and let the Drak magic take me.

It was going to take me anyway. My vision blacked in and out, my world turning into a strobe-filled nightmare.

A sharp, claw filled, nightmare.

Flashes of fire burned behind my eyes as claws dug into my skin. The echo of Wyn's fight drifted from somewhere not too far away from us, the sound mixing with Ilyan's yell right beside me, but I couldn't focus on any of it. All I felt was my own blood pouring over my skin.

I was in trouble. We had attacked the Vilỳs in the forest like cowards, burning the tent they were in to the ground. Facing them as an enemy that was able to fight, feeling their rotten magic press against my skin and swim in my mind; winning this fight was going to be a challenge.

A challenge, but not an impossibility. I would save this city. I would save the people it held. Even if it meant fighting to the death.

If I truly was born to defeat Edmund, then I had to make it through this. I couldn't defeat the self-proclaimed king if I was dead, after all.

There had to be a way to fight them.

And I think I had an idea as to how.

'Ilyan.'

He was there before I had said his name, ripping the creatures from my body and throwing them into the rough stone buildings around us. The screams of Vilỳ and mortal echoed in my ears, the ricochet of sound growing as the world dipped into the ember red color of sight again.

Let it come, mi lasko. His voice was loud in my mind as the red flared through me in heat and power. '*I will protect you.*'

Ember-filled light seeped into my mind, filling my sight with the same city streets we were surrounded by. Vilỳs ran rampant as they moved from human to human, devouring them, marking them, destroying them. Bodies lay battered in the streets as the Vilỳs tried to pry open windows and claw their way under doors. The screams of the humans were all but replaced by the high-pitched squeal of the monsters who had destroyed them.

The sight moved through the streets as if at a run, only to stop at an old, wood-slab door that was covered with the long scratches of the Vilỳs' claws, splattered with the blood of some poor soul who hadn't made it past the entry and into safety again.

I waited for the door to open, magic flaring in recognition of the dread that I had felt plague the earth, that sadness and fear that had been hidden in the city. It was the same, and it was hidden behind that door.

It wasn't the same as the terrifying enemy, however. The door screamed of safety. My magic promised that it was.

The vision ended with the snap of a crumpled Vilỳs body as it slammed into the cobbles right where I was folded over, the thing twitching once before it sagged into nothing.

I needed to find that door.

But first, we needed to get out of here. I would have to find the door on the way.

Vilỳs fell to the ground as I stood, a blast of blinding white light pushing away from me and scattering the vermin like twigs, giving us enough reprieve to catch our breath.

"It's no use!" I screamed above the animalistic battle sounds, sending a trio of quickly approaching winged monsters to the ground with a swipe of my hand, their once frenzied bodies looked like nothing more than crumpled leather. "We have to get out of here!"

'*I know,*' his voice ached, his jaw tightening as he continued to fight, desperate to save his home, to save the humans that he counted as his people, even if they didn't know he existed. The emotions that accompanied that knowledge gripped him, and with only those two words, he took my breath away.

I didn't want to leave either.

Pressing my back beside his, we stood side-by-side, igniting a destructive orb that gave us enough room to run through them. To run away from them.

It was the only choice now.

I could only hope that Wyn and Thom were smart enough to do the same.

Dragging Ilyan down the street, we ran. Vilỳ after Vilỳ dropping from the sky as we bolted toward where Wyn had been.

Burned remains of at least a hundred of the beasts littered the ground, the white stone of the building beside it burned away as if someone had thrown acid on the glistening surface.

I knew I was powerful, but that was like a little atomic bomb had gone off. And I hadn't even been trying. Creepy. I didn't want to know what would happen otherwise.

Ilyan's grip around my hand tightened as he pulled me away from the blackened space and down a narrow alley that lay all but hidden in the shadows.

'They will be at the clock,' Ilyan said as we ran into that claustrophobic depths of the alley, the ever-increasing screams of the massacre rattling the stone behind us.

I thought the battle in Rioseco had been bad. This was a nightmare. I couldn't even summon another acid attack when the whole world shook and the sound of another bomb dropped through the alley, screams of every kind hitting against my bones.

'What was that, Ilyan?'

'Wynifred. It's the fire magic.'

I guess I wasn't the only one with a bomb inside of me.

Ilyan pulled us into another wide road, the same white buildings stretched before us. But any sign of a calm street was gone. The buildings were a rainbow of death, the street a river of red.

It was all I could do not to scream.

The mortals were screaming as they ran from the things, trying to escape into the hopefully safe buildings, but it was in vain. Most were already infested by the Vilÿs, their wings flapping against windows and breaking through glass as they went after their prey.

I tried to stop, to help, to rip every last one of those demons from the sky with my bare hands if I had to, but Ilyan pulled me on. I didn't need his internal monologue to understand why.

There were more here, more Vilÿs than humans. If we were to stop and fight here, we would be lucky to escape alive.

We needed to get to the clock.

The building was perfectly projected in his mind—the old building with the massive round faces placed against its façade. There was a door off to the side that would take us to the tiny safe house on the top story, the one that Ilyan had kept since the fifteen hundreds.

I could see it all through him, but I could also see the door from my sight. I could still feel the pull of that door and whatever was hidden behind its marred surface.

I knew the clock was safe, but the pull to that door was stronger.

I needed to find it.

Ilyan towed me along as he turned into yet another alley, only to find a wall of black wings, the mortal screams of a woman and a child echoing behind it in a pain that wrenched through me in a powerful vice.

Oh screw it! These ones I was going to kill! These people I was going to save.

"Freaking demons!"

Magic erupted in a whirlwind of power that spread over the alley like a rock thrown in a pond. The ripples of magic moved over stone and cobbles in an explosion of destruction that tore through the street, shredding the wall of Vilỳs crashing to the ground in troves as the bomb that I had become ripped through them.

In a way, it was beautiful, watching the once beautiful creatures fall from their prison, their broken bodies free from the poison that ran through them. The humans they had surrounded were quickly running from the death that they would have certainly found.

Well, at least most of them were.

One, a woman, still clung to a whimpering boy, although for good reason. The woman was clearly dead. The cries of her child the only sound in the silence.

The silence before hell opened even further.

The bomb may have been fun, but I wasn't an idiot. I knew what I had done.

The explosion had ripped the sky apart with a burst of light that had shown millions of Vilỳs our exact location.

Ilyan exhaled beside me with a chuckle, his hand running up my arm as I turned toward him.

"I don't care what anyone says," he whispered, "you were made for me."

His lips turned up in a tiny smile as the light from the blast faded back into darkness, his hands soft against my arms, his lips gentle against mine.

The moment couldn't last, however. It is never wise to steal a kiss in an apocalypse after all. The temporary silence was cut by the shrill shriek of the Vilỳs, a warning of what was coming reverberating off the stone we were surrounded by.

I should have been scared that they were coming right toward us. But that scared withering girl was gone.

"To the clock," Ilyan said as he lifted the small, whimpering child into his arms, pulling me deeper into the alley after him. The child was so scared, so injured that he did little more than cry as the tall stranger carted him away.

We said nothing to the child as we ran away from the lifeless body of his mother, past the flow of blood and into yet another street. This one was narrow enough to be an alley. If it wasn't for the intricately carved doors that stood beneath drawn postcard windows, I would have assumed it to be.

The old street was lined with the bodies of the creatures I had killed in the explosion. The one or two that had somehow survived sat clawing at doors as if they were a lost dog looking for a home.

One of the mud brown creatures clawed at the heavy wood of a door, its movements growing more frantic the closer we came. The thing was oblivious to our presence thanks to the shield, but it wasn't us that was making him agitated. It was the sound of wings, it was the high-pitched screams as the Vilỳs that were drawn to the light pushed through the alley.

Looking for us.

We needed to move, Ilyan's tugging hand was a plea for that, but I had slowed down, watching the tiny things insanity as it sought for survival. Staring at the empty street that had graced my sight moments before. Blood ran through the cobbles, windows were shuttered with heavy panels of carved wood; it was all from my sight, I had been here only moments before.

Ilyan's hand slipped from mine as I came to a stop, his panic accelerating alongside mine.

We need to move.

I barely heard him over the heavy thump of my heart, the pulse against my rib cage was almost painful. Fear and panic turning into a freaking stereo system inside my chest.

It was like Deja vu on steroids.

'Joclyn,' Ilyan pleaded as he took my hand, the shrieks of the creatures growing louder. *'We have to move. The clock is just here.'*

'We can't go to the clock, Ilyan.' I pulled my focus from the door to my mate, to his bright blue eyes that, although confused, would follow me anywhere, no matter what I said.

Death, destruction, or both: he was here.

He intertwined my fingers with his, the grip strong as his magic flooded me. The alley was full of the Vilỳs screams now, the creatures search growing closer.

Ilyan was right, we needed to move.

But not to the clock.

My magic fused with his as it swam away from me, soaring through the tiny maze of streets we were closeted in. Searching. Looking. The hidden fear I had felt in my sight rammed into me from somewhere off to our left.

I ran without looking, sprinting past more grimy doors and ancient stoops, each one splattered with blood and bodies. I ran, bringing us closer to the searching Vilỳs our footsteps and heaving breaths telling them exactly where we were. But I didn't slow, I pulled him forward until we faced the door so covered with scratches and blood I was surprised that there was any wood left to it.

"Here."

Ilyan said nothing, he only pushed the door open with a single pulse of his magic and pulled us into the dark space as a warm, pungent wind moved past us, the door closing just as a dozen tiny bodies hit against it.

The sound of the thuds, of the screams, and of claws as they ground against the wood was deafening in the pitch-black. The noise flooded us, the frustrated screams of the monsters growing in intensity before they began to dissipate. The tension in my back loosened as I forced myself to breathe, though I still wasn't sure it was safe to.

It came out in a massive exhale while Ilyan's free arm wrapped around me, pulling me against him, his mind still swimming with questions. But he said nothing, choosing instead to pepper the top of my head in grateful kisses.

"It's okay..." I gasped, my words heaving with the fear that I hadn't registered until now. "We're okay..."

"Who's there?" The voice shook through the dark with an intensity I hadn't been expecting.

I jumped, and Ilyan's arm became nothing short of a vice as he held me against him, the limp body of the child pressing against my shoulder.

Ilyan's mind moved as fast as mine as we stared into the dark trying to figure out what we had walked into. What we were trapped with.

Where my sight had brought us.

"Answer me!" the voice came again, this time the decidedly female tones shaking with fear.

Ilyan relaxed a bit at the shake, even though his arm still stayed tight.

"We mean you no harm," Ilyan began, his voice that gentle calm I remembered from the first day I had spoken to him, his accent thick as he rolled his consonants around. "We needed shelter..."

"Ilyan?" the voice interrupted, the shake entirely gone now as the one word expanded into a babble of whispers in the dark.

I tensed at the use of his name, while Ilyan relaxed, a

swelling joy moving through him as his heart rate thundered in my ear.

"My lord?"

"Yes."

With that confirmation the darkness erupted in light and color, flares of magic tingling against my own as concealed magic broke free of binds that I didn't even know you could place. I cringed against the light, pressing my face into Ilyan's chest as he held me, his hand a wide span against my back.

The torrent of noise, of surprise, of awed whispers only grew as the light did. The rustle of amazement was so loud that I turned my head enough to see the battle worn people that littered the dilapidated space, their faces gaunt and haggard, their clothes singed and torn, but their eyes were bright with a hope so strong I was sure they hadn't felt the emotion in ages.

They looked at us, at Ilyan, in awe before, as one, they bowed to the ground, their bodies bending the same way I had seen in the courtyard so long ago. The respect was so deep I could only stare in open-mouthed wonder.

Where in the world had I brought us?

"Our lord, the king of our people," they said in harmony, their voices loud as they swelled inside of me. Ilyan's body was a tense calm underneath me. "We bow before you in allegiance, in devotion. We serve you now and for as long as the magic flows within the earth."

"Accepted," Ilyan growled, his voice deep in what I could only assume was a formal ceremony.

Their heads lifted with the word, the respect only growing as their vision shifted from Ilyan's tall frame, to the tiny simpering child, to my shivering body that Ilyan held against him, and then to the long ribbon that trailed down my back and the intricate braid that still graced my head.

"My lady," they gasped as their heads snapped back down in reverence. "Our Queen."

Well, crap.

15

JOCLYN

I HAD NEVER HATED the term "my lady" as much as I did in that moment. I hadn't wanted to hide in quite some time. Hell, I didn't really want to hide right then. But with the way they were all looking at me, I was starting to reconsider my options.

We had been here for over an hour, and they were still looking at me, the sidelong glances full of awe and wonderment that felt misplaced. Well, maybe not as misplaced as the few who kept coming up and kissing my hands, pressing the long length of ribbon against their foreheads.

Weird was one word for it.

Uncomfortable was another, and I don't think I had ever felt both so acutely before.

Even with that, I wasn't going to take this moment away from them. As much as it made me uncomfortable, I could tell by the look in their eyes, by the look in Ilyan's eyes, that this meant more to them than even I could understand. So, I smiled in awkward thanks, glad when the formalities ended, and I was given the opportunity to sit sandwiched between Ilyan and a wall.

And I did.

I mean, I wasn't going to hide, the hood on my blood-soaked sweatshirt was going to stay stoically down - but having a bit of a buffer was nice.

Becoming a queen overnight was overwhelming. I had an inkling of that before, with Wyn, Thom and Dramin's reaction. But this was like a trial by fire.

Add to that the fact that everyone was speaking a language that I hadn't mastered yet, magic and mouths and everything moving way too fast around the unfamiliar space and I couldn't have been more happy to make best friends with a wall and take the role of observer. Even if I was a royal one.

The ancient furniture looked derelict in the dim light, something that was probably only enhanced by the screams that echoed from the streets outside, the pleas for help ripping at my heart. I had tried to get up to answer their calls several times, but I knew it was foolish. Just because time had passed, it didn't make it any more probable that I would defeat the little beasts.

At least the screams were getting farther apart now, although I wasn't sure that was a good thing.

Ilyan was tense as he spoke to the pretty girl who had apparently taken over Talon's role after everything had happened. She was now second in command, and desperately trying to keep the few remaining survivors safe. It was no wonder she was excited to see Ilyan.

I would be, too.

The woman was as tall as Ovailia and Ilyan, her body lanky but lined with sinewy muscles that coiled around her attractively. I never thought of muscle as being sexy, but this girl pulled it off. Her sheet of strawberry blonde hair was definitely helping with how it fell down her back, much the way Ovailia's did. Well, maybe not like Ovailia's. No one should be compared to that irritating specimen given our current situation.

From what I could tell from the Skříteks I had seen, however, they all looked fairly similar—tall, slender, oddly ethereal people.

Besides, this girl, Risha, had a kindness in her eyes I knew at once Ovailia could never obtain, no matter how hard she tried. Even through everything that had happened the past few weeks, she didn't look nearly as careworn as the rest of them.

Risha stood over what they had been using as their strategy table, a hand drawn map carved into the old, wooden surface. Small, everyday objects were scattered around to display where camps, Vilỳs, or Edmund and his men were.

At least, that was what I would assume. They were speaking Czech so fast I couldn't make out individual words. I knew I could pull the words out of Ilyan's head if I really wanted to, but at this point, it was becoming abundantly clear that I needed to learn the language. "Pass the leaves" and "Where is the bathroom? I'm going to explode from eating these leaves" was no longer going to cut it.

Risha said something at an inhuman speed to Ilyan before glancing to the mark on my neck. Then her eyes widened in wonder before they darted away as quickly as if I had caught her doing something dirty.

It shouldn't bother me. Everyone outside would have a nearly identical mark in just a few hours, after all. It was beautiful, normal, but her look was way too similar to the looks that had scared me for so long.

My palm covered the raised, dragon-shaped branding for the first time in what felt like years, the skin softer than I remembered it.

For the first time since I had left those fears and insecurities behind, I was aware of it there, open for everyone to see, just like the boy we had rescued whose mark was already blooming on his cheek.

The child was curled up on a pile of blankets in a little nest in the center of the room 'where there is more light.' While I understood the reasoning, it still left the child in the middle of the floor, writhing in pain for all to see.

His whimpers echoed through the dark as the refugees cared for him, my heart twisting in a hope that there was something I could do to help him.

I could already feel my magic take over in a pulse that stretched through every muscle, every bone, in an attempt to pull me toward him. Just as it had when I had healed Dramin and Wyn. My magic told me what to do. It told me where to go and paved the path of what to do. I could feel the same pull, but this time it wasn't for healing. It was almost as if the child had something that my magic wanted, something that it was going to get no matter what.

My magic wanted something. It scared me.

The thunder of my heart mixed with his cries, with the screams of those outside until it was all an echo of sound that trapped me underneath it, pulling me toward it...

"Joclyn," Ilyan's thick accent pulled me from my focus with a jump as everything jerked back to life.

"Yes." I whispered, needing to say something, even though I could hear the conversation in Ilyan's mind, well the Cliffs Notes of what had happened anyway.

I already knew what he wanted of me.

All the random corks and buttons that were littered all over the table suddenly made sense. Buttons for other refugees, corks for pockets of Edmund's men that he had hidden all over the city.

"You need to know if there are any more corks?" I asked, knowing the phrasing sounded odd, something that didn't go unnoticed.

Ilyan laughed, while that wide-eyed stare came back to Risha's face far too quickly, many of the others around her looking just as confused.

Thankfully, this time I didn't care quite so much, my magic was already flooding away from me, my heart pulsing in excitement.

I closed my eyes, grateful to get Risha's worshipful expression out of my mind and let my magic stream away from me. I tried to keep it restrained, to keep the intensity at bay and not cause a whirl wind like I had in Rioseco, but it didn't seem to work.

The power came anyway, moving out in a rush as it streamed away in a powerful gust that moved through the room, lifting my ribbon and the loose pieces of my hair as paper and bits of fluff swirled around me.

The room filled with cries of alarm as the whirlwind grew, only to have Risha speak in what I supposed was a request for calm.

A ripple of embarrassment moved up my spine, but like last time, it was all a million miles away. They were all in another world, just out of touch from the world I was moving through, the one that was filled with darkness and blood. Filled with fear. They were two very different realities, and I was trapped between them.

My magic sped through the city, my mind following through streets, through alleys, streams, sewage systems. It all should have been beautiful. It had been before, when I stood behind that door, but now everything was dark.

Walls were splattered with thick blood, bodies lay haphazard and forgotten in the streets, and through it all, the Vilÿs flew, looking for more victims. Except these ones were different than the ones who had rampaged through the city, biting anyone they came in contact with. They didn't have the same blood red tint in their eyes. They didn't gnash and snarl as they flew through the air. Their movements were too organized, their eyes too clear.

A heavy weight lodged itself in the pit of my stomach. There was a difference for a reason. They were still the same creatures but the way they had been mutated was different.

They were different.

They were patrolling, I realized, my heart tensing with understanding of what Edmund had done. What he had really done.

He had created a police state. More than just using the Vilÿs to create an army, he had created guards to keep everything in line. As perfectly planned as his attack had been, he had done it all knowing he would draw us here, knowing he would trap us inside.

Where are the boundaries of the city? My voice was panicked as it plunged into Ilyan's mind, the conversation in quick Czech that he had been having stopping abruptly.

'Follow the river in either direction.' His voice was a rumble as his magic grew, moving through the city right alongside. *'There is a freeway that circles the city...'*

His instructions vanished as we saw it; the rubble of what once had been a roadway was now a ruin. Cement, trees, and portions of buildings were piled high in a barricade that towered far into the sky. It was more than a barricade, however. It was a wall that stretched into a wide shield of glittering red; a dome that spread over us, dimming the sky beyond and casting the blood red sheen over the city.

Everything was covered in the blood of what Edmund had done, trapped behind walls and a shield that I knew I would never be able to penetrate, not on my own.

Ilyan's anger grew, his emotions raging in a heat that was more than dread. It was a panic that took over every part of my body, every part of my mind, and tensed through me in a painful rage that ignited my magic further. I wanted to reach to him, to grab his hand and comfort him, to bring him close to me. But I was still trapped under the glare of the wall, under the screams of those who had tried to flee the city, only to be blocked by not only the wall, by the army of angry Trpaslíks Edmund had placed beside it.

I guess now I knew where the rumble of the first explosion had come from.

Edmund had closed off the city, trapping us all inside.

Any attempt at escape had been pointless, right from the start.

Bodies were piled before the barricades, cars crumpled against each other. It was the same scene of war that I had been shown in history classes for years. Pictures of a past I had never really understood to be real until that very moment.

I had never truly comprehended that one man could cause so much destruction. So much death.

That one man could hate so much that he would destroy so many.

I understood now.

"How far does it go?" Ilyan asked, his voice distanced through the tunnel of my mind and magic.

His hand pressed against mine, his magic surging alongside, the connection not necessary yet so very welcome. I rejoiced at the warmth of his touch, at the strength of that support as he followed my magic as it sped around the wall, through the endless destruction, and the line of Edmund's men. The constantly flowing river slowed, the brown and blue fading to a crimson color that was only enhanced by the shield that smothered the city.

It was a solid mass of men, of wall, of death.

'*Ilyan*.' The word was a plea for understanding that I knew I would never get. Not with the way I could feel the thunderous pulse of his heart within mine.

My eyes flashed open to the dark room, to the kind face of the woman who sat across from me, her shock smothered by the shadow of the destruction I had come from, my head spinning with recollection, my body weak from exertion.

"They are lining the wall," Ilyan's voice rumbled in English as he held me against him, his voice filled with the same anger I felt rule him.

"The wall?" The heavy accent in Risha's voice made it to where I could barely understand her. No wonder they had been speaking in Czech.

It was obviously more than a familiarity issue.

"My father has turned the freeway into a barricade. Nothing is getting out of the city."

"You mean we are trapped here." Risha slipped into Czech at her alarm, but Ilyan's mind translated it for me instantly. Not that I needed the help—her tone was enough, the fear behind it almost crippling.

"Ano."

Yes.

The room shifted into panic, the already battle worn refugees' hope squashed moments after it had been fed.

Ilyan lifted his hand, and without a word the room fell to silence.

Everyone looked at him in expectation, in fear, in reverence, in emotions I didn't understand. Ilyan sat in silence, his eyes closed in calm, though I could feel the waves of uncertainty and panic move through him.

I let my magic fill him, the warm tendrils moving through him and wrapping his fears in a mask that, while it did not calm him completely, made the tension in his body loosen. His eyes opened to look at me with that deep admiration that always took my breath away.

I barely restrained the sigh. I wasn't quite ready to let him sweep me off my feet with this big of an audience.

"That doesn't mean there is no escape," Ilyan's somber voice rumbled through the silence. "We came here fully expecting to fight. We fought in Rioseco, and we will fight here. Even if it ends in our death. We are Skříteks. We have been born to protect the magic of the world, to protect the wells of Imdalind. That is why we have come. That is why you still live. It is our duty to protect this world and all the power it holds. We may be trapped here, but it is not in vain. It is for the safety and security of all."

I tensed at his words, at the admission, at the possibility. We had only barely escaped in Rioseco, and the idea that we would flee only to come here and die without reaching our end goal—without killing Edmund—rattled me.

It was the fear of the prophecy that I had been fighting for so long.

I cringed, even though everyone else relaxed, the heavy

fear that had impregnated the room lifting with each word he spoke.

They were the Skřiteks—the warriors and protectors of magic. They had been born for this. They had trained for this. It would be easy to say that I was not one of them, that this was not my fight.

But it was.

Because I was one of them.

"What do you suggest we do, my lord?" Risha asked, her fear tapering as she leaned across the table.

"We know where Edmund's men are, and I think we can ascertain his plan based on how he has acted and what he has done. If we gather who is left of our kind together, we may be able to find a way to infiltrate his ranks and get Joclyn and I close enough to defeat him."

The magic in the room surged at the power in his words, my own strength, my own certainty growing stronger with each syllable.

I didn't think it was possible for me to forget how powerful Ilyan was, but watching him command and motivate so many people, his people, it was remarkable.

Murmurs of excitement swirled through them all as they broke into conversation, the quick Czech increasing as Risha and Ilyan moved to fortify a plan and find a safe space large enough for all of us on the odd, makeshift map.

I knew I should be paying attention, picking apart the words and understanding what came to everyone else so easily, but I couldn't focus. Ilyan's words were lingering in my mind, his magic pressing against mine in a lightweight bubble that was making my head spin one way, and the ground spin another.

The sensation was familiar, but here, among all these people, I did not know if it was one I should be having.

'*Cover my eyes,*' I pleaded, knowing what was coming and not wanting anyone to see. Not wanting them to know the full extent of my powers.

Instead, Ilyan wound his arm around me. With a soft laugh his lips pressed to the hollow beneath my ear.

"I will only cover your power if you truly do not want them to see, mi lasko," he whispered, his voice deep and heady. "There is no need to hide anymore."

His grip against me was a comforting weight, the love that swelled from him full of pride and a desire to show his people the Silnỳ they had all been waiting for. It was a deep-rooted love and support that worked to build me up, to set me free, and to let me be without fear of recourse, of judgment.

It was a wonderful feeling to be loved as I was. To be supported as I became what I needed to be. What I wanted to be. He corrected, his grip around my hand tightening.

I clung to him as the dizziness grew, as the strength of his arms around me increased, and the awed support swelled.

I didn't move. I didn't turn into him, despite the fact that I so desperately wanted to. I let the sight come. I let it swell and grow as my vision burned red and my magic surged, pulling my mind away from the present, away from the stale air of the room and the faded screams of the massacre that was slowly dying. My vision faded from red to black as the startled gasps of Ilyan's subjects faded to nothing, the sound of screams and fear in the sight overtaking them.

I braced myself for the sight, for the guidance, for the future, for some new insight into what we were facing.

However, nothing was new. I had seen this before when we had stood around the map, in the sight that Sain had pulled himself into, the vision that had made me question everything.

How sights work, if I could trust them, if I could even trust my father.

If I could trust anything.

It was the same sight, yet something about it was different. Something was pulling at the deep threads of my magic and begging me to watch, whispering at me to see.

The red roofed skyline of the city we were now trapped in drifted into view, the wide river glittering through the buildings in a trail of gold. I had seen this city. I had walked through it as the sun had cast its last rays.

I watched it set now, waiting for the next piece of the sight to come, waiting for the towers of Vilỳs to erupt into the sky. Then, like a movie, like a camera set too far in on zoom, that vision panned back, speeding away from the red rooftops to the roadway I had only just seen, except this time it was whole, and the sun was high in the sky.

I had seen it set. I had watched it dip down, the sky turning as red as the rooftops.

No, I realized with a panicked fear. It wasn't the sun. It was the shield. It was the magical barricade that Edmund had cast around us.

Moments after the realization, the world exploded with noise, the earth shaking as the Vilỳs exploded into the sky, the roadway collapsing in on itself, the buildings and people that surrounded the once safe structure moving into what quickly became a prison wall.

Screams reverberated in my mind as the attack began, the people running far below, the dingy brown Vilỳs tracking each of them down.

The whole thing was much more frightening from this

angle, the dimmed colors of what I knew to be a sight of the past mostly unnoticeable.

I had lived this, after all.

The screams echoed as my mouth opened, my voice dead against the scream of death within the sight and the gasps of surprise without. "The death will come; the sky will fall."

The same words seeped out like syrup. The words were not different, though the meaning behind them was. The barrier that covered the sky shimmered in the bright sun before I was sucked back into the city, right to the group of people who were huddled in the alley, the ones I had seen minutes before.

The boy that now lay unconscious behind me was amongst them, his face stricken in fear as he clung to his mother.

The river came next, or at least it should have. Instead of the wide river that ran through Prague, however, it was the same room we now sat in, the same boy on the floor where he now lay, my hand pressed against his skin. I only saw a glimpse of the magic, felt the pull of my own move beyond the barrier of sight when the vision shifted.

The same boy stood in the darkened city, the buildings crumbling and derelict as he fought a mutated Vilỳ, his hands sparking with light and magic. The knowledge of what would happen to him, what he would become, and the possibility that he wouldn't be as infected as Edmund had hoped was a balloon of possibility inside of me.

My hands against his cheek, pure magic from his hand. My magic could do this.

I could feel it.

"The war begins in the dark of night." I didn't even have

time to register what I had seen before the rumble of my voice filled the room. The river stretching toward the barricade before the sight flashed to the same cliff face from before, the one with the man on a horse carved into the high rock face.

Blood dripped down the intricate carving, the man and his horse bleeding from stone as though the stone itself had been cut.

It hemorrhaged as the vision shifted, myself and more than a hundred others standing on the roofline of the city, our cloaks beating behind us as we faced the barricade before we took off into the air, toward the wall of rubble and the red sheen of Edmund's wall.

We soared toward it, my hand extended as I shattered it with a pulse of energy so wide and powerful I wasn't sure where it had come from, or how I was capable of producing it.

"With hell behind and hell before," I said as we moved through the barrier, fire devouring the buildings behind us before we streaked through the bleeding cliff face. One after another, the sights came, the quick succession of them spinning through me before they once again slowed to the same river of blood that poured through the deep grey rock of a cave floor, spread over the smooth valleys of the uneven stone.

"One must fall before the light." My voice was dead as I followed the sight, as my heart raced at the image of the same hand, the fingers loose and lifeless. I expected the sight to fade to red as it had last time, for the vision to end and the final unfamiliar words to drift past my tongue, but it continued.

The hand turned into an arm, a strong arm with a wide burn of black water along the bicep, a strong shoulder that held me every night and wide empty eyes that I loved so much.

Ilyan.

"It is divided." The last words drifted past me, but I barely heard them. I couldn't even make them out against the scream that ripped out right after, the panic and desperation that had gripped me.

That had ripped me apart.

Ilyan's arms embraced me like a vice as the scream continued. I fought the need to fight the hold, to run away and find my father, to beg to know how to change what I had seen, to find someone to tell me that the sights were not infallible as I had once thought.

I had fought that acceptance so hard. I had fought my father as I fought to save my brother.

They couldn't be true.

I had wanted so hard to believe. To be able to use my ability to change the future.

I had before.

But something in this sight had changed. It wasn't like it had been before with my father. The magic was stronger, the truth of what I had seen screaming at me.

I didn't know how I could deny that strength.

But I needed to.

As I looked into the startling blue of his eyes and saw fear and worry reflected back, I knew I needed to. I couldn't let that happen.

I couldn't lose him just as he could not lose me.

I could feel his magic grow as he calmed me, feel his panic and worry fill me as he searched for an answer that, while I knew he needed it, I would not let him see.

Before he could find it, before he even had a chance to

see, I pulled the sight out of my mind, locking it away in a bind that even he could not break.

I would protect him, even if it meant sacrificing my own life.

I loved him that much.

You would do anything for the ones you love.

I would do this.

16

WYN

MAKE IT TO THE CLOCK.

Ilyan's instructions were clear, and I wasn't about to question them. Especially now that Ryland was calm enough to at least walk and not freak out. The city was calm, full of laughter and bustling families as they rushed home after a long day.

Getting to the clock should be easy.

We just had to get there before his attack mode triggered back into full assault mode and he tried to avenge the mortals or something. This place was full of too much ancient magic and even though he was calm, the danger of his insanity was buzzing in the dark of his eyes.

We had walked into a danger zone.

Which was awesome.

The closer I got him to the clock before any eruption occurred, the better. Easier to drag him one block instead of twelve.

Of course, I was already dragging him behind me as I followed the gentle pull of Thom's magic as we weaved through the last of the shoppers and businessmen as they rushed home at the end of the day.

"You bastard!"

The scream broke through the calm city chatter like a grenade and I jumped, recognizing the angry shout as one would recognize a punch to the gut.

Thom.

People turned in confusion at the shout, only to have their bewilderment turn to panic as two blood-covered men appeared out of nowhere, screaming and fighting against each other. The calm street exploded in fear as Thom and Sain screamed as sparks of color flew from Thom's fingers, the magic aimed right toward Sain. Thom screamed louder, his eyes twisting to me in a horror that I had never seen before.

A horror that I didn't think was possible for him.

"Thom?" I asked, knowing he was too far away to hear, and gripped Ryland tighter, dragging through the now fleeing mortals in a mad race to reach him.

The people grew thicker, my shield pushing them around and adding more fear to the already fleeing masses.

Screams ripped at my ears, blocking Thom's shout, blocking the last of my logical thinking.

It would be easier to just kill all these irritating mortals to reach him, they kept coming, kept pushing.

So many more than I had seen a minute ago.

It took me one too many heartbeats to realize that they were no longer running from Thom and Sain, that their fear was deeper than just two magically appearing men, and that the screams were everywhere.

They bounced off of every building, they rained down from the sky and roared through the cobbled roads below me.

The earth shook, and everyone looked above to the winged storm clouds that were descending on us.

Towers of Vilỳs streaming through the sky like towers of smoke, arching over us before darting back to the ground like javelins.

No wonder Thom was screaming.

This was bad, so bad.

I grabbed Ryland, ready to make a run for it, when the boy screamed like a wild man, his magic erupting in an uncontrolled attack.

So much for making it to the clock tower without an explosion. Attack mode had activated and I was now surrounded on all sides.

Thankfully, this time Ryland didn't seem to see me as the enemy. His frightening eyes were turned toward the monsters that were falling from the sky, his face turning tomato red as he screamed. Magic sprayed from his hands, lunging like bombs toward the bastard bats that were now circling us.

Like vultures.

Thousands and thousands of vultures.

There were so many of them, but I wasn't about to curl up in a ball and whimper my way into death.

Bring it on.

Ryland went into full attack mode as the creatures reached us, his magic exploding right alongside mine in an orb of white that sent at least a hundred of the freaky things back into the sky.

As quickly as they were gone, however, more took their place, waves of dirty rat birds coming in for the kill, trapping us in a cave of leather wings. My heart pounded alongside the lingering screams of the defenseless mortals around us, and I sent a blast toward what I was sure was crying, sure I was going to find Thom and a whimpering Dramin.

But the street where they had been was devoid of magic, attacks and beings alike. There was only a bleeding man, the poor fellow screaming as Edmund's creations destroyed him.

"What the...?" I gasped, red light bathing over me as Ryland continued his attacking tirade.

We needed to get out of here, and take down as many as those psychotic things that we could in the meantime.

Maybe find Thom and the others on the way.

Luckily, Ryland had already gotten the message. Magic was flying out of him in all directions, slamming against the creatures and buildings and who knows what else as he attacked.

Who knows what he was fighting now, but this was still better than the alternative.

Placing myself as far away from his line of fire as I could, I let fire sparks from my fingers, ripping no less than a dozen Vilỳs from a poor woman and throwing them into the air away from her, right into a flare of my magic, the sparks of violet ripping them apart. Gritting my teeth, I snatched others from the air, my magic flaring into them the moment my fingers wrapped around their gnashing bodies, burning them alive with one touch.

Mortal screams increased as Ryland and I fought the wicked beasts, their minds unable to comprehend magic among the horrors that were raining down on them. They ran and tried their best to fight, only to be felled with a scream.

I ripped the things from the frightened people, vaporized them into air as they reached me. The world was swallowed by stained leather wings and browning fangs. The world was drowning in screams.

But I didn't stop.

Fire streamed from me, waves of attacks rippling through the darkened, stagnant air as one after another, the creatures fell to the ground.

It wasn't enough. They kept coming. Fighting the airborne creatures with an earth-based magic was nearly impossible. As much as I tried, my magic couldn't reach them through the air. I needed the physical contact to burn them. It was the only downfall of the fire magic. I could use anything else as a conduit but air. And water, but that was a given. Even though the fire could travel on the back of my regular ability, it lessened the power somehow, something that I didn't need right now.

I needed that power.

Ryland's screech broke through the sounds of the Vilỳs as he ripped one of them from his shirt, throwing it through the dirge of creatures that were as heavy as locusts.

A mortal ran between us, blood oozing from a bite on his neck as he ran through the door of a shop, only to have the monsters break through the windows after him, his scream increasing as he was devoured.

"No," Ryland sobbed as he turned toward the screams, the sound pulling him from his madness for one shallow breath.

The agony on his face was clear, he knew what would happen when the mutated things bit a mortal, and he knew what danger awaited him if they got to us first.

A bite to awaken their magic, but more than that, a bite to poison you, to pull you under Edmund's control.

A freaking army. And with the way Ryland was panting,

his eyes growing ever darker, he was quickly on his way to joining that club.

We needed to get out of here.

The clock tower was close. Please be close enough.

Ryland moved from laughing to screaming to fighting to helping so fast his actions were distorted, his voice broken as the scream left before returning a moment later. He was like a television with a broken controller, and I had no way of knowing what show would come on next, or if it would kill me.

My heart beat in a rapid tattoo as I blocked another of Ryland's attacks before wiping several of the monsters from the sky, trying to pull Ryland after me and closer to the safe house. If I was lucky, Ilyan, Jos or Thom would come back for us, help me herd the crazed teenager.

I wasn't dumb enough to hold my breath.

It was only us, surrounded by the wicked creatures, the magical echoed of what I assumed to be Joclyn and Ilyan mixing with the screams.

We were on our own.

This was Edmund's plan all along, just as Jos had said.

Freakin' mad man!

If I survived this, which was starting to feel slim, he was sure as Styx going to pay for this mess.

First, I needed to get the incredible hulk under control.

Without killing, I reminded myself.

"Snap out of it, Ryland!" I yelled as I dodged his attack, and sent out another. "I need you here right now!"

A greasy smile spread over his lips, his eyes darkening into the demonic grin that would have scared me, if I wasn't so pissed.

"You psycho," I snarled, letting my fire ignite in a flame that burst from me in an orb that streaked through the air toward him. He batted it away easily, the thing smacking into at least ten of the winged rats and knocking them from the sky, knocking them into nothing.

At least the attack wasn't useless, but the black-eyed monster was now laughing maniacally as he attacked me, and then a Vilỳ. His brief lapse in focus was just enough to let me get close enough to tackle him into the blood-soaked cobbles.

We went down hard, even with the boy underneath me my neck jostled at the impact, my knees slamming hard into the stone.

"Get your head on straight!" I yelled as I slapped him, my magic plunging into him and quickly turning him off.

One hand on his chest, I flailed the other toward the bats, trying to keep them at bay as I locked Edmund out of Ryland's heart.

"You have to fight him," I pleaded as Ryland's wide, black eyes stared into me before his mouth opened in a scream, the blue rushing back to the wide orbs that clearly reflected the monsters flooding the air behind us.

Now or never.

"Sorry, kid," I said, as I once again knocked him unconscious and shielded his body.

Freaking disaster zone!

I jumped to my feet, holding him by the levitating ankle as I bolted down the street.

I was not one to run, and as much as it pissed me off, I knew I didn't have another option.

I knew I wouldn't be able to evade them for long. I was still several blocks from the clock, and the more I moved, the more their numbers increased, like snails after a rainstorm.

Except they were freaking fast snails, and that gross slime stuff wasn't getting rid of any old ladies' wrinkles.

The rats clawed at windows, they sat atop fallen bodies, biting over and over as strange gurgling noises came from their mouths.

I didn't stop to look. I didn't dare. I ran through the still fleeing mortals, dodging cars as they careened out of control, every inch of the frames covered with the things. Ryland's elevated body bobbed beside me as I grabbed the diseased things, throwing them away in little balls of fire as I ignited them. The hot, burning embers exploded others, and they went down together, the snow ball of my magic working in a way I hadn't expected.

It was madness, everyone running in zig zags in their attempt to escape, even though I could tell by the look on their faces that they knew there was nowhere to turn.

The streets were littered with belongings as a foolish few had tried to take valuables in their flight, only to end up bleeding and writhing beside their memories.

The street ended at a yellow flower shop, the building I clearly remembered being a church at one point in history blocking the street, leaving only two narrow alleys on either side.

The pitch black caverns called to me, screaming anything other than safety. I had to trust that was what I would find. Perhaps, mercifully, the forgotten spaces would be forgotten by the rats, as well.

Ebony blackness enveloped us as we ran into the narrow side road, the screams of the battle dimming as the high stone walls swallowed everything whole. I fought the urge to flare my magic, to bring light to this space, but it would only call them to us. The dark was almost too much for the shadowed sounds of terror.

Gravel crunched under my feet as I walked with one hand against Ryland and the other against the cool brick surface of the buildings. Taking us forward step by step, closer to the clock.

Beyond this alley was another narrow street. Beyond that was the large courtyard that would connect us to the famous attraction. Only a few more minutes, and we could be there.

That was, if nothing else went wrong.

I would say jinx, I would knock on wood or throw salt or whatever else superstitious people did, yet given the situation everything had already gone wrong.

Someone had handed me moldy lemons, but I was definitely going to make the best of it.

I expected a wall of the poisoned Vilÿs to erupt and take us down the second we left the alley, but there was nothing. Nothing except blackness and the haunted echoes of the battle I was doing my best to escape.

Keeping the shield tight around us, I ran to the next road the screams growing as we reached it. At first glance the disheveled road was empty, but even without the buzz of my magic I knew better.

The freaking monsters were hanging from the eaves of every building, the creatures immobile, except for the subtle sounds of their teeth gnashing together.

The street was only empty because the Vilÿs had done their job. Bodies—alive or dead, I wasn't sure—were strewn over the walkways, limp figures were draped over chairs and tables and broken cars. Rivers of their blood streamed from them, they lay in them. But nobody moved. Everything was still.

There was nothing other than the mutated bats as they waited.

Waited for movement. Waited for something else to attack.

And, of course, we couldn't go back the way we had come. We could only go forward.

Luckily, I had magic on my side.

Tightening the shield around us, I made sure we were still blocked from view and took one step into the dimly lit road. The sound of my feet against the pavement was soft, and yet, somehow, they heard.

They heard it as if it was a battering ram.

Tiny heads snapped toward us, beady eyes narrowing as they searched for the owner of the sound. For one terrifying moment, I was sure they could see us, until their lazy focus snapped back to the bodies that already littered the street, the desperate hope they would somehow awaken and give them something else to bite clear on their face.

This street was a death march.

I guessed I should have said jinx.

Luckily, I already had a way around this.

You know, that whole magic thing.

Wind swirled around me with one pulse of my power, the element growing warm as it intercepted with my magic, creating a small whirlwind of hot air that lifted me up enough to soar through the street. If I was lucky, it would take us all the way to the clock.

The flags and overhangs that lined the buildings whipped around, the fabric pulling dangerously as I began my flight.

One after another, the little beasts turned their heads. Eyes wide as they searched, several of them hissed into the air as they tried to decide what was going on, as they desperately searched for something else to attack.

It only took a moment for them to figure it out. We had

soared past the store fronts, past the bodies, past the carnage; Ryland at my side as I towed him along, but we weren't quite far enough.

Their screams echoed behind me as they descended from the rafters, speeding after the wind, past the enemy they couldn't see.

Okay, time to speed things up.

The force of the wind grew into unstable gusts that pulled at my hair and clothing, shifting the flow of my own powerful surge until it almost sent me off course.

It almost would have been better if it had.

Even through the blindness of my location, the rats had thought ahead, forming a wall of black claws and leather wings, their fangs already gnashing at the ready. A web of Vilỳs, ready to catch us.

It was a good plan.

You know, if it wasn't for magic.

The shield around us dropped with only a flick of my magic, the tiny creatures screaming louder at our sudden appearance, only to have their hungry calls silenced by the ball of fire that flared from my palm in an orb of red and black. It grew to the size of a small car in seconds before I released it into the air toward the monsters, burning a hole in the web in a ring of flame that moved through the rest of them like burning paper.

The smell of singed flesh assaulted me as we flew through the carnage, my feet hitting asphalt as I skipped back in to a run. They would still be following us, but I really didn't care at that point.

I was kind of enjoying burning the little things.

We turned a sharp corner into one of the many courtyards that riddled the city, the stone square one I had visited many times throughout my life. It had always been beautiful, full of life, full of laughing lovers and tourists.

Now, it was red and black, and full of pain.

People screamed as they ran through the open space, frantic to reach the buildings and the supposed safety they offered, only to end up pounding on doors that were already barred against them. Some ran, but so many more had already fallen, curled into themselves as they writhed, as they screamed, as the tiny things ripped into them, awakening their magic, turning them into another of Edmund's pawns.

The large statue of Jan Hus stood on the other end of the square, the green copper of her face streaked with the blood of those who had tried to escape, her body covered with the tiny creatures.

I would end those bastards first.

With a burst of orange fire, a wall flew away from me, rumbling over the old cobbles toward the Vilỳs, and their ugly distorted faces, and the fangs that dripped with blood.

I wished I could stay and watch the carnage, but the clock was so close, there were only a few precious paces until safety.

If I could just get them there, then I could come back.

At least that's what I told myself, with the screams of the beasts right behind me I knew there was only one other option.

Humans screamed as I passed, their bodies writhing as I ripped the creatures away from them as I went. There was nothing else I could do, besides putting them out of their misery.

It was only screams.

Only fire.

Only blood and the sound of my shoes squishing against

the bloodied cobbles, Ryland beginning to writhe in the air beside me as he woke.

But the door was there, just ahead.

The old, wooden slab was covered with claw marks, a few dead creatures huddled to the side.

Almost as if someone had already made it inside, as if someone else was safe.

Hope of Thom's arrival flared inside of me like a beacon, bright and powerful as the door swung open, and I flung Ryland into its depths without a second look.

"Wyn?" The voice came from somewhere above, and I calmed. Even though Sain's was not the voice I wanted to hear, it would do for now.

I didn't stop to see if Ryland was safe, if he was waking up, or if Sain was coming to help the boy. I only turned on my heels, framing the door as I faced the wall of creatures that had followed us, faced the blood and carnage I had left behind. Now, it didn't matter if they followed the flame.

Let them come.

I would burn them all.

My magic reacted with a flare that ravaged into the darkened road in an explosion that rocked the ancient building. Flames of the brightest red rippled down the old stones of the streets and the stores that had stood there for hundreds of years. Fire burned and cracked the stone, melting the rock and the tiny, winged beasts as though they were nothing. The poor people who still walked fled from it, the ones who lay bleeding were put out of their misery.

A pang of guilt I never would have felt before roared through me as I stepped back into the darkness, the heavy wooden door of the tower closing with a thud.

The regret at what I had done was strong. I didn't want to take the lives of all those people, mostly because I knew they weren't all dead. They had writhed in their pain as the poison Edmund had engineered moved through them, awakening their magic, infecting it and turning them into just another of his puppets.

I had lived that nightmare for years, and I didn't wish it on anyone.

It was better this way. They were free now, whether they knew it or not.

I held to that as I battled the regret. The painful tinge that made me wonder if I could have helped instead of destroyed.

We would never know.

Ryland's disoriented grumbles and grunts echoed through the dark as he writhed back into consciousness, pulling me from the alley and to the kid who was trying to push through exhaustion and insanity to stand.

If I didn't know any better, I would be screaming about zombies, but instead I sighed, grabbed him and plunged him back to sleep before throwing his massive body over my tiny shoulder and carrying him awkwardly up the stairs toward Sain and the men who hadn't left my mind.

Really, just one of the men, but I wasn't ready to admit that just yet.

I needed to know they were okay. All of them. I needed to see him with my own eyes.

My heart pulsed with each step, sprinting my way up the narrow stairwell before I burst through the ancient, carved door at the top and to the three men.

They were all there, but not how I had expected. They weren't laughing, they weren't joking about the spoils of war.

And only one of them was standing.

Dramin's neck was bleeding profusely, the red, glistening

fluid seeping over shirt and floor from where he was hunched against dilapidated wall. Thom was unconscious, sagging against the opposite wall, his head lulled forward onto his chest, everything covered in blood I prayed was not his. Standing in the tiny room between them was Sain, the man cowering like a beaten dog, his hair mussed, his eyes wide as he looked at me with the green that was darker than I had ever seen it. A green so haunted that everything around me froze.

My shoulders hunched in fear as my heart accelerated. The panic at seeing them, at needing to know if they were okay, froze against my bones as I looked at him.

Then a voice more ice than fear passed from his lips.

"I've made a terrible mistake."

17

WYN

"What mistake?"

I was sure I heard him incorrectly, or at the very least I was making a terrible assumption about whatever this mistake had been.

You don't walk into a room that is covered in blood and not jump to really crazy conclusions.

You don't stare at the limp body of a man you still aren't ready to admit feelings for and not feel like the room was closing in around you.

Every muscle from my shoulders to my toes tightened in coils of frustrated energy, my pounding heartbeat swallowing all other sound until I was trapped in a tunnel of panicked pulses and the screams of the dead and dying.

I was surrounded by death. Surrounded by pain. Sain standing in a trance while I was stuck staring at Thom; Sain's 'terrible mistake' echoing in my head.

"What happened?" I gasped when it was clear Sain wasn't keen on answering me and rushed into the room, Ryland's body dropping to the floor with a hollow thunk.

The sound of his flesh smacking against stone added to

the echoes of screams and heart beats that slowed everything down until I was tripping over my own feet to reach him.

Nothing was moving fast enough, I wasn't moving fast enough. But, when I collapsed beside Thom and his pale, limp body I would have given anything for it all to just to slow down.

He leaned against the flowered wallpaper, the old forgotten design peeling away from the wood and dipping over his hand like a crown. I tried to move the paper away, to move the long dreads that had fallen over his face, but my hands were shaking so badly it did little more than send them swinging.

Shaking like a leaf, I leaned toward him, pulling his limp body against me as hot, burning tears falling down my cheeks. I should hide them, the assassin wanted to hide them, but I just didn't care. He was too cold for me to care. His skin was like ice, his body limp and lifeless as though he was dead.

Please don't let him be dead.

The thought was a battering ram against my heart, one angry explosion that threatened to rip out of me.

This couldn't be happening.

"Thom," I asked, dreading the answer, or the lack of one.

My magic pushed into him, flooding him with all the strength of a tsunami, the fiery power rushing through bones and muscles and right to his toes. I checked for organ function, for signs of life, and for his magic. It was a checklist in my head—what to do to save a life or some such nonsense. Except, right then, I couldn't have been more worthless.

They were all there—the gentle pulse of his heart, the low gasp of his breath, the calming waves of his magic.

He was alive.

Or at least he should be.

Something was off. Everything was there, but it felt like it was sleeping.

No, like it was numb.

Weird. I don't think I had ever felt anything like that before. That was really not helping me to calm my panic levels. I was going to start accidentally starting fires soon.

"Was he bit?" I asked, giving Sain a glance in hopes of an answer, but the guy was now mumbling and pacing.

I would be glad that he had least got them all here, but he was really proving himself to be a whole lot of useless right now.

If I could peel myself away from Thom I would smack some sense into him, but I wasn't about to leave him. Not now.

"Sain! What happened?" I yelled, causing the man to shriek and step back.

I really didn't have time for this, I was too focused on my magic as it searched through Thom for some kind of injury. To find what was wrong, or a way to heal him.

Only to find nothing.

No cuts.

No bites.

No scary internal bleeding.

Just nothing.

It was as though he was asleep, but dead. Asleep and dead. That battering ram slammed against me again, this time with the strength of a freight train. A really angry freight train.

If I got hit by one more freight train I really wasn't going to survive it.

"Thom?" The question came much louder than I had intended, my frustration arching.

My magic pulsed with the emotion, causing the power to surge through him in a sharp jolt. It wouldn't have hurt him, well not much, I had done the same thing to him centuries before.

I never liked getting up with the baby.

Normally he would jerk awake, swear a bit, and rush off to Rosaline. This time, he didn't so much as twitch.

"Thom?" My fingers wrapped around his arms in a vice, my magic pouring into him like some kind of jump start.

Nothing.

"Thom!" I was getting hysterical. My voice lifted much higher than was safe with those little demons outside, but I didn't even care. I shrieked and shook him, his limp body jostling against the wall before he flopped forwards, long dreads draping over his face like they were the stems of the aged printed flowers behind him.

No response, not from his heart, not from his magic, not from him.

I was officially pissed. Pissed at him for doing this to me. Pissed at Sain for letting this happen. Pissed at me for not being able to fix it.

Worse, I knew I was dangerous. Worse yet, I didn't even care.

"What happened?" The growl ripped out of my chest as I turned to Sain, my magic turning into a full-on inferno as I fought the need to catch something on fire.

It wouldn't be the first time my anger would equal burn victim.

"Sain!" I wasn't going to let him stand there any longer. "What happened?"

The irritating ancient jumped as my hand wrapped

tighter around Thom's arm, afraid he would fall through the floorboards and be lost to another dimension.

"Answer me!"

Sain cowered, dropping on the floor as his hands continually moved one over the other as if he was trying to rub the skin away. The movement was agitated, fearful, and my skin prickled at it, the heat growing. If he didn't answer me soon, I was more than happy to burn that pesky skin from his hands, he clearly wanted it gone.

"I've made a terrible mistake," he said again with that same, horrifying icicle of a voice.

"What mistake? What did you do?" I bellowed and he jerked, looking like he had when we were trapped underground, and they had threatened to take away his mug.

Stupid Drak. If Joclyn ever started acting this way, I would have to take matters into my own hands.

Sain was not one to show emotion, but seeing him like that, seeing the fear in his eyes and the panic in his body, I knew.

He was afraid.

Weird. Even when Edmund had been only yards behind us, he had done little more than walk calmly forward, doling out subtle instructions like he was doing nothing more than making a pie.

Now, however, the emotions came off him in waves, infecting me like a virus. My magic sparked as he leaned closer, the foul smell of his breath drifting through the stagnant air.

"I've made a terrible mistake," he repeated the words again, and I lost it.

"Yes, I got that you loon! What mistake?" The words exploded as I reluctantly left Thom and crawled over to

Sain, the sound of my knees scraping against the dust covered floor loud in the echoes of war that dripped from the window. "What did you do to him? To Dramin? Tell me, Sain, or I will end you right now!"

Sain flinched as if he had been punched, and I froze. The movement was so similar to Ryland, to Joclyn, that it made me wonder what I was seeing. *Who* I was seeing.

The idea that Edmund had somehow infiltrated and manipulated him as well was so not what I needed right then. Not with the echoes of screams and wings that was seeping through the grimy glass. We were already trapped in here with the bomb that was Ryland. I really didn't need to add to that.

Luckily the youngest among us was still unconscious, although he looked like a tangle of limbs on the floor.

My heart raced as I stared at him, waiting for an answer that never came.

"What did you do, Sain?" I was already getting tired of asking, and the man was wilting like an unset gelatin. He clearly wasn't going to tell me anything, no matter how hard I asked.

Stupid Drak!

Fighting the need to either punch him or set him on fire, I jumped away. Everything was too hot, and too angry to be that close.

"Calm, Wynifred," a gentle voice moaned from the other side of the room.

I half-expected Ryland or Thom to be stirring. Instead, it was a man so calm, and so injured that he pulled me right out of my anger. In my panic I had been so focused on Thom and Sain's ridiculousness that I had stepped passed him.

I had vowed to keep Dramin safe, to get him through this, yet here he sat, blood dripping from his neck.

Giving Sain a glare to end all glares, I rushed to Dramin's side trying to ignore the blood the covered his front, the rivers of it still clearly pouring from his neck. The old man was just as limp as Thom, but at least his eyes were open, and the low hissing that came from his throat promised consciousness.

"You can't ignore this forever," I hissed to Sain, grabbing Dramin and helping him to sit so that he looked a little less like a broken marionette.

His skin felt like ice, the cold chill pulling the heat of my magic into him like it was starving. I let it swell into him, going through the checklist like I had with Thom, but this time those check marks turned into giant, red X's.

Broken leg.

Bruised lungs.

And, of course, right to his neck, to the gaping wound and the poisonous magic that was already infecting him.

He had been bitten.

My eyes snapped to his, the fear adding to the panic I already felt. A woman's scream rang loud and clear from right outside, the high note a twisted orchestra to the empty stare Dramin and I were locked in.

There was nothing I could say, he already knew he had been bitten. He already knew there was no way to fix it.

Normally, the bites sent you into a coma fairly quickly, but he still sat before me, very much awake, his painfully weak magic not so much as reacting to the infiltration. Not that it could heal him or stop it.

"Dramin, I—"

"I am fine, Wynifred," he cut me off, his weak voice riddled with a plea that he didn't need to speak aloud, an acknowledgement that, Drak or not, he had known all along.

He had known from the moment the sky had exploded with those things. When you can't run, and you can't fight, there is only one other possible outcome.

He may be accepting of whatever fate he had become trapped in. Too bad for him, I wasn't quite ready to give up on him just yet.

I wasn't going to tell him that, though.

Instead, I nodded once in faux understanding and his face cracked into a sad, little smile. Pooling my magic into his neck, I let the power surge around the open wound that blood still poured from and began stitching the skin back together. The process was slow and arduous as I fought against the tainted magic, fought against a wound that didn't seem to want to be healed.

Not as if I gave it another choice. Edmund's poison may be stubborn, but it obviously had never come in contact with me.

"I can fix things as well as I can destroy them," I said as the bleeding stopped, the skin continuing to weave itself together until it was nothing more than a fine, pink line; sealing the poison and the possible death sentence inside.

"One neck is hardly worth the trouble." He sighed.

My pride prickled a bit at the depth of his deceivingly kind voice.

"It is to me." I could barely get the words out. "Are you okay?"

He knew as well as I did that 'okay' was relative at this point.

"I'm fine," he repeated, his frail hand moving over mine in a motion that looked more like a slowed down replay rather than reality, the contact was heavy and somewhat calm as he tried to comfort me without magic.

He had been weak and tired in his room back at Rioseco. Now, he looked as though all life had been sucked out of him. His eyes were wide and searching, although the way he stared into space I had a feeling he wasn't looking for something that still existed on this planet.

Or someone.

I understood that all too well.

"Dramin?" I was surprised at the shake in my voice, the way my hand clung to his arm, a fear I didn't fully understand moving into me.

He said nothing. He only looked at me with the same confusion I felt, the screaming from outside seeping through the shuttered window like a fog.

I felt more of a responsibility toward this man than I had anyone before, with the exception of one. Despite keeping him alive, saving him wasn't going to repay what I had done. But I was still going to try, even if it was starting to feel like a failure.

"We will survive this," I said, the promise feeling more like a lie than I had meant it. "But I do need to know what happened. Did something attack Thom? And what in the world is your father on about?"

Dramin opened his mouth to speak, the fear in his eyes growing before the loud boom of Sain's voice shook through me, my muscles tensing back to their panicked knit.

"It is not the way of the Drak, son," Sain heaved from behind me, but there wasn't a drop of that deep, echoing sight in it. This time his arrogance was dripping with the reverence he always seemed to think he was owed.

"Oh, now you talk!" I roared, turning on the Drak and

his gross regality as though it was an ignition switch. A freaking, flame flying from my fingertip's ignition switch.

Sain flinched at the sparks that were twitching from my fingers, his eyes growing wide. But even with the fear there, he was no longer cowering like he had been. Now, he stood tall, much taller than me, and puffed out his chest as if he was an animal going to battle.

I guessed, in a way, he thought he was.

Let him try.

I would tear him limb from limb.

Or burn him limb from limb, because fire magic.

"*What* is not the way of the Drak, Sain?" I spat, my voice dripping like bile as I faced him. My patience had evaporated before we had even left the cave, it had snapped when I had seen Thom, and now it was hanging by a thread.

He really shouldn't be pushing me. He was clearly going to embark on this dangerous journey anyway.

"We do not reveal what was seen in sight, unless it is asked of us." Pompous, arrogant...

"I'm not asking about sight." My words were more growl than actual English. "I am asking about now, and what happened to Thom, and whatever freaking mistake you made."

"It is the same," he continued with a smile that made me want to slap him. "We cannot disclose that which deals with sight unless it is asked of us."

His voice was that conceited calm again, the same tone he had used on Joclyn only days before. I was beginning to understand why she had reacted the way she had. I didn't think I had ever been spoken to in such a derogatory way. Even when we had run from the dungeons of Prague, he had been kind as he directed me. But this? This reeked of some underlying pretentiousness that I must have been allergic to.

I was breaking out in hives. At least it felt like it with how my skin was all prickly.

"Well, I am asking."

"You did not touch the water, Wynifred." Sain smiled, the same underlying slime shining through before it was gone, washed away with the echoes of murder that drifted up from the street.

"Do you really think that matters anymore?" I didn't restrain the snarl.

It still didn't make sense. Not with what he had always done for Ilyan, not with the way his face was contorted in such a desperate way.

Why wouldn't he tell me?

"The rules will always matter, Wynifred," Sain said with that same hard line. "It is all we have, and they will always matter."

"I don't care, Sain! Not anymore, not after this," I was yelling now, gesturing to where Dramin sagged lazily against the wall, and where Thom had collapsed. "You need to tell me, and you need to tell me now!"

I was louder than I should have been, and I knew it. The human sounding shrieks of a Vilýs erupted right outside the boarded-up window, and I jumped, the scratching of claws joining right behind as my voice drew them right to us.

Sain and Dramin turned to the window as I did, our eyes wide for a moment as we waited to see if the ancient shield Ilyan had placed around this house would hold.

A three-hundred-year-old shield, at that. Dramin shifted away from the window, clearly doubting it. Ilyan was strong, but I would be impressed if that thing didn't have more than a few cracks. I couldn't leave a shield up past a few decades, after all.

The light that slivered through the wood planking that covered the window flickered as the little beasts moved over it, shimmying over the window to see inside. To see us. Light strobed over the room we waited, staring at the figures just behind the heavy wood planks.

My heart was beating so fast my chest hurt, the tension tight through every muscle as I waited, magic at the ready.

The flickering lights slowed, even though the creatures remained. Waiting, as if they knew we were still here. Dramin released a ragged breath. I would love to join him, but I was still locked in that tightly bound coil, those things were still right there.

Normally I would make some bad 70s reference, or quote a song, but nothing was coming.

Leave it to rat birds to suck the 70s right out of me.

"You can't keep this to yourself, Sain," I whispered, looking back at him as the terrifying sounds of the rats that flew outside the window grew louder, helping to drive my point home. "We just came through a massacre, Sain. Ryland is damned, Thom's down for the count, your own son was injured, and you are spouting the 'rules of the Drak'?"

His reasoning was all the more ridiculous now, a fact that he was clearly aware of. His eyes grew wider with each word, his body shaking as though he had been struck down by some ten-second flu, the symptoms leaving as soon as they came.

Stupid Drak with his stubborn Drak-ness.

"What do you know, Sain?" I whispered, barely louder than the rats outside the window, the darn things beginning to scurry around again.

"I know nothing."

"Bullshit." Could I just shoot fire at him now? Nothing serious, just enough to make him jump. Anything to get a sensical answer out of the man. Hell, come to that maybe, if I threw him out the window or dangled him in front of the little monsters, he would talk.

I pinched the bridge of my nose in agitation, hating how the old tendencies so quickly came to mind.

Torture. Pain. At least I wasn't trying to seduce him. Even the thought brought a fresh wash of bile to my throat.

I hated more that I could make it work.

I wondered if I could get the same result by making him listen to Bruce Springsteen.

Doubtful.

"You obviously know something, Sain. You did something wrong, remember? You saw this and then lied to us that it had already happened, why?"

I didn't dare look away from him, I let my glare fly free, waiting for him to flinch, waiting for him to cower. He did neither.

Where's Bruce Springsteen when you need him?

"We need to get out of here."

So much for forced calm, any attempt at stability snapped in half like a popsicle stick. My magic pulsed, and I could smell the smoke, even if I had no idea what I had set on fire.

"Excuse me?" I was sure my voice had hit an octave that wasn't natural, but I really didn't care anymore. "Answer the question, Sain."

"It's not safe." The suggestion was not only ridiculous, but an obvious side-step.

Must. Not. Burn.

"Nowhere is safe!" More rat birds joined the first as I

roared, and both Sain and Dramin flinched. I looked to Dramin, desperately hoping he would back me up, but the man was clearly scared of his own shadow and he sagged farther against the wall in an attempt to stay upright.

"Ilyan told us to come here. He will be here. We aren't going anywhere." I was firm.

Why couldn't he answer the freaking question?

"We need to leave," he repeated the same phrase like someone had skipped back a chapter. The inflection and everything was the same. Everything except my reaction.

"Answer the question, Sain. What did you do? What did you see?" I yelled. I raged. And I called more of those things to the window, Sain's eyes growing wide as he turned to them. I may not be able to dangle him in front of the beasties, but I could sure dangle them in from of him.

"We need to leave."

"That's it!" I lunged at him before he had a chance to move away, my tiny hands wrapping around his arms and holding him in place. Sheer strength kept him there as I locked my magic inside of myself, afraid of what it would do to him. I was sure, by the pain in his face, that he could feel the heat against his skin. He could feel the warning.

Rats. Fire. Pick your poison old man.

I needed my answer.

"Knock it off, Sain," I growled, fully aware my voice was feral from behind the clench in my jaw. "We can't go anywhere. Even if you saw something, we are still stuck in this tiny room full of invalids. I can't wake Ryland up without risking him bringing the whole building down; Dramin can barely move, let alone walk; and Thom… Thom. What did you do, Sain?"

"We need—"

"No!" I snapped, cutting him off with a crack that mixed

with the screams from outside, the rats that still clawed at the window. He flinched from the outburst, and I was certain I had accidently pushed some magic into him. I really didn't care anymore. "No more. You need to tell me. I can see in your eyes that something happened. I don't care about your asinine rules. I respect them, but if you keep this up, more people are going to get hurt. Someone is going to die. This time, you have to tell me. I'm not going back out into that massacre with this many useless bodies unless you talk. So, talk."

Sain stared at me unblinking, his body frozen where I held him. The dim light of the room wavered as the rats continued to claw at glass and wood, surrounded by their tiny screams and scratches in a room that was as much like a prison as the one we had met in.

A prison that had forged a bond, a trust, that I don't think anything could break. Now, I was starting to question it. Styx broke up for a reason, after all.

Of course, it probably wasn't quite as world-ending. Well, apocalyptically world-ending, anyway. I could still feel that sting.

"Talk, Sain." My voice was soft, a fact he noticed right away, his body relaxing under mine as my hands dropped. "Talk."

"The sights are broken, Wynifred," he whispered the same thing he had for days. I still wasn't one hundred percent sure what he was talking about, but after being accosted by winged monsters I was starting to get an idea. "I have seen things since the earth was nothing but a barren waste, and men and magic existed together in peace. Millennia of sight. And only now do things break. Things that I have seen centuries before are now nothing but a Zlomený. Things seen are now broken with lies. I saw the city under attack, yet it was not. I saw the end of Edmund, yet it failed to come. Nothing is certain anymore."

He looked away from me to Dramin, his eyes hooded with guilt as I waited in the faded symphony of pain and fighting that drifted through the walls.

A shiver moved over my spine, the fear of the uncertain feeling raw and cold against my bones. My life had always been influenced by the Drak. For hundreds of years, Sain had guided my movements as Edmund's assassin, and even after he had gone, we still relied on the sights he had left us with. Prophecies that one after another had come true. Infallible truths that we had followed. Even with Ilyan, we followed his sight, knowing, without question, what would happen.

Now, there was question.

Now, there was fault.

Now, there was death.

My heart pulled to Thom as though he had called my name, the shaking organ thundering against my ribs. Darn heartbreak, I was trapped in far too much agony than I would like to admit. I may be a powerful assassin, but right then I wanted to just grab Thom, run away, and make everything all better, through crying or hysterical fit I wasn't sure.

I guess I had been reduced to a blubbering teenager.

Instead, I was going to settle for answers.

"What happened to Thom, Sain?" I asked, forcing myself from Thom to Sain, fixing him with a scowl that I hoped was enough to hide the glistening in my eyes.

Blubbering teenager indeed.

"I received sight while we walked through the city, and it told me of the dangers of this place. Of where we were heading..." I tensed as he paused, the incessant claws of the

Vilỳs sounding louder for some reason. The danger Sain spoke of seemed far too close. "I tried to tell him to stop, to convince him to find Ilyan, but he refused. He began to yell, and the shield dropped only moments before the Vilỳs tore the sky apart."

I nodded, I had seen this after all. I had seen the shield fall, and the screaming. It made sense, but it also stunk to high heavens. I may have seen Thom yell, but it was so out of character for him that even the memory made me uncomfortable.

"They were everywhere..." His voice was hollow as his eyes drifted out of focus, his memory pulling him back as mine did.

Faint screams echoed from outside, making it easy to remember, to feel the fear that was infecting air and souls. "Thom and I tried to fight them off, but then he was hit with an attack from behind us. From you, from Ryland, from Joclyn? I don't know. But he fell to the ground. It took all my strength to escape those things and drag them both here. I had to keep them safe. He's my best friend, and my son..."

The power in his voice left as he sagged down to the cower that was quickly becoming his trademark. His shoulders hunched over as he slunk down next to his son, the guilt clearly raging through him.

I wanted to tell him everything was okay, remind him that he had gotten them here, but something about his story was gnawing at me. Digging into my bones, until I was questioning everything I had seen.

Sain couldn't be lying, he was trustworthy. He had helped me. but nothing was fitting. Nothing was adding up.

Sain had said Thom had been hit with an attack from either Ryland, myself, or someone near us. However, I hadn't been shooting out attacks, and even though Ryland had, by the time he had started to do so, Sain and the others had already been gone.

I wanted to say I was remembering wrong, that they were still there, but I had seen the empty street moments before Ryland had gone bonkers. I could still feel the panic when their magic had vanished, when I hadn't been able to find them, of not knowing where they had gone.

I stared at Sain blankly as I tried to push the questions from my mind, only to have Joclyn's voice fill my head—the deep conspiratorial whisper as she confided in me about her father and how she didn't trust him.

She had stood in that hallway and looked at me, begging for me to understand her, to trust her about Sain and whatever it was he was hiding. But, I couldn't. I had been locked in that prison with him. I had escaped the city with him. He had saved me. How could I not trust someone who had gone so far for me? She just didn't like her father was all.

Then why was it grating on me right now?

She didn't trust him.

I was starting not to trust him, either, even more with this whole mistake thing he was still avoiding.

"What did you do wrong?" I needed him to answer, I needed to know he was trustworthy, and as much as I hated saying it, I needed to know that Joclyn was wrong.

She couldn't be right.

Not now.

Not about him.

Because that would mean... my heart pulled me to Thom, but I couldn't look away from Sain, his focus looking from Dramin to me in obvious confusion. It was a look that was so out of place for a Drak that it took all my strength not to laugh.

Or punch him in the face. Probably punch him.

Prove her wrong Sain, please.

"What was your serious mistake?" It took everything to keep my voice low and calm, but my panic was reaching a boiling point. My frustration rumbling right back into being as the bastard stared at me, his wide eyes dropping briefly before he jerked so fast he may have well been zapped.

"Dramin," Sain rumbled in the deep, heady tone that was his. "There is a room over here if I remember correctly. I think it's time you lie down."

"No, Sain," I hissed, jumping up as he did. "You don't get to run away from me."

"I need to assist my son."

"You need to answer me." My snap was as hard as the scowl I was giving him,

Poor Dramin was trapped between us, his body sagging, his eyes hooded. He didn't so much as say a word as his father pulled him to standing and half dragged, half assisted him to a room I was sure hadn't been used in a decade and would be so dust covered you wouldn't be able to tell the rats from the dust bunnies.

"We will talk in a moment, Wynifred."

That was so not good enough for me.

"Sain!" I hissed, careful to keep my voice low, not that it mattered.

The little beasts already knew we were here. I hated to admit it, but Sain was right, we needed to leave, which made perfect sense seeing as he was taking Dramin away from where he had insisted we needed to get to. You don't lay down when you need to leave.

My confusion was turning into a beast in my chest, that same gnawing feeling digging deeper.

I didn't trust this.

Everything was falling apart, and it all rotated around one very unconscious and possibly dead guy.

Geeze, even thinking that was a stab in the heart.

Shuffling across the floor, I collapsed beside Thom, desperately hoping that I could just roll him over and he would grin at me, but he still slumped against the wall, like he was dead.

That iron fist punched me in the gut as the thought shoved its way back into me. My hand pressed against him, my magic plunging into him in a desperation to feel something, to feel some trace of an injury.

Still, there was nothing.

No sign of an attack. Nothing to heal.

It didn't make any sense.

If he had been attacked as Sain had said, there should be some sign of that happening, some trace of what had hurt him and was keeping him trapped in whatever this was. I couldn't even find a bite, however.

The tension that had taken up residence in my chest tried to dislodge itself, but it wasn't working, so I sat, listening to the low buzz of Sain and Dramin's voices. The nondescript argument bleeding through the old door and supercharged through my agitation.

Fingers shaking, I grabbed his hand, wrapping my fingers around his, only for ice to drench my soul as my fingertips grazed a dozen raised bumps on the palm of his hand. Turning his hand over, my eyes widened at what appeared to be slowly growing boils.

What in the multiverse was this?

I had searched his body for injury. I should have felt this. I should have seen it. But there was nothing to feel, nothing inside of him.

I was staring right at it, but my magic couldn't find it. There was nothing there to feel.

Clinging to Thom's hand, I tried to pick out something, anything, that would give me a clue as to what was going on. On what game Sain was playing at.

There was nothing.

Nothing but the questions and inconsistencies that piled up the more I tried to ignore them.

It didn't make any sense.

Sain's story. His reaction. Thom's injury.

And still the irritating Drak hadn't even answered my questions.

I've made a terrible mistake.

What terrible mistake, Sain? What have you done?

I kept trying to push my doubts away, yet they kept coming back like the waves on the beach, faster and farther in every time. I had to trust him.

I had to.

After everything, I didn't have any reason to doubt.

Still, something wasn't adding up. That was what was hurting the most.

What hadn't been said was almost louder than what had.

18

WYN

I SAT on the dust covered floor, my hand wrapped around Thom's as I tried to decipher the voices that came through the door, a task that was proving to be impossible thanks to the sound of the Vilỳs that were still trying to get in.

The room was full of the sound of scratches, mumbles, and screams.

Even though the attack was wearing down and the sound of screams were coming farther apart and from farther away, the Vilỳs that clawed at the shutters still remained. Scratching claws pulled at the wooden barrier of the walls in a desperate attempt to get in.

Ilyan's barrier was holding, but listening to the endless scratching and the tiny screams of the rats was increasing my agitation level. What I wouldn't give to open the window and rip their heads off.

The tiny little things had haunted my last few days, they had it coming.

"Wyn?" The weak voice drifted through the dark from behind me, and I jumped. Like full-on head to ceiling, landing on my feet in a warrior stance, jumped. I was ready for the attack, instead there was only Ryland, his tangle of limbs twisting back to life.

Dust twisted through the air, spreading over the floor in filthy snow banks as he began to wake. He groaned my name, attempting to pull himself out of the drunken stupor I had placed him in. His mind was muddled enough that he wasn't a danger at that moment, but that meant very little when it came to him.

Thom's hand fell from my hold, landing on his chest with a soft thud as I scuttled to his side. My blood-soaked jeans scraped over the rough wood floor, bare feet gripping through the dust as I reached him, the moans of confusion beginning to twist into the sounds of pain and fear.

Compared to Thom and Dramin, Ryland was boiling hot, his magic way too close to the surface, ready to explode. I wanted anything but to touch his furnace, but he was too dangerous to leave alone.

My magic rushed right to his heart, to the battered organ that was the gateway for whatever Edmund was still doing to him. Placing a tight shield around his heart, I locked away whatever power he had been infected with. I already knew it might not be enough to help him, not with the screams that were dripping in the air. But I had to try, loud noises would attract more of the little beasts, and Ryland could be as loud as they came.

The last thing we needed was a swarm of the rats right outside our window, the few that were there were making a big enough dent on their own.

"Ryland," I soothed, my voice calm as I leaned toward him, hand and magic pressing against him in way that I hoped was comforting.

Thankfully, he reacted to it. His whimpers fading until

he curled into himself with a snap, his voice ripping out of him loud and angry.

Well crap, so much for being comforting, I was in trouble.

First comes panic then comes magical explosions. Then comes a missing wall and little winged rats ripping at your flesh.

It was like those rodent cookie books, but with death. Well, and my mouse had wings.

"Ry," I tried again, furiously trying to strengthen the shield around his heart before all hell went down. "It's Wyn, Ry. I'm right here."

"Nononononononono." He ripped at his hair, writhed on the floor, and tried to pull away from me, but I held on like he was my life raft rather than the other way around.

He was a sinking ship and he was going to take us all down.

I knew I should knock him out, but with both Dramin and Thom unconscious, and us needing to get out of here, he really needed to be less of a log and more of a walking zombie.

Hopefully the kind that doesn't create magical explosions.

"Ryland," I tried again, careful to keep my voice low as I leaned closer to him.

I was sure he couldn't hear me over the moans and panicked mumbles that were dripping from him as he pulled at his hair.

"No, Father, I won't, I won't."

He was moving closer to insanity instead of away from it. Great.

"It's okay, Ryland." Yeah, it wasn't completely true, but I was more focused on shielding his heart and his mind from freaking Edmund right then. It had been so easy before, but it was almost like the infection had grown, Edmund's control was everywhere.

I needed to shield him, and not burn him from the inside out. Well, I always said I enjoyed the challenge. I would probably smile at it if we weren't stuck so deep in this whole end of the world apocalypse.

Magic wrapped around his heart, smothering him in comfort. He instantly calmed and quieted. Seeing as his body was relaxing and not writhing in pain, my fire magic hadn't attempted to eat him.

I was counting this as a win. Well, I did.

Until the laugh.

The childlike laugh froze through me, tensing every muscle, breaking my heart into a million shards of anger and pain. It took everything in me not to burn him to a crisp.

Not now, anytime but now.

Rosaline.

I had grown used to the pain of hearing her in my dreams and nightmares, but here?

In the middle of a war?

She laughed again and my magic slid, a flame of power or fire twisting right into Ryland and sending him screaming before I could slide the powerful wall back into place.

My heart was a freaking rock as the laugh echoed so perfectly that I was sure she was lying right next to Ryland. I turned, expecting to see her, to see the blood slither down her face the way it had in the last moment of her life.

It was only Ryland. Only Ryland and the sound of my child that was coming from inside of him. No, not inside of him. The sound was clearly in my head... but how?

Faced with the end of the world, and I lose it, I had expected better from me.

I could do better. My heart may as well have been dying as I ignored the laugh, keeping the shield around Ryland, the guy thankfully calming as his bright blue eyes shifted to look at me in thanks.

Thanks that were drowned out by the laugh, the sound still drifting from inside of him.

Okay, something was clearly going on.

"Mommy." Her voice was clear. It was calm. It was beautiful.

I couldn't stop the way my magic flared, and my heart crashed inside of me. I would never be free of this, free of this loss that was trying to rip me in two jagged pieces.

I tried to move away from the sound, from the voices, but Ryland's hand was like a vice now. No matter how hard I pulled, he wouldn't let me go. It was no longer Ryland we needed to be concerned about. It was me.

Tears trailed down my face, as my magic caught fire to the floor, long flames licking over the surface in twisting snakes that circled around us as if there was a trail of gasoline there, I tried to keep the sobs trapped inside. But they exploded the same as the fire, a pop of light and flame that reached toward the ceiling. Ryland jumped, gripping my hand as the voice came again and again.

"Mommy."

Jerking, I turned to Ryland, ready to yell at him to release me, to let me run as far away from here as possible. Instead, the kid was calm. Calmer than I think I had ever seen him. His eyes were, innocent, the plea for help clear without him so much as saying anything.

It froze me.

"Take it out," he moaned, his voice an echo alongside Rosaline's laugh. "Take it out."

"Take what out?" My voice warbled as his hand tightened around mine, his face trailing with fresh tears.

"Take him out. Take it out of me." His voice was calm, his eyes pleading, his scarred hand pressing against his heart, and I knew.

I had seen the detestable thing enough, I should have known it was there. We all should have.

No wonder Ryland was a man condemned. He was possessed. Controlled.

The blade.

The blade that had been made from Rosaline's soul... it was inside him. It couldn't be.

I didn't want it to be, but I already knew that was a fool's hope.

"Mommy?"

I cringed against the voice, the way it echoed in my head and pulled at my heart.

"Can you hear her, too?" I won't deny there was hope there, hope that he would understand.

Hope that someone would finally understand.

But he couldn't, the pain, the desperation in his eyes, it was all there for another reason.

"Where is it?" I asked, keeping my voice low, as if I could stop the awful truth of his response that I already knew was coming.

He only continued to press the palm of his scarred hand against his heart.

Dread infected me and I closed my eyes, embracing the black behind my lids as both scream and laugh rumbled in my mind.

From the moment Edmund had destroyed her life, I had vowed to release Rosy from the prison she had been entombed within. And Ryland held one of the pieces of her soul.

There wasn't any question about what I was supposed to do. There never had been. I would have moved mountains to help her, despite the pain.

It just so happened that this mountain involved cutting open an innocent boy's heart, removing a piece of my child's soul, and miraculously putting said heart back together again before his magic died, taking him with it.

I had removed hearts for centuries, keeping them beating for Edmund's use, keeping the magic alive so he could devour it. Given that, this should be a simple task, like breaking into a Pink Floyd concert.

Yeah, I so got this.

"Okay, Ryland," I promised, letting my magic swell around him as he smiled, and I pushed him back to sleep.

His head hit the floor with a painfully loud smack as a held breath seeped from his now relaxed lips, and plunged the room back into near silence. The scratching of the Vilÿs was somehow becoming comforting, it was the chicken scratch whispers of Sain and Dramin that was setting me on edge.

Sain. He was being anything but trustworthy right now, his actions were the equivalent of a blazing warning light. I would knock him out and restrain him, you know, if I could handle four invalids on my own.

I couldn't have him walking in on this, I needed to get to work.

Ryland's chest was riddled with the same scars I had seen in the dungeon, the same scars that moved through my palm. Line after line, one over the other as the blade had been plunged into him again and again, a reminder of what he had been forced to do.

The kid was scars inside and out. Ryland's life had been stolen before it had even had a chance to begin.

It was time to take that back.

"Mommy?"

My magic reacted at the sound of her voice, plunging into the beating organ that held the core of his magic, his life.

You weren't supposed to let your magic enter another person's heart, strictly speaking. I knew Ilyan did it all the time, but he was insanely strong and could control his magic so perfectly that there wasn't any risk. He could defend himself against the soul's automatic defense system, you know, that little response that tried to destroy anything that entered the heart of another. That powerful wave of magic that was currently trying to beat me down.

Painful pricks of energy zapped against my magic, surging through me in a warning that I already knew I couldn't heed. I needed to find the blade.

For Ryland. For Rosy.

The magical assault punches were coming fast now, his magic doing anything it could to stop me. I didn't have much time. I sliced into his heart, searching for the shard, for the poison that was infecting me, my magic reaching everywhere in its search.

"Mommy!" Her yell of excitement rang through me as though she was standing right next to me, her arms opened wide, ready to jump on me.

And then I realized why.

I hadn't felt her magic in centuries, but there it was, embedded in a shard of blood mixed with souls and magic so small I wasn't even sure Ilyan could have found them. I had only found it because of Rosaline.

She had showed me the way.

Her magic was as beautiful as it had always been, incredibly strong, so joyous. It was like coming home again to feel it so close. Yet, it was tainted by the other souls that had been stolen to make the blade, the malice that ran off them so strong it was like bile against my tongue.

Nasty and bitter.

My chest constricted painfully as I pushed my magic farther, wrapping it around the tiny shard as though it was precious, cradling the malice alongside the beauty.

With one strong heave, I pulled it free from the softly beating tissue that it had been lodged in.

Ryland's magic recoiled as the toothpick-sized object was released, his power rebelling against what it was and what it had done to him.

His wasn't the only one.

Even with the strength of Rosaline's magic within the precious cargo, the malice and poisoned magic that ran through was like an acid against my own. My magic rebelled, attempting to pull away from the heady toxin. To leave it where it was and get out of dodge.

No, I couldn't do that. Not to her.

"Mommy?"

Hatred infected me as I pulled and carefully twisted the shard away from his beating heart and through his body until it pressed against the skin from the inside, a point of pressure that grew outward. His grey-tinged skin tented before it pushed through, a thick ribbon of the brightest blood coming behind.

Blood trailed over his skin, dripping onto the floor in a great pool of red. I didn't see that, however. I only saw the tip of the blade, the shard of knife covered in his scarlet blood, the piece jagged and broken as though it was nothing more than sandstone.

I didn't dare touch it, yet I couldn't fight the pull as it dragged me closer. Begging me to hold it, to take it into me. I had never felt anything like it, this need. It was as though the blade itself was power, as though it could give that power to me.

His warm blood rolled over my fingers as I pulled it from his chest, the tiny blade resting in the palm of my hand in a streak of crimson. Staring at me.

Ryland's magic worked to heal him as mine recoiled back into me, but I was trapped, staring at the blade in both a fear and a need I didn't understand.

Yes, I knew I should be afraid of it. Afraid of what it was, what it did. But this fear was different. It was rooted in possibilities. I had no intention of using the thing, but part of me... Part of me couldn't help wondering what it meant, what would happen if I did.

I shook my head as her laugh echoed in a haunting void that I hadn't heard before, and I shivered, letting the last of the ill-placed power leave me.

I held a piece of my little girl's soul in my hand.

That was all.

Nothing more. I was better than that.

I felt dirty for thinking of it in any other way, for letting those thoughts infect me as they had.

I sat quite still as I closed my fingers around the precious piece, holding it close, as I had held her so many times before.

"I'll set you free, my darling girl," I whispered, my voice drowned out by the creatures who clawed at the windows, their voices loud in their desperate haste to find entry.

"Everything all right?" Sain's voice erupted behind me.

I jumped, pulling Ryland's shirt over the now healed wound, my fist tightening around the shard. My heart was thundering inside of me, a slither of vile secrecy snaking its way over me, a fear I hadn't expected following behind.

The shard.

I couldn't let anyone know I had it. They would take it away. They would take my daughter away. They would use her soul against someone else. I couldn't let that happen.

"Wyn?"

"Yeah, everything's fine." My voice sounded dead. "Ry woke up, so I put him back out. I figured that's better for now."

I tried to bring as much life back to my voice as I could, but I wasn't sure it was working. Everything around me was moving in slow motion, my magic flaring abruptly as I over-critically inspected my surroundings. Everything from Thom's unconscious body to the dust mites seemed untrustworthy.

What was happening to me?

I understood a basic need to protect something so precious. However, paranoia had never been my thing.

I shook my head again and pushed the emotion away, glad when it slipped away and took some of that darn tension with it.

"Dramin's asleep, too."

At the mention of Dramin, my mind pulled away from the shard of the soul's blade, right to the conversation before. Frustration and anger followed right behind.

"Does that mean you are going to tell me now?" My voice still shook with residual anxiety as Sain's focus snapped to me. His eyes were dark as I pulled him right back into the conversation, I was sure he had hoped I had forgotten.

"Tell you what?"

"Don't treat me like a fool, Sain. You may be one of the first, but that doesn't make you any better than the rest of us."

"That is a debatable opinion."

"And yet, you are capable of 'making mistakes' like us all." My voice was laced with teenage angst, but I let it flow, grateful when his eyes narrowed disdainfully at me. "Stop playing games, Sain."

He continued to glare at me, his eyes harder than I had ever seen them. The same fear was back in his eyes, but I didn't look away. I didn't dare.

"As I said, I have made a terrible mistake. But it is not what you assume," he began again, his eyes continuing to glare into me a look of pure anger and horrified fear running over his features. "I thought they were gone... but they aren't. They are going to find me. They are going to find you."

"Who is going to find you?" I was scared to ask, scared of the answer, scared of what it might mean for us, and why he wanted us to run.

"They know what we did—" Sain's words fell from the air as the door below us opened, the yells of the Vilỳs rang clear as the heavy footsteps echoed up the stairwell, large and heavy.

"He's found me. He's going to kill us all." Sain's voice growled through the dark as the door opened, my magic reacting before I had a chance to stop it.

19

WYN

A RIBBON of flame streamed from my hand like someone had embedded a flame thrower inside of me, the powerful attack intercepting the door and turning it, and whoever stood behind it, to dust.

Well, it would have if the people behind the door weren't two of the most powerful beings in existence.

The attack flattened in mid-air as though it had hit a glass pane, ribbons of heat and flame fanning into spirals of harmless smoke. Rings spiraled before they vanished, revealing the scowling, blonde-haired man right behind.

"Wynifred!" Ilyan's voice was a snap of scolding as he walked into the room, Joclyn right on his heels.

Yep, Ilyan was pissed, and it probably wasn't just that I had shot fire at his head. I mean, that could have been part of it, but you know... I just blew up a door, in the middle of a frightening Vilỳ invasion.

So, now they were coming and we had one less line of defense.

Well, darn it all.

"Sorry, Ilyan." I was sure I wasn't going to get any kind of forgiveness from him.

Not with the low scoff of frustration that rumbled from him as he took stock of the room, the lines of his face deepening.

I could only guess how this looked to him—Sain and I facing each other as if we were about to attack, Thom and Ryland unconscious on the floor, and a still fresh pool of blood glittering in the corner.

Well, multiple corners. Dramin, and now Ry. Let's hope no one asked about Ry.

"What has happened here?" His accent was thick, and while I wanted to recoil in expectation of his temper, the other side only stood up taller, facing him as my eyebrow arched uncomfortably.

"In case you haven't noticed, my lord, the city is under attack by about a million of Edmund's flying rats. Dramin was bit, Ryland's a mess, and Thom..." My voice lost its sass as it caught on the emotion in my throat. I stopped, staring at him with wide eyes as everything I had said clicked into place.

"Dramin was bit?" Jos' voice was a shriek through the dark as her eyes grew so big I half-expected them to pop out of her head, but she only blinked and ran into the adjoining room. For anyone else, it was a reaction that might border on insanity. For her, I was sure her magic had told her exactly where her brother lay.

Sain jerked forward as if he was going to follow her. It's a good thing he didn't because I would have full-on tackled him.

I wasn't letting him out of my sight, especially now that Ilyan was here. Sain seemed to understand that, either that or he just liked to glare at me. Which would be great if he wasn't staring at me with that same dark look in his eyes, the fear and warning playing deep into my soul.

Ilyan rushed to his brothers' side, moving from Ryland to Thom as he checked them, trying to heal them. Meanwhile, Sain and I were locked together, the unspoken message screamed at me from where I stood.

The old man kept looking from me to Ilyan as though the king was the enemy, as though he was afraid of him.

As if Ilyan was the one who was coming for him.

That couldn't be right.

"Sain? Wynifred?" I jumped as Ilyan said my name, finally pulling me away from Sain's death stare.

My magic tugged uncomfortably as Ilyan's shoulders tensed as he pressed his hands against Thom's. The pulse of his magic was so strong I could feel the shadows weave through the room like a radiant heat.

"Ilyan?"

"What happened?" He didn't even look at us when he said it. His focus was only on Thom.

My stomach was officially twisting itself into a pretzel, "I saw them right before the Vilÿs attacked—"

"He was hit by a stray attack from somewhere behind us," Sain interrupted, his voice stronger than it had been for the past few minutes. He was nearly yelling, his gravelly voice lined with a power that made me want to smack him. What happened to his cowering nonsense? "I don't know what it was or where it came from. It looked unfamiliar to me. But he's been like this ever since."

Unfamiliar to him? That was not what he had said before.

I couldn't figure out what in the world he was playing at. Nothing was falling into place. Everything was too tense— Sain was acting like a loon, my daughter's voice was talking to me, Thom was injured so badly no one could tell what was going on...

I was going to develop a hump from the tension that was pressing against my spine.

"Is he all right, Ilyan?" I asked, ice trailing over me as my hands writhed together.

"I'm not sure." It was an honest answer, but the honesty was so not helping. The panic was lingering, spreading as it snaked around us like acid, pricking against me.

"His magic is fine. He is fine..."

"But you just can't wake him," I finished his thought for him as he stood, the sloppy braid that trailed down his back only a foot away from me.

Ilyan nodded, and my stomach dropped. I knew I should at least be happy he was okay, but the mysteries kept adding up, just like the little rats that were clawing at the window.

"That doesn't explain the scabs, though," I grumbled, my mind still trying desperately to put the puzzle together.

"What scabs?" Ilyan asked in Czech.

"Perhaps scabs is the wrong word." I said nothing more as I moved to the other side of Thom, his limp hands soft against mine as I turned them over.

The palms were covered with the boils I had seen before, except now they were more akin to open wounds, each angry, red mark a perfect circle. The raw flesh looked as though someone had dropped acid onto the tender skin and melted it away.

Ilyan's face hardened, his jaw tensing into a tight line. "Přetížení dávka."

My heart seized. I knew exactly what that was, even though I had never seen it. But seeing it on Thom... The world must have stopped spinning on its axis.

"But how?" I asked even though I knew. There was only one way to get Přetížení dávka.

An overstimulation of magic.

It was much like what could happen if you pushed too much magic into someone who couldn't handle it. They would drown in it, their bodies essentially exploding from the inside out. I had done something similar a few times on weaker opponents. It was a fascinating way to die.

This, was different though... If magic was heroin, this would be the equivalent of an overdose. Taking too much, or stealing too much.

I had seen the same sores on Edmund for years, and now it was starting to make sense. He was burning himself from the inside out as he gorged on the magic in the hearts I had brought him, strengthening as he pushed himself right to the limit, only to bring himself back, stronger than before.

But Thom?

Even after all the centuries we had lived and worked by Edmund's law, I didn't think he would ever stoop to that.

"He wouldn't."

"I agree. I do not see Thomas engaging in such darkness." Ilyan's voice was heavy and distanced, his hand soft against Thom's jaw before he stood. "But there is only one way for this to happen..."

"I don't want to believe this, Ilyan." The words barely made it out through the clench in my teeth.

"I don't know what else it could be. The boils, the inability to wake..." Ilyan whispered, his blue eyes sparking with a hope that I could completely understand.

Sain, however, didn't seem to feel the same pull. The man was strangely quiet considering we were talking about his best friend. For having been through so much together, he didn't seem very broken up.

"Did you know, Sain?" Awe, disbelief, and a hurt I didn't think I could fully explain rushed out.

He shook his head.

That's it, he just shook his head. The lack of emotion was unsettling, especially given the last few minutes with his panic and need to run.

My distrust of him was turning into a festering boil.

Ilyan rushed over to check on Ryland again, shifting the two men around until they lay side-by-side like bodies prepared for burial.

It was creepy. No, it was downright terrifying.

"We need to move," Ilyan announced as Joclyn squeezed back through the old cracked door, rushing over to me and wrapping her arms around me.

"Move?" I asked as I hugged Jos back, although it was halfhearted, everything was a bit too numb right then for me to explode in unnecessary emotion. "Move the bodies?" The word was painfully wrong. "Move from the city? Or move to a new safe house? Because, after everything we went through, I would be all for leaving the city and letting me burn it to the ground. We can rebuild. But not with the flying rats trying to rip our throats out at every turn."

Joclyn and Ilyan stared at each other, lips pressed in tight lines, as eyes and jaws and everything worked far too quickly for them to merely be standing and not having one of their ever-irritating mind-meld sessions.

"Spit it out, you two," I scoffed, unable to keep my irritation at bay. "The whole internal talking thing is fun and all—"

"We can't leave the city."

They were five dumb words, but they sliced through my ramble like a knife.

"What are you talking about?" The shrill sound of my

alarm cut through the stagnant air, sending swirls of dust into the shallow light beams that drifted through the window.

Through the darkness of the room, everything was alive with fear. We all stood still, staring at each other in that irritating expectation that was normally reserved for bad daytime TV.

And the father is...

No one, because we are all going to die.

"If you don't answer, I may accidentally set this whole building on fire..."

Jos' lip twitched at my partially serious ultimatum, her grip on me loosening enough so she could turn to face me.

"Edmund has blocked us in. He has built a wall and placed a domed shield over the city. I can't find a way past it."

"Great," I snapped, knowing I was way too loud. I also didn't care. "Three of us against a million or so Vilỳ? Well, at least we are powerful and will put up a good fight. Fire magic, Silnỳ, King of the Skříteks. Sorry, Sain, I would include you in this powwow, but we all know Draks are useless. Unless you have something to see, that is. Anything you would like to tell us."

Yes, I was baiting him.

"I have nothing to see in the interim," Sain growled, his voice bristling a bit.

"You have no use in the interim," I spouted what came to mind, not worrying if I hurt him, my sour voice striking through each of them as my magic flared angrily.

Negativity was leeching off me like a virus. I didn't think I had ever felt so outnumbered before. Even when I had destroyed that nest of Drak...

I pushed the thought away, willing some Styx song to

come into my head and take it away. It was the best palate cleanser if ever there was one. Well, at least my choice to live was good for a little bit.

"Calm down, Wynifred," Ilyan growled, his voice rumbling as Joclyn's arm weaved around my shoulder.

"There's more," she whispered, her voice low as Ilyan went into the room she had come from.

Sain was looking at me with that same panicked fear but this time he followed his king. I looked after him, trying to decide if I should once again pull him back. At least Ilyan could take him down if it came to that.

"We found some refugees..."

"Refugees?"

"Some people got out of Imdalind. It's not just us anymore..."

"How many?" I should be more focused on the fact that people had made it out of the blood bath Edmund had unleashed on Imdalind. At any other time, I would, but not now.

A distant scream filtered through the frantic scratching of the Vilÿs as if on cue. My head turned to it, almost expecting the victim to be standing behind us with dozens of Vilÿs ripping at their flesh. There was nothing except the old, dust covered table that had been pushed up against the window probably before Joclyn had even been born.

"Numbers don't matter. There will be enough." Her voice had deepened the way Sain's always did when he was *seeing* something.

Ugh. I really didn't like seeing her that way.

And after the last few minutes I didn't want to associate him with her.

"I am guessing you aren't going to tell me how you know

that..." I rolled my eyes at her, something she laughed at and pulled me closer.

My irritation begged me to move away from her, to move away from hug and contact. But I was trapped in the hug, in a dust covered room, staring at the immobile bodies of Thom and Ryland.

"Well, I would," she sighed, her own irritation blazing through, "if I knew one hundred percent. But I don't. I just have a dumb sight with things that may or may not happen..."

That sounded like the Jos I knew.

I laughed as she huffed in irritation, the diplomatic attempt she had made all but gone now.

"I guess I'll have to take it," I said as my laugh faded away. "As long as you saw it, I suppose, then I know it will happen. My best friend's sights are the very best sights..." I spoke as nonchalantly as I always had with her, the laughter rolling off my voice. Her reaction wasn't as humorous.

She flinched, her shoulders pinching together in a tight, little spasm that reminded me so much of the broken girl I had seen only days before, the broken soul Ryland still fought.

My stomach dropped in fear, expecting the roving eyes and the manic movements to return. But she only stood, her eyes wide with the same fear she'd had when she had first walked in.

"Jos?" I expected her to recoil, but she only stood with wide eyes staring far away from me, through me. "Are you...? Are you seeing now?"

I didn't think I could make that sound any more awkward. All of this still kind of felt like finding out a cat you had raised really had two heads, and it had been hiding one all along.

"No." Her voice was dead, dead enough that I almost didn't believe her. "Just worried about getting all of these unconscious and injured males out of here and to the next safe house." Her smile grew with each word, the fear leaving her eyes, even if it was a little bit.

"Why is it always us girls who have to clean up after their messes?" Jos put her hands on her hips with a smile, looking so much like a house mom complaining about messy toys that I couldn't help but laugh.

Sadly, it was true. All the boys—save Ilyan—were useless.

At least we got one of the best of the bunch.

It took everything to keep myself from looking at Thom right then.

"Watch yourself, Jos," I cautioned, letting a smile spread over my face. "Ilyan will hear you, and then he probably will make us do it all on our own."

I said it in jest, but I already knew how true it was. I had been on the receiving end of Ilyan's 'I'll show you who's boss' temper tantrums too many times. I wasn't really interested in a repeat, especially when thousands of ravenous rat birds were involved.

Maybe I could conjure that giant two-headed cat to eat them all.

"Nah..." Her smile only grew. "He wouldn't try. He knows I can kick his ass."

I laughed as she did, the sound lingering before a very loud and painful cough came from the other room. The laughter died as we looked toward the sound, listening to Ilyan's loud mumbles drift through the heavy walls of the house.

"Wyn?" Her voice was so soft that I was surprised it had scared me so much.

"What is it, Jos?" I asked, watching her jaw clench and unclench as she fought with some question that seemed to have gnawed off her tongue. I waited, her jaw chewing increasing to the point I was sure she was going to lose her nerve.

"Do you think the sights are infallible?"

"What are you talking about?" I asked, this was not where I had expected this to go. "You were the one who told Sain they weren't. That they couldn't be."

"I know, but... this one... I mean... They feel different..."

"Feel different?" The question wasn't right, but I didn't know how else to ask, how else to understand. I had no basis for sight.

Her eyes widened as the voices beyond the wall grew, the heavy footsteps making it clear they were coming, and it was time to get all these broken boys out of here. To get to the next safe house and see exactly what numbers we were dealing with.

"I don't trust him, Wyn. Something's off, something he's not telling me."

"Sain?" I asked, my stomach tensing at the connection. It was one I didn't want to make and one I didn't fully understand.

She nodded as the door opened, the three men shuffling through the large gap with Dramin supported between the two more able-bodied.

Jos looked at me once more before she walked off to help the poor men, leaving me standing in the middle of the dark dust motes, staring at the four people that, in some weird way, had left me questioning everything I had thought to be clear and concise.

Hours.

It had only been hours, and now everything was not

only filled with a frightening danger, but more questions than I cared to think about.

It was such a fine line and confusing haze of knowing whom to trust and whom not to. After hundreds of years, I knew I could trust Ilyan. After everything in the prison, I knew I could trust Sain.

But now, everything was somehow becoming muddled. I could almost see a line being drawn before me, sides being chosen, knowing my turn was coming.

The only problem was, I was beginning to doubt which side I should choose.

20

OVAILIA

Ilyan had always been predictable, and having chosen the clock as their safe house only proved it.

There were dozens of safe houses littered throughout the city; larger ones, nicer ones. But he chose this one, the ancient one that wasn't even furnished and hadn't been used in something near sixty years.

It was concealed visually and close enough to the river that it provided a quick getaway should things go south.

It was perfect.

It was also disgustingly predictable.

My brother never had been the smart one, no matter what anyone said.

I exhaled in disgust as a Vilỳ flew before me, its teeth gnashing in obvious rage, the tiny, sharpened points ready to dig into my flesh.

"Zdechnout." The word ground from behind my teeth, and the filthy thing fell to the ground with a thunk, its now lifeless body curling into itself as it hardened to stone.

It was nothing more than sediment now, the contorted face was already falling away to sand.

The trigger-word might have been based in rudimentary magic, but at least my power-hungry father had the good sense install the thing. One word equaled instant death for the buggers. Without the safety switch, I wouldn't have been able to lead Sain and his two, now lifeless companions through the street.

Of course, one was lifeless thanks to some handiwork I had been working on for a while. A little bit of arsenic for his mortal body, some omezující stone extract for his magic, a good helping of stolen soul, and he was good as dead.

That had been the easy part, of course—poisoning Thom. Convincing Sain to trust me and follow me had been a bit harder, but not by much. From the moment he had walked into the city, I had no doubt the voices in his head had grown louder, the internal manipulation my father had plagued him with for centuries igniting as though someone had flipped a switch.

In a way, that is exactly what had happened.

If he had thought he had been in control all this time, he had been very, very wrong.

He had never been in control. And he never would be again.

With one touch of my skin against his, my magic flooded into him, and his magic reacted even if his heart did not.

The force of the heart is strong, but magic could be stronger.

I made sure mine was.

Now, he was eating out of my hand, just as my father had asked. Even though I was sure he was fighting it, what could he say? *Ovailia helped me get the battered boys here, and now she knows where we are.*

He was in my web.

Everything was working out perfectly.

A wide, malicious grin spread over my face as my heart rate accelerated, my next target speeding into view as if she had been summoned here. I guessed, she had in a way.

Ilyan had commanded them to regroup here, and here she was, my useless brother floating beside her as though she had him on strings.

Another of our puppets.

Wyn rushed from one alley to another, beelining for the clock tower with a herd of the filthy things right behind her.

It would be wonderful just to step out now, down the filthy creatures with a word, and let her run right into my path.

It would take only a flick of my magic to steal her heart, her magic, as I had been commanded.

Doing so now, however, would not play in our favor. The timing for Wynifred's end must be perfect. Just as Thom's had been. Just as Sain's would be. A perfectly orchestrated dance, ending with my elder brother's head on a pyre, his ridiculous mate's right beside him.

The thought made me smile, if only because it would be here sooner than they would know.

My targets were all happily closeted away in a safe house that I not only knew about, but thanks to the magic Ilyan had implanted inside of me, I could easily gain access to.

It was almost too easy.

My brother *was* a fool.

Wyn reached the door in a rush, throwing Ryland past the threshold as she turned toward the Vilÿs, her eyes sparking with a flame I had seen all too many times before.

I smiled as she began to glow, flames flicking to her fingers as my own reacted in warning. As much as I would love to stay for the show, I had bigger things to attend. Besides, I liked these boots too much to risk them burning.

Turning, I walked down the side alley I had closeted myself in, my heels tapping and hair swishing as I felt the heat of her fire grow behind me.

I didn't even look. I only pulsed my magic to life and pushed myself into the void of a stutter with the faintest pop. The tapping of my shoes changed from the clang of the old cobbles to the heavy snap of leather against stone as the streets of Prague faded to the caves of Imdalind, leading me towards the room that had once been Ilyan's and was now the central hub of Edmund's operations. The massive space was made for a king, and now, after all this time, the rightful one had returned to take up residence within it.

At first, I had thought the choice to be pointless. It was only after Edmund had begun delving into the depths of the cave in his search for the mud that I realized why that room was the best choice for our objective.

It was the perfect outlet to relieve the anger that Ilyan had built in him. What better way to calm the nerves than to destroy everything your bastard son possessed?

The hall that led to the ornate set of rooms had once been lined with polished walls, now they were full of divots of a magical coup, perfect outlines of ash detailing where Skříteks had once stood. Thick lines of their blood were splattered against the walls and pooled in dried patches against the floor.

Ilyan's immaculate belongings burst from the many doors, the clothing that was specifically designed for Council and weddings now ripped and soiled with blood and body matter, precious stones ripped unceremoniously from the once elegant fabric.

Everything stunk in the warm scent of death, the putrid aroma wrinkling my nose. A small smile twitched at the corner of my lips at the thought of Ilyan's face if he was to ever see this hall again. To see what we had done and where the remains of the last of his people had ended up.

I wanted to witness the beauty of his agony. To watch his heart break from within his body as we added his precious half-breed to the remains.

My father stood right inside the last set of doors, his guards standing at attention from every door, window, and wall of the massive room. Even if there was a chance at someone getting this far into the maze of Imdalind, they wouldn't be able to get at him.

Massive stone buttresses stretched over the ceiling above him, crisscrossing over the natural light that was filtering in from the mirrored shafts that stretched through the mountain to the daylight above.

Those serpentine tunnels were only mildly less confusing than the ones we had been trying to infiltrate for the past two months in our search for the mud of Imdalind.

A search we were no nearer to completing.

It was no wonder that what had once been Ilyan's main living space was in disastrous shambles. Furniture lay in splinters; feathers, cotton, and glass were spread over the floor in a maze of texture that was covered with crimson blood and ebony ink. It was art in a way.

It was beautiful.

The smell was even worse in here if it was possible. However, after walking through the hall, my body wasn't rebelling against it as much.

My hair flew over my shoulder with a flip, the tap of my shoes against glass echoing painfully as I approached my father. His focus was on the detailed model of the tunnel system he had been working on since I first had been able to gain him access to the caves below the city.

Of course, it hadn't been without recourse.

It should have been easy. My father had built many of these caves; he knew them. Or at least, he had.

Unbeknownst to everyone, Ilyan had been working to expand and move the tunnels, changing the paths and trails until they were unrecognizable.

My lips curled in disgust.

At least Ilyan was in the city. Even if the Vilÿs weren't able to take control of his mind and power, he would still be of use to us. He could still take us to the wells of Imdalind.

"They are above the clock." My voice reverberated off the white, stone walls, the large acoustic space making the sound much louder than I had meant it to be.

Edmund remained hunched over, his hair falling over his eyes as he studied the diagram. His fingers drawing lines of magic as he attempted to ascertain the correct path to where he hoped the wells were.

"All of them?"

"I know for certain Sain and Wynifred have taken refuge there with Dramin, Thom, and Ryland." The tap of my shoes moved in time with my words as I walked around the room, lifting what was once an elegant tunic with my toe. The serfs had given the filthy thing to Ilyan right after he had declared their debts paid.

An irritated scoff spilled from me at the disgusting memory. I would never understand why anyone saw him as a saint, or why he would keep something so vile.

"But not Ilyan." His eyes darted to mine for the briefest of seconds before settling back down on the model. The disappointment in that brief glance was so clear that I could almost feel his hand press against my spine, and I straightened

The start of fear rolled through me, but I pushed it away. Fear was only a weakness that would get you killed. Sadness would only show the easiest way to dispose of you. I would do neither.

"Not that I saw, Father." My voice was level as I stood before him, my confidence clear, but it still wasn't enough to keep his rage at bay. It rippled down his back like a cat curling in preparation for attack.

"And why didn't you wait to make sure my son had made it to the supposed safety with the others?" His voice was a growl as he rose to meet me, the depth of his hatred rolling through the room in waves of green.

"Wynifred ignited the city."

Edmund jerked at my statement, his eyes wide with greed as his lips curled into a smile, the malice in his eyes seeping into me and igniting my own.

The gluttony grew, the desire for what he so desperately wanted coloring him along with the smile that spread over his face. He walked toward me with that slow, calculated step he always had when he was plotting, when his mind was working far ahead of the cold, stone walls that held us.

My own greed grew with each step he took, my own desire to see that magic in his hands swelling until I was regretting not having taken her then. With her power, it wouldn't have mattered if we had Ilyan. With the fire magic, we could boil the stone down, and then Edmund could walk a straight path to the wells that held all the magic we needed to control the world.

"She used it again?" His voice was a snake that wound over my spine.

"Yes, Father."

His smile grew, and this time, I stepped away. Foot falling over foot as I backed away from the fearful need that lined his face, an act that only fueled the desire that rampaged through him.

"The same as last time?"

"If she did the same, do you think I would still be standing here?" The words flew out without so much of a thought, the quick sass slipping out in a barb.

He blanched at my tone, the smile vanishing from his face before it returned, even more sinister than before.

"Tell me of Sain," he snarled, his voice more of a warning than I would like to admit.

I could not misstep again.

At any other time, I might have tried to find my way out of the situation with flattery or lies, but this time, I had at least been able to give him what he wanted.

"It was as you said," I whispered, careful to keep my voice low, to draw him into me with the news I had for him. "Sain has not escaped the bind you have on him, no matter how much he pretends to be free. Whatever you have done was enough, and he slipped. He slipped enough that I was able to find him before the attack began, incapacitate Thom, and draw him back in."

"So, he is in love with you, then?"

"No," I admitted, surprised to see his face fall.

My father prided himself on wooing and bedding women in record time, a skill that was passed on to none of his children. For whatever reason, he was not pleased with it, either. I had come close with Cail on his instruction, but the fool had died before I'd had a chance to complete the task. I still took his magic in the end.

"But his magic is still attempting to fuse with mine, something that I helped along. The possibility of a restored bond is too much for his weak energy to resist. Give it time, Father. He will feed into our hands, just as you wish."

"So, he has seen you, then?" Edmund's eyes flashed with

greed again, desperate and needy as he watched me, unwavering as he held me in place.

"Yes."

I would have thought the single word would have brought him joy with how he had taken the news so far, but in no more than a flash of light, the desire that had filled him departed, leaving a mask of fury.

His eyes were dark, as he growled at me, "And what do you think will happen if he chooses to give Ilyan the information of your visit?"

I flinched at the ice in his voice, the carefully masked disgust that rang clear. I knew he had meant to manipulate me with the fear, but I felt none of it. It only ran through me like water as my own smile spread.

I took a step closer to him, his body stiffening in expectation of what, I wasn't sure. He should know I wasn't foolish enough to attack him. No matter how much power my body held, it still would not be enough to face him.

I wasn't foolish enough to try.

I *was* foolish enough to face him for this, however.

He thought I had failed, slipped. He shouldn't be so naïve. He was the one who had raised me, after all, trained me, turned me into what I was.

"That won't happen." I was sure of myself, a fact that only enraged him more.

"How can you be so certain, Ovailia?" It was a snap that bit through me, but I ignored it as well as the warning in his eyes. I ignored the way his guards flinched and moved against the wall in preparation for what was coming.

"Because of what I did to Thomas."

His rage froze in place. His face was stuck in confusion until what I had said slipped into place, his dislike for Thom fueling a whole other set of emotions.

"Ah, yes, the most foolish and useless of my children. I'm always surprised to hear he has evaded me," he sneered. "Tell me, what did you do to him?"

"I poisoned him."

"Poison? From the Vilỳs?"

My smile only grew, the complexity of what I had done, of what I had created, swelling through me. Even my father with his brilliant mind could not see it.

"No father, with something the mortals do. It reacts to the body like a Přetížení dávka but cannot be healed the same way. If Sain missteps even a little bit, I will destroy his dearest friend."

"Control." It was one word laced with so much emotion I could have bathed in it.

"Yes. And I have all of it."

He looked at me, processing what I had said, his hand lifting to press against my cheek. I froze, waiting for what would come next.

A pat or a slap.

Pride or distaste.

"Just as you have taught me, Father." It was my last plea, and I was certain the tone in my voice revealed that. Right then, I didn't care.

"And I couldn't be prouder." He smiled at me, his lips curling in a long, greasy line that oozed into me in a relaxing warmth I hadn't felt from him in what seemed like centuries.

Right then, I couldn't have been prouder to be his daughter.

I would do anything for him.

21

JOCLYN

YOU WOULD THINK that with a million flying bats hovering just feet from us we could stand to be a bit quieter. Or at least not so loud that every step was met by the deranged beady eyes of one of Edmund's freaky little creatures. Ryland's whimpers drifted back from where Ilyan was holding him just a few steps ahead of me. One tiny little sound and no less than twenty of the things turned to stare and search for their next victim, or food, or whatever it was that they saw the people of this city as.

Considering we had pulled their focus from what appeared to be a mostly eaten carcass I would say it was a little of both. I really didn't want to think of it beyond that, just as I really didn't want to know what kind of carcass they were feasting from. My stomach was already twisting itself into a nervous pretzel as I turned away, focusing on my shield and keeping it strong around our little group.

Just me, my shield, and my tiny army of invalids.

Ilyan and Ryland brought up the charge, Wyn and a hovering Thom brought up the rear with me, and Sain took up the middle. The old man was practically carrying an equally old and limping Dramin on his back. The two old men were stumbling so much that I already had to send out a few blasts of magic in an attempt to keep the Vilỳs beady eyes off of us. Thanks to the Drak and their sudden inability to shield themselves I had been delegated to protection and shield detail, my magic spreading through the air and masking us from view.

Which seemed to be working, given that the two old men had now crashed sidelong into a forgotten bicycle.

All of the Vilỳ around us turned, many more popping out of windows and doorways where they had been hiding so as to investigate the sound. No amount of evil sidelong glares could really convey how frustrated I was with the two of them.

I was pretty sure Sain was doing it on purpose, the jerk. He falls into a flower pot and sends dirt and terra cotta scattering over cobbles, and I get a glare of accusation.

Yeah, thanks dad. That's really helpful.

'Ignore him, my love,' Ilyan's voice soothed into my mind as he glanced back, his slight smile fleeting before he turned back to guiding us through the street and toward our destination.

'Ignore the fact that he is a pain in the butt? Or the fact that if he keeps that up we are all going to be dead before we get there?' There was no point in trying to hide my hostile anger, it all rolled out of me in waves of frustration so loud I was surprised the little rat monsters didn't turn away from the flower pot they were still inspecting.

Both. And we are almost there, the Castle complex is just ahead. Hopefully Risha and the others have already secured a temporary shield. Ilyan returned, turning his head just enough to give me the tiniest of smiles. I might have mistaken it for a warning glare if I wasn't doomed to deal with Sain, who was once again giving me some gnarly side eye.

'Seriously. If he keeps this up I'm gonna to lose it.'

'Ignore him, mi lasko.'

'Oh trust me, I am going to ignore him so well that he might just fade away into oblivion, just like yesterday's farts.'

Ilyan coughed in an attempt to restrain the laugh that was now rumbling through my thoughts.

Here we were, walking through an apocalypse and Ilyan's bubbling chuckle was shining through the red tinged light like a beacon. The sound was so carefree that if I closed my eyes I was sure I could just wipe out the world. Well, I could if it didn't smell like blood, anyway.

Blood or not, I was officially smiling, something that Wyn noticed in seconds. She gave me the trademark 'what's up with you' look, glancing between me and Sain as though she had missed something besides the guys sour expression. I kept smiling, refusing to look at my dear old dad again. Luckily my best friend had a good amount of brains and she rolled her eyes.

Guess Ilyan and I had been caught again.

Except she didn't seem to find it as funny as I did. Her face fell, her hand tightening around Thom's, the still unconscious man floating beside her. She had been so adamant of Sain's trustworthiness before, something had clearly happened in the room above the clock. Both of them were acting very weird.

'I couldn't agree more,' Ilyan whispered into my mind, although I didn't know why, it wasn't like anyone else could hear us. *'We can figure it out once we get inside.'*

'Inside?' I asked as Ilyan led us around the corner and into an adjoining walk way, the long lane lined with what appeared to be the tiniest houses I had ever seen. They were

adorable, or they would have been if the street wasn't littered with bodies, the houses splattered with a bright crimson that still dripped down the multicolored facades.

"We are here," Ilyan said aloud, his voice firm and commanding and causing most everyone around me to jump.

I may have, a little bit, but I wasn't about to own up to it. I knew what he was doing, even if I had no idea where we were.

Seconds after he had spoken, the air before a tiny blue house began to shimmer, the air itself falling away to reveal Risha and about five others. Wyn gasped, and said something in quick Czech before pulling herself up to her full height. If I had to guess I would say she was swearing, and turning into assassin Wyn. It was a little unnerving watching her shift into someone else.

"Don't go on a rampage," I warned as Ilyan began to lead us forward, the air shimmering around us as the shield they had placed around wherever we were moved to encapsulate us.

"I am suddenly realizing why none of those people were very nice to me while I was married to Talon. I am pretty sure that blonde guy tried to get me kicked out a few times. And here I was thinking it was just because I was a Trpaslík." Wyn was still stoically staring forward, although Thom was noticeably floating a bit closer to her as her hand tightened. I half-expected him to open his eyes make some wisecrack about her complaining.

"I take it you weren't very nice to them?"

"Before Talon? I was the worst. Murder, death, mild infidelity. I deserve everything they have done to me. I expect that it is about to get a whole lot worse." She gave me a smile that didn't quite reach her eyes, the hard light I had seen a few times before making a grand return.

Welcome back, scary Wyn. It was almost like looking into mirror at a carnival fun house and seeing a different person look back. I would have to thank the entourage of grade B horror movies that Ryland and I used to binge on for that one. Yes, I totally shivered. And, there was Ilyan laughing in my head again.

'If you could see this glare you wouldn't be laughing.'

'I have seen it, my love. I am still laughing.' His chuckle was clear in my mind, although his face was nothing but stoic business as he turned to me giving me a lone nod.

"Shields down, Můj kamarád."

I let the shield pop like a soap bubble, the shimmering air falling away and revealing us to Risha and the Skříteks. Each of them instantly moved from being on guard to a befuddled mess.

The reactions weren't anything like what I had expected. Everyone had assumed Dramin and Thom to be dead, although they were not far from that. The last anyone knew, Ryland and Wyn were as good as that, locked in a dungeon. The reaction at seeing all of them was immediate; shock, joy, and fear rushed through them before they all moved to help, which would have been fine if a particularly scruffy looking man hadn't tried to take Thom from Wyn.

"I've got him, Deterim, but thank you so much for your assistance." She spat, pulling Thom back over to her and sending his dreads swinging. "I think I am quite able to carry him where ever we need to go."

The man's face fell almost immediately, his eyes narrowing and drooping as he looked down at her. "So you are back are you?"

"Hands off my man or you are going to find out." She was

saucy, snide and the guy took one quick step back before I hit her so hard on the arm that she jerked. The guy, Deterim, froze in place, looking between us. He clearly expected Wyn to lob my head off or something.

Jeeze, I really hope that wasn't a thing she used to do. But yeah, assassin. Clearly she had done that and worse.

"Don't be such a jerk, Wyn. I highly doubt that there is a song about a woman pining to death while her hot boyfriend is in a coma."

"You clearly haven't listened to enough music in your life," she said with a snort, her eyes flashing to mine before darting back to Deterim who was looking like he both wanted to throw up and pick a fight. I really hope he didn't decide to do both, because that would be a bit too gross.

Blood was one thing...

"And you clearly haven't allowed people to help you. We need to clean up, Wynifred, and Thom needs things you cannot give him." I was careful to keep my tone harsh but not so regal I sounded stuck up.

It was a line I clearly wasn't walking well, because both Wyn and Ilyan, who had allowed one of his men to carry Ryland away, were now chuckling at me.

"Wynifred?" Wyn mocked, her giggles turning into a belly laugh as she threw her arm over my shoulder and pulled me into her. "We gotta work on turning you into a badass. Only pushovers call me Wynifred."

She was clearly talking my tall, foreboding, mate, her face twisted up in a smile, but his was narrowing into a firm-eyed stare, his magic buzzing through our connection like a live wire. "Well, I guess I'll be a pushover, then," I teased, poking her hard in the side.

'You should ignore her too.'

'Easier said than done, my love.' Yeah, he had totally

earned the look I was giving him, it was all twisted smirk and furrowed brow.

'Tell me about it.'

"You can take him, Deterim," Ilyan said, obviously changing the subject as he turned to the still shocked man. The poor guy looked like he was going to bolt before he dared step between Wyn and Thom again.

But Wyn nodded and released Thom's hand, her fingers dragging over his chest as he was moved away from her. I could hear her heart crack and shatter over the floor as the tall Skříteks led Thom away.

"Where are we taking the injured?" Ilyan asked when Risha appeared on his left, looking a bit cleaner if not more windswept than that last time I had seen her.

"We are using the cathedral for now." She said in quick Czech, although I was only able to pick that much out of Ilyan's head before she bolted into a full explanation that I couldn't even try to follow.

A few words popped out every now and then, like 'window' and 'bathroom', and what I think was 'bed', but the rest of it was a mystery. Ilyan's response was just as fast, just as strained and I sighed. I was exhausted after everything, and trying to decipher the sea of words in his mind was not working.

As they talked we walked passed the tiny houses, following everyone towards what I now recognized as the cathedral. Or rather, the massive spires of what my mind was trying to tell me was a fortress. Yes, I am pretty sure my jaw dropped, straight to the floor.

"St. Vitas." Wyn provided from beside me, her voice a hiss over the quick Czech of Ilyan and Risha. "It's one of the oldest cathedrals in Europe, in one of the largest and most secure complexes anywhere in the world. At least with what I know, but I could be biased."

She was clearly smiling, but I didn't turn to look. I couldn't look away from the spires of the beautiful building, the tall points stretching toward the sky until they were looming over us like needles protruding from the earth. A deep green roof came into view as we rounded a corner, buttresses and intricate stained glass windows gleaming against the discolored sky and making everything look like a sun set.

Each window was intact, by some miracle. No wonder we were all headed there.

"It has a monastery, now a museum. A large estate known as the Castle, basically it is just a big museum." Wyn might as well have been talking to herself with how I was staring at the cathedral. I just couldn't get over the beauty of it.

I had been so out of it in Rioseco that I hadn't been able to admire the ancient beauty, and the bits of saw of Prague before it turned in a war zone were now just blood-covered memories.

But this, I was sure nothing could replace this moment in my mind.

"A museum hardly seems safe." I wasn't sure if I was mumbling or just overcome by awe.

"It's a compound," Ilyan said as he dropped back from Risha to flank my other side, his arm around my waist and Wyn's around my shoulders. With their height differences I was feeling a bit like an accordion folder. "The entire estate is surrounded by high walls and living areas, it makes it easy to shield, and easy to defend."

"We need a bit of a better shield that I can provide, however," Risha said with a wave toward the sky, the motion finally pulling my focus from the beautiful buildings that we were surrounded by and the deep red sky.

The problem was staring at me like some heavenly warning. The glimmering air from before was starting to fade, little cracks shimmering over the surface like red tinted spiderwebs as the haunted world behind it began to peek through.

"Oh, I so got this," I said, cracking my knuckles as Wyn chuckled beside me.

"Forget being all proper. You might be the first queen I'll actually like, Jos."

"Well, consider the source." Ilyan grumbled, his voice echoing in my ears in my magic began to buzz, his moving to join it.

"True. Your step mothers suck, Ilyan."

Ilyan grumbled, Risha gasped, and I just smiled, shooting my magic into the sky and showering the world with stars as my magic stretched over us, joining with Ilyan's in a barrier that spread over us like a blanket.

For a moment it washed out the red of the sky.

For a moment, everything looked normal, well until a Vilÿ smacked into the side of the barrier and slid down it like a bug on a windshield.

"Well," Wyn said, her face spread into a wide smile, "it's not inconspicuous, but it will sure keep us entertained for hours."

I slugged her in the arm and sent her tumbling to the ground in a fit of giggles. I'm sure it hurt. I had no regrets.

22

RYLAND

"TAKE IT OUT."

The words were mine. They seeped out in a moan that sounded more pleading than pained, nearly the exact opposite from what I expected with the agony that was ripping through my body.

Everything hurt so intensely that I was desperate to go back to sleep, although I wasn't positive why I had been sleeping in the first place.

Hadn't we just been in the cave? Weren't we just running down the streets of Prague?

I didn't know anymore.

I didn't know anything, really, except for the dim, red hue that cast over my closed eyes and the rough feel of old cotton sheets against my skin. Those I was sure of, but why there were warm sheets in Prague, or even how I had found these amazingly warm sheets remained a mystery.

My muscles throbbed as I shifted my weight, trying to roll over, only to be wrapped in a deeper ache in protest. So, sitting was out.

I shifted one last time, eyes fluttering a bright red light that burned through me as my focus attempted to adjust.

Not that gaining focus helped, nothing around or above me was familiar. I was laying in warm sheets, on a soft bed, underneath tall, sweeping ceilings and old buttresses that I wanted to say were familiar.

Even though I had never seen them before.

Nothing about this was familiar.

Well, unless I was dead, and I was sure I had not led a life good enough to go to heaven. This space reminded me far too much of a cathedral to be hell.

You're home.

I jerked.

The voice rumbled through me, although it had changed somehow, mutated into a hollow sound that echoed until it became something deeper. Something more frightening.

Listening to the voice, it all came back.

The sky turning black with those winged creations of my fathers, the smell of fear in the air, the explosions of magic, the feel of my blood as I begged Wyn to remove the voices from my heart.

Remove the knife.

Now, I had awakened in this strange place surrounded by shallow breathing and distant footsteps. All of it echoing through the cavernous space.

The cavernous cathedral.

It was then I recognized it. I had never been here before, but I knew. I had heard of this cathedral all my life—the massive holy place that stood in the center of Prague. And now I was here.

I'm here, too.

You can't be here. Wyn took the knife.

I'm still here, you can't escape me. Not until you kill them all.

"No." I was firm, even if the word was calm, my heart an agonizing weight as I pushed the madness away. Shoved it out of my mind.

I lay still, staring at the ceiling as I listened to the voice that had once been so loud become distanced and fragmented, like the transmission was broken.

No.

Like the receiver had been removed.

The shard had been removed.

You can never escape me.

I think I already have, Father.

He yelled in anger at my reply, but the sound was an echo of what it once was, my mind almost peaceful. It was like waking up from a deep sleep and having everything around me change for the better. Even if the voices were still there, they were only a distant memory now.

My hand shook as I lifted it to my chest, fingers fluttering against my bare chest as they trailed toward my heart, toward the dozens of scars that had been cut through the skin to pierce that battered, beating thing my father had used to control me and everyone around me for so long.

For the first time, right in that moment, my heart was mine once again.

Not completely. Not quite.

Yes. Mine.

The taunt was too faint to matter, and I couldn't help but smile in reply.

I had won.

I could win.

Everything had changed.

The remote control they had instilled in me was no longer controlling my every move.

There were only scars left, and even if they were ugly, I could live with those.

Suddenly, the large stone archways that hung above me did not seem so old. The stone seemed brighter, the red hue of the sky giving everything a glistening, rosy glow.

You are still right where I want you.

Strangely, I didn't care.

"It's the St. Vitus Cathedral." I had only heard the depth of his kind voice once or twice, but even now, in the strange place, it filled me with calm.

I had only met Dramin once before, and then I had been so bogged down by my demons I hadn't really seen him. Not really. His memory was only shadows of my subconscious, a mutated reality that had been handed to me.

I turned, expecting Dramin to be sitting calmly beside me, drinking out of one of those ugly mugs. There was only the cavernous space of what had obviously been turned into a dorm. Pews, prayer stools, and whatever else normally occupied the space had been removed, replaced by rows and rows of identical white wrought-iron bed frames and sagging mattresses, each one made up with over-washed crisp sheets. It was like something I had seen in a million movies.

An orphan grew up in some church setting, only to be inducted into some bizarre adventure. There was a book one of my nannies would have read me about that. Something along the lines of girls and lines and a tiger with bathroom issues.

I couldn't remember.

The beds lined either side of the large hall, stacked one after another like dominos. Most of them were empty, with the exception of one a few feet away on my left where a small, dark-haired boy slept. Another was on the other side, where my brother, Thom, lay sleeping as if he were dead. The image was a weird jolt to my spine, one that probably would have grown into a panic if it wasn't for Dramin who sat in the bed beside him, looking as unconcerned as though Thom was simply sleeping. I hoped that was the case.

Dramin was propped up against piles of pillows as if he could no longer support himself. Then again, judging by the bandages that were taped to his neck, I was sure he couldn't. Not that he minded. He sat, beaming with a positivity I didn't think was possible given the situation. It was like someone had taken Sain, taught him to laugh at a young age, and then wiped the irritation out of his brow with a damp cloth.

Something about the man was intriguing, like family I didn't know I had had.

"Excuse me?" I could barely get the words out; my throat was raspy and dry.

"St. Vitus," he said without looking, his focus on the ornate architecture that stretched above us. "I knew you were wondering, so I am answering. Also, you were brought here by Ilyan. Wynifred had to put you under after your little... shall we say, *episode*?"

Episode, he says. If only they knew what you are really capable of.

If only they knew I created you to kill them.

To kill all of them.

Not a chance. Not anymore.

Dramin turned as if he had heard the battle inside my mind, but said nothing. He only lifted his ugly mug to me with a chuckle. It's not like he needed to say any more. I had been around Sain enough over the past few months to know how a Drak's mind worked.

So have I, son, so have I.
And I know more than you ever will.
I am still in control.
No, you aren't.
Not of me.
Not anymore.
We shall see.

I shook my head as the voice laughed, as if the motion would be enough to clear the insanity. The laugh echoed in my ears as it faded, the sound moving back into the dark recesses of my mind and leaving me to stare at my brother. Thick cords of his hair spread around his head like briars in an ugly garden. It would have been comical if it wasn't for the situation.

"What happened?"

"Well, that boy there," he lifted his mug to the boy on the other side of me, but I didn't turn, I couldn't look away from my brother. "He was bitten by the nasty things, as was I."

"And Thom?"

"Well, that is a mystery." Dramin sighed dejectedly, his mug dropping into his lap with a splash of the amber brown liquid. "No one is quite sure what happened to him."

I know what happened to him.

The voice was a dark chuckle, a dim menace that sent a shiver over my spine.

This time, it was in fear.

I pushed it away. I was unwilling to admit the emotion had found me again, that my father could truly know anything of what was going on.

Instead, I tried to push myself to sitting again, but my muscles were even less interested than the last time. As if they had a say. I managed it with a grunt, and the heavy blanket fell away from my torso, letting the cold fall air of the cathedral drift over my bare skin.

"Ilyan brought everyone here to figure out our next move." There he went again, answering questions I hadn't been able to put voice to.

"And where is he?"

"Speaking to the heads of the houses," a new voice answered my question.

I jerked, turning toward the new arrival with a furious trepidation that tensed through my muscles, as if I needed to be ready to attack.

My magic reacted as the distant voice within me laughed, dark and deep, almost in expectation of the fight that was coming.

It never did.

It never would.

When I faced her, I knew at once that would never happen.

Not because she was a woman. No, I had battled enough women. Hell, I had killed enough women in my past to make that argument invalid.

No, as I turned to face this stranger, there was something else there. It was something deep and foreign, something that scared me.

"The head of the houses?" I repeated her phrasing like a question. I knew the answer, though. My brain was going into overdrive, so I foolishly said the first thing that slipped into it, a fact that didn't go unnoticed by her if her smile was any judge.

"Yes, there will be a council in a few days. He is speaking with the last surviving heads of each family in preparation."

I could only nod, the old information stagnant, after all.

"I'm Risha."

"Ryland." My voice was much softer than I had meant it to be.

Maybe I will have you kill her, too.

I fought the jerk at the phrasing, startled by my emotional reaction to the voices. I hoped she didn't notice.

"Nice to meet you, Ryland."

I hadn't thought something so formal could be so beautiful.

We stared at each other, the minutes ticking away until it seemed they had gone by long enough. Then Dramin chuckled, the deep, rich sound pulling me out of whatever reverie I had been stuck in and right to the old man who sat with an ugly mug and the biggest smile I had ever seen plastered to his face.

"Risha is serving as Ilyan's second until someone can be chosen to take Talon's place." I stared at him, trying to figure out why he would tell me this while still attempting to recover from the embarrassment of having stared at the girl for so long. "I figured I would answer the question that was burning on your brain. That, and she's single."

I didn't think it was possible to choke on something when you were neither eating nor drinking, but I somehow managed it, gasping and coughing loud as I attempted to figure out how to breathe again.

Risha, however, laughed. The sound was rich and joyful, and just like that, I was forgetting how to get saliva down the right tube again.

How embarrassing.

As if on cue, the door to the hall opened again, and Joclyn walked in, followed by a thoroughly agitated Wyn.

"I don't understand why you can't tell me what you plan on doing to that kid. You never know, I could help you." Wyn's gravelly voice laced with enough whine that it pulled me right out of my embarrassment and into what I should have been certain was hell.

But it wasn't.

It's her.

Kill her.

The voice was louder than I had heard it the last few minutes but I pushed it from my mind as I stared at them, my mind quick to find its path again.

Yes, it was Joclyn. And, yes, in some ways, I wanted to hurt her. However, in reality, it was just Joclyn. It was just Wyn. It was just two girls. One who used to be my best friend, who I used to love. One that, until that moment, every time I would come face-to-face with her, I would see nothing but blood and death.

Kill them now!

The voice grew louder, but it didn't matter anymore. In this one frightening moment, I knew for sure that everything had changed.

I stared at them in bewilderment as they walked in, Joclyn stopping in her tracks at seeing me staring at her.

"You're awake." I could hear the fear and anger behind her voice.

I expected her own trepidations to ignite mine. Hell, everyone around us obviously expected the same things judging by the way Risha moved closer, her body squared in a guard stance. Wyn was looking between the two of us as if she was trying to decipher who to stop.

Kill them now!

The voice could barely make it through the static.

I wanted to tell him it was useless.

I felt nothing, and I could tell by the look in Joclyn's eyes that she felt nothing, too.

For whatever reason, by whatever divine wonderment, we had defeated it.

You will never defeat me.

I said it before, Father, I already have.

"Yep, I'm awake."

She could only nod in understanding, a move so like her I couldn't help smiling. She returned it so quickly that, for a brief moment, it seemed like everything was going to be alright, that I would get my best friend back.

"I'm here to heal him." She nodded her head toward the boy.

I should have been grateful for the change, but I was more grateful for the change in us and what we had regained.

She smiled before she moved to the mysterious boy on the other side of me.

Wyn laughed and jabbered on about who knew what at such a low decibel that, even if I tried, I wasn't sure I could make it out.

I looked away from Joclyn, my focus pulling right to the tall, strawberry blond who stood at the foot of my bed with an elegant smile pulling over her face.

"I am glad you are feeling better," she whispered, her voice laced with all the knowledge in the world, something that, for the first time, I was happy I didn't have to explain. She already knew.

But, more than anything, I was happy that it was true.

"So am I."

23

ILYAN

THE DRESS WAS the palest yellow, like the memory of sunflowers left too long in the sun. The fabric was a soft velvet that was intricately stitched and embroidered in a design that I had run my fingers over far too many times in my youth, but the stitching was just as perfect and solid as it had always been. The dress may have been worn thin in some places, but you could still see the intricate workmanship, the artistic designs or flowers and trees. It was easy to see the care that had been given to this dress when it was first stitched over a thousand years ago, and the love it had received since the last time it was worn.

All of that was for good reason and as I carried the beautiful dress down the hall, I was glad for it all.

The dress had been my mother's.

It was only by a sheer miracle that the dress had been stored somewhere I could reach it, that it wasn't buried in the depths of Imdalind with all my other treasures that I had surely lost. Until about an hour ago it had hung in a museum in the center of Prague, protected by mortal measures of airtight containers and dimmed lights, and by my shield of magic to keep both age and rats away.

I had donated it to the museum shortly after the second World War. I had wanted the residents of the city to see the dress, to gain even the tiniest of inklings of their origins. Even if they would have no idea what it would mean.

The dress was the one my mother had worn the day she had been bonded to my father, and then again on the day that the new lines of lineage and ruling had been drawn and they had been elected king and queen.

The first of the Chosen Children and the daughter of the original Skříteks.

Before then, it had been the firsts of each branch of magic that had overseen our society. They had ruled as one. Skřítek, Trpaslík, Vilỳ, and Drak. Frain, Chyline, Rinax and Sain.

But with the creation of the first Chosen, a being with all branches of magic within them, they had made the decision to change the ruling and future of our kind. No one knew at the time what it would mean, but right then it hardly mattered.

My mother, the amazing, powerful woman that she was, had worn this dress when she had been crowned queen. It was the dress I would have Joclyn wear today. On the day she would stand before our people and be officially accepted to rule them, by my side.

My steps echoed as I walked down the old stone hallway of the cathedral, past the store rooms, and old priests quarters that now sheltered the wide majority of my people, and tapped on the door near the end, the old wood echoing loud and abrasively through the icy silence of the sacred place.

I don't know why I knocked, she knew I was standing

there. Her smile was bright in my mind at the formality, her welcome spreading through me like fire.

My heart swelled with pride as her magic filled me, the door opening all on its own and revealing a startlingly empty room. There was only the small bed we had pushed into a corner and a dresser that was covered with char.

I had felt her magic. I had expected her to be there.

The room was void of her sunny smile, however, as well as the aroma of vanilla that wafted around her thanks to the shampoo we had found. I stepped into the room in a rush, my nerves pushing into high alert as the door snapped shut behind me.

The room was not the one that Risha and the others had attempted to give us. That one could have housed at least twenty refugees and had a bathroom the size of a small hospital. We didn't need it, and I had quickly refused the extravagance. This room may be small, and the bed may take up most of the space, but it was just the two of us. We didn't need any more than this. No matter what my people would have me believe, we were not any more deserving than any of them.

Of course, the tiny space was even more small and lonely without her in it.

"Joclyn," I called as I stepped toward her magic and to the open bathroom door that was tucked into the corner.

She stood before the mirror, staring at her reflection with a look of pained confusion on her face. She looked so lost that I let my magic fill her as I searched for some injury, as I calmed her fears. But nothing was there, nothing but the sadness as she looked at her reflection, her hand lifting her shirt as she inspected the scar that cut through her abdomen.

"Můj kamarád," I whispered as set the dress on the

bureau, just out of sight, and stepped behind her, her magic pulling me toward her so abruptly that I was amazed I was able to move as slowly as I did.

Her focus didn't leave the scar, however, her mind moving through the moment the sword had cut into her on repeat. Her fingers trailed over the mark that covered almost the whole circumference of her waist, the scar from the blade that had poisoned her, that had almost sliced her in two having left what almost appeared to be a raised brand of rotted skin behind.

"I didn't think it would look this bad."

I stepped closer, placing my hands over hers, our fingers intertwining as together we traced the scar.

"It's so long." Her memories flitted over to me, the moment of the strike replaying once again. The feel of the blade was so sharp in my mind that I could almost feel it penetrating my own skin, my spine tensing in the shadow of pain that was overtaking me. I may not have felt the blade when it first pierced her skin, but I felt her agony then, and I felt her worry now. Each emotion so strong that it felt as if we would drown in them. I was sure she already was, so I let my magic swell, wrapping my arm around her and pulling her into me. She dropped her shirt, concealing the scar from view, her own arms coming to compress against me as we stood, cheek to cheek, staring at ourselves in the mirror.

"Most would have succumbed to that poison in minutes," I whispered in her ear, my accent thick in my awe of her. She shivered into me, her eyes fluttering closed in a gentle sigh as I felt the tension in her shoulders ease.

"It's all that super powerful magic that's buzzing through my veins." Her fingers flicked against mine, letting the magic swell and burn between us as if to emphasize a point. The mischievous look in her eyes cemented it, sending my nerves spinning. Well, before the mischievous glower faded into frustration.

"A magical anomaly."

The admission had more pain and anger in it than it really should. She had clearly been around her father lately. I was running out of options on what to do with the man. He had never been so callous before, and the way he was behaving was making me question his loyalty. I wasn't one to thrust people out for simply behaving like a vile miscreant, but he was clearly walking on thin ice.

I would push him through it myself if it came to that. For now, I needed to keep Joclyn away from the worry that the man brought.

"No. It is nothing as ridiculous as that. You are simply stubborn, my love. That is all." I spoke in Czech, translating the words into her mind as I pressed my lips against her temple and sent another pleasurable shiver down her spine.

The ripple of her energy made me smile and for a moment I nearly lost track of my reason for rushing here.

"I'm not stubborn," she retorted, wrinkling her nose like a little rabbit as she glared at me through the mirror. The look was so beautiful I couldn't help but kiss her again, this time letting my lips drag down to her cheek. Another kiss, another shiver, and this time I chuckled.

"I am, however, going to be one giant scar by the time all of this is over." She laughed a bit, but the sound was forced as she lifted her shirt again. The silver in her eyes flashed so dark that for a moment I expected the burn of sight to come, but there was only a harsh laugh, a forced smile, and a sigh that stretched through the air in a heart-wrenching frustration.

"That may be true, but you will be one beautiful giant scar by the time this is over." I may have smiled at her, but the lifted brow and frustrated grimace I received in return hardly seemed to appreciate the humor.

"My beautiful mate," I whispered in her ear before stepping away, my focus only on her as I stripped off my shirt, baring my chest to the woman I loved.

It may not be the first time I had been stripped before her, but somehow, this time, I felt more bare than I had at any other. The useless piece of fabric crumpled to the ground as I revealed the dozens of scars on my chest, the burn on my arm, and the dozens of other little nicks and holes in my skin that I collected over the centuries. I was sure she could not even see those ones, but each one was as bright to me as hers was to her.

If only because I remembered where each and every one of them came from.

The same look of awe, pain, and sorrow that she always had when she saw the raised marks that littered my skin lifted in her brow, her hand hovering before me. She had traced the raised lines dozens of times, but now it was as if she was afraid. As if she was seeing them for what they were for the first time.

Stepping forward, I placed the hot palm of my hand over her scar, letting my touch linger as her hand fell to my chest, her fingers hot against my skin. We were bare, both in scars and in soul. Perhaps we were seeing the depth of each other for the first time, the vulnerable fear that makes your knees shake.

"I see you, my love," I whispered in Czech, letting my heart translate as our magic swirled together and I brought her into me, her hand still against my chest, mine still on her hip as I pressed her against me, our joined magic sparking against both skin and air. "Don't let this scar cut too deep. It is on your body, it is not a part of you."

My heart was a heavy drum as I dragged my fingers over her back, across her neck and pressed the palm of my scarred hand against her mark.

Our magic erupted at the touch, the lights of color that were so normal for us filling the room with spots of color and magic. The fireworks of our connection sped around us like a tornado, rushing through everything as I pulled her into me, and pulled her lips against mine.

She answered the desperate touch with her own passion, her hands twisting over my chest to grip my hips, pulling me closer as she lifted onto her toes, trying to bring her small frame to my taller one.

That I could help with. My arms were bands over her torso, over her waist as I lifted her, a deep groan rumbling through my throat as she wrapped her legs around me, sending my heart and my magic into overdrive.

This beautiful woman was truly testing my self-control.

There was no way I could get enough of her. I resisted the urge to carry her into the other room, or to hold her against the tile wall of the bathroom and taste her lips for all of my eternity. Even the aroma of her hair, the taste of sweet mint and salt that lived on her lips, on her neck, on her brow, were causing an internal struggle that I was already accepting defeat over.

I would win every battle against my father's men. I would keep my people safe.

But this woman? My wondrous mate? I would gladly lose myself to her every time.

I knew I had other business here, but I couldn't wait anymore. I wanted her connection, her soul, to drift beside mine. If only for a moment.

"Come with me." My whisper moved over her skin, goose pricks moving over her neck at the heat.

She shivered beneath me as I gently pressed my lips to hers once again, a lingering spark of color erupting beside the mirror in a blast of white that rippled in the air. The heat of her magic burned against her skin as deeply as mine, everything shifting as the bathroom faded away. Neither of us moved, even though we were both aware of the change, aware of the connection the was deepening beside the passion and taking us far away from here.

"Ilyan?" Her voice shook as she whispered my name, her head lifting from my chest to squint through the bright sun of the beach we now stood on. The waves were an orchestra of calm, the sound swallowing the pain and uncertainty from her eyes.

Her wide, silver eyes were smiling as she clung to my hand, the sound of her heart a deep bass drum against the caw of the gulls. I had seen the beautiful silver of her eyes harbor so many emotions, so much pain, and hope, and joy, and fear, and laughter.

And power.

It was the love and admiration that looked back at me now, however, that was taking my breath away.

"I'm nervous, Ilyan," she admitted, the words clear even though her face did not project that same uncertainty.

"Nervous?" My mind searched hers as I looked for meaning, for understanding about what she could possibly be nervous about.

"Yes. For the council, for what comes after…"

"There is only us in the after," I whispered, my fingers soft as I brushed the long strands of hair out of her face, the unruly locks dancing through the air like tendrils of sea foam.

"What if it is an end?"

It was the same fear. The fear of death, of losing each

other to the great void beyond this world.

The fear followed her like a shadow, it haunted her as she slept and as much as I tried to chase it away, to mask it, I knew that I never could. No matter how much I wanted to keep this from her, to protect her, this fear she had to face on her own.

"You and I are covered in scars, deep ones, and shallow ones. But each of these scars has healed and created something stronger. I hold your scars," I whispered as I pressed my fingers over the surface of my chest. "And you hold mine."

I kept my fingers soft as I ran them over her abdomen, the delicate touch and the gentle beach breeze shimmering through our intertwined figures and causing her to shake beneath me.

"They make us stronger, but not only on our own. Together, too. These are the bonds that have weaved our connection together like iron and created something amazing. There is no end to this."

We stood there, eyes locked, magic swirling and growing. I wished I could stay in this calm forever, but I already knew we had to leave.

I didn't dare look away from her as our beach dissolved, our minds pulling us out of the Tôuha and into the disheveled bathroom, the dimmed red light from the sky streaming through the window and over us like rose-colored water.

Even though the red of the sky was a frightening reminder of what we were surrounded by, and the battle that we had yet to fight, right then it was beautiful.

"I will always be by your side." I promised, her eyes glossing over as she lifted herself up on her toes, her lips a firm pressure against mine.

24

RYLAND

THE BEDS of the makeshift hospital had all been pushed aside. Thom and Dramin had been moved to a private room near Ilyan's, tucked away to where they could be cared for better. Where Ilyan could keep an eye on them, I assumed.

Besides, this space was the only one big enough to hold everyone, to fit the large diamond-shaped platform that was required for council.

I stared at the platform as if it had offended me, the sheets of burned, black wood something I had learned about from my father, from a ceremony I had seen enacted many times before. Or a twisted version of it, anyway. As my father had completed it, time and time again, declaring himself as king.

I am the king.

I had a feeling, however, that this time I was going to see the real ceremony performed by a council as it was originally devised and created all those years before even Ilyan was born.

Which was a long, long time ago.

I didn't dare move from where I had been placed near

the platform, the small boy Joclyn had healed yesterday standing beside me with a combination of both fear and excitement on his face. He writhed his hands before him as he fidgeted, his subtle movements so small that, for a child, they should have been seen as common place. However, as he was surrounded by the calm and powerful magical beings of the world, he stuck out like a sore thumb.

Not only because of his subtle movements. Not only because he was new magic.

But because he was a child.

A child.

A child with a mark on his cheek, the raised brand looking as though his grandmother had kissed him and left lipstick there. It was a unique gift. But, just like Joclyn who had hid her mark from me for her whole life, he didn't see it as such.

I could tell by the way he kept rubbing his hand over it, covering it as though he was ashamed.

He stood beside me in the place reserved for Chosen Children. The line that I was sure at one point had been littered with dozens of those who bore the mark. Now, however, there were only three.

Me, with a hole in my back where my father had cut the precious mark out, the boy, and on the other side of him, a girl who stood in a yellow dress so old she looked like she had been pulled out of painting. A girl who, only months ago, would have cowered in nerves. Now, she stood with a confidence I hadn't seen from her before.

I never could have guessed from the girl I knew that she had this in her. That she could find this.

She really had been born for this.

I could tell by looking at her, but so could everyone else.

Dozens of eyes kept glancing toward her with a revered

awe that she reflected with either grace or fear, probably more fear, but even that was leaving her. Just as it was leaving everyone else.

Hope and joy grew on the crowds' faces with each moment we stood in the silent space, the eager anticipation devouring the haggard, gaunt fear that had riddled them.

I was certain I looked the same.

Here I stood amongst them, not as a token of the battle they had fought for centuries, but as an ally. A fact that was probably made more obvious given my uncanny likeness to my father.

So, I let them look, their eyes darting between Joclyn and me as we all waited for things to begin.

You are my twin in more ways than looks, son.

I twitched a bit at the voice, shaking it away as the buzzing of conversation in the hall grew.

These were all who remained of the last of the people my father had spent centuries hunting. No more than a month before, he had taken control of their last remaining sanctuary, sending them all scattering into the crevices and hiding places of the city that was now little more than a blood splattered maze of fear. Until Ilyan had arrived to gather them all.

These were all who were left. No more than thirty of the tall and fair beings I had been raised to decipher as my enemy.

My father's voice rose inside of me before I squashed it down, eyes lingering over the small crowd until they came to rest on Risha, the woman who was as tall and fair as all the others. I didn't see her as an enemy.

She stood with a few others near the platform, talking in low, excited whispers. She was as composed as she had been yesterday, her gestures short and sure as she spoke. Even from here the gentle, powerful nature of her soul was drawing me in.

I stared at her openly, knowing I should look away yet not really caring. Something kept me there, glued to her as her eyes lifted to mine, the intense conversation she had been having lost and forgotten as her gaze drifted to me. A soft, red color covered her cheeks, an identical one seeping over mine at the look, at the way she smiled, at the way my heart beat in response.

It was one glance, one blush, one moment, and then she looked away, her eyes cast to the floor as warmth flooded my cheeks. Sweat built at the base of my neck in what I was sure was either excitement or joy. It didn't matter what it was, though. It was there, and I liked it.

Well, I liked it until I heard Joclyn sigh from beside me, the joy deflating like a balloon. A guilt I didn't want to feel seeped into me.

No, it wasn't that I didn't want to feel it. It was that I shouldn't.

Joclyn was no longer mine.

Yes, I wanted her as my friend. More than that was closed to us. We had talked about it. She was happy, and I wanted that for her.

But then why did I feel so guilty? Why did I shy away from this joy that was so free?

Why did I feel like I needed her permission?

Because she still belongs to you. She hurt you, remember?

She's so close...

What are you wait...?

Oh, shut up, will you?

The internal scolding was loud as I looked at her curiously, trying to make sense of everything that was moving through me, trying to filter through the emotions and confusion, only to have her eyes dart toward mine. The beautiful, silver eyes that I had fallen in love with so long ago. The eyes that were filled with so much more emotion, joy, and strength than they had ever held.

A million unspoken things passed between us, a million things that could never be said lingering in the air.

Right then, staring at her in a way that felt more friend than fancy, I wanted to talk to her the way I always had. I wanted to tell her what had happened.

Before I even had the chance, the large, wooden doors at the end of the hall slid open with a grind. All the lights in the hall extinguished at once, leaving us standing in the dim red light that filtered through the tall windows, pools of crimson hitting the floor in shimmering lines.

"All hail our king, our lord, our guide," the voice rang out in Czech from behind, loud and booming as it echoed across the walls.

As one, everyone moved down to their knees, their heads hung low as myself and the other Chosen Children remained standing, watching Ilyan stride into the large room, looking like something out of a historical drama.

Tunic, tights, even a crown—it was all a little ridiculous. I wanted to laugh since it was a stark contrast to my father, who always wore the same black and purple velvet robe, a crown much larger and gaudier atop his head.

Compared to that, Ilyan's choices seemed regal, perhaps even humble.

Exactly like him.

I might not know my brother well, but I knew that, above all else, he put his people before his needs, possibly more than he should.

Ilyan climbed the small steps to the platform, moving himself to the direct center of the space right as the same voice cut through the silence. The role that would normally have been taken by the second in command was temporarily occupied by one of his many followers.

I knew I should be ruffled that I hadn't been asked, but part of me was grateful. Especially given my past, I didn't know what these people would do if I was given a role so high. Best not to push my luck.

I would rather prove myself, my worth, and my loyalty to them, anyway.

"Our lord, the king of our people," the voices rang out in unison. A shiver moved up my spine at the deep magic that was infused with them. "We bow before you in allegiance, in devotion. We serve you now and for as long as the magic flows within the earth."

"Accepted," Ilyan said, his voice a deep groan through the room.

"He has taken his place," the voice came again, not so much of a beat following before the reply resounded through the space. The Czech words reminded me so much of what I had seen and what was going on that I forgot to respond.

"Speak, our king."

I am the king.

You know this, son. Don't let them convince you otherwise.

Seriously. Put a sock in it.

"Ilyan, son of Edmund, third of the first of the Skříteks, and savior of our city. He stands before us, ready to rule, and as one, we will accept him. Do you accept him?"

The deep rumble of the voice continued, but I didn't dare look away from my brother. I didn't think I could if I tried. I was frozen, seeing Ilyan for what I had always known him to be, for what everyone else in this room saw him as.

More than king.

More than ruler.

More than brother.

He was their guide.

I accepted that as they did.

As one, everyone in the large space raised their hands above their heads, one loud clap smashing through the revered silence as the sign for acceptance rang loud.

"It has been accepted," the voice came, followed by a silence that was impregnated with anticipation.

Ilyan shifted, his eyes moving over everyone—over the last of his people, over the confused child who stood beside me—before finally resting on his mate. It was an acknowledgement that didn't smother me for the first time.

I waited alongside everyone else for him to speak as the dim, red light of day became nothing more than shadows.

"My people," Ilyan began, the power in his voice carrying over us, "we have been scattered, but now, we have been found. While our numbers are few, they are still strong. *We* are still strong. And now we gather not only to cement the rule of my people, but to strengthen our numbers and to move toward our goal, our birthright, and our heritage. We have been graced with magic for a reason. For this reason, we will take back the wells of Imdalind. We will defeat Edmund Krul, first of the Chosen, and take back the magic of the world."

The magic in the room boiled in excitement and anticipation, mine included. I fought the need to scream, yell, and stomp my feet as was always done in the councils my father held. Instead, I raised my hands above my head, clapping once alongside everyone else, sealing the words with a calm agreement, a powerful bind falling over me as I did so.

I could feel the weight of the ancient magic shift over me

like a warm blanket, the calm looks on everyone else's faces making it clear that they felt the same things I did. The magic was affecting them the same way.

"Edmund has taken control of not only the wells of Imdalind, but also the city. He has plagued the calm creatures, the Vilỳ, with a poison that infects not only the precious magic they hold, but also the magic that is awakened in the ones they bite.

"Joclyn, daughter of Sain, first of the Drak, has found a way to reverse the poison in these souls, making their awakened magic as safe as the magic that was awakened in her and in all the other Chosen Children to date. This can be shown in Jaromir, the child we pulled from the streets. Not only is his magic pure, but he has awakened much faster than is usual. His power is now a strong force within him."

Ilyan's voice was strong, yet still not enough to drown out the excited babble that was growing into a fountain of sound, the voices bouncing off the old, stone walls.

I looked around as the sound continued to swell, my own excitement lost as the small boy in question took a step into me, his tiny frame almost trying to blend into mine.

"Hey, there," I said in Czech, my voice soft as I bent over to him. "It's okay."

"They are scared of me." His voice was so small.

"No," I said a little louder as he looked at me with scared eyes. "They are excited that you exist."

I didn't expect him to understand right away, and judging by the wide eyes that looked up at me, he didn't.

I smiled softly as my focus left the scared little boy and went to the strong woman who stood beside him. The parallels between them were so funny I couldn't help laughing.

"What?" He was obviously upset at my laughter.

I stopped the chuckle and looked at him, jutting my chin toward Joclyn so he would know what I was talking about.

"She was the same way. She hid her mark for years. She hid herself for years. Now look at her. She will be queen today."

She should still be your mate.

No. Not anymore.

"She will be an amazing queen."

The boy's eyes grew into large saucers full of so much disbelief. He looked at me before turning toward her tall, sure, frame. The mark on her neck was proudly displayed for all to see.

"Silence." The command in Ilyan's voice rumbled through us, silencing the room as Ilyan's magic sealed it, and everyone was forced to follow orders.

While the use of his magic in such a way boiled under me a bit, it was short lived. After all, I could see the same irritation in Ilyan's face. He didn't like using it, either. Everyone else, however, now stood in a humbled silence, their heads bowed low as they waited for him to continue.

"It is the suggestion that we gather as many of the injured as we can, bring them here to be healed and trained, and then give them the option to move forward with us. To help us fight for the freedom that is not only ours, but will be theirs, as well. What say you all?"

Ilyan had barely finished before the resounding clap echoed through the room, confirming his request.

It's a good plan.

Too bad...

"Thank you, my friends," Ilyan continued, the heartfelt words rumbling over me. "Now, for the true purpose that we have gathered in this council."

He paused, his lips breaking into a wide smile as he walked toward where I stood, his look thankfully not reserved for me, but for that same powerful woman the little boy still stared at.

Ilyan extended his hand gently, his long fingers reaching toward her as her delicate hand settled in his, pulling her onto the platform and into the middle of the space.

"As many of you know, I have found my mate, and the ceremony has already been performed. It is for that reason I bring before you Joclyn DeSpain, daughter of Sain, the first of the Drak; bearer of the kiss of the Vilÿ; and a child chosen by them as my mate, my companion, and your queen."

He spoke to those around him, but his eyes never left hers, a deep, desperate longing in his gaze so deep that it moved through me with such an emotional wash I was having trouble breathing.

"Do you accept?"

You are a fool, son.

And here I was, beginning to accept you as my child.

You are no better than the rest of them.

I clapped my hands above my head as all the others did, letting my father's taunt wash over me as if it was nothing.

It was nothing.

The sound of my clap was one booming noise with all the others, the simple movement sealing my agreement of Joclyn and placing her as my queen.

For one brief moment, the joy in her face blanched, her skin paling as she took a step closer to Ilyan, her hand wrapping tightly around his.

That same warm balloon swelled within me and I turned toward Risha without thinking. My stomach twisted at what I had done, but more at what I was now seeing.

Standing behind Risha in the shadows against the wall

was Sain, his dark hair falling over his eyes as he mumbled to himself.

Mumbled.

He mumbled the same way I had as my father's voice had tormented and dragged me down into insanity.

Now, there stood Sain, his hands writhing one over the other, his head pressing into the cool stone as he fought the same demons I had.

He had mentioned before that he knew what I had battled, but it was in the past. It was something he had already defeated. Yet, seeing him there, the way he moved, the way he mumbled...

He was battling them *now*.

He always has been.

My father was fighting for control of him, too.

Who's to say I don't already have it?

I might have won, but I was seeing another fight right in front of me.

And seeing it from this angle, I wasn't sure how I had won.

Or if he would.

He won't.

They all clapped again but I didn't even turn, I just stared at the old man, something wicked twisting in my gut.

25

WYN

I REALLY SHOULD BE at Joclyn's celebratory feast, toasting to the new queen. She was my best friend, after all, it made sense for me to be there. But everyone else was there, even Dramin had been taken down in an old wheelchair someone had found.

Judging by the remains of dried blood on the seat and back it wasn't as old and forgotten as they had been trying to pass off. None of that really mattered when the whole world is covered by blood and death, though.

The only thing I cared about right then was that the room that Thom and Dramin had been moved to was lacking one Drak, and I could actually talk to Thom, and not keep everything in a whisper as I tried not to disturb Dramin and his fake snoring. Yes, I might be missing the feast, but seeing as we were in the middle of an apocalypse it was less feast and more 'eating beans out of a can.' I was pretty happy right where I was.

Sitting here. In the silence. My hand wrapped around Thom's.

I clung to him as he had to me when I was healing just

days ago. My fingers wrapped around his wrist, careful not to touch the boils that covered his palms. But even that was getting a little tricky, the boils were spreading up his arms now and a few of the bigger ones of his fingers had begun to break and seep a dark fluid that smelled like rancid gasoline, which I wasn't even sure was a thing. But if it was this is what it would smell like.

And this was horrible.

Ilyan had said that he was not contagious, but I wasn't going to take any chances, at least not until we could find enough gauze to wrap them. There had been talk of a few of us heading to the nearby hospital to get some medical equipment, but no one was really ready to journey out into the rat-infested red world quite yet so the bits of gauze and supplies we had found in the old monastery were earmarked for Dramin and Jaromir, and the few others that we had found alive in the complex.

There weren't many survivors, but now that Joclyn could heal them, the numbers were bound to jump. Which meant fewer supplies and less food.

And fewer of the precious things I needed for Thom. It had been a near miracle that I had found some of the Brash Clay in a flower garden in one of the main squares. That, a bit of onion, and a drop of the ash from my flame and maybe I could get the boils on his hands to clear up.

Maybe. Even with the ancient magic of the Brash Clay I knew the chances were slim, but I was still in stubborn acceptance mode.

"We got to the castle complex, okay," I whispered, as I began to smear some of the dirt onto his hands. "Jos did some of her badassery and she and Ilyan shielded us. It's like we are in a snow globe inside of a snow globe. All we need is little flakes of dandruff falling around us and we would be all set. I wonder if Sain has enough dandruff on his ugly mug to do the trick."

I laughed to myself, my heart clenching at the shadow of Thom's chuckle that was filling my mind. I could hear him so clearly, but he still lay as still and impassive as he had the past few days.

"I wish I could talk to you like Jos does to Ilyan, to know if you were still in there. If you can hear me. To ask what happened..." My rambling faded away as I shifted, the clay still on my fingers even though my focus had drifted a million miles away.

Well, not a million miles, but on Dramin's bed and everything that had happened the other day.

"So I can ask you who we can trust." I was fully aware I was talking to myself now, not that it mattered. "Sain's been..."

I swallowed my words as voices chattered right outside of the door, the quick Czech sounding like chicken scratches through the door. I went back to smearing the mud on his palm as I focused on the heavy steps of the stragglers, waiting for them to get far enough away that I could continue.

"Why can't people get to feasts on time? It makes it really hard to have secret conversations with your first love." Or your still love, I corrected, but just to myself. Saying it aloud to an unconscious man rated as super weird on the how weird is your relationship scale. "It makes it impossible to ask the cosmos if the guy who got me out of what was certain death is, in fact, working for the enemy."

'Working for the Enemy'. It sounded so wicked, like I was trapped in a weird spy movie. My eye brow tweaked, pulling into my hairline as I watched his face, practically begging for a groan or a blink or something to tell me I was on the right track.

Still nothing, not even a relaxing sigh from the goo I was smearing on his palms. I was sure the boils hurt, and this stuff made everything feel great, even my fingertips were happy, and I didn't even realize that they had been achy.

"He couldn't be, though," I continued in my banter, "I mean, if you had seen him in that dungeon. Edmund has always been a beast... but dude." I shook my head.

I had been stuck in the same roundabout rationalization about him for days. The whole episode in the room screamed at me that something was wrong. He seemed to be downright terrified of Ilyan for some reason, but to be working for a man who abuses everyone he comes in contact with. No one would willingly do that.

"Well, no one but Ovailia," I whispered, finishing my thought out loud. "Who he was mated to."

Thom's hand dropped to the blanket, leaving a smear of mud behind as it slid forgotten to the edge of the bed.

"Well, crap," I grumbled as my fire jumped through my veins, my fear sending it into a ripple of magic that was just dying to escape. I pushed the magic into submission, eyes narrowing at Dramin's still empty bed as if he had something to do with it.

No, not him, just his dad.

More voices started to drift through the door, these ones moving fast in the opposite direction, the heightened excitement pushing through the door as if the two men were speaking through a megaphone.

"We are so lucky to have one of the firsts with us. I thought they were all dead."

"So did I. Sain has been missing for centuries, and

Joclyn? I can't believe she is his daughter! We will surely survive this mess with the power of the Drak on our side."

"I hope so," A third voice popped in just as the voices began to fade again. "I heard from someone that Sain is concerned his daughter's control of her sights is lacking and that..."

Their voices faded away, not that I really needed to hear more. Sain had been going on about how Joclyn was destroying and breaking sights for a while. Something I easily believed until his sight was wrong, and Joclyn's sight was correct with the attack on Prague. Thanks to Sain we had walked into a death trap.

Sain and his terrible mistake.

"I wish you could tell me what happened to you. I have a bad feeling Sain was involved somehow," I whispered to Thom, replacing his hand on his chest as though it was made of glass, I clung to it that gently too. Which took some work, I was more likely to break glass with a stare. "I have a bad feeling that Sain did this."

Mommy! Rosy's excited call jumped through my mind, breaking the silence and jerking through me. The formally soft touch of my hand against his turned into a vice and I froze, ice and agony dragging through me as more steps began to filter down the hall. The torrent of steps grew as I glanced at my pocket, the slight lift of jean revealing exactly where I had placed the shard of blade that morning. I shifted my weight, as if I needed to conceal the tiny bulge from the quickly growing sound of voices that was heading my way.

As if they could see through walls, and bed, and jeans to discover what I had done.

The feast couldn't have been over so soon, could it? Of course it could. Without the food to constitute the word "feast" it was more like a snack and go. It seems as though we had already hit the word "go".

"I will figure this out Thom," I whispered to him, as more scrapes and scuffles of worn down shoes began to echo through the door. What could clearly be explained as the squeak of an overworked wheel blending among them.

"I can't say it aloud, but I think I have found something that might solve this. That might fix this..."

"I want what is best for them. I know her intentions are honorable, but I worry about her skill." Sain's voice boomed down the hall with the strength of someone giving a speech to a mob and cut me off.

"She can hold Ilyan's magic, sir. I think that says enough about her skill." I didn't recognize the voice, but the question in it was clear, as if whoever was speaking was starting to wonder if their assessment was right or not.

"Just because a clay pot can hold water does not mean that it knows what to do with it," Sain answered with a strange calm that didn't quite match him. Well, except for the pompous, riddle-induced part of him, that matched perfectly. His trite response was immediately followed by whispered mumblings and the groan of hinges as the door opened.

My hand tightened around Thom's wrist as Dramin's blanketed chair was pushed in his downtrodden expression drifting to Thom the moment they entered. Well, Dramin entered. Sain was still turned and facing whatever horde had followed him down the hall. Something that Dramin seemed downright upset about. Upset, but not surprised.

"With the right training she can do amazing things. I only hope that she chooses to accept what I have to offer."

My heart turned into a rock that had forgotten how to beat as Dramin's eyes met mine, guilt and worry wrinkled in his brow. Dramin may have been surprised to see me there, I wasn't sure, but it mattered very little, if only because of the way he was looking at me.

As if he was asking for help.

"I, however, am always here to help any of my people who need it," Sain continued to address the people as though he was some kind of TV evangelist, the creep's weird proclamations meaning nothing with the way Dramin was now staring at me.

"Are you okay?" I asked Dramin in a hushed whisper, his eyes drooping to his lap, just as his chair began to move and he was pushed the rest of the way into the room.

"Wyn!" Sain called the moment he saw me, "I didn't expect to see you here. But of course... you missed the feast. If you could call it that."

There was a bit too much bitterness in his voice, this tone was usually reserved for anything that concerned Joclyn. I chose to ignore it.

"Believe it or not, there are two people in this room. I wanted to sneak a few minutes with one of them, seeing as the other was gone."

"Well, I hope you didn't do anything foolhardy while we were gone." There was no smile in his voice, and unless I was truly losing it with my assumptions on him, I could have sworn there was a warning there.

Or rather, a threat that was already winding up my spine. Good thing two could play at this game. There was no way I was letting him keep me from this room. Keep me from Thom.

"No terrible mistakes for me." All of us knew exactly what I was referencing, and each of our reactions perfectly matched that.

The nefarious killer inside of me smiled, even as

Dramin jerked and straightened, his sagging jawline tightening. Sain, however, met my grin head on, pushing Dramin right up to his bed, facing the dying man away from me.

"I'm glad of that," Sain said through the grin that was plastered to his face. "Now, if you will give me a few minutes to help my son back to his rest..."

He gave me no room for recourse and I stood, carefully making sure that Thom was comfortable before I stepped to the door.

"Be careful, Sain," I hissed as I stepped past him, the laugh of my daughter echoing in my head like some kind of demented soundtrack. "I wouldn't want you to make any more mistakes."

"I don't make mistakes." I heard Sain say from behind me, his voice ice as the door snapped shut.

I whipped around, but the lock was already latched, the voices on the other side reducing to hisses and mumbles. I stared at the door, listened to the panic of the men and knew one thing behind a shadow of a doubt.

Dramin knew exactly what had happened.

And Sain was his keeper.

26

SAIN

I SHOULDN'T BE HERE.

Not after everything I had heard. I knew what they wanted of me. It was the same thing they always wanted, the same thing I had given them for years.

My mind was full of it.

Information.

Information I knew they could take with only a few words.

Well, that they thought they could. Not that I had ever given them everything they desired.

I should leave, focus on my own agenda. On the plans I had spent thousands of years carefully weaving together, manipulating the sights and magic of my progeny in order to accomplish.

This choice could upset all of that.

Yet, I stood, shrouded by the dark of night, the moon a blood red orb as it glimmered through the powerful shield that shrouded the city. The shield that was slowly heating the city. Even the air was growing warmer by the minute.

The ancient stone pillar I leaned against however was cold, and nothing near living up to its name.

The Golden Gate.

The archaic arches were built in the 1300s as religious zealots created towers to their gods. The popular tourist attraction was now smeared in blood, the bodies of those same sightseers littering the ground around us, forgotten souls who had passed before their magic, their true ability, had taken hold.

It was pathetic in a way.

It had been less than a month since I had walked through the gilded archway, since I had guided Wynifred away from the massacre, from Edmund and his ridiculous plan of control.

I had told him years ago that his goals would only lead to ruin. As much as he relied on the manipulated sights I handed him, however, he hadn't listened.

It was better for me, for what I wanted.

Now, I only needed to find a way to continue to use Ovailia and her father for my benefit while they thought they were getting what they needed.

I had done it for years. I would do it again.

For those I loved, to protect them and change the future I saw, in order to control the magic in a way that I was born to do. They would see what I had done soon enough.

They would be grateful for it.

They would bow before me because of it.

This choice was another step on my path. Even though the pull I felt deep inside was only creating a deeper complication.

It had first awakened when I had held Ovailia as an infant in my arms and again when the bond with her had been completed.

It was a need that I was sure I had forgotten, that I hadn't needed.

Not since Angela.

But now...?

I can see you, Sain.

The voice came, the same as it had for centuries before I had tricked Thom into providing my escape, the sacrifice of his child necessary to use his abilities to break me out of Edmund's control. I had heard her voice all through my imprisonment and for decades after until it had finally faded into nothing. Until my memories returned and the bastard daughter I had seen hundreds of years before put my entire plan in jeopardy.

Foolish girl, I would have to end her as well.

The voice had started to return when Edmund had found me, days after delivering the birth stone to the Silnỳ, when I still thought myself to be her mortal father. Then, even though my memories hadn't fully returned, the whispers had begun, piecing together my past before my mind could put everything together on its own.

It was nothing like it was now, the consistency only increasing with the first step I took back into the city.

Instructions, commands, orders.

All delivered straight into my mind.

Just as they had been for so long.

As they would until the end.

Even Edmund was playing into my plan, in a way.

The courtyard glimmered with the shadows of red and black, the hot breeze pulling at the tree's and trash, sending all the forgotten belongings from the massacre rolling through the courtyard.

My sight pulled at me as it tried to show me visions of future and past and things I didn't really care about right then. I pushed it away as the bell from the high tower of the cathedral rang loud and clear, the sound awakening the ravenous Vilỳs that were left hunting, the nasty things taking flight and zooming right for the sound.

One of the vile things flew at me, my body not so much as tensing as it continued on its path, ready to devour me.

"Zdechnout." I spoke the word aloud as it rattled in my head, and the Vilỳ dropped to the ground with the thunk of stone on stone.

"One down, ten million to go." Her voice was as smooth and sweet as it had always been, the sweet tones sending my heart into a rage and my magic into a frenzy.

I looked up to her as she approached me, her hair swinging behind her, the tap of her high heeled shoes loud and hypnotic. My heart rate accelerated at the sound, the deep need for her growing out of nowhere.

"Ovi," I sighed, fully aware that the despicable longing had seeped into the word. Oh well, it would only help me in my plan.

She smiled at the nickname that had always been hers, her face lighting up with a joy I had missed from her.

The clicking of her shoes stopped as she came right up to meet me, her eyes a white-hot heat as she stared into me.

"Hello, Sain."

My magic boiled at the honey in her voice, her body bending toward mine as her arm trapped me against the gold inlaid stone of the archway.

We stood, staring at each other as the Vilỳs calmed down, my magic moving in a desperate attempt to reach hers.

"So, Sain," she began, the whispers of the voice picking up in my ears, "tell me what Ilyan has decided."

I knew I shouldn't have come here, but I didn't have a

choice, just as I didn't have a choice about whether or not I was going to tell her.

Although, not for the reasons she would assume.

With one gentle press of her lips against mine, all the secrets that Ilyan had trusted me with came free.

He had trusted the wrong person from the very beginning.

Both Edmund and Ilyan had. I had learned from the moment Dramin crawled out of the mud that this world was mine for the taking, mine to mold, mine to create.

And I would.

All these bastard kings were just a means to an end.

ALSO BY REBECCA ETHINGTON

THE WORLD OF IMDALIND

THE CIRCUS OF SHIFTERS

Flame of the Phoenix, Book Four

The Dragon Queen Series
Rising Flame (coming March 2019)
Books 2-4 TBA

THE OTHER WORLDS

The Through Glass Series
Book One: The Dark
Book Two: The Blue
Book Three: The Rose
Book Four: The Cut
Book Five: The Light (Coming 2019)
Book Six: The Ascended (Coming 2019)

Of River and Raynn, The Series
The Catalyst: Act One (Rereleases 2019)
The Requisite: Act Two (Coming 2019)

ABOUT THE AUTHOR

Rebecca Ethington is an internationally bestselling author with almost 700,000 books sold. Her breakout debut, The Imdalind Series, has been featured on bestseller lists since its debut in 2012, reaching thousands of adoring fans worldwide and cited as "Interesting and Intense" by *USA Today's Happily Ever After Blog.*

From writing horror to romance and creating every sort of magical creature in between, Rebecca's imagination weaves vibrant worlds that transport readers into the pages of her books. Her writing has been described as fresh, original, and groundbreaking, with stories that bend genres and create fantastical worlds.

Born and raised under the lights of a stage, Rebecca has written stories by the ghost light, told them in whispers in dark corridors, and never stopped creating within the pages of a notebook.

Find me online
www.rebeccaethington.com
contact@rebeccaethington.com

ACKNOWLEDGMENTS

This book was written in one of the darkest times in my life – and without the loving support of my dearest of friends, and the understanding from the most amazing fans – it may not have happened. So I thank you. I thank you for holding my hand, for cheering me on, for watching my videos, for crying with me, and for understanding as my life fell apart, that the story could still live on.

This book would not be without the amazing support of each of you.
So I thank you.

And a very special thanks to those who were there through it all.
Jen, Lila, Ricky, Spencer, Shaina, and Kris

You have saved me.

THE IMDALIND SERIES, BOOK SIX
THE FULL SERIES IS AVAILABLE NOW

www.ingramcontent.com/pod-product-compliance
Lightning Source LLC
Chambersburg PA
CBHW021522250626
47154CB00006BA/1933